GHOSTS

Peter Cawdron
thinkingscifi.wordpress.com

Copyright © Peter Cawdron, 2023

All rights reserved. The right of Peter Cawdron to be identified as the author of this work has been asserted in accordance with the Copyright, Designs and Patents Act 1988. All the characters in this book are fictitious, and any resemblance to actual persons living or dead is purely coincidental.

Cover image: Leonardo Da Vinci's Vitruvian Man (1490 AD).

Disclaimer: No Artificial Intelligence (AI) was used in the creation of this story. Some would argue that no intelligence was used at all. I'll leave that for you to decide.

Imprint: Independently published

ISBN: 9798863817590 — Paperback

ISBN: — Hardback

Uncertainty is an uncomfortable position.
Certainty is an absurd one.

Voltaire

Intern

Deep red carpet softens Molly's high heels as she rushes to keep up with the aide in front of her. Molly's been to the White House before as a high school student on a scheduled tour, so she's seen the lofty ceilings, the grand columns, and the white marble busts of Washington, Jefferson and Lincoln before. She's admired how each statue is set in its own alcove, often flanked by flags on polished wooden poles with golden spikes and ornate tassels. The polished floors, the life-size paintings in the style of Dutch masters like Rembrandt, and the ornate cornices on the ceiling, along with the crystal chandeliers, have a beauty that transcends mere politics. Molly knew what to expect, but working in the White House as an intern has her heart racing at a million miles an hour.

Day one, she thinks, steeling herself for the challenges that lie ahead.

As her father's a US senator, she's supposed to be accustomed to the fabled halls of power, but her palms are clammy. Her purse hangs over her shoulder, bumping into her hip as she walks. She's wearing a puffy cream blouse and a plain black skirt. Her mother told her, "To be and not be seen is the goal." As a young woman with a master's degree in foreign affairs, Molly thinks of herself as assertive and independent. She's a feminist. She's attended protests on the Mall in support of women's reproductive rights, gun control, prison reform, LGBTQIA+ rights and climate change. Is there any cause to which she hasn't lent her voice? And yet, on walking into the White House, the lioness has curled up like a kitten.

"Molly Sorensen," the aide says, handing her folder over to the receptionist in Human Resources.

"Please, take a seat," a young woman of similar age says to her, gesturing to a row of chairs set against one wall. "Director Greene will be with you shortly."

Molly sits. She cups her hands in her lap, with her legs held together, pointing straight in front of her. She's tempted to pull out her phone, but she wants to come across as professional.

"Molly," the director says a few minutes later. She didn't even hear the door open beside her. "This way."

Molly greets the director with an enthusiastic handshake. At a guess, he's in his forties. He's clean-shaven with a receding hairline and could be any one of hundreds of similar men she's seen wearing dark suits within the White House. His eyes glance down at her breasts. It's as though she's wearing a sandwich board advertising sex, even though that's not what she or any other woman wants on meeting a senior manager for the first time. He lingers a little too long on shaking her hand, which causes her to avert her eyes and look down at his grip. As if he's only just realized, he releases her fingers, waving her into his office. He was lost in thought, preoccupied with something about her personally, but what? Is he a creep? Or is she reading too much into her first, fleeting impression?

Mahogany panels line the office walls. There's a bookcase, even though the dozens of books arranged there appear to be unread textbooks.

"Have a seat," the director says, pulling back an ornate wooden chair with a plush cushion and a high back. Molly thanks him, taking her seat. Before she can scoot a little closer to his desk, he rests his hand on her shoulder, touching not only her blouse but the bra strap beneath the fine fabric. She freezes. His fingers flex, feeling the textures beneath them before peeling away as he walks past and rounds his desk. The director sits in a faux-leather office chair and swivels to face her with a smile.

Molly is shaking, but she's not sure if it's with anger, fear or disbelief. It's slight. She doubts he notices, but her heels lift off the floor beneath the seat. She raises her knees, pivoting on her toes. She has to make a decision. Right here. Right now. With no preparation or forethought. She has a mere split second to decide what she's going to say, and she knows she'll have to live with the consequences. Molly hates herself for it, but she remains silent. She tells herself she's overreacting to a slight touch. She clutches her hands in her lap, hiding her fingers from sight and forcing a smile.

"Congratulations. You've been assigned to the Office of the Chief of Staff. You'll report there each morning, but on Mondays and Wednesdays at noon, you'll check in here with HR and debrief with me personally. I want you to..."

The director talks for several more minutes, outlining her duties and responsibilities, expectations and reporting lines, but Molly can't focus on his words. She nods in agreement, but she barely hears him. She's still trying to process what just happened. It's as though there are two different worlds operating in tandem, one in which she's going through an onboarding process at the White House, the other where her personal space has been violated. The clash between the two leaves her feeling a sense of cognitive dissonance. Is she imagining unwanted sexual advances? Is she too overly sensitive and dreaming up conflict?

"Any questions?"

"No," she snaps in quick reply, wanting to get out of the HR office.

The director stands, and she matches his pace, not waiting for him to round his desk. Molly reaches the door before him and is tempted to grab the handle and open it, but that seems wrong, almost rude. Molly's not sure why, but etiquette seems to demand she pause and allows his outstretched hand to get the door.

The director opens the door, saying, "If you have any issues or need any support, please don't hesitate to stop by my office."

His hand rests on the side of her hip. Within fractions of a second, his fingers run across the small of her back and the top of her buttocks as she rushes to get through the door.

"I look forward to seeing you again."

Molly is in shock.

The receptionist is oblivious.

Molly stands in the middle of the carpeted reception area, looking back at the director and his half-smile. He knows. He understands she's powerless. Denial and plausibility are his allies. Were she to say something, it would be his account that's believed. Molly wants to scream at him. Her fists clench. Her knuckles go white. But what has he done? Each slight was mere seconds in length. Each was harmless on its own and could be dismissed as accidental. She's helpless and he knows it. And he'll use that to push the boundaries further next time they meet. Molly feels sick.

"The chief of staff's support office is down the hall. Fourth door on the right," the receptionist says.

"T—Thank you."

Molly walks back out into the grandeur of the White House, but the marble has lost its shine. The polished tables have lost their luster. She feels sullied, dirty, but why should she? Molly hasn't done anything wrong. Instead of walking proud, she hangs her head, looking at the fall of her glossy black high heels. Molly ignores the embossed wooden signs, counting the doors. A tear forms in the corner of her eye, but she fights the urge to cry. Self-pity is a luxury she cannot afford. She's been ambushed. She has to bounce back.

On walking into the Office of the Chief of Staff, Molly takes a deep breath. She pins her shoulders back, raises her head and strides in with the confidence she wishes she actually had.

"Molly Sorensen?" an almost identical receptionist in a seemingly cloned reception area asks with the same timbre of voice as back in Human Resources.

"Yes," a reluctant Molly replies.

"Please. Have a seat."

"Of course."

Molly feels as though she's fallen into the grips of a machine with gears turning methodically, grinding coarse wheat into fine flour. Once again, her hands are in her lap, only they feel heavier now. She resists the urge to pull her phone out of her purse, but this time, it isn't out of temptation so much as depression. She knows the messages that await her online. Her mother will be on the family group chat, asking how her first day is going. Her father, brother and sister will all offer encouragement and be curious about her day. Molly has no desire to lie to them. She will, but not right now. Lies are pleasantries. Lies are conveniences. Lies are ways of avoiding uncomfortable truths. Why should she lie to protect that asshole? And yet she will. Even though she's entirely innocent, the truth sullies both of them. She sighs.

"Molly," a voice says beside her. Like the Human Resources director, the President's Chief of Staff, Susan Dosela, has mastered the art of opening doors without anyone noticing. The hinges must be greased nightly. "Please. Come into my office."

Those few words strike with a sense of déjà vu. Molly swallows the lump rising in her throat. She stands but with less vigor than before. Reluctantly, she follows the middle-aged woman into her office.

Most of the women Molly's seen within the White House either have their hair back in a ponytail, up in a bun or pulled back with a hair band, keeping their face clear, but not the chief of staff. Her long brunette hair is dead straight, hanging down either side of her face. Her fringe looks as though it was cut yesterday. She's wearing lipstick but no blush. In any other context, she'd look assertive, but she comes across as kind. Susan Dosela is wearing a pantsuit, which Molly's father says is a power move. Molly's not so sure. She thinks it's more practical. And comfortable. And damn, it has pockets!

"Have a seat."

"Thank you," Molly says, sweeping her skirt under her as she sits. Try as she may, she can't make eye contact.

The chief of staff doesn't sit down. She stops behind her chair, sensing something's wrong. She grips the headrest, peering over the leather seat back at Molly.

"Are you crying?"

Molly's lips tighten. Her eyes dart around, unsure where they should settle. She clutches her fingers in her lap, determined to be strong.

"Fucking Greene," the chief of staff says, shaking her head. She takes her seat and leans across the desk with her arms stretching toward Molly. Her fingers splay out across the polished wood. "It's okay. You can talk to me. You're not in trouble. You haven't done anything wrong. You're not going to lose your internship or anything like that."

It takes all of Molly's might to make eye contact. She breathes deeply but doesn't say anything.

Susan Dosela leans back in her seat. "Power is... intoxicating. And like a drunk, people do dumb shit when power goes to their heads. And you. You've walked into a classic power move."

"I don't understand," Molly says, feeling confused and yet genuinely relaxed in her presence.

"It's a game."

"A game?"

"Not to me. Not to you. But to those like Greene, yes. Absolutely. And he's using you like a chess master sacrificing a pawn to trap a bishop. Did he lock eyes with you before you left?"

Molly has to think for a moment. She recalls standing on the carpet in reception, not wanting to look at him but feeling compelled to raise her eyes.

"Yes."

"Bastard."

Molly says, "Why did you ask about that particular moment?"

"Because, to him, your reaction is reward in itself. The look on your face told him he'd won."

"But why would he do this to me?" Molly asks, fighting back tears.

"Because, like players in any game, he relishes the next move."

"But you know," Molly says, feeling indignant. "You know what happened, even though I haven't said anything."

The chief of staff points at the wall of her office, saying, "And he knows I know. He knows damn well you wouldn't be able to hide it from me. And he knows he walked a fine line. Let me guess; he lingered when he shook your hand. He touched you, but it was borderline. He only touched your shoulder or your waist. And in a way that could be construed as friendly or haphazard, but with undertones that made you feel uncomfortable."

"Yes."

The chief of staff hangs her head for a moment. When she looks up, she says, "Welcome to the White House."

"I—I," Molly says, stuttering. "Aren't you going to do something?"

"Greene's a relic from the last administration. He's already on notice. He doesn't want to be here. What he wants is a severance package. He wants us to pay him out. Money for nothing."

"And me?"

"You're a means to getting under my skin. You're a nudge. You're a reminder that he wants me to push him out the door with a golden parachute."

"But you can fire him," Molly says, feeling angry. "For sexual harassment."

"Sexual?" The chief of staff looks over her glasses at Molly. "Really? It was a few steps shy of that. None of us want to go into independent mediation, right? Do you really want to sit before a tribunal to testify—probably for hours, perhaps even days—about something that took mere seconds? And have your character questioned? To drag your name through the mud? No. Greene knows exactly what he's doing. It's calculated. He's a psychopath. He's dancing the tango."

Molly shakes her head in disbelief.

The chief of staff picks up a folder and hands it to Molly, saying, "Okay. We need to change gears. Time to move on. You'll feel better with something to do."

Molly accepts the nondescript folder, feeling unsure about herself. Everything is moving too damn fast in the White House.

"Press Secretary Collins is sick," the chief of staff says. "I need someone to act as a placeholder. You don't have to do anything other than shuffle documents between his office and the Oval. Understood?"

"Umm, yes," Molly says, still wanting closure on the incident with Director Greene.

"Read it. Make sure you're across all the details, especially the footnotes. Then take it to the President. If she has any questions, your job is to point her to the appropriate notes in the briefing. Understood?"

"What are you going to do?"

"What I should have done months ago," the chief of staff says. "Push Greene out with a termination package. Oh, I'll make sure there are enough rumors to muddy his reputation in the marketplace, but most of Washington won't care."

"He's done this before?" Molly asks, realizing she's not the only pawn in this game of chess. "He shouldn't be rewarded for his behavior. That's not fair."

"No, it isn't. But it's the best of a bunch of bad options, and that's politics!"

Training

Aleksandr walks along the main corridor within the vehicle assembly building in the Russian Vostochny Cosmodrome. An aging Soyuz rocket lies on its side on a series of railway carriages. Its four distinct booster rockets are already attached to the fuselage. The sight of so many rocket engines sitting there idle has Aleksandr longing for the skies. The upper stage has been prepped for a deep space flight. Although secrecy surrounds the mission, with international observers guessing at a flyby of the asteroid *3753 Cruithne*, Aleksandr knows it's destined for the Moon. Russia has long spied on the Moon with jealous eyes. After the failed attempts in the '60s and the colossal destruction of the N1 rocket, Russia seemed to give up on lunar exploration. Deep down, though, the stain of losing the space race to the Americans remained. Now, it's become a generational embarrassment.

Following the loss of the Russo-Ukraine war, the Russian Federation fractured and threatened to break apart. Space was seen as a point of national pride. Cosmonauts were a rallying point for patriotism, providing politicians with a way of unifying the people. Russia has *always* succeeded in space, or so Russian media told its people. Sputnik lead to Laika, to Yuri Gagarin becoming the first man in space, and Valentina Tereshkova becoming the first woman in space, beating the American Sally Ride by twenty years. Alexei Leonov was the first person to conduct a spacewalk. Lunokhod 1 was the first rover on another celestial body, exploring the Moon remotely years before Apollo 11 touched down. The Russian space program took the first photos of the far side of the Moon and conducted the first flyby of another planet. The Russians were the first to land robotic probes on both Venus and Mars.

Aleksandr longs for the glory days again. He wants his name to be etched alongside Gagarin and Leonov.

The Luna mission has been designated as вечность or *Vechnost*. Like so many terms in Russian, *Vechnost* has contextual meaning. It can be used to signify an eon or an age in time but is most commonly taken to mean eternity. Aleksandr, though, thinks of it as a colloquial term meaning immortality.

The fairing at the top of the Soyuz reaches out well beyond the surrounds of the rocket itself, giving it a bulbous head and providing plenty of cargo space for satellites or, as is in this case, an enhanced, crewed Soyuz space capsule. For the astronauts, it means they launch in darkness. They have a video feed from cameras mounted on the fuselage of the rocket as well as from mission control, but just once, Aleksandr would like to see the launch from the windows of the capsule itself.

Western media mistakes the Russian word *cosmonaut* as being synonymous with astronaut, but they miss the heart of the concept. Russians have the word *astronavt*. If they wanted to call their celestial sojourners astronauts, they could. Cosmonaut, though, encompasses the Russian philosophy of cosmism. As far back as the 1850s, Nikolai Fyodorov advocated for science as the key to the future and to reaching human immortality. In 1903, Konstantin Tsiolkovsky developed the rocket equation, allowing humanity to reach for the stars. He longed to see Russians colonize not only the planets within the solar system but the galaxy as a whole. Cosmism influenced the October Revolution of 1917, launching the Communists into power. In Russian thinking, a cosmonaut is one who "*strides forth from the earth to conquer planets and stars!*"

The West may see no difference between astronauts and cosmonauts, but Aleksandr holds to the old ways.

He steps outside, walking over to the administration building. A stiff wind blows grit across the ground. The sky above the horizon is a ruddy brown, resembling Mars more than Earth. It's the desert. The Eastern Steppes of Russia are grasslands bordering the deserts of outer Mongolia. When the wind whips up, it carries dust and dirt for thousands of miles. It's good for the grasslands but irritating for people. Aleksandr hates the Far East. He signed up to go to space, not to some inhospitable region beyond Mongolia. He detests his role as a trainer. With four spaceflights under his belt, he's being called on to raise up the next intake of cosmonauts, but this isn't what he signed up for. To him, it's frustrating. Ninety-nine percent of being a cosmonaut is walking around with feet planted firmly on the ground.

"Fucking steppes," he mumbles, turning into the wind and lowering his head.

Although the facility is called the Vostochny Cosmodrome, it's nothing like the Baikonur Cosmodrome. The facilities here are rundown and second-rate. As Baikonur is in the old Soviet Republic of Kazakhstan, which is now an independent country, Russian pride demanded a Russian space center. The problem was the only suitable site was in the Far East. Vostochny is four thousand miles from Baikonur, almost five thousand miles from Moscow itself. Aleksandr had to drive to Vostochny, towing a trailer with his possessions. It took fourteen days, driving for seven to eight hours a day. Fourteen days of seeing nothing but forests and the occasional village.

The nearest town is Uglegorsk which has a population of five thousand people. In winter, Vostochny is a frozen hell, while in summer, it is plagued by swarms of mosquitos that darken the sky.

The nearest major city is Blagoveshchensk, which is precisely as enticing as it sounds. Although it's only three hours away by road, the city is divided by the Amur River, with the southern side of the city becoming the Chinese border town of Heihi. Trade is common. Smuggling is a way of life. Heihi is the only place where there's any decent food or any chance of buying new electronic equipment for use at Vostochny. European embargoes are meaningless to the Chinese. The only thing they understand is hard currency, either US dollars or yuan. Bartering with the Chinese is the only way to circumvent the corruption that siphons off cash from the Vostochny Cosmodrome. Buy a laptop from Heihi, and it'll incur a 20% markup for *"transportation."* Requisition it through the quartermaster at Vostochny, and it'll cost twice the going rate in Heihi and arrive with half the advertised RAM and a secondhand hard drive.

The Vostochny launch center has been built on the outskirts of the majestic Zeya River. It's the one redeeming quality of the region. Its deep blue water is hypnotic, meandering rather than flowing. It's good for fishing, which provides some relief from the monotony of the isolated cosmodrome on weekends.

Aleksandr walks into the administration building. He walks past a security guard at the front desk. The guard is dressed in camouflage fatigues. A rifle leans in the corner. A pistol is set in a holster on the guard's hip.

Aleksandr holds up his ID as he storms past without any intention to stop. At a distance of almost twenty feet, it's impossible to make out his picture, let alone his name or position. He's been stopped by guards before, and it's a mistake they've collectively chosen not to make again. With indignation, Aleksandr demands they know who he is. Their job is to guard against unauthorized personnel, not to harass regular staff.

The guard nods, knowing better than to incur Aleksandr's wrath.

Several people stand before the elevator, waiting for the doors to open. Aleksandr has no patience. He marches to the stairs and jogs up two flights. Most days, he'll beat the elevator. Today, he doesn't. He opens the stairway door, stepping out onto the floor as the elevator doors open beside him, allowing those he saw downstairs to walk out behind him.

"Hmm," he grumbles.

Aleksandr storms up to his secretary. Technically, she's an administration officer assigned to the cosmonaut office itself, but he's made it clear not just to her but the others that he considers her his personal assistant.

"Has everyone arrived?"

"Just two more to come," she says, leaning past him and looking at those walking down the corridor from the elevator. As far as Aleksandr is concerned, if they've come in after him, they're late, regardless of whether the introductory meeting has begun or not. He's tempted to scold them, but he doesn't say anything as they rush past, entering the meeting room. What little patience Aleksandr has is reserved for scorn.

He drops his bag in his office. Of all the cosmonauts, he's the only one that isn't confined to a cubicle or a hot desk. Seniority has its perks.

"Good morning," Aleksandr says, walking into the meeting room at exactly 9 am, and not a minute too soon or a minute later. The two candidates from the elevator are still putting their bags beneath their desks and in the process of sitting down when everyone else rises to their feet.

In unison, the twenty cosmonaut cadets reply, "Good morning, sir."

"Have a seat," Aleksandr says. It's subtle, but even with those few words, he's asserting his dominance. He may smile. He may speak with a soft voice, but their futures lie with his assessments, and he's already making mental notes.

Aleksandr is 5'6" in height, which puts him below the average height of men in Russia at 5'9", but he's still above the average female height of 5'4". His height shouldn't matter. Intellectually, he knows that, but his pride demands a bigger stature. Aleksandr knows Napoleon's small-man syndrome is a myth. Napoleon was also 5'6", which sounds short by modern European standards, but he was the average height for men in France in the 18th century. Napoleon's adversary, the Duke of Wellington, was 5'9", while Admiral Nelson was shorter than Napoleon, measuring 5'5", but the narrative in the British press painted Napoleon as insecure about his height. It was a simple way to mock him, and the public loves nothing more than simplicity when it comes to slander. That Napoleon was a megalomaniac should have been enough, but being short made it easy to despise him, regardless of whether he was short at all. For Aleksandr, though, being short is demeaning. It's not, but he hates people looking down at him. He much prefers sitting at a boardroom table where he can raise the seat and stare someone square in the eye.

As the son of the Russian ambassador to the US, Aleksandr was raised in privilege, only to have that privilege negated by a bunch of uncouth football players and the lanky high school basketball team. Up until the age of fourteen, they were all roughly the same height. By fifteen, the differences were showing. By sixteen, Aleksandr was physically looking up at his US male classmates even though, mentally, he despised and looked down on them with disdain. By seventeen, he was the only boy still in line with the American girls. When he hit eighteen, the difference was insufferable, angering him. It wasn't fair. Why should genetics bless some and curse others? And, what's worse, the blessed were oblivious. They lived as though they somehow deserved the prowess brought on by their height.

For Aleksandr, the towering bulk of 6'2" American jocks with muscular chests is still intimidating. He won't admit that to anyone, but it provokes a backlash from him. It's fight or flight, and Aleksandr has never run from a fight. Fight is all he knows. And being short, he learned to fight dirty. In college, he learned fighting need not involve fists. Words are more effective than punches. Now that he's in a position of power earned by his own merit as a cosmonaut he wields words like a sword.

The candidates are seated in five rows of four. The actual room is quite spacious and could easily accommodate sixty people. Those present could be seated in just two rows, but last night, Aleksandr deliberately set the seats well apart, spacing only two seats at each table. It gives them plenty of room to spread out, but more than that, it makes them uncomfortable. They're isolated. Most people want to blend into the herd. Aleksandr wants the candidates to feel exposed and vulnerable. He's looking for how they respond, especially when they don't know they're being watched.

The candidates either have laptops open or paper pads out, ready to take notes. Aleksandr walks along the front row and, without warning, closes the lid on the first and third laptops.

"Stand," he says, and the meaning is implicit. Just these two should stand.

Sheepishly, a woman and a man rise to their feet. Both of them clutch their hands in front of them, bowing their heads slightly, not daring to make eye contact with him.

Aleksandr asks the audience, "Do you see these two? Look at them. Look closely."

Aleksandr is aware of the fear surging through the room. No one knows quite what to expect or why these two particular candidates were singled out. His selection was random and arbitrary, and that kind of uncertainty carries a clear message with it. *Never let your guard down. For better or for worse, you'll never know when you're about to be singled out.*

Aleksandr waves his hands around. "After eighteen months, this is all that will be left of your intake. Two cosmonauts. Everyone else will return to their offices or military units. Everyone else will be but a memory. Only two will remain. The question I have is, where will you stand? Will you be one of these two? I don't know, but I do know the pass rate for this course is 10%. To succeed, you must be the best. I expect your best. Nothing less. Over the next year and a half, you will learn to put Roscosmos first in everything you do. You will eat, sleep and breathe the cosmonaut ethos."

He turns to those standing and gestures with his hands. They sit but with the care of someone handling a live grenade.

Aleksandr remembers his intake class well over a decade ago. His instructor was kind. She wanted everyone to succeed. She was weak. Being nice is for street performers and clowns. Cosmonauts need to be disciplined. If he scares the class, that's good. They should be scared. Aleksandr has been into space. He understands what it means for a thin sheet of insulated metal to be all that separates life from death. Being nice is for first dates and family dinners. Being nice will get someone killed in orbit.

"I am friendly, but I am not your friend. I will mentor you, but I will not carry you. I will teach you what I know, but I cannot answer for you. It is for you to show the steel and resolve of a Russian cosmonaut. It is for you to prove you have the intelligence, the dedication, the drive, the knowledge, the discipline and the consistency to wear the Russian flag on your arm and the Roscosmos patch over your heart.

"I believe in objective measures. Each of you will be given a starting value of a hundred points. Every time you succeed, that will be increased. Fail me, and you will lose credit. Reach zero, and you will be sent home."

Aleksandr addresses the two candidates from the elevator, saying, "Katya Myshkin and Alexsei Rogov, you will both be docked fifty points for being late."

Neither of them complains. They hang their heads. Eyes go wide around the room. No one speaks. For a moment, no one breathes.

Aleksandr says, "No one arrives after me. Is that understood?"

In unison, the cosmonaut corps candidates reply, "Yes, sir."

And Aleksandr allows a faint smile to escape his lips. Fear is his to command. He will mold this class into his image. Aleksandr may be confined to the Russian steppes, but he will rule as emperor over the candidates—*his* candidates. It will be as though he were ruling in the palace at St. Petersburg in the days of old. He will have the respect he deserves.

That he's being unreasonable is irrelevant. Their responsibility is to obey. Technically, Katya Myshkin and Alexsei Rogov were in the room before him, but not the floor. Aleksandr walked out of the stairs before they stepped from the elevator, and for Aleksandr, that is insolence. Anyone that is dedicated to excellence would not risk being late. And he can see it in their eyes. The fear of failure looms large. Neither will take such risks again. They will please him. They must. They have no choice.

Briefing

Molly isn't nervous so much as overawed at the prospect of meeting the President of the United States on her first day working in the White House. It's difficult to think straight. After the fiasco with Director Greene and Chief of Staff Dosela, it's nice to be doing something constructive. Molly's not naive, but she is a little star-struck by President Elizabeth Smith-Knowles.

As a Democrat, Molly campaigned for the President in Boston, door-knocking and handing out fliers at the mall for nine months leading up to the election. She joked about politics being the liberal surrogate for pregnancy. When the election finally came, celebrations began early in the evening when it became apparent that the United States had elected yet another female President. Since then, there have been the usual termites in the news cycle, constantly undermining the President's agenda. Congress has been hostile, but somehow, the President has still pushed through Medicare reforms that have helped millions.

"What's she like?" Molly asks, sitting on a chair next to the President's receptionist, a well-dressed woman in her early thirties.

The receptionist looks up from her laptop screen and thinks for a moment, probably not about Molly's question so much as whether she wants to get drawn into a protracted discussion.

"Busy. Insanely busy. Two minutes with her is like two hours with anyone else. And she expects a lot. She demands a lot."

Molly nods.

"It's the job," the receptionist says. "If she's blunt with you, don't mistake it for being rude or unkind. She's not like that. She's got a bazillion priorities tugging on her, pulling her in different directions. She has to decide what she prioritizes. So she'll deal with something, and then," the receptionist snaps her fingers, "she's on to the next critical issue. And there's *always* another critical issue."

Molly nods again, looking down at the folder in her hand.

"What are you here to talk to her about?" the receptionist asks.

"Oh, I'm a gopher," Molly says, belittling herself. "Go for this. Go for that. Ah, the Press Secretary is sick, so I'm here to deliver this."

She holds up the folder as though it were an exhibit in a court of law.

"Well," the receptionist says. "Make sure you understand what's in there because she *will* have questions, and she will expect answers."

"Yes, of course," Molly says, realizing she's not at ComicCon waiting to meet a celebrity to get an autographed photo. She's here to do a job. Interning. Is that a verb? Molly thinks about it and realizes the noun and verb forms have entirely different meanings. Or do they? She opens the folder. Five or six pages have been bound together with a metal clip. At the top, someone's stamped *Eyes Only* in red ink.

Office of the

Director of National Intelligence

Object of Interest BDO 2033-495 Observations

BDO[1] 2033-495 was originally detected by the NASA ATLAS observatory by grad students at the University of Hawaii[2] on Feb 14th of this year.

"Valentine's Day," Molly mumbles to herself, knowing she should probably think a little more deeply as this briefing clearly isn't about red roses and chocolates.

The BDO's distinct spectra[3] ruled out classification as a comet or regular C-type[4] asteroid, and it was designated[5] as an Object of Interest[6], possibly an M-type[7] solid metal core asteroid such as 16 Psyche[8].

The tiny numbers next to various words are links to the copious footnotes at the bottom of each page. Molly pities anyone who wears glasses, as she has great eyesight and, even for her, the font borders on microscopic. She reads the entry for footnotes one and six, wanting to understand the acronyms and terms that have been used.

BDO *is a Bright Data Object, sometimes referred to as a Brilliant Data Object. BDOs are candidates as OIs (Objects of Interest) as they stand out from the background noise/static in broad-spectrum astronomical data dumps. They are bright/brilliant in that they are anomalies among the chaos and require further investigation to properly identify. After analysis, a BDO may be reclassified as an actual Object of Interest (OI) or may be relegated as a ghost image or artifact of the collection process itself, being a false positive reading. Examples of false BDOs include the use of wifi to stream video within an observatory, causing an extended spike in radiometric data, and inadvertently appearing as a real object in deep space.*

Object of Interest *(OI) is the designation used for any BDO determined to be an actual astronomical body. OIs have an unknown, unpredictable or unconventional orbit or unusual composition requiring additional investigation. OIs are often reassigned as long-period comets or near-Earth asteroids and may require ongoing monitoring of their orbital paths.*

"Oh, my eyes, *my eyes!*" she mumbles, pretending they're about to bleed from sheer bureaucratic-induced tedium. The receptionist looks sideways at her with a knowing smile. Molly smiles in reply and returns to reading the briefing quietly.

Subsequent observations of BDO 2033-495 determined it to be an extra-solar[9] Object of Interest with an interstellar origin[10] with a hyperbolic orbit[11] approaching from the solar apex[12] at right ascension $18^h\ 28^m\ 0^s$ and declination 30° north.

"Now, that last part should have had a footnote," she mumbles, pointing at the words *right ascension*. She looks up at the receptionist, asking, "Who writes these briefings? They know this is for the President, right? She's not going to care about technobabble."

The receptionist shrugs, saying, "That's why you're here. Your job is to make it plain."

"Oh," Molly replies, re-reading a couple of the footnotes to ensure she comprehends the briefing. "And the Press Secretary normally does this?"

"He's really good at cutting through technical jargon and bullshit. If anything, he's a little too good at it."

Molly returns her gaze to the document, thinking this is way beyond her remit. There's no way Chief of Staff Dosela knew what was in this folder. She was probably given a summary by someone else. If she'd read even a single sentence, Molly's sure she would have sent it back to the ODNI and asked for a revised version without the jargon. Dot points, that's what's needed. Just a series of salient facts. They could leave all the footnotes for anyone wanting more clarification, but the whole memo needs to be rewritten for clarity and simplicity. Molly may be a gopher, but she's a gopher with a master's degree. She knows her way around the absurdium of academia, and this whole briefing is dancing around details without actually making a point.

The point of origin[13] is identified as an unnamed star on the border of the constellations Lyra and Hercules[14].

"But what *is* the point?" Molly mumbles to herself, not referring to the BDO's point of origin but the reason someone sent this mumbo jumbo to the President of the United States of America. And why does the Director of National Intelligence care about an asteroid or a comet or whatever?

It seems the receptionist is getting used to Molly talking to herself as she smiles but doesn't look up from her own work. There must be a lot of colorful characters passing through the reception area, waiting to see the President.

The appearance of out-gassing[15] directed toward the Sun rather than as a cometary tail[16] appears comparable to propellant exhaust[17], altering the inbound velocity[18] at a rate of 28m/s. Current trajectory[19] is consistent with gravity-assist deceleration[20] around the Sun itself, resulting in an unknown subsequent orbital profile[21].

The door to the Oval Office opens, and a naval officer leaves with his head hung low. Raised voices seep through the walls and out of the door.

The secretary looks up. "The President will see you now."

Molly swallows the lump in her throat. She closes the folder and gets to her feet. Out of habit, she straightens her skirt, checking that her blouse is neatly tucked in. Molly clutches the folder in front of her like a shield.

The inside of the Oval Office is breathtaking. Around the edge of the room, the polished wooden floor glistens like crystal, catching the sunlight streaming in through the tall windows. There's a plush, inset woolen carpet matching the shape of the room with the insignia of an eagle in front of the Resolute Desk. Around the edge of the carpet, various quotes have been embroidered in words roughly a foot in width. Molly steps over rather than on the words of Martin Luther King Jr., saying, *"Injustice anywhere is a threat to justice everywhere."*

Oil paintings of past US Presidents adorn the walls. Bronze statues rest on ornate wooden cabinets spaced around the room. They beg for closer examination, but Molly cannot comply. There's one of a cowboy on the back of a bucking bronco, with the wild horse kicking its rear legs high in the air, another of a US soldier in a World War Two uniform charging with a rifle in hand, and yet another of an Apollo astronaut standing on the lunar surface in a bulky spacesuit. He's saluting a bronze replica of the Stars and Stripes on a thin pole.

The President is wearing a pantsuit not unlike the one worn by the chief of staff. She's leaning against the Resolute Desk, facing several military officers seated on the chairs and couches at the other end of the oval carpet. She has her hands folded over her chest.

"Is this it?" she asks, throwing out an impatient hand.

Molly rushes over, handing her the folder, then she stands silently off to one side as the President skim reads the first few pages.

"I don't get it," the President says, addressing the generals. "This is what Bill's upset about? This is why you want an Executive Order to fund space-based weapons in defiance of the UN Outer Space Treaty? I'd like to think the ODNI has more to worry about than a few stars down the end of a telescope."

Molly speaks before she thinks. "It's an alien spacecraft, ma'am."

"What?" the President says, turning to her with eyes that go wide.

"That's what they think. That's what they don't want to tell you. Someone in ODNI thinks there's growing evidence to suggest there's an alien spacecraft out there."

The President slaps the folder on her leg, saying, "Well, why didn't anyone tell me that?"

One of the generals replies, "No one believes it, ma'am. No one wants to call it. I mean, it's on the fringe of being a conspiracy theory."

The President says, "No one wants to look stupid, huh?"

Molly can't resist. "No one but me, ma'am."

She's expecting a laugh. She doesn't get one.

The President hands the folder back to her with the actual document hanging out of it and on the verge of falling to the carpet. "Explain it to me."

"Ah, shouldn't this be coming from NASA?" Molly asks.

"ODNI isn't waiting around on NASA."

One of the other generals says, "Besides, there are already leaks hitting the media."

Molly flips open the folder and scans the contents. "Okay. It's quite technical, but the footnotes explain a lot of the terminology. Basically, the University of Hawaii spotted an object coming from outside our solar system. They tracked it over several months, thinking it was a comet, but instead of vapor streaming out behind it, they saw vapor in front of it like the exhaust of a rocket slowing down to land. And it's slowing fast, at several times the strength of gravity we feel on Earth, which isn't something a comet would do. Ah, there's also some additional details about where it came from and that it's heading for the sun and not for Earth."

"Well, that's good, right?" the President says.

"It's going to use the sun to slow down."

"Slow down?"

Molly isn't an astrophysicist. She isn't even in the Press Secretary's office. She's an intern, but she's intelligent. She understands the footnotes. She applies herself, thinking of an analogy.

"Imagine a tennis ball bouncing off a car driving into the parking lot at the local tennis club. If the ball didn't hit the car, it would keep going across the main road. But when it collides with the windshield, it absorbs the car's momentum and bounces back toward you."

Molly's quite proud of her succinct example, but it takes only a few words from the President for her to realize it wasn't quite as applicable as she thought.

"They're going to crash into the Sun?"

"More like swing around it as though it were a pole they were running past." Molly looks at the notes, adding, "It's called gravitationally-assisted braking. It will only work because the object is coming head-on at the sun as it orbits the Milky Way itself. So, yes, it's more like grabbing a pole as you run past."

The President is quiet, considering those words.

There's movement behind Molly. Out of the corner of her eye, she sees Chief of Staff Dosela. Molly's not sure how long she's been standing there. She didn't hear the door open or close.

"I'm sorry," the chief of staff says to the President. "I didn't realize how sensitive this was. I thought I was giving her a standard press briefing pack."

"Nonsense," the President says. "She's brilliant. She understands all this star stuff."

Molly feels as though she should interrupt to qualify that she *barely* understands what's written in the briefing and no more of the generalized *star stuff* the President is referring to. Molly's using the skills she picked up during her master's degree, where she was often forced to rephrase and interpret complex documents on the fly. It doesn't mean she's an expert at anything beyond what she's read. If anything, she should speak up, as silence is a lie, but the moment passes before she can respond.

The President turns her focus back to the military officers. "If this thing is a threat, can we defend ourselves against it?"

Several of the officers shift nervously in their seats. A couple of them start to speak, but from the lack of conviction, it's obvious to Molly they'd waffle on about uncertainty, offering only vague answers.

The army general, dressed in drab olive with golden stars on his lapel, says a blunt, "No."

"Explain."

"Our military is focused on land warfare. Tanks, soldiers, artillery, helicopters—they're all about achieving land-based objectives. Our air force is geared toward air supremacy to protect our land assets and bomb the hell out of anyone else's land assets. Our navy supports the army. It can fight its own battles, but no one lives at sea. It, too, is geared toward supporting maneuvers on land, especially when it comes to the Marines."

One of the other officers says, "General Morley is right. Even our subs and our strategic nuclear forces are geared toward hitting targets on land."

The President leans forward, resting her head in her hands for a moment. "So unless they land and walk out in front of us, our army is…"

"Useless," General Morley says. "In the sky, we might get in a few licks. In space, no chance in hell."

Molly forgets where she is and the rank and position of those around her. To her mind, this discussion is premature. "Why are we assuming they're hostile?"

The President looks at her, but not with disdain. This is what the receptionist was talking about. President Elizabeth Smith-Knowles is brisk, but she's not unreasonable. She points at Molly, saying, "What she said."

"It's not so much an assumption," General Morley replies, "as a precaution. Winning wars is 90% logistics and only 10% battle. We are unprepared. At the moment, we could not go to battle as we have no logistics capable of supporting warfare in space."

The President nods, accepting that point.

"But this is marvelous," Molly says as the Chief of Staff steps up beside her, touching her forearm and wanting her to be silent. Molly can't fall quiet, not at this moment. "This is First Contact. Our world will never be the same."

"And that's what worries me," General Morley says.

The President is quiet, but she nods in agreement with the general.

Looking at those present in the Oval Office, it strikes Molly that change is scary because it represents the unknown, and that does not sit well with her.

Molly's family hails from Ireland. She's visited the Emerald Isle twice with her dad. Their ancestors were the Taverners and came from Howth, a rugged peninsula on the outskirts of Dublin. In 1846, the Taverners fled the Great Famine, arriving in New York as part of *the tired, the poor, the huddled masses yearning to breathe free.* From there, they moved to Boston. Over time, marriages blurred the lines of descent. Molly's grandmother was the last of the Taverners. They'd been in Howth for over eight hundred years before fleeing to America. Local folklore attributes Rob Taverner from the 1300s as coining the phrase, "*Something bad—but known—is better than something unknown.*" It became the unofficial family slogan.

Over time, the devil was added to the phrase because sensationalism is like writing a blank check. There's no better way to make a point than invoking Lucifer, Beelzebub or Satan. It always struck Molly as a little perverse that her family is best known for coming up with the phrase, "*Better the devil you know.*" She heard that cliché way too many times as a teen. As proud as her father was of its origins, to Molly, his pride seemed misplaced. For better or for worse, the devil is still the devil. Can the devil really be better than any alternative? Are there degrees of demons? Do they come from different circles of hell? Regardless, the phrase has become iconic not only in her own life but within European culture.

Standing there in the Oval Office, Molly can see the same perverse logic of "*Better the devil you know*" holding sway over these military minds. Change must be the worst of the devils, not Baphomet with his goat head, horns, wings and pentagram charms.

As bad as things might be on Earth, with annual heat waves, climate refugees causing instability, the decline of wildlife, famines and viral outbreaks rippling around the globe, these people *know* this particular devil and they know him well. They're comfortable with the devil. If it comes to a choice between devils, this one is better as, at the very least, it's quantifiable. But aren't there angels *and* demons? And why does it have to be either black or white? Is the current devil really that desirable? Why is change scary? Why can't change be for good?

The whole *better-the-devil-you-know* concept strikes Molly as shortsighted. It favors the status quo over change as though somehow change were a fallen angel rising from the fires of Hades itself.

Molly's lips tighten, betraying her disgust.

"You don't agree," the President says to her, and Molly feels utterly intimidated.

Molly's no one. She's nothing. She shouldn't even be here. Were the Press Secretary not sick, neither of them would be having this conversation. If Chief of Staff Dosela hadn't taken pity on her following her run-in with Director Greene, she would have never been handed that folder. Molly doesn't have a fancy uniform or decades of command experience. She hasn't risen on merit. She's here because her dad pulled some strings with the chief of staff. Nepotism much? If Molly were honest, she would rather be on the other side of the ornate steel fence surrounding the White House, carrying a sign, protesting for something, anything—for change! Oh, the irony. She should be standing shoulder to shoulder with those of her generation, challenging their elders. Change is no devil. That's where she belongs, not here in the Oval Office, and certainly not in a discussion about the arrival of intelligent beings from another planet.

Molly is soft-spoken in reply. She's hoping reason rather than volume holds sway in the President's thinking.

"Regardless of whether we're talking about ET or the economy, change is inevitable. It's not something we can ignore. Somewhat ironically, change is the only constant in life. And the general's right. We should be prepared, but not only for war, for peace."

The President wags her finger at Molly. She clenches her jaw, raising her cheeks and tightening her lips. She's thinking rather than speaking, which Molly finds intriguing. The President is the one in charge. Six months ago, a hundred million voters decided to put the power of an entire nation in her hands. She has the final say, but she doesn't seem to want to say anything at all. Molly can see the machinations of her mind at work. Like a grandmaster sitting before a chess board, watching their opponent's opening gambit unfold, the

President is playing through dozens of scenarios in her mind before settling on her response. To the untrained eye, the move of a pawn from C7 to C5, exposing the bishop, might seem innocuous, but it's the strategy, not the move, that counts.

The President turns her attention back to the military leaders.

"War and peace. That's our approach. I'll sign your Executive Order and lean on Congress to formally recognize the funding requirement, but we need to be seen to be operating within the constraints of the UN Outer Space Treaty. Prepare for war. Hope for peace."

The generals nod, along with two admirals from the navy.

"Dismissed."

The officers get to their feet. Molly and the chief of staff are closest to the door. They should be the first ones to leave. Molly turns away from the President, but the chief of staff takes her gently by the arm, leading her away from the door. Nothing has been said between the President and the chief of staff, but Susan Dosela seems to be able to read the President's mind.

The officers leave, closing the door behind them. Molly swallows the lump choking her throat. As intimidating as it was being in the briefing, being alone with just the President and her chief of staff is terrifying.

The President walks around her desk and takes her seat, dropping rather than lowering herself into it, revealing her exasperation. She gestures to two ornate but uncomfortable seats set to the far side of the desk. The two of them sit as well. The cushion is firm. The carved wooden back is knotty in shape and doesn't align against Molly's back. Her shoulder blades aren't sure where they should be or what they should rest against.

The President blows air from her cheeks.

"Well, that was interesting," the chief of staff says. Both women laugh, which Molly finds perplexing. She's the only one not in on the joke.

The President addresses Molly, saying, "I will be having words with your father, young lady."

Molly must look mortified as the President follows up with, "You did great."

"Next steps?" the chief of staff asks.

The President thinks for a moment before replying, "We need to get out in front of this."

"You're worried about domestic optics?"

"Rednecks firing their AR-15s at lights in the sky? No, it's Russia and China that worry me. Humanity is fragmented. I'm worried this is going to end up as every man for himself. We're going to need the UN to step up on this issue. We need a coordinated response."

The chief of staff says, "Getting international agreement is going to be tough. The Security Council is anything but secure."

"If we don't, this is going to get ugly."

"I know."

"Get me in front of the UN General Assembly. Tomorrow."

"Yes, ma'am."

"And you," the President says, addressing Molly. "Talk to NASA. Talk to ODNI. Be discreet. Find out *everything* you can about this damn thing. No surprises. I need to be surfing ahead of the wave, not crushed by it as it breaks over me."

Molly nods. She feels electrified to be part of the team.

T-38

Chris 'Crash' Williams walks down the yellow and black line on the white concrete taxiway. The line curls in a smooth arc as it leads to the hangar, but he's a little OCD and doesn't mind walking along it instead of taking the most direct route. Airports are built on the principle of *safety through repetition*. Everything is prescribed to minimize accidents. The dual yellow/black line is a taxi guide for aircraft entering and exiting the hangar, allowing them clear space while on the taxiway, keeping them away from parked aircraft and the paths used by tankers and ground crew.

Ellington Field is barely twenty minutes from NASA's Johnson Space Center in southern Houston, making it ideal as an airport for astronauts and their T-38 jet aircraft. Although technically, it's a civilian airport, the government uses part of it as a joint base for the US Air Force, reservists and the Texas Air National Guard. NASA has to squeeze in its flights around everyone else. As an astronaut, Crash needs to clock a minimum of ten hours of airtime in a T-38 each month. It's no hardship as he loves flying high-performance twin-engine jets.

Over on one of the other taxi lines, he sees another T-38 being rolled out. Andrea Barman is training one of the new intake of candidates for the astronaut corps. She's walking around the sleek jet aircraft, running her hand over the fuselage and talking to the trainee. Rather than heading in to get his own jet, which is being prepped by the ground crew, he jogs over to say hello.

The T-38 is an old design, first coming into production in 1961, but the airframe is proven. As it has twin seats set in a line along its high, sloping fuselage, it's used as a trainer, but it's not sedate. The T-38 is the Ferrari of the skies. Whereas most modern jets, including 5th-generation fighters like the F-35 Lightning, have an overstuffed aerodynamic design, allowing for internal fuel tanks, internal weapons bays and all kinds of electronics catering to navigation, targeting and counter-electronic warfare, the T-38 is bare bones. It's streamlined. Being a trainer, it doesn't need the extras. It's built for one thing: speed. Its wings are stubby, protruding barely 25 feet.

The T-38 is a baby. At 45 feet in length, it's as long as the F-22 Raptor is wide. Two T38s lined up nose-to-nose would still be shorter than an F-35 Lightning, but Crash loves his T-38. The Air Force pilots he knows joke about it being a prize toy from a box of Cracker Jacks, but he thinks the T-38 is underrated. Any aircraft that can stay in use for well over half a century has his admiration. And he loves the fact Neil, Buzz and Collins all flew in one. Crash may never ride in a Gemini or an Apollo capsule, but he feels an affinity with the astronauts of yesteryear when he climbs into a T-38. They've left something of themselves in the cockpit.

"Hey, what's your flight plan?" he asks, jogging up to Andrea. She's standing in front of the aircraft, reaching up and running her hand along the smooth lines of the elongated nose cone, no doubt giving the trainee an appreciation for the history captured by these underestimated jet aircraft.

"Hi Crash. Liz is about to have her first hands-on training flight."

"Oh, a virgin, huh?" he says, looking at the embossed name tag velcroed to her uniform: *L. Browne*.

Liz doesn't look impressed by his comment. Like Andrea, she's dressed in an olive flight suit. Her hair has been meticulously pulled back. Gusts of wind rush across the runway, but not a single strand of hair moves out of place.

"Crash, right?" Liz says, offering a cautious hand. "Your reputation, like your nickname, precedes you."

"He's not that bad," Andrea says.

"You're French," Crash says, picking up on her slight accent.

"I'm from Sussex," Liz replies, not that Crash would know where that is. The perplexed look on his face prompts further explanation. "It's in England. My father's British, while my mother is French. I bounced between the two countries while growing up."

"Ah," Crash says, finding her accent alluring.

"I'm here on exchange from ESA."

"Flights?" he asks, meaning spaceflights.

"Three. Including an aborted Soyuz launch that dropped back four hundred miles downrange."

"I heard about that one," he says, smiling. "Seems I'm not the only Crash."

Liz says, "I have to admit, it was bloody terrifying. I thought I was going to die."

Crash nods.

This is the unspoken truth of spaceflight. Death is never more than a heartbeat away. The difference between life and death comes down to the precision and consistency of engineering practices developed over decades. One slip-up, a single lapse in concentration or an overlooked quality check during construction and disaster can unfold within fractions of a second during a launch. Trying to quantify the insane engineering feat that is spaceflight is nigh on impossible. Even something as simple as the sheer amount of fuel being consumed is difficult to comprehend. Seeing a glowing flame reaching several times the length of the rocket it's pushing into space gives some idea of the ferocity involved. Someone once calculated that when Apollo 11 launched, it was throwing out the equivalent of four elephants worth of fuel every second. It's a crazy mind picture, but spaceflight itself is crazy. NASA, Blue Origin, Boeing and SpaceX make the extraordinary look ordinary, but it isn't. Crash knows he and the other astronauts are sitting on top of a powder keg while waiting to launch.

With genuine affection, he says, "I'm glad you were okay."

"Thanks," Liz replies, having softened her own tone of voice.

At that moment, all the banter and jostling is gone. There's nothing but respect shared between them. They both know the difference between them and those whose names are engraved on bronze memorial plaques comes down to mere time and chance. For all their training and dedication, nothing can compensate for faulty equipment. Get a flat on the freeway and it's annoying to change a tire on the side of the road. Get a loose nut in the fuel lines of a rocket engine and the turbo fans will disintegrate, destroying the entire rocket in seconds.

Andrea says, "We've got a 45-minute flight out over the bay. We'll take in the sights. Perform some basic maneuvers and be back in time for the briefing at Johnson. And you?"

"Me? I'm joyriding. Clocking hours."

"Come and join us for some formation flying."

"I might just do that," he says, smiling and turning away from them, leaving them to complete their preflight inspection. As an afterthought, he turns back to Liz and says, "Remember: no rudder when landing."

"What do you mean?" she asks, narrowing her eyes as she stares at him with curiosity.

"He's right," Andrea says.

"No rudder?"

"On the T-38, the rudder is like a sail sticking up behind you," Crash says. "Even a light touch will put you into a roll when close to the ground, fighting wind gusts. Trust me. It's not something you want to do."

"And you've done that?"

Andrea laughs. "That's how he got his nickname."

"You crashed a T-38? And survived?"

"Almost," Crash says. "I *almost* crashed a T-38."

"Go on," Andrea says, setting her hands on her hips. "Tell her. You started this."

"I was on my fifth flight with an instructor in the back. They tell you the instructor can take over at any point in time, but don't be fooled. From the back seat, they can't see shit."

Andrea nods. "It's true. I get a great view of the sky, but I can't see what's in front of or below the aircraft, just the solid back of your ejection seat and your helmet."

Crash says, "I was lined up on approach, but I was off-center. My instructor told me to straighten up or go around. Fifty feet up, coming down at a hundred and fifty knots, and I was hit with a crosswind, pushing me further from the center line. I tapped the rudder."

"And?" Liz says, intrigued.

"And I panicked when the airframe tilted. I meant to counter the initial roll, pushing back with the opposite rudder, but I pushed too hard. Way too hard."

Andrea says, "He performed a barrel roll at thirty feet with his undercarriage extended."

"A barrel roll? Like—all the way around?"

"Yep." Crash laughs. "The instructor froze. He could have taken control, but he was sure we were already dead. He figured there was nothing he could do but hold on for dear life."

"And?"

Andrea says, "And Crash set the T-38 down as though nothing out of the ordinary had happened. It's on YouTube. He rolled that baby on approach and then his back wheels both touched down at the same time. The nose flared, allowing for aerobraking, and then the nose wheel touched a few seconds later. Apart from the barrel roll, it was a textbook landing."

Crash says, "I faced a board of inquiry. They grounded me for three months. They were sure I was showboating—like I was some hotshot showing off. I wasn't. It was a genuine mistake, but once I was committed to the roll I knew I had to complete it or I'd lose flight stability."

Andrea says, "Replays showed the wingtips cleared the ground by about three feet, and the wheels touched down less than half a second later. And that's how he got his name: *Crash* Williams."

"But I didn't crash!"

"You came too damn close."

Liz says, "I heard you crashed an Orion while docking with the Lunar Gateway."

"Now, that wasn't my fault," Crash says, getting defensive. "The investigation proved it was down to instrument failure. And I docked. Just a little hard."

Liz raises her eyebrows, clearly trying to reconcile what she's heard with what he's saying.

Crash says, "And I never lost my flight status."

"That's true," Andrea says.

"Anyway," he says. "Line up your approach and don't touch the rudder."

Andrea turns to Liz, saying, "It's good advice. Once we're out over the bay, we'll perform some barrel rolls and you'll see what he means about the rudder. It's far more sensitive than what you'd be used to in a propeller plane, like a Cessna."

United Nations

Molly is in awe of where she's standing. She's at the back of the General Assembly Hall within the United Nations Building in New York with Chief of Staff Sue Dosela. Staff move down the rows wearing vacuum cleaners on their backs. The desks are wiped down. Security guards stand by the doors, watching.

To Molly's mind, the hall is a cathedral. Instead of a deity, the god is geopolitics itself. The ceiling is easily a hundred feet overhead, with a broad blue dome stretching across the auditorium as though it were the sky. The emerald-colored marble rostrum at the front is massive, but it looks small against the sheer size of the hall itself. The rostrum has been set below a brilliant, golden panel reaching from the floor to the ceiling. The gilded UN logo is in the center of the panel. Olive branches surround a polar projection of Earth looking down from the north, including every continent except Antarctica, which, technically, isn't a country.

Although olive branches represent peace, they do so only for a few of the world's major religions: Judaism, Christianity and Islam. For the Hindus, Buddhists and Taoists, olive branches are meaningless. For atheists, they're demeaning as they perpetuate a myth. And with those few thoughts, Molly gains an insight into the absurd complexity of unifying the world. The only thing everyone on the planet shares in common is their humanity, but humanity is the one thing no one cares about. They care about their heritage, their religions, their political ideologies, their money, their influence over neighboring countries, and their natural resources. Being human isn't enough. Looking at the logo, Molly cannot but feel the futility facing President Elizabeth Smith-Knowles. The approach of an alien spacecraft should unify everyone, but it won't.

"This place looks like a movie set, like something out of *Star Trek*," Molly says. "It looks like the *Federation of Planets*."

The President's chief of staff laughs. "Oh, you've got this all wrong. The fictional *Federation* was modeled after the UN, not the other way around."

"Ah."

"Do you know why you're here?" the chief of staff asks.

"No."

Molly's perplexed. Her father sold her on the internship as a summer spent shuffling paperwork between filing cabinets and archive boxes. It was supposed to be a shiny star on her resume. Nothing more.

"You're invisible. And that makes you invaluable to us. If the President or I approach someone, it'll attract attention. We can't have an off-the-cuff conversation with anyone. Everything we say is an official position. But you. You can mingle. You can make suggestions. You can probe and ask questions."

Molly nods. She's not sure anyone is going to take her seriously, but she'll try.

"Come. I want to show you the UN Security Council. You'll be watching from the observation deck, but you've got to get beyond the awe of this place. I want you to ignore the pomp. Ignore the ambassadors. Ignore anyone that looks and acts important. They're actors on a stage. It's their aides that hold the real power. Often, the front men are just marionettes. It's the puppet masters we're after."

The chief of staff leads her down a corridor and into another vast room with a crescent-shaped wooden table. Out beyond the circular table, matching the broad, curved wood, there are dozens of chairs arranged in two rows.

The chief points at a row of windows halfway up the far wall.

"You'll be up there. Ignore anyone at the desk. Watch those in the back seats like a hawk."

Molly says, "Shouldn't this be something the CIA does?"

"The NSA. And yes, they will be watching and listening, but you're the ace in the hole."

Molly doesn't understand. A guard within the security council room walks over, waving them out.

"The UN is a den of thieves. We know all the players. We know their spooks. And they know ours." She raises an eyebrow. "But an intern on her first week in the White House? They'll look at you and figure you're on *work experience.*"

"I'm a nobody."

"Exactly. No one will notice you."

The chief of staff pulls out her phone and sends Molly an encrypted list of names and photos.

"I've got a bunch of people I want you to keep an eye on. Talk to them. We need to know what they think about the BDO—what they really think."

Molly looks at her phone. She scrolls through a dozen images, wondering how she's supposed to remember so many names and faces when everyone looks the same to her: *important.*

Molly says, "I won't be able to talk to half of these people."

"You don't need to. The diplomatic corps will cover the regular bases. We need you to rove. We need you to sweep out wide, looking for anything that might be missed by our dragnet. You're an extra set of eyes and ears. We're hoping you might pick up on some unguarded comments."

"Most of these people are Chinese," Molly says, flicking through the list.

"And a few Russians. We're confident we can get Europe and India to participate in an international mission. We'll invite the Russians, but historically, there's always been tension between us. We expect they'll want to go it alone. Russia is the wildcard. Their economy was crippled by the war with Ukraine. They're still on the UN Security Council, but they've been humbled before the international community. We don't want them making trouble. They have nukes. Lots of nukes. And they have a long history of spaceflight. We really don't want to be squabbling with them over the arrival of an alien spacecraft."

"And the Chinese?"

"The Chinese are prickly. They, too, will want to go alone as a matter of national pride. We need them to see the bigger picture, that this is about humanity as a whole and not any one nation. If anything, the Chinese are more of a worry than the Russians."

"Why?"

"Because they can afford a mission like this. The Russians will struggle. The Chinese could pull it off with ease. We need to get both of them on our side or First Contact is going to be a nightmare."

The chief of staff looks at her watch.

"Okay. We've got about an hour before the President addresses the General Assembly. From there, she'll go on to address the Security Council separately. We've got diplomats greasing the wheels, but it's the random comments that will be most revealing about what they're actually thinking. And how they report this back to their leadership is going to be crucial to the outcome. We cannot afford to alienate these people."

"Alienate," Molly says, smiling and trying not to laugh at the chief of staff's choice of words. The chief of staff suppresses a smile of her own. She drops her head, shaking it slightly, apparently caught off guard by her own joke.

"Okay," Molly says, still feeling overwhelmed but a little more upbeat.

"And don't worry about language barriers or anything like that. Everyone here speaks English. Everyone. Especially those that deny it."

The chief of staff leaves Molly in the cafeteria.

Molly sits in the corner, pretending to sip coffee from an almost empty cup, acting as though it were full. She watches as diplomats wander through the broad main corridor talking with each other. They send their underlings for coffee, but Molly notices the gophers like her chat among themselves while in line. The coffee shop is a melting pot within the United Nations. It's easy to see relaxed smiles and laughs while getting coffee. Their defenses are down. Molly spots a few of the people on her list. One of them, Wú Jīng, walks around between tables, looking for a seat.

"You're welcome to join me," Molly says, offering a friendly smile. She turns off her phone, noting that Jing specializes in foreign affairs for the Chinese Ministry of Public Security. Her father is a senior advisor in the politburo, having survived the purge following the ousting of Premier Zhū. Jing is pretty, but Molly's sure that's a convenient distraction. Pretty girls are always underestimated. Beauty blinds people to brains.

"Thank you. My feet are killing me."

Molly glances under the table.

"High heels? Oh, you're more dedicated than I am. It's flats for me."

Jing asks, "What are you doing here at the UN, Molly?"

Damn, she's good. Molly's wearing a photo ID with her name on it, but the type isn't overly large and Molly didn't spot Jing glancing down at it.

"Me?" Molly says, feigning ignorance. "I'm a summer intern. Day two. I'm here to run errands for the White House staff."

"Oh," Jing says, and Molly can see the machinations of her mind at work. She's trying to assess whether Molly might surrender important information inadvertently. Meeting Jing *before* the US President's appearance in front of the General Assembly is perfect as it disarms the Chinese advisor. They're both playing a game, although Molly feels as though she's one step ahead. As far as Jing is concerned, their meeting is purely coincidental.

Jing sits. She sips her coffee, hiding behind the rim of the disposable cup for a moment, although her piercing eyes never leave

Molly's. "Do you know what all this is about?"

Molly clutches her hands in front of her, wanting to appear sincere. She leans forward and speaks in a soft voice, saying, "It's all those rumors... about a spacecraft."

"They're true?"

Molly nods. She figures she's not revealing anything too sensitive, at least, nothing the President herself won't be discussing within the hour.

"What are they going to do?" Jing asks with the seasoned practice of a professional.

Molly's always loved gossip. She's never had to do it as a job before. For her, this is fun.

"NASA's going to launch a mission to intercept the spacecraft. The President wants a multinational crew, with someone from each of the permanent members of the UN Security Council onboard."

Jing narrows her eyes. For a moment, Molly thinks she's blown her cover. Molly was a little too quick to divulge very specific information. There's an awkward silence. Jing lowers her hands to her lap. Her phone rings. She raises it to her ear and speaks in Chinese. The stunning woman gets up, taking her coffee with her, saying, "I need to take this call."

"Sure," Molly replies, watching as Jing walks away between the tables. Molly's left wondering who played whom. Did Jing feign looking for a seat? Was Molly the mark all along? Did someone really call her at that exact moment, or did she fake an incoming call while her hands were out of sight? The whole James Bond thing is way beyond Molly. This is *not* what she imagined when she signed up as an intern. Molly thinks she did the right thing. She hopes she hasn't said too much.

A couple of the Russians on her list are standing over by a vending machine on the edge of the cafeteria. One of the men inserts a five-dollar bill, but the machine rejects it, spitting it back out. The man straightens the bill and tries again. Molly sees an opening as the bill is rejected yet again.

"Swap?" she says, coming up beside Dimitri Pavlov, who is in his mid-fifties and does not need a Snicker's bar. Molly holds out a crisp five-dollar bill, and he laughs, bows slightly, and accepts, swapping bills with her.

"Thank you," he says, inserting the note and finally getting his absurdly overpriced candy bar.

"You are with the US delegation?" he asks, retrieving his prize from the metal tray at the bottom of the vending machine.

"I'm an intern," Molly says, smiling. "I'm just here to get some work experience."

"Ah, yes. Experience is a good thing."

They chat for a few minutes, with a couple of the aides on either side of Dimitri looking deeply suspicious.

When it becomes clear the conversation isn't going anywhere, Molly says, "Well, it's nice to meet you. I hope our countries can cooperate more. Perhaps in space, if not on Earth itself."

"Yes, yes," Dimitri replies, but he's guarded, not giving anything away.

The doors to the main hall open. Diplomats begin entering. Molly finishes her drink and heads to the bathroom. As she exits the stall, Jing comes up to her. Molly ignores the Chinese woman, washing her hands as though she hasn't noticed Jing in the mirror. Molly's expecting Jing to make small talk, but she jumps straight to the issue at hand.

"Are you sitting in the observation area?"

"Yes," Molly says, lathering soap on her fingers.

With a sickly sweet voice, Jing says, "Let's sit together."

"That would be nice," Molly replies. "I don't know anyone else here."

They make their way to the stairs and head up to the balcony looking out over the General Assembly Hall. The Secretary-General of the United Nations is standing to one side with the US President, waiting to walk out onto the marble rostrum. Dignitaries take their seats. Behind them, translation teams make notes on their laptops, speaking softly through microphones mounted on headphones.

As everyone waits for the proceedings to start, Jing asks, "Why do you think they're doing this?"

Molly isn't sure what she means. Is Jing talking about why aliens are coming to Earth?

"I—I'm not sure I understand your question."

"A multinational crew. Why would the US President want that? It must be difficult to coordinate such a response."

"Oh," Molly says, trying to sound innocent and realizing Jing took the bait. She lies. "They want to ensure equal access for all nations. Not everyone can be on the mission, but the Security Council represents our best grouping. The President wants to get beyond politics. She sees this as an opportunity for humanity to come together as one."

In reality, the US wants to avoid conflicting approaches to the alien vessel. If there's a single mission, it's easier to manage actions and expectations, but Molly is *not* telling Jing that.

Jing's thumbs ripple over the screen on her smartphone. She's madly sending out multiple text messages, probably echoing Molly's words, but to whom? Whoever's on the other end, Molly hopes Chief of Staff Dosela is right. There's no way anything Molly says is going to convince anyone about the need for international cooperation, but she can reinforce the overall message. Hopefully, the Chinese are getting a consistent message through multiple channels, and that should be reassuring, despite the uncertainty of First Contact with an unknown intelligent extraterrestrial species.

Molly says, "The President is concerned about being transparent. She wants to be inclusive and make this a scientific expedition rather than a political one."

"Hmm," Jing replies. Molly notices a tiny, flesh-colored hearing aid in Jing's ear. She wonders if it is bi-directional. Jing fires off another message on her phone, but the text is in Chinese, making it indecipherable to Molly. Jing could be reporting on their conversation or ordering a pastrami sandwich for lunch.

The UN Secretary-General walks onto the broad, marble rostrum beneath the golden emblem of the United Nations and introduces the US President. Once the applause has faded, the President addresses the assembly.

"Mr. Secretary-General, esteemed ambassadors and representatives from around the world. Thank you for coming here today at such short notice.

"Over the past ten thousand years, there have been a handful of key moments in time that have changed the very course of our civilization. Among these is the rise of agriculture. The wheel. The invention of gunpowder, the printing press and the telescope. The combustion engine. Science. Antibiotics. The right to vote. Vaccines. Computers. And it's these pivotal points that allow us to advance as a civilization. Today, we face another such turning point. We stand at the crossroads of history once more, but this time, it's not an invention of our own hand that will transform us, but one of another."

The silence within the auditorium is palpable. Even the translators seem in awe of what's unfolding before them, whispering quietly into their microphones.

"I've come here before you today with news that will forever shape our future. And I ask that we—the people of this world—band together to cooperate and work together, for today, we have learned we are not alone in the universe.

"As I speak to you, NASA, ESA and various space agencies around the world have trained their telescopes on the skies, tracking the path of an extraterrestrial spaceship entering our solar system."

Jing raises her hand to her mouth. She leans forward. Although she knew this was coming, the shock still hits her. She could be play-acting, but Molly doesn't think so. There's a tremor in her fingers.

The President speaks to a stunned auditorium.

"At first, the idea seemed outlandish to me. Then, as more and more evidence came to light, it became undeniable. Now, we must prepare for First Contact with an advanced extraterrestrial species.

"For many, the initial reaction will be one of fear—the fear of the unknown, but I ask you to consider the alternative: with each advance we've embraced, our world has improved. First Contact offers promise. Hope. First Contact gives us a chance to step forward into a bright, new future.

"Our place in the universe has forever changed. In the annals of human history, there will be everything that came before this moment set in contrast with all that comes after.

"In 1543, an Augustinian cleric working for the bishop of Frauenburg in Poland published a book that would forever change the way we view our world. Nicolaus Copernicus had the audacity to challenge the notion that Earth was the center of creation. Although sunrise and sunset make it seem as though Earth is stationary and it's the Sun that's in motion, he proved that all the planets in our solar system revolve around the Sun.

"Copernicus forever changed the way we look at the universe. And in the same manner, First Contact will forever change the way we look at *life* within the universe.

"We are not alone. We are part of something bigger, something grander, something even more magnificent—the evolution of life scattered throughout the cosmos. The light we see through our telescopes carries with it not just the cold, sterile radiation of stars but the promise of life arising on other planets like our own.

"I stand here before you today not as the President of the United States of America but as a fellow human being. There are eight billion of us on this planet. Although we inhabit different countries and cultures, different stations in life and society, we're united by one common attribute. We think. We reason. We conclude. And together, we act. Regardless of race, creed or country, our societies are built on cooperation—and we need that now more than ever. We need to look out for each other. First Contact should unite us like never before."

Molly swallows the lump in her throat, knowing this is precisely what the President fears, that First Contact will divide an already fractured humanity.

"I have come here today to share with you the evidence we have gathered and to invite you to join us on this historic occasion."

On either side of the marble rostrum and the intimidating golden backdrop, there are screens as large as any found in a cinema. They're so big and imposing they appear as though they're part of the overall futuristic design, being some abstract representation of blank space. It's not until images are projected on them that heads rise.

The first photo is grainy. Blots of grey appear scattered like snow in the background. Dozens of stars are visible, but their arrangement is peculiar/unnatural. They're grouped in three concentric rings clustered around a bright star in the center.

There's a date/time stamp in the bottom right-hand corner of the image. It advances in increments of four hours. As it does, the group of stars moves at an angle, shifting from top-right to bottom-left over easily eight to ten images, drifting against the backdrop of other stars. The effect is similar to stop-motion photography, with the cluster skipping between positions at a steady rate. Static crackles within the image like snow in a winter storm, but the motion is unmistakable.

The President turns her head sideways, looking up at one of the screens. "What you are seeing here is a starship firing its engines to slow down as it approaches."

She gives those present a few seconds to absorb what they're looking at and then returns to her notes. The short clip replays over and over again.

"Dr. Jonathan Wheeler at NASA's Jet Propulsion Laboratory has analyzed the chemical signatures in this image and tells me this is a Direct Fusion Drive. It's something we can model on paper but cannot yet build. The exhaust plume is a form of plasma hotter than the surface of the Sun."

The President pauses, waiting for the image to change.

A single static photo comes up, but the contrast is high, washing out the exhaust so the various individual plumes blend together, forming a lumpy, glowing blob. The high degree of contrast, though, reveals something of the shape beyond the engines.

"Based on our calculations, the starship is roughly 3500 feet long and 900 feet on each side. To put it in perspective, it's far bigger than our largest aircraft carrier. It's approximately the size of four or five ocean cruise liners with a total of around 8,000 rooms. Now, we don't know how much of the starship is dedicated to the engines and fuel tanks. If the ratio is similar to our spacecraft, as much as 90% of this vessel might be fuel tanks, but this craft is far larger than anything we can put in space."

She waits. A few seconds later, the screen changes to show a zoomed-out image of the inner solar system. The Sun appears as a yellow blob in the middle. Mercury, Venus, Earth and Mars all appear as tiny colored dots with lines that trail behind them in a curve, reaching halfway around their respective orbits.

A solid red line swings in toward the sun, curling in so close it appears to graze the surface before peeling away much slower. The alien spacecraft seems to perform what is essentially a u-turn around the sun itself and then turns toward Earth. As with the earlier animation, there's a date/time stamp in the bottom right-hand corner; only this one moves by days rather than hours.

"The vessel is not heading directly toward us," the President says. "It's going to use the sun to slow down. Once the starship has rounded the sun, we expect it to continue on to Earth in approximately six months' time."

The President is still staring sideways up at the screen when it goes blank, returning to a white canvas. She takes a sip of water before continuing.

"If you're like me, you have a million questions. I wish I could answer them. This is an emerging situation. As we learn more, we will share what we know openly with the international community. Above all, I believe this is a scientific event with relevance to all of humanity. I want to avoid politicizing the arrival of this starship. I want to ensure equal and unfettered access to the scientific community, regardless of country or culture.

"The official position of the United States of America is that the existence of intelligent extraterrestrials does not pose a threat to Earth.

"When Neil Armstrong first set foot on the Moon, he left a plaque saying we came in peace for all of humanity. In the same way, we believe this too is peaceful exploration."

From somewhere off to the side, someone yells, "How do you know?"

The President isn't flustered. She says, "This is not the forum for questions. I will be addressing the Security Council this afternoon and will speak to any concerns at that time. What I can say to you now is that this is not an invasion fleet. It's a single spacecraft. If they wanted to attack us, they'd begin by hurling asteroids at us like the one that wiped out the dinosaurs. That is *not* happening. They are approaching us as visitors. We should greet them in the same spirit.

"For now, I ask for patience. I ask for calm. I ask for time to allow our scientists to better understand what's unfolding. When faced with the unknown, it's always tempting to think the worst, but rarely does the worst unfold. At this point, we have no reason to believe our extraterrestrial visitors are anything but curious about the exotic forms of life that inhabit the third planet in this particular solar system. We suspect they're explorers, much like Darwin, Cook and Magellan.

"Thank you for your time this morning. I look forward to briefing you again in the near future as we learn more about this remarkable event."

With that, the President turns and walks from the rostrum. Throughout the auditorium, ambassadors get to their feet, calling out questions and yelling to be heard, but she's undeterred. She walks with confidence toward the side door and shakes the hand of the Secretary-General before disappearing into some backstage room.

Molly turns to Jing. She's in shock. It's the glassy look in her eyes. Even knowing roughly what was coming, seeing the images made it real. Jing rests her hand on Molly's forearm, saying, "Thank you, my friend."

Molly nods, unsure what to say in response to that. For her part, Jing seems genuine. The silly games of global political wrangling seem to have fallen from Jing's mind. For a moment, she's not Chinese; she's human. Molly hopes the President's speech has a similar effect on the rest of the Chinese contingent as well as the Russians. For Molly, this is exciting. She has no doubt, though, that for a lot of people, this news will be terrifying.

Disbelief

"Crash," Andrea says, rushing into his office in Houston, Texas. "Have you seen this?"

Crash Williams slams the lid of his laptop shut with a rush of adrenalin that must raise questions in Andrea's mind. He's not looking at porn. That would be the natural assumption given the vigor of his motion, and he can see suspicion in the slight narrowing of Andrea's eyes and the subtle twist of her head, but it's not porn that embarrasses him.

Crash was playing *Wordle,* and on his sixth and final guess, he failed. Yet again. He was looking at his miserable stats, which tend toward an average of four to five. Crash enjoys the Scrabble-like online game, but he's not very good at it. And if there's one thing Crash doesn't want to admit, it's failure. It's a perplexing character trait and one forced on him out of necessity, being a larger-than-life senior astronaut. So the big tough guy can't solve *lover,* getting stuck on *lo_er:* who cares? But what does it say about him that he went for *loser* and *lower* before *lover*? Crash cringes at the thought. There are a lot of words that use those letters, he tells himself. In reality, there are only a handful, and if he'd swallowed his pride earlier and shoved in an unrelated word to flush out other consonants, he would have probably stumbled upon the answer in three or four attempts.

Crash smiles. It's fake and forced and far too rushed, but Andrea seems more concerned about whatever had her charge into his office.

"The President…"

"The President?" he replies, wanting slightly more context.

"She just announced they've spotted an alien spacecraft."

"She what?" he says, getting to his feet and laughing. "You're kidding, right? What is this? April 1st?"

"It's no joke."

Crash joins her in the open-plan office. As part of NASA's appeal to a better work/life balance, there are a smattering of regular offices, breakout rooms and meeting rooms scattered around the outside of the vast floor, but most of the office is an open plan. Green, leafy plants droop over dividers. They're everywhere, creating what the astronaut corps affectionately calls *The Jungle*. To be fair, seeing computer screens and keyboards dotted between palms and hanging leaves is far easier on the eyes than the old grey chest-high dividers.

In the center of the floor, there are a bunch of stylish red and blue couches along with comfortable swivel chairs grouped around circular coffee tables. It's a retro-fifties feel that matches the oversized NASA meatball logo on the wall by the elevators.

Several years ago, someone brought in a shiny chrome Italian coffee machine worth several thousand dollars and placed it in the kitchen opposite the seating area. As such extravagance can never be justified in a US government department, it's always a talking point whenever dignitaries visit the astronauts' office. Once they're assured public funds haven't been misused, they're happy to enjoy a macchiato or a café latte with generous amounts of steamed, milky foam floating on the top of their coffee.

Above the coffee machine, there's an 80" flat-screen television Crash has only ever seen playing NASA TV. Someone's switched it to MSNBC. Astronauts and support staff gather around the open area as someone turns up the volume. Crash looks around. No one is at their desk. They're all in the central area, staring up at the television.

He and Andrea walk up to the back of the crowd.

Liz Browne from ESA turns to Crash, asking, "And this is for real, right? You're not playing a prank on me as the new kid on the block."

"No," Crash replies, but his voice isn't convincing. He's staring at the screen, trying to understand what the grainy images mean.

"You're not punking a gullible foreigner?"

"I..." Crash shakes his head, unable to answer. He's trying to hear what's being said on the television, but several people are on their phones, talking as they stare up at the screen. There are subtitles, but he's arrived mid-conversation. The MSNBC anchor is talking to a panel of experts, none of whom he recognizes.

"*...important we don't rush to conclusions. That's the temptation we face. It's all too easy to jump to unsubstantiated outcomes. To rush off on a tangent. What we need are facts. We need to stick to the facts.*"

"But we won't," the anchor says, preempting the reply from his guest.

The elderly man opposite him says, "*No, we won't. We'll take one extraordinary fact and we'll weave dozens, perhaps hundreds of unfounded scenarios from it. We'll embellish. We'll guess. We'll exaggerate. We'll react. We'll be defensive. We'll give in to our fears. And we'll be convinced our particular take is right—if only everyone else would listen to us. We'll fabricate our own reality. It's what we do best.*"

"I don't understand what you mean by that," the anchor says, intrigued by that last point. "*How are we going to fabricate reality?*"

"*We're not rational. We like to think we are, but we're not. First and foremost, we're emotional. We think with our hearts, not our heads. We feel rather than think. And we'll go with what we feel is right regardless of the evidence. This has been the case for tens of thousands of years. Superstitions, religions, myths, biases, prejudices—these dominate our history, not science. Science is an outlier. Science is a latecomer. Science is the exception, not the norm in society. Misinformation travels at the speed of light through fiber optics and satellite connections while scientists are still analyzing data.*"

The anchor asks, "And you think misinformation will dominate First Contact?"

"*It already has.*"

"*What do you mean?*"

"*Check your phone during the break,*" the aging professor says. "*I don't need to look to know Threads, Facebook, Reddit and WhatsApp will already be swamped with conspiracy theories. It's human nature. And that's the danger when it comes to First Contact. Forget about them. We need to look at ourselves. Look at how we react. How we overreact.*"

As if on cue, the show switches to an ad break and the people standing in front of the TV raise their smartphones, checking their social media apps. If they're like Crash, no one doubts this guy is right—they fear just how bad such misinformation will get. During the pandemic, lies cost hundreds of thousands of lives.

NASA Director Angela Summers walks out of an elevator flanked by aides, and those that notice her arrival begin to scatter, heading for their desks. Perception is nine-tenths of reality. Even though the director has a reputation for being kind and soft-spoken, she's the most senior executive on the NASA board. Smiles can be friendly, but they can also precede daggers.

"Please," she says, both announcing her presence and appealing to those on the move. "I know this is unprecedented. I came down here to talk to you and answer any questions you might have."

The director stands in front of the television as everyone gathers around, wanting to hear what she has to say. As she's 5' 6", the screen is still visible above and behind her. Someone mutes the sound, leaving the subtitles on.

"We've all got questions," she says, sweeping her long, brunette hair behind her ears. "And you, more than anyone within NASA, are going to be facing questions from an increasingly curious media in the days to come. Please. If you're approached, direct questions to the NASA Press Office. Let's keep a unified voice on this."

Around the room, heads nod in agreement.

"The media are not going to like the answers we give them—

because we have none. They're going to demand answers we don't have. We need to avoid rumors. We need to manage expectations. We need to keep the science first and foremost in this discussion."

Someone calls out, "Are we going up there?"

It's an anonymous question conveniently delivered from the back of the crowd of astronauts and support staff. Not even Crash recognizes the voice, although it was male. The director lowers her gaze. For a fraction of a second, she catches his eye, looking briefly at Crash. She straightens, eyeing the crowd. She must know she can't lie to anyone here. Save the lies for the media.

"Yes."

No one speaks. They all wait for her to continue.

"The President wants to put together a joint mission with ESA, Roscosmos, ISRO, JAXA and possibly China as well."

Crash and Andrea look at each other. Liz raises her eyebrows, turning to look at them. Crash still doesn't know what all this is about other than prime advertising slots for Coca-Cola and Snickers playing in the background on the TV. America is nothing if not obsessed with news cycles. It doesn't matter whether it's war, pandemics, a school shooting or the antics in Congress, the media thrives on regurgitating the latest heart-stopping tragedy. They say sex sells, and it does, but fear sells more. Uncertainty is a cash register for news corporations.

The director says, "I have mission planners working on a number of options, but we won't know which one will be used until the craft approaches Earth."

"Damn," Crash mutters under his breath, still not having seen anything of the actual announcement yet.

"Oh, and here it is," the director says as MSNBC returns from its ad break.

"*If you're only just now joining us,*" the anchor says in subtitles, "*we're unpacking the news that an alien spacecraft is approaching Earth. Earlier today, the President confirmed the presence of the craft in an address to the United Nations.*"

Director Summers points at the screen. She reaches up and across in front of the anchor, tapping the grainy image of dozens of glowing dots arranged in the shape of concentric circles, with the central smudge being the largest.

"So this is it," the director says. "Although we don't know the mass of the spacecraft itself, that it is decelerating at over 3Gs means these engines are undergoing a serious, sustained burn. To reach that rate for a craft that's the size of several ocean liners, this would have to be a fusion drive.

"If you're accelerating propellant to slow down, you don't want to waste a drop. You want to throw that propellant out as fast as you can to maximize its worth. As best we understand it, this is beyond chemical or even a standard nuclear drive. It would have to be fusion to run for days, possibly weeks."

Crash nods, appreciating how the director is giving them detailed insights, probably taken from briefings she's been given by JPL.

"Although we can't see any detail on the craft itself, the arrangement of the engines is symmetrical, and that suggests a balanced, symmetrical shape beyond them. The ratios of length to width and height confirm that. The craft is long rather than squat or fat."

The image changes. The anchor and his guest are talking about the approach to the sun.

"Now, this is interesting," the director says, and she has his full attention.

Crash has given up on reading the subtitles. Director Summers is the only one he wants to hear from.

"Look at how it's coming head-on toward the Sun. What are the chances of that? Think about how many approach angles there are in three-dimensional space. What are the odds they would originate *exactly* on the same angle on which the sun is orbiting the Milky Way? It's just not likely.

"The gurus at JPL think they've come from roughly thirty degrees off this approach. Like a bullet falling to the ground, they've shot out in front of the Sun and curled in toward it, wanting to use it to help with their braking maneuver. So don't buy this junk about them coming from the border of the constellations Lyra and Hercules. They probably came from much further afield, and they're using a hyperbolic approach, curling in toward us. This maneuver could have been conducted over a distance of light years, and we're only seeing the final stage of the approach. It's like looking at the end of a tangent. The graph might look dead straight at that point, but that's only because you're sampling such a small segment."

The image on the television changes to a high-contrast shot blurring out the engines and revealing dark shadows that suggest the overall shape of the spacecraft.

The director says, "They're talking about this thing holding a crew of thousands, but that's nonsense. That's like looking at the Saturn V launching Apollo 11 and saying, *look how damn big it is—you could get hundreds of people in there!* Well, you could if you didn't need fuel. As it was, we could barely get three people to the Moon and back.

"I would be surprised if there's any crew at all. The most likely outcome is that this spacecraft is a long-range probe akin to Pioneer or Voyager. We can go much faster and farther with lightweight robotic probes like Cassini and New Horizons. Compare any of our deep space missions with crewed missions and the effectiveness of a robotic probe is somewhere in the order of ten thousand to a hundred thousand times more efficient. So my money's on this being robotic, perhaps powered by some kind of AI we can interact with."

"Hot damn," Liz whispers beside Crash.

"But I'm spitballing," the director says. "We lead with science, not guesswork. We look at the evidence, arrive at an idea, and test that idea, right? That's good science. All too often, people take the first two steps and forget about the third. Science is nothing without testing ideas. We've got to be willing to change our minds as new information comes to light.

"If test results agree with our thinking, wonderful—then we'll test something else. We'll keep probing and prodding and poking until there's nothing left to try. If the results disagree with our ideas, we need to change our ideas and change our minds. It's this last step—changing our minds—that has tripped up humanity for tens of thousands of years, but we can do better. We're NASA. We need to be an example to others."

Around the crowd, people nod and mumble in agreement.

"Okay," the director says. "That's enough from me. I'll be down here for a while, mingling, answering questions. If you have any concerns about this, talk to me."

With that, the director walks over to the guy holding the remote for the television and signals for him to turn it up. She starts talking to some of the young interns grinning from ear to ear. For them, she is the stuff of legend.

Crash knows the director well enough to realize this isn't a social visit. She wants to talk to someone without anyone noticing and without there being an electronic trail. Given the way she looked at him earlier, he decides to grab a coffee and loiter.

"Are you thinking what I'm thinking?" Andrea asks, standing beside him at the counter. Both of them have their backs to the director and those milling around.

"Uh huh," Crash says, stirring some creamer into his coffee and shuffling along so the ESA astronaut Liz Browne can shuffle in beside Andrea at the counter. Liz grabs a tea bag, drops it in a cup and adds boiling water.

Quietly, she says, "Not just a drink break, huh?"

"Nope," Andrea replies, keeping her head facing the chrome coffee machine. The distorted image of the director shaking hands is visible in the shiny metal.

The three of them peel away from the counter and form a small group standing on the outskirts of the crowd. They sip their drinks as the director smiles, shakes more hands, and slowly works toward them.

"Left hand," Crash says.

"What?" Liz asks.

"Hold your drink in your left hand."

"Why?" Liz replies, switching hands anyway. Barely a second later, the director is in front of them with her charismatic and disarming smile. She shakes hands with each of them, but it's what she says rapidly while in passing that causes Crash to take a deep breath.

"Liz, you'll be one of the mission specialists representing the UK and France. Andrea, you're CapCom. Crash, you're mission commander, representing Canada and the US."

In among the buzz within the open-plan floor, the director's words are lost on anyone standing more than a few feet away. The director's smile never fades. It's as though she's a politician kissing babies for the cameras.

"Plan accordingly."

With that, the director turns and walks away. She stops to shake a few more hands before heading for the elevators.

Without being too obvious, Liz points at the director while turning to face Crash and Andrea, confused. Crash signals with a subtle turn of his head, leading them back to his office. He leaves the door open, not wanting to attract attention to their impromptu meeting. Andrea leans on the door frame, blocking the entrance. Liz sits in a chair. Crash sits up on the edge of his desk, swinging his legs as though he doesn't have a care in the world.

"What just happened?" Liz asks, shaking her head.

"Flight selection," Andrea replies.

Crash says, "The director's telling us as much as she can."

"I don't get it. What did she just tell us?"

"That she's worried about leaks. Very worried."

"From her own office?" Andrea asks.

"Or ours," Crash says. "She wants to keep this quiet until she's ready to go public."

"Why?" Liz asks.

Crash laughs. "Once this is public, you won't be able to drive home without the paparazzi hounding you."

"And the crazies," Andrea says. "Don't forget the conspiracy theory nut jobs. They sure as hell won't forget you."

"Oh."

Crash adds, "And remember her opening words about deferring questions from the media to the NASA Press Office. She said that for us, for our benefit. We have to deflect attention away from ourselves."

"Got it."

Andrea says, "Don't underestimate the lengths the media will go to in order to get a scoop on this flight. Don't tell anyone what she said. Not your friends. Not your Mom. No one."

From the way she speaks, Crash can tell Andrea's saying this as much for her own benefit as for him and Liz.

Crash says, "If they've got a crew, they've got a plan. If they're telling us, it's been approved by the board and probably the President."

"Who else is part of the crew?" Liz asks.

"At a guess," Andrea says. "The space agencies she listed. Us, North Americans. You, Europeans. The Russians, Chinese, Indians, maybe the Japanese and Russians."

"That's quite a crew," Crash says, shaking his head, knowing how difficult it will be to manage.

"She ticks a few boxes between the two of you," Andrea says, pointing at them.

"Four countries," Crash says. "It goes a long way to making the list multinational."

"You're Canadian?" Liz asks.

"My Mom."

"Ah."

As an afterthought, Crash says, "And no Jack Schmitt."

"No Jack Schmitt," Andrea says, agreeing with him. "Not yet, anyway."

"Probably never if we have to accommodate all of these other space agencies."

"Jack who?" Liz asks.

"Jack Schmitt was the geologist on Apollo 17," Crash says. "Out of all the Apollo astronauts, he was the only scientist. He was a geologist. He's the only one that wasn't selected because of flight experience."

Liz is curious. "An alien spacecraft is approaching us, and we're *not* sending scientists? Ah, doesn't that strike anyone else as a mistake?"

Crash says, "The US isn't going to give up its leadership role on the flight. And no other country is going to offer a scientist over someone they feel they can trust up there."

"You can trust scientists," Liz says with vigor in her voice.

"You can," Andrea says. "Everyone else, though? Not so much."

"Jesus. He was right."

"Who?" Crash asks.

"The guy on the TV. *Forget about them. We need to look at ourselves. Look at how we react. How we overreact.*"

"Yep," Crash replies to Liz. "And that's our job up there. To keep things level. To avoid overreacting to our own fears and prejudices."

Andrea raises her eyebrows, saying, "Well, that sounds like fun."

Russia

Aleksandr is furious. After hearing the US President's address to the United Nations, he storms up to the top-floor executive office within the Russian Vostochny Cosmodrome's admin building. On stepping out of the elevator, he's greeted by the vast logo for Roscosmos, the State Space Corporation, which is anything but a corporation as it is run exclusively by the government. The logo is mounted on a polished wooden wall. To anyone else, it's impressive to behold. To Aleksandr, it's an insult.

Regardless of whether it's the US Space Force, the Chinese National Space Agency or Roscosmos itself, the influence of American culture on space logos is unmistakable. All of them use some derivative from Star Trek iconography, and that makes Aleksandr sick.

Being greeted by a delta-shaped badge reminiscent of those worn by Kirk and Spock is frustrating. That was science fiction. This is science reality. Why should the Russian vision of the exploration of space be subordinate to American mythology? The thought running through his mind is, do we not have our own dreams?

The Roscosmos logo is a skewed version of the Star Trek badge surrounded by an oval. Aleksandr prefers the red star that dominated the agency in the 90s, even if it did hail back to the Soviet era. Gagarin needed no such Americanized logo. He wore the Soviet flag on his shoulder—blood red with a hammer and sickle. The first formal logo was of a stylized rocket launch sweeping up toward the sky with a red star at its zenith. If Aleksandr had his way, he'd return to that original logo.

For Aleksandr, the current logo is a capitulation to American ideals. The assumption that dominates Western thinking is that the future belongs to America and her allies within the United Nations—particularly those that speak English. But the future is yet to be written. Russia has always held sway over European politics, and it will again if Aleksandr has his way.

Seething with anger, Aleksandr marches past a befuddled receptionist who knows better than to try to stop him. She watches him, scrawling notes in the visitor's book, jotting down his name and his date/time of entry.

The flight director's office is at the back of the broad floor. There's no direct path as the open plan design has been built in the shape of interconnecting circles. Aleksandr has never been impressed by the fanciful imagination of the architect who decided to force twists and turns on the staff. How is confusion desirable? Aleksandr was told the intent was to make the office less intimidating and more conducive to informal discussions. He doesn't agree. He steps between curved partitions, essentially walking through cubicles as he weaves his way to the director's office. There's a straight path in front of the windows, but such a diversion requires walking in an L-shape from the reception area, and that demands patience. Aleksandr has none. He will take the most direct route.

Through the internal windows of the director's office, he can see the aging man talking on the phone. The director's personal assistant sees Aleksandr coming and gets to her feet, holding out her hands in a feeble attempt to slow, if not stop him.

"I need to see Director Olenev," Aleksandr says, not slacking his stride.

To her credit, the receptionist is brave. She steps in front of him, blocking the door with an outstretched hand, but for Aleksandr, she's merely a speed bump. She's not going to use physical force to stop him. She couldn't. He steps around her and opens the door against her protests.

"We need to talk," he says, bursting in while the director is still on the phone.

Director Olenev holds up a single finger, wanting silence. He points at the chair on the other side of his desk. Aleksandr takes a seat as the receptionist bows in apology before closing the door behind her as she leaves.

The director is a gruff man in his sixties. His grey hair is thinning on top. The folds of his eyebrows have sagged over the decades, leaving him looking as though he's squinting. Age spots mar his cheeks. Skin sags beneath his jaw. He's overweight. He leans back in his chair. The springs squeak.

"Huh," he says with more of a growl than a voice. "Ah... Ummm... Yes, yes. Okay... I will make it happen... Understood."

He hangs up the aging black plastic desk phone with its tightly curled cord looking as old and worn as him.

"You," he says, turning to face Aleksandr. "You should not be here. Not without a scheduled meeting."

"Bullshit," Aleksandr says, even though the director could ground him or even run him out of the cosmonaut corps.

"You've heard?"

"Everyone has heard. It is all that is being talked about on the news."

For a country with such tightly controlled media, it is surprising the censors in Moscow are allowing the news of an approaching alien spacecraft to dominate the headlines. If anything, it's probably the result of paralysis-by-analysis. The executive team involved in vetting Russian news is probably waiting on an official position from the Kremlin. In the meantime, the assumption is that such news is not harmful to the country's international position. Aleksandr is expecting a grand retraction or change of focus once those paralyzed with indecision have been given a sharp nudge.

The director swivels in his chair, reaching for his laptop and turning it around so Aleksandr can see what he's been looking at while on the call. The image on the computer screen is stunning. Aleksandr shifts his chair closer.

"This is much better than anything the Americans have," he says, leaning forward and taking a good look at the imaging of the alien spacecraft. The distinct signature of dozens of engines is both crisp and clear. The grainy shadows have sharp lines. Pipes crisscross the darkness. There are bulges and forks disappearing behind the glare of the rocket engines.

The director corrects him, saying, "Much better than anything the Americans have released."

As this image has been taken at an angle, like all of the photos taken from Earth, the side of the vehicle is partially visible. Aleksandr is interested to see if it has sleek, smooth lines, which would suggest a spacecraft that has or will enter an atmosphere, or if it is more reminiscent of the clunky Russian space probes such as Venera or Zond with their oversized radio dishes and cumbersome solar panels. The American Pioneer and Voyager probes, along with the US Lunar Modules, were distinctly unimpressive to look at, favoring function over form, while the US Space Shuttle and the Russian Buran had no choice but to succumb to the demands of sleek aerodynamics. To his surprise, the alien spacecraft seems to be a blend of both approaches.

The lower portion of the alien vessel, down near the engines, has a smooth cylindrical shape, probably because it houses fuel tanks. Farther along the craft, there are spherical protrusions which may represent separate types of fuel being stored under pressure. Beyond them, a variety of shapes are visible, including the faint outline of what looks like scaffolding extending from the fuselage. The sunlight catching them is indistinct, but there's a slight, matching image on the far side of the craft, suggesting symmetry on either side of the vessel.

"Solar panels?" Aleksandr asks, tapping the screen.

"We don't think so," the director says. "Their fusion drive would produce excess heat that could easily be converted into electricity. We think this is an antenna array, probably to listen to us across all frequencies."

"Ah."

The director is smart. Once again, he's effectively disarmed Aleksandr as he so often does in various meetings. With the steam fading from his ire, Aleksandr is left struggling to be defiant. Defiant against what? The director openly sharing classified information with him?

"Russia must go alone," Aleksandr says, leaning back in his seat and ignoring the temptation to continue examining the image.

"Alone?" the director asks, leaning forward on his desk with his elbows resting on the polished wood. He splays his fingers wide, pressing them together. He's intrigued.

Aleksandr says, "The Americans. They want a multinational mission, right?"

The director nods. For all his flamboyant outbursts, Aleksandr knows the old man likes him and his insights. He respects Aleksandr because Aleksandr gets results.

There's silence between them for a moment.

The director says, "It has been suggested that cooperation could be good for us."

"No," a strident Aleksandr says. "We don't need them. We don't want them."

"We don't?"

"Russia is the largest nation on Earth. Russia spans not only numerous time zones but numerous cultures. We have the greatest ethnic diversity. It is we who should make First Contact."

"Largest?" the director says, chuckling. "Are you proposing we take a default position based on our size alone?"

Aleksandr ignores his jab. "We should not be beholden to the Americans. This is imperialism! Colonialism! America wants to control First Contact. They should not be allowed such impunity."

The director listens with interest.

"It's their narrative. That America represents freedom. They don't. They represent money. There is nothing that speaks louder in their culture. Oh, they call it freedom to fool the masses, but it is greed that drives capitalism. We should not surrender our autonomy to them."

That last point gets the director's attention. He nods and takes a deep breath. Aleksandr can see he's being guarded with what he can and cannot say, and yet Aleksandr knows the old man will speak freely with him nonetheless.

"The Duma," the director says, measuring his words with care. "They are considering the American offer of a combined mission."

For once, Aleksandr is quiet.

"We are one world divided by mere chance alone. It is our place of birth, not our intellect or rationale, that determines who we are and what we believe. If you had been born in Iowa or Connecticut, you would condemn Russia for going alone."

Aleksandr doesn't like that point. He blurts out, "Russian culture is continuous over thousands of years. It stood supreme as European nations rose and fell."

Aleksandr points at a banner containing ornate calligraphed Cyrillic characters proudly displayed on the wall of the office. "Rus' Khaganate predates every other European culture, being an extension of the Mongol empire itself. While the English and the French were muddy peasants in villages, the Slavs were building palaces. As the Byzantine Empire fell into ruins, Staraya and Novgorod were flourishing with trade, but does the West recognize that? No, they see only their own grandeur. They flatter themselves. They rewrite history. They inflate their importance. They despise us. It is arrogance that drives them on. They cannot represent us to an extraterrestrial species any more than they could represent us to the lost tribes of the Amazon. They represent only themselves."

"You are very persuasive," the director says, making notes on a pad of paper.

"Russia is at the heart of modern civilization. We are the past, the present and the future. America's day has passed like that of the British

Empire. From here, they will fade, but Russia and China will rise, forming a trade block to rival Europe and the Americas. It is we who should meet with those from another world. Our scientists. Our engineers. Our diplomats."

The director smiles, wagging a finger at Aleksandr. "You. You should have been a politician, not a cosmonaut."

Aleksandr is so engrossed in his own logic he barely hears the director. "Our name itself, Russia, comes from the Greek *Rho* meaning *to steer*. It is our calling to steer humanity forward. Our origins are found in unity. Our future lies in unity. It is we who will unify the people of Earth, not the Americans."

The director laughs. "It's not me who needs convincing."

"You must convince the Duma," Aleksandr says, clenching his fists in his lap.

The director laughs again. "They do not listen to me. They tell me what they want done."

"Then give them options. Guide them."

"What would you have us do?"

"Send me," Aleksandr says, barking his response at the director, but that he only speaks two words reveals this was his true intent all along. Gone are the flowery words and appeals to reason.

"Oh, and there it is," the director says, pointing at him. "Aleksandr, you do not disappoint."

Aleksandr ignores him, saying, "We must be strong. Strength is all America understands."

"And you would do this? For Mother Russia?"

"Send me and Genji Sokolov. We send a man and a woman. It is like the old times, Gagarin and Tereshkova."

"The Americans will send a woman."

"We will go further. We will make Genji the mission commander. She will be in charge. She will be our leader. I'll be the mission specialist."

"Hah," the director says, wagging his finger in front of Aleksandr. "And so she remains with the capsule while you make First Contact?"

Aleksandr cannot answer him. The director has seen through him as though he were a ghost. Aleksandr simply nods, offering false modesty.

The director says, "I will take your proposal to the prime minister for discussion with President Sheremetev."

Aleksandr purses his lips. He knows this is it. He's played all the cards in his hand. Now, he must watch as the other cards in this game of poker fall to the table. The lack of control does not sit well with him. He wants to say he'll talk to the prime minister himself, but such insolence will not get past Director Olenev. There is only so far Aleksandr can push the old man. It takes all his will not to speak. If he could just—no. To speak now would be to fail. Words hold no power beyond stirring others to action. At a certain point, they lose even that influence. If words aggravate those listening, they undo themselves. Aleksandr clenches his jaw.

"That is all," the director says. They both know which boundaries can and cannot be crossed. For all of the director's patience, there are lines that even Aleksandr dares not step over. Director Olenev is focused. Even before Aleksandr has risen from his seat, the old man has turned his laptop back toward him and is checking emails.

Without saying anything, Aleksandr stands. He nods out of respect and leaves quietly.

Invisible

"You really are invisible," President Elizabeth Smith-Knowles says, sitting behind the Resolute Desk in the Oval Office.

"Have a seat," the chief of staff says to Molly, gesturing to one of the couches.

Molly cannot get used to being in the presence of the President. She feels like an imposter. Correction. She *is* an imposter. There's no doubt about it. She does not belong in the Oval Office, let alone talking openly with the President. Her fidgeting fingers betray her. She tries to clutch them in front of her skirt but to no avail. The chief of staff understands. The older woman sits on one of the couches, pointing at the other couch opposite her.

Molly sits on the edge of the opposite couch. The cushion is firm, refusing to give under her puny weight. She dares not sit back.

"There's one more thing we want you to do for us," the President says, sitting behind her desk. She has a laptop open, but it's resting to one side of the desk next to the phone.

"Anything," Molly says. She should wait and hear the President out. Prudence would demand an understanding of the finer details of any request before agreeing to unspecified demands, and yet Molly wants to help. She enjoys the praise of these powerful women.

"We picked up Wú Jing's calls and texts while at the UN. She bought the whole thing. The Chinese were skeptical about our intentions, but Jing convinced her father that we were sincere. Our ambassador made similar overtures before I addressed the assembly. By the time the UN Security Council met a couple of hours later, he had tacit agreement from Beijing to participate in the joint mission."

"That's a relief," Molly says.

"It is. Now, if we can just get the Republicans onboard, we'll be set."

Molly's confused. "Republicans?"

In her mind, they're discussing an international mission. Why would an internal American political party have any bearing on that? Are they going to put a Republican on the spacecraft? Why do US political affiliations matter in First Contact?

"Congress holds the purse strings," the President says. "I need to swing at least three Republicans to secure the vote for funds."

Molly is silent. She hadn't given finances a second thought. She just assumed NASA would have rockets ready to go, but from the way the President is speaking, she suspects this relates back to the earlier discussion with the military.

The chief of staff says, "Conspiracy theories are already circulating on the Hill. They're saying we've manufactured this crisis to justify executive overreach. Between Jewish space lasers and QAnon, they're now claiming we're in league with the aliens, that we're surrendering to them."

"Hang on," Molly says, confused by what she's heard. "Is it overreach or surrender? They're contradicting themselves."

"They do that a lot," the chief of staff says.

"But it's not true."

"Oh, Molly. Don't you know? This isn't about truth. When it comes to politics, it's never about truth; it's about the tribe. And the tribe demands we take sides."

Molly is aghast. "Sides? But isn't there just one side to this debate? Humanity? Doing what's right? Can't they see what's actually happening here?"

The President says, "There's our side, and there's their side. In a two-party system, they're the opposition. They *have* to oppose us. It's their whole reason for existing. They have no other motive. There is no other option. If they ever agreed with us, their side would dissolve."

"But... But the arrival of aliens should be a non-partisan issue."

The President laughs. "Oh, they hate that. No, they must oppose us. And it's always been this way. If we promote vaccines, they'll oppose them as unnatural—as though sickness and death are nice, natural alternatives. If we suggest tax reform for the working class, they'll push tax breaks for the wealthy. If we want to build up the economy, they'll say no, let wealth trickle down. If we want to expand Medicaid, they'll protest against big government. It never ends. There's no debate. No discussion about merits. No consideration of the pros and cons. All that is offered is resistance. And that's all their followers want. They don't actually want resolution or compromise or explanations or progress. They want a scapegoat. They want someone to blame. They want someone they can focus their anger on."

"That's really sad."

"It is, but it's simple. And simple communicates. Simple avoids misunderstandings. Simple is easy to grasp. It's easy to sell."

The chief of staff says, "The opposite of light is darkness. But what is darkness? It's nothing. Of itself, it doesn't exist. It's simply the absence of light. In the same way, they pride themselves not on being right but on opposing us. They're the yin to our yang."

The President laughs, adding, "And they'd say the exact same thing about us, only we really do want to do what's right. Mostly."

That last word stings. It's a little too telling for Molly. She'd like to think of the President—*her* President—as being beyond reproach, as being driven only by principle, as always taking the high road. Sitting there in the Oval Office, she realizes she's naive. *Mostly* suggests there are compromises for the sake of donors and supporters. Molly would rather her heroes, or heroines as is the case, were pure. Reality demands otherwise. Politics is pragmatic.

"What do they want?" Molly asks. "Everyone wants something. What do they want?"

"Power," the President says.

The chief of staff is even more blunt. "Money."

"Money?"

Money has always been an abstract concept for Molly. She grew up in a reasonably wealthy family, so much so she never lacked anything. For her, money is a means to an end. She's never been able to reconcile the accumulation of money for its own sake and has even challenged her father about his eight-digit stock portfolio. Why bother with more? What? Is it like collecting baseball cards or something? Why not help others? Molly studied foreign affairs in college because she wants to make a difference in this world and not because she wants to make money. She screws up her face. It's only slight, but it doesn't go unmissed by either woman.

The chief of staff says, "It's somewhat ironic that money comes before morals in the dictionary—because that's the same damn place it holds in most people's lives."

The President concedes to the chief of staff, saying, "Money dominates *both* sides of politics. Unfortunately, it's the one thing both parties have in common."

"And me?" Molly asks, unsure how she fits into this discussion.

"You," the President says. "You're the invisible woman."

The chief of staff opens a folder and hands her a piece of notepaper with the Presidential Seal at the top. It's a handwritten memo, but the President is left-handed and has a distinct writing style, leaning back to the left. This is written in cursive, sloping to the right. The note is unsigned. And it's been rushed. It's been written on an angle as though someone leaned across a desk and quickly scrawled a comment.

If Speaker Emmet doesn't approve, Russia will go alone.

"Take a photo with your phone," the chief of staff says. "We need you to leak this to the media."

"I don't understand."

"Remember, this is about money," the chief of staff says. "Power."

The President explains. "After the corruption scandals of the twenties, Emmet campaigned on an anti-Russian platform, but even he concedes we need Russia onboard. He'll lose face if the Russians launch their own mission. He'll be blamed because he stalled the appropriations bill. He does not want to be the one everyone curses for a fractured mission. It would be politically devastating for him."

The chief of staff says, "And if his reputation is damaged, he'll lose both money and power within the Republican Party."

"And Russia?" Molly asks, feeling she deserves to know the whole story before playing political saboteur.

"The prime minister has reached out to me through back channels saying he supports a joint mission."

The chief of staff says, "The leak serves two purposes. It backs Emmet into a corner, and it tacitly announces Russia's cooperation—neither of which we can push from the Oval Office itself."

"Huh," Molly says, realizing she's a patsy. "And how do I do this? How do I leak this to the media?"

The chief of staff says, "Approach John Walters from *The Washington Post*. He's in the Press pool here at the White House. Tell him you're troubled by something you've seen. Tell him you don't know who you can trust."

"Won't he smell a rat?"

"From an intern on her first week in the White House?" the chief of staff asks with a grin on her face. "No, he'll see the concern of an outsider. He'll think this was written during an intelligence assessment. And he'll be thinking about himself. He'll smell a Pulitzer Prize in the making."

"Politics, huh," Molly says, shaking her head at the Machiavellian intricacies she's being exposed to on just her fourth day in the White House.

Molly's father warned her about what he calls the *sleight of a magician's hand* in politics, but even he never suspected she'd be drawn into this level of deception. As it is, Molly realizes it's her family association that gives both the President and the chief of staff confidence in her. Have they ever considered that she could betray them? They're not the only ones that can use someone to further their ends. From their perspective, she's useful, but they haven't considered the reverse is also true. They're useful to her.

Molly's invisible. And that makes her powerful. They may think she's a patsy and willing to be run around to do their bidding, but she's biding her time. For Molly, morals come before money. At the point her morals are tested, she has no doubt about her resolve. After all, to extend the chief of staff's analogy, morals come before both politics and power in the dictionary.

Going Alone

Aleksandr hovers behind the technician in control of the long-arm centrifuge within the cosmonaut training center in the Vostochny Cosmodrome on the eastern edge of Russia, barely a hundred miles from the Pacific. The controls are rudimentary, being mounted on a stainless steel panel. The dials look as though they were installed in the 1950s, while the switches are bulky and widely spaced to avoid confusion. Their various functions have been engraved on plastic tabs and stuck beneath each switch to avoid ambiguity. A big red button with the words '*Emergency Stop*' is within easy reach of both Aleksandr and the technician. Several other engineers and support staff are in the room, sitting at consoles with actual computers displaying metrics on the simulated gee-force loading along with the medical metrics from the cosmonaut candidates swinging around within the centrifuge.

A glass window allows them to look out over the floor. The regular, rhythmic swish of the iron arm of the centrifuge accompanies the capsule as it swings around. At the other end of the arm, there's a counterweight. A red warning light flashes on the warehouse floor, although how anyone could walk in and not notice the behemoth in motion is beyond Aleksandr. The doors have magnetic locks controlled by the technicians, but they're not fail-proof.

In the movies, these rooms are circular. In real life, there's no need for aesthetics. Any large room will do, so long as it can be isolated. As it is, the candidates can't see out of their dummy space capsule, and if they could, the constantly changing sight would make them sick.

A screen mounted above the window shows two trainee cosmonauts strapped into their seats.

The capsule is set at an eighty-degree angle relative to the floor. When stationary, the cosmonauts are lying rather than sitting sideways with their heads in line with the iron arm of the centrifuge. Once underway, though, this configuration simulates the crushing sensation of reentry, with the apparent force pushing down through their bodies. For them, it feels as though they're about to be thrown out through the floor of the capsule.

"Two gees," the technician says.

"Take them to four," Aleksandr says. Then he keys his microphone, saying, "This is what Neil felt when returning from the Moon."

The two Russian cosmonaut candidates in the capsule are Katya Myshkin and Alexsei Rogov, the two students he penalized on day one. They're enthusiastic. They both smile, offering a thumbs up.

Although the inside of the centrifuge is an exact replica of their spacecraft, the outside is altogether different. The capsule is mounted on gimble-like swivels with electric motors allowing it to be moved into any particular orientation required for the training exercise.

Aleksandr is a bastard. He knows it. All of those in the control room know it, as does Director Olenev. No one cares. Katya Myshkin and Alexsei Rogov, though, still haven't figured that out. He can tell that from the cheesy grins on their faces as they sit there, strapped into their seats, wearing their spacesuits and Snoopy caps. They're about to learn this is not a rollercoaster ride at the local fair.

"EMS failure," Aleksandr says. "You're tumbling."

He reaches over, leaning past the technician and initiates a one-meter-per-second roll on the x-axis, followed by a half-meter-per-second roll on the y-axis. It's not a crazy blackout roll, but the combined effect of rotating on two different axes at different rates is disorienting.

With steely determination, Katya Myshkin takes the yoke and

fights the roll. She flicks the appropriate switches to initiate a reaction control thruster. Within the confines of the test bed, they won't do anything. Whether they work now is up to Aleksandr. For the trainees, the shifting capsule spinning at the end of the long-arm centrifuge causes the perceived gravitational force to change. Instead of pushing down through them, it slides to one side, simulating the sensation of tumbling.

Both candidates follow their training and lower their visors. Barely a second later, while they're twisting into an upside-down position, Alexsei Rogov vomits. Spew plasters the inside of his helmet. Aleksandr smiles.

"And you have regained control," he says, returning the x and y-axis controls to zero, allowing the capsule to return to its original position swinging round and around within the centrifuge.

Alexsei Rogov's head leans back, sinking into the headrest behind him. At a guess, he's unconscious, but he'll live. The technician and support staff also realize what's happening. They all turn away from their consoles, looking at Aleksandr but not saying anything, wanting him to initiate an emergency stop. Aleksandr, though, isn't finished with his assessment.

Katya Myshkin shows no regard for the discomfort of her companion. She can see the distress he's in as his arms shake, spasming beside her, but she focuses on the control panel in front of her. Katya reviews her flight metrics, talking through the simulated altitude and attitude of their theoretical descent to Earth with a fake mission control. She's following procedure rather than reacting emotionally. Her first concern is the health of the spacecraft, not Alexsei Rogov—and that's as it should be. In real life, if the problem isn't properly understood and rectified, they could fall back into a spin, and both die.

Aleksandr waits a little too long. Everyone knows it. No one speaks. Finally, he leans forward and hits the emergency stop button.

The centrifuge decelerates. Several of the support staff, including the medic, are up out of their seats and running down the stairs toward the warehouse floor. They wait for the centrifuge to come to a halt and align itself with the staging platform.

Aleksandr is intrigued by Katya Myshkin. Now that the simulation is over, she turns her attention to Alexsei Rogov. Katya raises his visor and releases the five-point harness holding him in his seat. She's preparing for the medical team, but she's doing it without panicking or overreacting. She's methodical. Aleksandr likes that.

Katya Myshkin and Alexsei Rogov were the late-comers on the first day of training. As they come from different branches of the armed services and different regions within Russia, they didn't know each other before that day. Since then, Aleksandr has had them bound by fate. He was ready to flunk both of them, but Katya Myshkin has shown him what he's looking for—cold determination. To most, being ruthless is inhuman. Aleksandr disagrees. For him, cruelty defines humanity as much as compassion. It's as necessary as kindness. All too often, bleeding hearts will say love is all that's needed, but Aleksandr knows that's a convenient lie. They, too, will be ruthless if their survival hinges on it; they just won't admit to such instincts. Aleksandr is pragmatic. How would hominids have survived without being ruthless? Natural selection knows no kindness, and neither does he. If he's trapped inside a metal box hundreds of thousands of miles from the safe, warm embrace of Earth, he wants to know he's with someone who will do whatever it takes to survive.

The capsule is opened. The medic clambers inside. Alexsei Rogov has choked on his own vomit, breathing it in during the exercise. He coughs up blood as he's dragged out of the capsule. Katya Myshkin shows no emotion, only professionalism. She cares. She must care. He's her partner. But it's then Aleksandr sees what he's been looking for all along. Katya Myshkin offers a brief glance at the camera. She knows Aleksandr is watching her. She's playing to him as he once played to his instructors, manipulating them without them realizing it. Aleksandr smiles. He likes Katya Myshkin. She will go far within Roscosmos.

There's movement behind him, but he's distracted by Katya clambering out of the capsule, being helped by technicians.

"Are you done torturing your students?"

Aleksandr grins. He turns, greeting Director Olenev.

"She," he says, pointing at the screen. "She will reach orbit, but not him. He is weak."

"Hmmm," the director replies, but they both know he didn't come here to talk about training exercises or Aleksandr and his unorthodox methods. "Have you heard?"

"Why do you think I'm torturing them?" Aleksandr replies with a wicked smile.

"Hah."

"So, it's true. We're going to join the Americans?" Aleksandr asks, but even as he speaks those words, he doubts them. The director wouldn't be down here if that were the case. He'd be waiting for Aleksandr to storm once more into his office. No, some other strategy is at play, and that intrigues Aleksandr.

One of the support staff walks back into the control room. On seeing Aleksandr and the director, he reverses back out, bowing as he leaves and signaling for the others to remain outside.

The director points at the monitor and the vomit seeping from a helmet left inside the capsule.

Aleksandr says, "I never run these sims in the mornings. Only ever early afternoon. After lunch."

The director laughs. He's carrying a folder. He opens it and hands Aleksandr a glossy photograph. It's the same image as before but with a variety of lines highlighting different parts of the vessel. It's guesswork, but good guesses. Aleksandr purses his lips. He nods, thinking about the broader implications.

"It's a star shot," the director says. "By our calculations, based on the deceleration we see, our scientists estimate it would have taken roughly ten thousand years to get here from any of the six nearest star systems. We think the craft used all its fuel to accelerate and then gathered hydrogen while in flight, effectively refueling on the fly, and that's what it's using to slow down now."

"So it's older than the villages of the Volga."

"Older than the pyramids or Stonehenge."

Aleksandr doesn't like non-Russian examples of antiquity, but he accepts the director's point.

"And there's no crew."

"Not unless there were thousands of generations, no."

"It's a ghost ship," Aleksandr says, pausing for a moment. "What do our scientists expect? Why do they think it was sent here?"

The director leans against the control panel. Aleksandr sits up on one of the desks, handing the photograph back to the director.

"It's not so much what we expect as what *they* expect. They would have sent this spacecraft long before there was evidence of technological intelligence on Earth. They're expecting an uninhabited island—just birds and trees."

Aleksandr nods.

"They're after samples," the director says. "We expect robotic probes. And then we expect it to depart."

"Hah," Aleksandr says. "That won't happen."

"What do you mean?"

Aleksandr is surprised by how naive the director is on this point. "No one is going to let them leave. The Americans will junk that thing before they allow it to fly off. It's too valuable. Imagine all that could be learned."

"Director Zukov said you would be skeptical. He says we should not interfere with the alien mission."

"We," Aleksandr says, spreading his arms wide and encompassing the whole room. "All we humans do is interfere. For ten thousand years, we have interfered with nature. To interfere is to make progress. Back then, we built rock walls to keep goats in and wolves out. We dig up metals; we cut down trees; we harvest the seas. Nothing we do can be described with any other word than *interfere*. Why stop now?"

"I told them," the director says, shaking a finger at Aleksandr. "I told them you were the man for the job. They doubted. They wanted Mikhail Ilyin or Lidija Kozakov, but I said science comes after reason, not before. I told them you would not rest until Russia once again reigned supreme in space."

Aleksandr is intrigued. "You want me to go with the Americans?"

"Oh, no. We will send Mikhail to train with the Americans. You will lead *our* mission."

"I'm confused."

"We must be seen to be a responsible member of the international community. We must be seen to be cooperative."

"But?"

"The Duma agrees with your reasoning. Why should America be first? Why not Russia? What reason is there for the West to dominate First Contact?"

"There's none."

"Precisely. They may think they represent humanity; they do not. No one can. Not America. Not China. Not any one country. In truth, we must represent ourselves."

"They will feel betrayed," Aleksandr says.

"They will. And they will stand down our contingent from their mission, but we do not care. We will muddy the waters. We will blame them for the breakdown. We will say we were forced to go alone. We had no choice but to prepare an alternative."

Aleksandr smiles.

He likes what he's hearing.

First Contact

"Crash, right?" Professor Andrew Morecambe asks, holding out a friendly hand in greeting. Reluctantly, Crash accepts. He'd rather be known as Chris Williams, NASA astronaut, but he's learned to accept the public has fallen in love with his moniker, Crash. It's become a term of affection, not derision.

Andrea and Liz both grin. They know. Each of them shakes hands with the professor as they sit at a wooden picnic table on the vast park outside the nondescript NASA financial administration building on the outskirts of the Johnson Space Center in Houston, Texas. Suburbs roll into the distance. Joggers run around the public park. Couples walk dogs. Kids feed ducks swimming in the pond. In the parking lot, a custom van sells coffee and snacks. It also has packets of dried peas and corn on offer as an alternative to bread for the ducks.

Clouds dot the sky, breaking up the brilliant blue with what could be wisps of cotton candy floating in the distance. As it's late afternoon, shadows stretch from the trees. The table is partially in the shade, with the shimmer of leaves causing light to dance on the wood.

"Please," the professor says, and they sit on the bench seats, with Andrea sitting next to the professor while the others sit opposite him. Liz has a notebook. She opens it and draws a line across the middle of the page and writes the title *First Contact*. For someone that scrawls in a hurry, her handwriting is meticulous. The faster Crash writes the more his notes resemble a kindergartner playing with crayons. There have been far too many meetings where he's gone to review his dot points the next day only to feel like he's deciphering hieroglyphics. He'll leave the note-taking to Liz.

Andrea places a paper bag on the table and pulls out several cans of soda. As they're cold, the condensation has soaked through the bag. If she waited any longer, the cans would have torn through the flimsy brown paper and fallen on the grass. She hands them out. To anyone watching, it's innocent. A bunch of co-workers and friends are sitting outside on a beautiful day, enjoying the warmth of a summer afternoon. For the astronauts, it's a way of meeting with a senior SETI scientist without attracting attention.

"Thirsty?" she asks, offering the professor a Coke. He accepts it. She pulls out a can of Dr. Pepper, offering it to Liz, who waves it away. Crash isn't a fan of the Doctor either, but he accepts it, allowing Liz to have the can of Sprite. Andrea keeps the remaining Diet Coke for herself.

The professor pops the ring on his can, saying, "First. You all have my admiration and respect. I'd give anything to be going up there."

Crash grits his teeth. He doesn't reply to that comment. He's an imposter. For him, this isn't imposter syndrome, where someone feels unworthy when they're actually quite competent; he really *is* unworthy. He may be an experienced astronaut, but to his mind, that's nothing compared to what they face in the unknown of deep space. Is there anything that can prepare any of them for First Contact? It's the unknown that unsettles him. After considering the topic for decades, even the professor's insights could fall short as there's no way to know what's been missed until they set foot on that alien vessel.

From the other side of the picnic table, Andrea glares at Crash, wanting him to say something. Liz tips her pen sideways, tapping his hand and prompting him to speak.

Crash says, "It's humbling." He thinks for a moment and then adds, "I'm not sure I would have been my first choice for this mission."

"And that," the professor says, "makes you the ideal choice."

"I'm not sure I follow," Liz says.

"Everyone I know wants to go up there. Anyone could go. I'd love to go, as would all my colleagues. Every single one of them. But it's those that *don't* want to go up there that interest me."

Crash pops the tab on his can of soda, unsure where the professor is going with his point. A rush of air accompanies the twist of metal. He raises the rim to his lips and sips. Bubbles dance on his tongue. The professor is soft-spoken.

"The absurd difficulty of First Contact should not be trivialized or underestimated. And that's the danger for someone like me. Oh, I wouldn't want to misinterpret First Contact, but I probably would."

Liz makes notes.

"We see what we want to see," the professor says, "what we expect to see."

"Like an optical illusion?" Andrea asks.

"Yes, precisely. Our minds are geared toward interpreting words, phrases and symbols in a predictable manner. We instinctively want to make sense of chaos. I mean, look at that cloud up there. To me, it looks like a man facing sideways, reaching out with one arm toward something, perhaps an item on a shelf."

"Or it could be a kitten extending a paw," Andrea says.

"Exactly. And this is how our minds work. We're blind to the mechanics of our own thinking. We don't see humid vapor condensing at a thermal boundary within the atmosphere to form an opaque network of microscopic water droplets."

Crash says, "We see the head of an elephant or a horse."

Liz says, "Expectations sure can be misleading. I was at the ESA gym a few years ago in Paris, working out with weights. I had a routine of lifting 4, 5 and then 6 kilograms. On one particular day, I really struggled with the 6. I felt so weak. I couldn't figure out what was wrong until I rolled the weight over and realized it was a 9."

The professor smiles. "Yes. Expectations blur our thinking. They rely on assumptions. And when it comes to First Contact, that could be dangerous. When you're up there, you need to see clearly. You need to see not what you want or expect or long to see. You need to see reality for what it is. And, to my mind, that makes you ideal. I'll be able to give you some ideas and strategies, but somewhat ironically, you're *less* likely to be fooled by them than me. I'd be too willing to see what I want up there."

Crash replies, "But isn't ignorance equally dangerous?"

"Ignorance is dangerous. Expectations are worse. Have you ever wondered why our minds gravitate to negatives? Why is our default reaction to being surprised fear instead of joy? Both emotions are built on excitement, energizing our thinking, so why are we so often afraid? Afraid of the dark. Afraid of failing. Afraid of the contents of an envelope from the IRS. Afraid of saying the wrong thing and making a fool of ourselves in front of our friends. Afraid of being abandoned by those that love us."

"I don't know."

"It's because negative expectations help us avoid consequences. And there's no real danger in getting it wrong. If you're in Asia, walking a jungle track, and the bushes rustle, what do you think? Could that be a tiger or a bush rat? Could it be a poisonous snake or a squirrel? Expecting the worst kept us safe for tens of thousands of years. Reacting as though it were a tiger or a snake kept our ancestors safe on those rare occasions when it really was a tiger or a snake. Most of the time, though, it's just the wind. Expecting the worst is literally a survival mechanism. As horrible as it feels, these reactions keep us safe—even though we're probably safe anyway. But up there, your instincts are useless. Up there, the rules will be different. Up there, you need to temper your natural expectations."

Crash says, "So I need to see leaves rustling and nothing but leaves rustling."

"Exactly. You can't let your mind jump to negatives as none of our terrestrial rules will apply. You've got to see things clearly."

Andrea turns to Liz, saying, "Well, this isn't what I was expecting from this meeting."

To which the professor grins. "You've got to be prepared to face the unknown without fear."

Liz asks, "But how do we prepare for something that's never happened before?"

"Oh, but it has," the professor replies. "Our history is replete with examples of First Contact, only not with aliens, with each other.

"Fifty thousand years ago, seventy thousand, a hundred thousand—it's difficult to say for sure—but we spread out of Africa. *Homo sapiens* ventured into Europe, Asia, Australia, the Pacific and the Americas. And not in one migration. In many. Then, for tens of thousands of years, we ignored each other. We're not sure why, but we did. It seems we were content until someone invented ocean-going sailing ships and the age of exploration began.

"Marco Polo teased Europe with the allure of exotic trade and spices on the Silk Road. We set sail, looking for safer, quicker ocean routes to the Orient and set off to discover new lands. Only there were no new lands. We simply rediscovered lands already conquered by *Homo sapiens*. For the most part, every island and continent had already been discovered by someone we then called a native. *Human* would have been a better term as native implies an intrinsic difference between us and them. And *all* the differences between humans are contrived. Genetically, less than 0.1% separates all eight billion of us. We're a single species divided by everything we have in common."

"And First Contact?" Andrea asks.

"Whether it's the Dutch in Asia, the British in India and China, the Spanish in South America, the Americans on the midwest plains or British colonists settling Australia and New Zealand, First Contact has *never* been in favor of the original inhabitants. Never. It has *always* favored the more technologically advanced civilization."

Liz says, "Well, that doesn't sound good."

"And you're going to be seeing a lot of this in the press and on social media. People are going to be afraid of what could go wrong. They're going to be worried aliens will do to us what we've done to others."

"Should we be worried?" Crash asks.

The professor thinks for a moment before replying, "I don't know. Possibly. In our experience, First Contact has often devolved into war and even genocide. Sometimes it was deliberate and systematic, like when the British wiped out the aborigines in Tasmania or Cortés invaded Mexico. Other times, it was haphazard and accidental, like when smallpox ravaged North American tribes, wiping out tens of millions of people long before European settlers spread westward into the now largely empty lands.

"Space is hostile. There are very few habitable environments. We only know of one: Earth. It could be that they see Earth just as the Europeans saw America—a land of opportunity into which they can spread. And they may want to establish colonies alongside us, just as we did with the Native Americans. If that's the case, I'd expect roughly the same outcome over time. An initial period of peace followed by conflict as they expand and we diminish."

"Fuck," Andrea says, beating Crash to that comment.

"Now, I don't think that's likely. But is it possible? Yes. It all comes down to their intent in coming here."

"Why have they come here?" Crash asks.

The professor shrugs. "That's what we need you to find out. Their journey could be akin to Charles Darwin and the voyage of the HMS Beagle, cataloging life throughout the galaxy. If that's the case, then we're the Galapagos. They'll observe how life has evolved here, perhaps take some samples, and then sail on to the next island.

"Earth is an oasis in the lifeless deserts of outer space. They might decide to set up an outpost and cooperate with us. That would be the best possible outcome. If they share their technology, it would catapult us into the future."

Andrea asks, "And how likely is that?"

The professor laughs at his own reasoning. "How likely is it a US nuclear-powered warship would share technology with Amazonian tribesmen?"

Andrea says, "So we can expect trinkets and candy, but no muskets."

"Exactly." The professor takes a sip of soda. "I don't think they're here to invade us or colonize our planet. It just doesn't seem like the kind of thing an advanced civilization would do. After all, civilizations are civil by definition."

"We're not," Crash says. "Oh, we like to think we are, but someone runs across the border, fleeing oppression, and we throw them in jail. We're the biggest exporter of arms in the world. What if they're *civil* like us?"

"They're not like us," the professor says. "That's the one thing we do know for sure. They evolved on some other planet, around some other star. Now, there were probably the same drivers behind natural selection, such as disease and predation, but they will have charted their own course to the stars. We can guess at motivations and drivers. We can look at our own past for clues, but there's only one way we'll know for sure."

"By making contact," Liz says.

"Yes. Our biggest problem is what they consider intelligent."

"What do you mean?" Crash asks.

"We're intelligent, right?"

"Right."

"I mean, we have no doubt about it, but they may not see our intelligence the same way. We're smarter than chimps and gorillas, but it's not intelligence that separates us from them; it's writing.

"Crows are as smart as any seven-year-old child, possibly smarter. They can solve complex problems, they use tools, observe behavior and learn. They even talk among themselves, telling each other about any nasty humans that threaten them. What they lack is the ability to pass detailed information *accurately* from one generation to another. They can't write."

"Write?" Liz says, jotting down that point.

"Roll back the clock a few hundred years to the point Europeans first sailed the oceans of the world and ask yourself why there was such a vast difference between the Dutch, the Spanish and the English when compared to the Aztecs, the Native Americans, the tribes of Indonesia, the Maoris of New Zealand or the Aborigines of Australia?

"It didn't come down to intelligence. Contrary to the stereotypes of the day, these people weren't savages. Hell, the Aborigines were weaving fish traps and building complex weirs and rock walls to farm wild fish for over forty thousand years! That's about twenty thousand years longer than Europeans. They weren't stupid or simple. The Brewarrina fishing pools span over half a mile, with intricate rock formations taking into account tides and seasonal flooding. Archeologists think those fish farms could have sustained a population of around three thousand people—which is as large as most medieval cities in Europe. No, the Aborigines weren't dumb. What the Aborigines lacked was writing, which allows precise knowledge to accumulate from one generation to another.

"We're no smarter than them. The difference is we have access to books. Writing allows us to stand on the shoulders of the giants that came before us."

Crash says, "It's the time traveler's paradox."

Everyone looks at him. The professor says, "Now, you're going to have to explain that one to me."

Crash says, "Send any one of us back in time to say one thousand AD or even the time of Christ, or when the Egyptians were building the pyramids of Egypt, and what difference would it make?"

"Hah," the professor says, grinning, knowing precisely where Crash is going with his point. "None."

"Exactly. We know about computers and bacteria, internal combustion engines and airplanes, but they'd never believe us. We could tell them to watch their hygiene, but they'd think we were superstitious.

"I can fly a Starship, but I can't tell you how to make the alloys in the rocket engine. I'd be useless back then. There's nothing I could contribute. Ironically, they'd know more than me. Their knowledge of that time would be more useful than my knowledge from now."

"Yes, yes," the professor says. "And this is the point. We think of ourselves as intelligent, and we are, but we've inherited *everything* around us. In the past, someone figured out how to clean the water that comes out of our taps. Someone else figured out how to treat the wood in the walls of our homes so it doesn't rot. Someone else figured out how to fire bricks in a kiln so they can support a home for centuries. Someone else figured out how to generate electricity from running water or burning coal—or fizzing atoms. And yet someone else figured out how to refine rocks in the ground, turning them into the copper wiring that allows power to reach our homes. Take all that away from us, and we're not that far removed from chimps and crows. If anything, we're more helpless than them."

Liz asks, "So these aliens, when they're looking at Earth...?"

The professor says. "They may not see our intelligence as all that different from other animals on this planet, such as cephalopods or dolphins. To them, we've simply mastered the ability to accumulate knowledge. And we benefit hugely from that, far more than our individual intelligence alone would suggest."

"Hmm." Crash finishes his can of soda, noting he couldn't even recognize aluminum ore in the ground, let alone refine it and produce a pressurized vessel for carbonated beverages. Hell, he couldn't even make the contents. How do you extract carbon dioxide from the air and inject it, under pressure, into some syrupy liquid to make Coke or Sprite or whatever? Lemons. There are lemons involved somewhere along the line—and sugar—but that's as far as he could take the process.

The professor says, "And we're not giving them a lot of reasons to think we're anywhere near their level of intelligence."

Andrea says, "Reality TV, huh?"

"Any TV," the professor replies. "We have an amazing storehouse of scientific research, but that's not what we crow about. We broadcast anything and everything but actual life. If they can decipher our electromagnetic signals, they'll see a species obsessed with sports, comedies, romantic movies, horror, cartoons—you name it. The one thing they won't find is science as we find that boring, so we don't broadcast it anywhere."

"Oh," Crash says as the implications reverberate in his mind.

"It's going to be difficult to explain our love of fiction. Hell, they may not realize that what we're transmitting is fake and purely for entertainment. They could think *Survivor* is how we resolve differences between people, voting them off the island. They could see dragons in *Game of Thrones* and think such winged, fire-breathing animals exist or at least once existed. They could watch *Star Trek* and assume we have a fleet of spacecraft with warp drives out there somewhere exploring the galaxy."

Liz says, "Ah, this is going to complicate First Contact."

"Oh, yeah," the professor says. "And what do you think they'll make of pro wrestling? Re-runs of *Jerry Springer* are going to require some explanation."

Crash hangs his head. "Fuck."

"Yes, porn's another issue. We over-sexualize our entertainment, amplifying our sexual appetites way beyond reality. To them, we'd look like peacocks with our feathers out, dancing in display, constantly trying to lure a mate."

Liz laughs. "So, we could get up there, and they're sitting around watching *Love Island*?"

"Maybe," the professor says, "Deciphering the intricacies of language and obscure encoded formats like our audio and video signals should be difficult. There's a good chance they just see static, that they know there's an intelligent message in the signal somewhere, but they can't interpret it. Yet."

"We can only hope," Crash says.

Liz says, "First Contact is our first impression."

"Yes, it is. And I think that's something else people forget. First Contact is the start, not the end. We have to see beyond the moment. We've got to consider what happens next month, next year, next decade. We can't just drift aimlessly through First Contact."

For Crash, this is a key point. And it bothers him. He doesn't say anything, but in the back of his mind, he makes a note: Second Contact might be more important than First Contact itself. The professor, though, seems to breeze through the idea. Liz wants clarification. Like Crash, she's unsettled by the concept.

"Why?" she asks.

"If we don't manage First Contact, someone else will. There are plenty of people that would like to exploit First Contact. They can't help themselves. It's about power. The temptation is too great. Forget about aliens for a moment; someone somewhere will figure out a way to weaponize First Contact. It could be a religious leader using it to sway the masses. It could be a political regime to oppress dissent. It could be one nation warring against another. I don't know, but I do know there will be misinformation and lies."

"Because there's so much at stake," Crash says.

"Exactly. And the aliens? They'll see all this. They'll watch the drama play out between us. Only, they're detached. They'll be able to watch us without being drawn into either side. They'll see us squabbling."

Liz says, "Like a teacher watching students fight over a ball at recess."

"Yes."

Crash says, "Now, I *really* don't want to be going up there."

The professor smiles. "And that's why you're perfect for the job. We need someone to represent us in a broad, calm, balanced manner."

"But no one can represent us," Liz says. "It's not possible for one person to accurately represent all eight billion of us."

"No, it's not, but we have to lead with science. We have to lead with curiosity. We have to show them that for all our flaws, we want to learn."

Crash nods at that point, taking it to heart. In the weightlessness of space, the weight of an entire planet will be bearing down upon him, but he has to keep First Contact simple. Already, there's considerable debate among the senior management team at NASA about who should physically make First Contact. Some are arguing for him, as the mission commander, to stay with the *Odyssey* and send out one of the other astronauts to explore the craft. Being English, Liz has been touted as the best candidate. She's a good compromise between the various nations represented in the crew. Others are arguing that America should not be sidelined. Politics rather than reason seems to be driving the decision. As commander, he agrees with the professor that, regardless of who opens the hatch, they should be driven by a desire for scientific exploration rather than a political stunt.

The professor pauses for a moment. His eyes narrow. He squints, but not at the sunlight coming through the trees. He's thinking deeply about something.

"Have you ever wondered what it's like to be a bat?"

"A bat?" Liz asks, sitting back, confused by the question. Crash raises his eyebrows. He, too, is bewildered by the comment.

"A bat," the professor says.

"I don't understand," Andrea says.

"It's a question of perception," the professor replies. "The gulf between us and an alien race may be so great they cannot conceive how we think. Imagining our lives might be as abstract as us trying to imagine being a bat."

"And we can't think like a bat," Crash says. "It's too abstract."

"Exactly. And that could be a barrier between us and them. The point is that it might not be language barriers that prevent us from talking to the aliens. It could be sensory barriers. We might be so radically different from each other that it would be easier to imagine being a bird or a bat than an alien.

"Oh, we can picture hanging upside down like a bat, flapping our hands as wings and screeching to form sonar images with our ears, but we can *never* really know what it means to be a bat. It's the extreme differences between us. We have roughly the same senses of sight, sound, taste, touch and smell, and yet life as a bat still escapes us. What senses do these aliens have for detecting the world around them? They may look at us with the same perplexed curiosity we have for bats and snakes.

"Butterflies taste with their toes. Snakes smell with their tongues. Bees talk to each other using pheromones. Spiders listen with their feet. Bats can detect a single strand of hair in a pitch-black room. It's not just that these aliens may have different senses to us, but that those differences may make it impossible, or at least impractical, to communicate effectively."

Liz says, "So it could be like trying to talk to a butterfly."

"Yes. You need to be flexible and able to adapt up there. Avoid fixed expectations, as they will surely let you down.

"All language is based on agreement. An apple is an apple because we all agree it's an apple. But consider the difficulty of telling a deaf person about apples. You have to find another medium other than speech. Or the difficulty of telling a blind person about apples and pears. You have to agree on touch and taste for definitions rather than images and words."

Liz says, "So if there's no overlap in our senses."

"It will be like talking to butterflies."

Crash scratches the back of his head. He came to the meeting expecting answers. Instead, he has more doubts than before. He understands the professor's intent is to prepare him for the most radical of scenarios, but if he runs into anything even remotely like this, he'll be helpless.

Crash likes to be in control. Even before he trained to become a pilot and then an astronaut, he was consumed by a desire to resolve problems. Understanding was the key. Regardless of their complexity, the bewildering array of dials and controls in the cockpit of a jet could be understood. They all had specific functions. Together, they told him what he needed to know to make split-second decisions. Now, though, he feels totally unprepared for First Contact, and that leaves him feeling overwhelmed.

Being an astronaut is simple. There are a million things to know, but they're knowable. They're details he can wrap his head around. And if he can't, he can talk to a specialist back in mission control. Everything's planned. Everything that unfolds in space has been meticulously rehearsed on Earth, either with a submerged mock-up simulating a spacewalk or by swinging from the ceiling to approximate weightlessness while repairing equipment. Uncertainty is eliminated by training on various contingencies and procedures. And it's never him up there alone. He's surrounded by hundreds of hours of simulations and scenarios, as well as specialists providing insights into equipment and potential failure points. Everything is discussed. Every angle is considered.

For once, Crash is unprepared. And he gets it. He understands why the NASA director wanted them to meet with the professor. The director wants them to understand that this mission is different. It's not that it's First Contact so much as the complete unknown. All of his instincts say preparation is the key to success, but he finally understands the professor's message: preparation is impossible. Flexibility is the key. Agility is the key. Avoiding fear, avoiding instincts, seeing reality for what it is—that's what's needed. For Crash, this is a change in mindset, but he accepts it.

Liz says, "As the last hominid species, we've always been alone. We've always wanted someone else to talk to. Now we're about to meet them, and yet we may not be able to understand them."

"It's a possibility we need to consider," the professor says. "And if that's the case, we need to be patient."

"Angels and cherubim," Andrea says.

The professor replies, "Yes. Whether it's the gods on Mount Olympus or the demons of the underworld, we've been obsessed with non-human intelligence for thousands of years. Finally, fiction will become reality."

Control

Chief of Staff Susan Dosela leads Molly downstairs within the West Wing of the White House, saying, "I want you to shadow me on every meeting involving BDO 2033-495."

Molly nods. "Understood."

Nothing about the White House feels natural. It's formal. Stuffy. The polished brass fittings on the railing and dark mahogany wood speak of grandeur. There's not so much as a stray bit of lint on the carpet. Everything screams serious, which sets Molly on edge.

Molly's not a fan of the acronym BDO, meaning Bright Data Object, but that's the term that seems to have caught on in the media and not OI or Object of Interest. She suspects it's because of the cultural preference for three-letter acronyms over two.

Molly has been fascinated by the way scientists, astronomers, media personalities and politicians have struggled to define the BDO in any other way. For some strange reason, no one other than the conspiracy nuts on YouTube wants to refer to it as *"the alien spacecraft."* It seems more sanitized and manageable as the BDO. Technically, it's not even a BDO anymore, as that acronym refers to anything unusual that stands out in the reams of astronomical data pouring in from various telescopes. Regular folk like her assume telescopes take pictures, but most of the information they collect is raw data—numbers indicating things like brightness, timing, location, chemical composition, etc.

The term BDO originally arose because spikes in these numbers could arise from something as simple as using a microwave oven to heat some pasta in the observatory kitchen. Confusing someone's hot lunch for an alien spacecraft isn't a good look. Incoming text messages to a mobile phone appear remarkably like some exotic form of alien communication because they *are* an exotic form of communication—just not from aliens. Most of the Bright Data Objects get filtered out of the record. From what she heard on CNN, only one in a thousand ever gets reclassified as an Object of Interest, and the BDO is interesting, but the term BDO 2033-495 is what made it into the news, and it seems to have stuck.

Ralph, why couldn't they call it Ralph? That's an equally unassuming, non-threatening name. Molly is tempted to casually drop Ralph in conversation just to see the reaction, but life in the White House is too damn serious.

Chief of Staff Susan Dosela is still rambling as they walk along the plush carpet in the lower corridor. Molly's distracted by her own weird sense of humor. She can't imagine everyone would be so stressed and uptight if the grad students at the ATLAS observatory in Hawaii had called it Ralph. Or Alohi. Molly had a boyfriend in high school called Alohi. He was from Waikiki. He said Alohi meant shining or bright and was similar to Aloha, so it would actually fit quite well. Molly can't wipe the smile from her face. She can't imagine anyone getting upset about an upbeat name like Alohi. Ah, what a missed opportunity.

"Are you okay?" the chief of staff asks, turning to look at her.

"Oh, um," Molly says, composing herself. "Yes. I'm fine. The BDO changes everything, huh?"

"I need you to focus in there. Your job is to ignore me and watch everyone else. You're invisible. No one will notice you. I want you to observe those in the meeting, looking for body language and reactions the President and I might miss."

Molly is quiet.

Her silence does not mean agreement. She doesn't like the idea of being a snitch. Perhaps she's being naive, but she cannot imagine anyone involved in these meetings isn't conscientious. They wouldn't be here if they weren't loyal and dedicated.

The two of them surrender their cell phones as they walk into the Situation Room. Being a SCIF or Sensitive Compartmented Information Facility, the Situation Room is shielded from external electronic surveillance and contains a host of countermeasures designed to detect any unauthorized electrical devices.

The chief of staff sits near the top of the table, awaiting the President. Molly distances herself, walking down the narrow gap between the conference table and the chairs pressed against the wall. She sits in the corner, giving her a good view of both those seated at the table and the spare chairs on either side.

A woman in a US Air Force uniform walks in as part of the attendees, only she's politely stopped by the Secret Service. An electronic wand is run over her right hand.

"Oh, sorry," she says, slipping off a FitBit bracelet and dumping it in a plastic tray. Molly's not sure whether the FitBit can record audio, but the security team isn't taking any chances.

Once everyone is present, the President walks in. Various officers from the Army, Navy and Air Force stand to attention. Civilians like Molly stand out of respect.

"Thank you. Please be seated," President Elizabeth Smith-Knowles says, holding her hands out in a friendly gesture.

As the meeting starts, the chief of staff steals a glance at Molly. For her part, Molly has her legs crossed and a pad of paper perched on her lap. As she's left-handed, she can rather conveniently obscure anything she writes simply with the placement of her arm and the twist of her wrist holding the pen. Not knowing who's present, Molly uses a numeric system to keep track of everyone, starting with the President as number one and proceeding clockwise around the room. Molly counts 32 people in the meeting, although 20 of them are all on the far side, leaving her side of the room unbalanced. For whatever reason, the various military officers have congregated together opposite the civilians. It's a curious clustering of personalities.

Number Four, sitting beside the chief of staff, says, "We need to have a clear plan in place for how we're going to control First Contact."

Control? Molly doesn't like that term, but she remains quiet, making notes. Control is the antithesis of freedom, but she listens, wanting to understand more about the intent behind that concept.

"We need to be thinking about the impact on the general population. The media are quick to pick up on dissenting points of view. Anything for ratings, right?"

"Right," the President says, agreeing with Four.

"Now, the media's fragmented. We've got socialist elements. We've got the hard right and conspiracy theorists. And we've got the fact-based orgs, like Reuters. I know we normally leak to the Post or the Times, wanting to steer reactions in key market segments, but I think we have to avoid our usual channels on this one. No favors. We need to release through Reuters to keep neutrality."

Molly makes detailed notes. She doesn't mind this kind of control. Four is trying to limit the tendency of various news organizations to run with their own agendas and—more importantly—for the White House to steer them.

"It's Pandora's box," Four says. "As tempting as it is to funnel information through our usual connections, it'll backfire."

"I don't like it," the chief of staff says.

"Me neither," the President says.

Four says, "If we show favoritism, we'll breed enemies."

The President rests her elbows on the table. Her chin rests on her propped-up hands as she considers that point.

Four says, "If we go exclusively through Reuters, we're sending a clear message to both the left and the right. We're not playing games. We're not playing politics, even on those occasions when it would suit us."

"And you think this will work?" the President asks.

"Nothing will work," Four replies. "We're sailing into a storm. All we can do is batten down the hatches. It's impossible to predict the chaos that's coming our way, but we can mitigate it by being smart with what we can control. And we can control how information flows from the government to the people."

The President nods. "Okay. Do it. But get the word out to our regulars first. I want them to know what we're doing and why. They won't like it. Everyone loves an exclusive. But if they know it's a level playing field, they'll respect that."

Four nods.

Molly notices Sixteen, who's sitting further down the table, shaking her head in disagreement. Sixteen writes something on a notepad and then rests her pen, sighing as the discussion moves on. Molly makes her own notes, realizing the chief of staff will know exactly who Sixteen is and will have a quiet word with her.

Thirty is a US Army General seated on the other side of the President. There's a pecking order to the seating. The general is close enough to reach out and take the President's water bottle if he wanted to, so he's clearly important.

"Ma'am, we need to talk about the possibility of civil unrest as First Contact unfolds."

The President is intrigued. "What kind of unrest do you expect?"

"Our modeling suggests unrest could arise from a variety of catalysts. We suspect there will be clashes between the far-right and Antifa as contact unfolds. Neither group is likely to sit on the sidelines if they feel threatened.

"You'll have the National Guard available to support local law enforcement, but this plays directly to John Hammond's earlier point: how information spreads is going to be important. The left will seize on literal interpretations and their implications. The right will be fanciful and flamboyant, making mountains out of molehills. Neither will be entirely correct, but that won't matter to their supporters. They'll come out in defense of their side, and clashes will ensue.

"I'd recommend we start with a National Guard presence in each state capital city before problems arise. If we show force, we're sending a message of our own—that violence will not be tolerated."

The President says, "I understand your intent, but I don't think we can do that. We'd be playing into the long-running right-wing narrative of the federal government seizing power. We'd fan the flames rather than douse them."

The general says, "We use a soft approach. We talk to the states about deploying unarmed Guardsmen in utility uniforms. We have them on the street, walking routes between federal government buildings. We have them mingling with people in Starbucks or whatever; it doesn't matter so long as they're seen. We drive trucks around, but nothing threatening, no hummers, no armored personnel carriers."

"I like it," Thirty-Two says, sitting directly next to the President. Thirty-Two is a slim man in a slightly oversized but immaculate three-piece grey suit. At a guess, he's in his forties. He's clean-shaven with light skin and unusually long hair for a man, curling just off his shoulders. Molly's seen him around in the West Wing hallway but doesn't know his name or position. He says, "People react globally but think locally. If they see a local presence, they'll feel safe. They'll feel as though the government is doing something to protect them—at least at the state level. If we can get the sate governors to support this approach, it could really help."

The President is skeptical. "While they're standing in line for a coffee?"

"It's emotional, not logical," Thirty-Two says. "And logic follows emotion, not the other way around. If you want to appeal to them with logic, you need to satisfy their emotional needs first. Show them they're safe, and they'll listen to you. It doesn't matter how illogical it may seem to us, but if Joe Brown in Little Rock, Arkansas, thinks ET is about to land in his backyard, he'll freak out. If he sees the National Guard on duty, he'll relax a little because there's someone standing between him and the unknown."

"Even if they're unarmed?" the President asks.

"Even if they're unarmed—initially. We need to appeal to

emotion, not logic, because no one, absolutely no one, thinks logically when they feel threatened."

The President nods, conceding that point. She addresses her chief of staff, saying, "I need to talk to the state governors before taking any action. Tell them what we're thinking. Get them on board." She turns to the general, adding, "And it had better be a soft touch. I don't want to give Fox or News Max any ammo to use against us."

"Understood."

"Coordinate with my office before deployment. Let's make sure we have everyone onboard before we start rolling out troops."

The general nods.

The discussion ambles, becoming caught up in the intricacies of international trade, airport security and cross-country transportation. Molly tries to stay focused, but after almost ninety minutes, her attention span is waning. Looking around the room, she's not the only one with glazed eyes. The President, though, seems to want to continue working through an agenda covering everything from border security to international relations in the age of First Contact.

Everyone is dressed formally. The guy sitting opposite Molly is in a US Air Force uniform. He picks lint off his trouser leg, but he doesn't drop it on the floor. Instead, he pockets it and then returns to sitting up straight and attentive. To her mind, he shouldn't even be in here as the discussion moves to budget allocations, which has nothing to do with the military.

At first, Molly was intimidated by absolutely everyone within the White House. Director Greene from Human Resources quickly destroyed that myth. Since then, she's reminded herself that nothing is as it seems. Outwardly, everyone's calm, composed and professional. They exude confidence. They belong. She's the imposter, the outsider. Only lately, she's begun seeing through the facade. Everyone in the Situation Room was woken from their slumber by an alarm clock this morning (probably as an app on their phones). They all dragged themselves out of a warm bed to pee and shower and get dressed. Then they ate a bagel or—if they're like her—skipped breakfast and went straight for coffee. They climbed into their cars, walked to the bus stop or headed to the subway and rode to work. If they were on a train, they sat or stood shoulder to shoulder with strangers. Physical boundaries are meaningless on public transport. Arms and legs brush as close as they would with any lover, but they ignored that, staring at their phones. Some would play Candy Crush. Others read the news or listened to podcasts. The diligent would be answering emails. Most of them would use the uncomfortable intimacy of strangers to shut down emotionally for a while before work demanded their all.

At the point they showed their passes to security and walked through the cordon, their personas changed. They became someone else. They were no longer John from apartment 2B or Susie, who enjoys yoga and live music on the weekends. They were now the Director of Communications or Liaison with the Department of the US Navy. At lunch, they'll be themselves again before transforming once more for the afternoon, only to finally relax on the way home. Then it'll be a quick run to Kroger's for salad dressing before popping some lasagna in the oven. After dinner, it'll be Netflix or some other streaming service entertaining their overworked brains before they fall asleep and recharge for another day of roleplaying.

Molly decides being an adult sucks.

Twenty-Four is sitting on an angle opposite her. He holds up his hand as though he were in class. Like her, he's not seated at the table but rather is in the supporting seats set against the walls of the Situation Room.

"Yes," the President says, looking past a bunch of heads to what must be a familiar face to her.

"We need to think about how we control the next few steps beyond First Contact."

That gets Molly's attention. She sees a few other people react as well, being interested in this point, so she jots down their numbers and watches how they respond to the point as it unfolds.

Twenty-Four says, "We're planning for here and now, but we need to be thinking about how we control the change that is to come."

The President gestures to Twenty-Four, introducing him to the rest of the room. "Jacob Billings is from the Department of Treasury's fiscal planning office. What are you thinking, Jacob?"

"Ma'am. The arrival of the alien spacecraft has the potential to cause long-term economic and cultural disruption. As an example, back when the internet first exploded onto the scene, we faced the dot-com bubble, where excitement outstripped reality and a lot of businesses failed. And it wasn't just small businesses. Nokia was once invincible, dominating the mobile phone market in the 90s. It looked unassailable, as did Blackberry, as did Kodak. Now, they're museum pieces.

"Then we had the social media bubble. For the first time, the world was united on one global platform. Facebook had more users than the ten largest countries in the world combined. And then disinformation set in, and the bubble of confidence burst, followed by a pandemic where lies took lives.

"Then we had the AI bubble. AI was the future. AI would replace all our menial jobs and usher in utopia. Only it didn't. It left the menial jobs untouched and stripped out the talent from where it was needed most. And then, like Ouroboros, the snake began eating its own tail."

The President says, "And you think something similar is going to happen with First Contact?"

"It's inevitable. Every time we open Pandora's gift box, there's chaos. We're going to see tectonic shifts in religious sentiment. We're going to see economic boundaries disrupted. As countries and companies scramble to understand even the simplest alien technology, we'll see an arms race develop. There will be winners and losers. A lot of losers. And it's the losers we need to keep in mind. It's those that find themselves on the sidelines of progress that are likely to lash out, and that will result in political instability."

"And you think we can control that?" the President asks.

"Not once the horse has bolted," Jacob says. "But before then? Yes, we can."

The chief of staff says, "Change is always upon us."

"It is, but it's the pace of change that's disruptive. We need to slow things down. We need to control *how* change occurs. We need to legislate *before* change is thrust on us, not after."

The President rolls her head to one side, looking down the table at her chief of staff. "I'm not sure we can do that. We're just one country among hundreds. We can't control what Russia, China or India does in response to the arrival of the alien spacecraft."

Jacob says, "We need to establish rules for communication with the aliens."

"Beijing is not going to play ball. Neither is Moscow."

"They don't need to. We need the aliens to understand that their arrival represents a point of social, cultural and technological change for us. We need them to give us exclusive contact."

The President leans forward in her chair. "You want the US to be the sole arbiter of alien technology? And you don't think that will lead to war down here?"

"We share," Jacob says. "But yes, we act as a filter. We act as a chokepoint. We slow things down. We control First Contact."

The chief of staff says, "And what if the aliens don't trust us? What if they decide Beijing is more closely aligned with their ideology? What if they think Moscow is a better bet?"

"We need to convince them," Jacob says. "Forget about physics and biology and all the academic inquiry surrounding First Contact, we need to strike a political agreement with them. That should be the first order of business."

The President's eyes go wide. "Well, that's a tall order."

Jacob is blunt. "If we don't control this, chaos will ensue."

Molly can see a variety of responses around the room. The military officers agree with Jacob. Most of the civilians nod, but there are a few dissenters softly shaking their heads. Like her, the idea of manipulating and controlling others is repugnant to them. The government should guide, not mandate. The whole notion of control is anathema to her. Molly rebels against the direction of the chief of staff.

She ignores those who disagree, refusing to draw the chief of staff's attention to them after the meeting.

And if this is how the US Government is dealing with its own citizens, what will it do when negotiations start with the aliens?

For Molly, the notion of controlling First Contact is horrifying. Humans should listen rather than make demands of their celestial visitors. Rather than forcing them to fit the machinations of 21st-century geopolitics, they should be free to decide what they feel is appropriate. There's no black and white. Whether it's the US, China or the tiny Pacific island nation of Tuvalu, politics is a murky grey. To think otherwise is worse than folly; it's to ignore the evil that has been done in the name of freedom over the decades. It's hubris to think humans could control an intelligent species from another planet. Or even to consider they'd need such control.

What the hell is everyone so damn afraid of? Yet again, Molly sees the worship of the status quo as nauseating. Change excites the young. It scares the old, but why? It's because life is a lie. Today is the same as yesterday, only it isn't. Yesterday is gone. Yesterday can *never* be revisited. Tomorrow need not be the same as today, but only if there's the courage to change today. And to her mind, that's what's lacking—courage.

Molly grits her teeth. Her nostrils flare. It's slight. She steels a glance at the chief of staff, hoping she hasn't noticed. Sue Dosela is making notes on her paper pad.

Molly has no idea what tomorrow holds, but she knows one thing: she has the courage to change today. For now, she'll bide her time, but she won't stand by as the President and her advisors attempt to control First Contact. If given the chance, Molly will create change for the better. She refuses to cower in fear before the future.

Second Contact

Branches shift with the breeze, casting long shadows over the park. Birds murmur in the sky, swirling in flocks of thousands. They ebb and flow like a school of fish evading a barracuda in the depths of the sea. They're looking for somewhere to roost as night slowly descends. Thin, wispy clouds high in the stratosphere light up with shades of pink and golden yellow.

The astronauts have been sitting with the professor for several hours, occasionally disappearing to use the bathroom and then returning to the picnic table. The professor looks as fresh as when they first started, but Crash is struggling. His attention span is waning.

"I might just—"

"Sure," the professor says, and Crash excuses himself.

As he walks away, he hears Andrea asking about how aliens will interpret our different cultures and various languages. The professor says they probably have similar differences themselves, as a monoculture isn't practical for a global species and isn't conducive to progress.

Crash jogs up the stairs to the NASA admin building and uses the bathroom in the reception area. Before returning, he grabs a candy bar from a vending machine. It's not the healthiest choice of snack, but he needs a sugar hit. He stands by the floor-to-ceiling windows, looking out over the sprawling park with its lush trees, picnic tables and children's playground. Ducks float on the pond.

As the park borders both the NASA building on one side and a school on the other, it's public property and popular with the locals. Two women push strollers along the pavement, talking to each other as they walk along the winding path. Runners jog past them, stepping off the concrete and onto the grass as they run on by, checking their smartwatches, no doubt for their pace and heart rate, and listening to music with their wireless headphones. For Crash, the message is simple. Aliens roll in—life rolls on. For him, Liz and Andrea, First Contact is all-consuming. For everyone else, it's a curiosity. It's an interesting byline. The circus is in town.

It's funny, but as important as it is talking to the professor, a bit of physical distance gives Crash a broader perspective. Movies and musicals make revolutions seem as though they unfold overnight, but they don't. They simmer before boiling. Whether it's a political revolution or a technological one, like the advent of the Internet, all revolutions need time to gather momentum. Most people only spot them once they're flattening everything in their path. What will happen when humanity makes First Contact? At the moment, that's all anyone's thinking about or talking about, but Crash is curious about what comes next. When is the steamroller going to flatten the road?

Crash walks back to the table with a couple of bags of Doritos from the vending machine, along with a bag of Skittles. If he's hungry, so is everyone else.

"Oh, thanks," Liz says, taking a bag of Extra-Cheesy Doritos from him. Andrea and the professor share the candy. No one wants the Hot Chili Doritos.

Crash sits back down, saying, "Something you said earlier bothers me."

"What?"

"Second Contact."

The professor stops chewing. He looks at Crash with astonishment. "Explain what you mean."

"All the hype," Crash says. "Ah, the President said it herself. This is a turning point in history, but all we're focused on is the fulcrum around which history will turn. We're not looking at how the seesaw is going to swing from one height to another."

"Oh," the Professor says. "So what comes next?"

"Yes."

"I don't know. We don't know."

"Do you have any ideas?"

The professor says, "I'm not sure we're in a position to guess. I mean, think about Copernicus publishing his work on the heliocentric theory or Newton describing how a cannonball fired fast enough would go into orbit. Neither man could have foreseen the Apollo lunar missions or the exploration of Mars, and yet that's where their work led us.

"Galileo spotted the moons of Jupiter and the smudged rings of Saturn through his telescope. He joked that the planet had ears or handles. He could have never imagined the grandeur of the images collected by NASA. Imagine if he'd seen Jupiter's Great Red Spot—a single, violent storm lasting for centuries and large enough to hold a thousand Earths! Or if he'd seen the stunning majesty of Saturn's rings and the icy moon of Enceladus spraying geysers easily ten thousand kilometers into space. Those geysers reach a height twenty times the size of the small moon itself. Even though Galileo peered at those peculiar points of light and realized they were moons, he could have never imagined what actually lay out there in the darkness."

"And neither can we," Crash reluctantly concedes.

"No," the professor replies. "But I think you have a valid concern. First Contact is like a first date. It's all roses and champagne, all smiles and warm fuzzy feelings. It's not until the second, third, fourth or fifth date that you get a feel for a potential partner."

"Once you're outside the honeymoon period," Andrea says.

"Precisely."

Liz says, "So we could come away from First Contact thinking everything went swell only to see things unravel?"

"A lot depends on how they view our intelligence," the professor replies. "Will they see us as equals or curiosities? Oddities? I mean, look at how we treat intelligent animals here on Earth. There's no doubt dolphins are smart, and yet we breed them in captivity, deny them access to the open ocean, and have them perform tricks for our children's entertainment."

Andrea says, "But the aliens must see we're more intelligent than that?"

"Must they?" the professor asks. "We know dolphins are highly social creatures with a complex language unbound by words. They can share sonar images with each other. That's like me sharing the mental image of my wife and kids with you through sound alone. And they can solve problems and use tools. They can even lie."

"How can a dolphin lie?" Liz asks. "They can't even speak."

"In one enclosure, staff would reward dolphins with fish for collecting litter that blew into the tank. The dolphins quickly realized they could use this to manipulate the trainers. They began hiding scraps of paper beneath rocks at the bottom of the pool. They'd tear off small pieces and present them for fish. We don't see that level of cunning in humans until they reach the age of ten.

"Dolphins are one of the few animals that can recognize themselves in a mirror, meaning they're self-aware. They know who they are. And they're socially minded. When a mass stranding occurs, it's the result of a pod trying to rescue a stranded dolphin and everyone ending up in the same mess. And why? Because they care about each other. They'll risk their lives to help each other."

Liz says, "And we beat them to death with clubs and spears."

"Yes," the professor replies. "We slaughter them in their thousands in the waters around the Faroe Islands. The bay is known to run red with blood."

Andrea asks, "And you think these aliens could do something similar to us?"

"No, but it is a possibility. We're chauvinistic. Even among humans, we're obstinate and biased, mistreating others based on race or gender or wealth when there's really no difference between us at all. When it comes to other animals, we refuse to see any other species as deserving of our rights. We even speak of *human rights* because no other animal qualifies for consideration. In the same way, they might see us as inferior to them."

"But we're intelligent," Liz says.

"Are we?" the professor asks.

"Yes."

"Hmm," the professor says, popping a few Skittles in his mouth. "Intelligence can be measured in different ways. I suspect they'll be more interested in our collective intelligence rather than any individual brilliance."

"I don't understand what you mean by that," Crash says, curious about the professor's reasoning.

"Bees form a collective intelligence that's greater than any one bee on its own. Together, they can build hives, regulate the temperature within their colony, and produce astonishing amounts of honey."

"And us?" Liz asks.

"Our collective intelligence is dubious at best. Individually, we're quite smart and rational and caring. Collectively, we're destructive. I mean, look at climate change. We've done that to ourselves.

"Since the mid-nineties, there's been a growing public awareness of the problem. Each year, the UN holds its COP meetings to limit the use of fossil fuels. We sign treaties and accords in Paris and Kyoto and wherever. We install solar panels and drive electric cars. And for what? Have you looked at the graph showing CO_2 emissions over the past three decades? It's a *smooth* curve upward. All the committees and interventions and protests have had precisely zero effect on the rate of change. We are exactly where we thought we'd be fifty years ago if nothing were done."

"Well, that's depressing," Liz says.

"That's humanity," the professor replies. "That's us. That's our collective intelligence or lack thereof. Our societies are driven by convenience, and that's exploited by greed. We call it capitalism, but it's really consumerism. So what will they see when they look at Earth? Will they see medical researchers looking for cancer treatments, or will they see rivers of plastic polluting our waterways?"

The professor laughs, pointing at Crash as he adds, "And your job? Your job is to make us look good."

Crash sighs and shakes his head.

Liz says, "So there's a decent chance they'll look at us with disdain?"

"They'll see us as we are," the professor says. "We may be able to fool ourselves into thinking we're the greatest, but they'll see us stripped naked. They'll see the petty wars and infighting. They'll see our various factions and the way people are abused and manipulated. They won't be fooled by any of the facades we put up. They'll laugh at our ideologies."

"Collective intelligence, huh?" Crash says.

"We're not as smart as we think we are," the professor replies. "We're not logical. We like to flatter ourselves, but we're easily fooled. We're creatures of passion—emotion.

"Logic evolved as a means of defending our passions in an argument. Most people reason to defend their position, not to change their minds or advance their understanding.

"When it comes to sensational ideas, we're like cats chasing a laser pointer. We'll pounce on anything that's shiny and new. Only unlike a cat, we can actually catch hold of these ideas. Then we turn and become like a dog with a bone, defending our newfound prize as though it were sacred.

"Look at the madness during the pandemic. No one wants to be sick. No one wants to suffer. No one wants to die in agony. No one starts out as an anti-vaxxer, but there goes the red dot of that goddamn laser pointer. It's racing along the carpet. Gotta chase it!

"Somewhere along the line, there will be some vague point that appeals to our vanity, to the passions we already hold—and that's all that's needed to believe a lie. We become convinced against all logic to the contrary. We throw out any logic we don't like. We have to. We have to justify the madness—not the logic, the passion! And the irony is, the smarter we think we are, the easier it is to be fooled.

"We overestimate our own intelligence when it's largely irrelevant. You don't need a blistering IQ to drive a car, do the laundry, play golf or walk the dog. Regardless of how smart we think we are, we rarely use our intelligence to its full potential. And it makes no difference anyway. Our collective intelligence is far more important than any one individual's intelligence. It doesn't matter how smart someone is, anyone can own an iPhone, but no one person can build one from scratch.

"And what will these creatures from another star system make of our idiosyncrasies? Will they have some of their own? Will they see through the thin veneer of logic we use to justify our emotions? How will that affect the way they deal with us?"

Crash says, "That's Second Contact."

The professor nods, agreeing. "That's Second Contact."

"Damn," Liz says.

The Plan

Aleksandr lowers his head against the bitter wind rushing across the Russian steppes. Tussocks of grass bend and sway. Flecks of snow and ice rush past. Winter is still weeks away, but Siberia listens to no man. Predicting the weather howling across the vast expanse that makes up eastern Russia is folly. Even with global warming, the frozen tundra keeps her anger. As does Aleksandr. He and the land are one in their hatred of the Vostochny Cosmodrome and their desire to see it swept into the Okhotsk Sea along with the bergs and ice flows.

Even with a down-filled coat and a traditional *ushanka* on his head, with the bear fur pulled down over his ears, the cold still cuts through him. This is what Siberia has been known for throughout history: the ice that bites. He can feel it in his bones. Enemies of the revolution were exiled here not for punishment but for reformation. Siberia breaks the spirit. It's unrelenting. Unforgiving.

Aleksandr rushes up the steps leading to the administration building. Ice hangs from the handle. He steps into the lobby and is greeted by a rush of hot air fighting off the cold. Steam radiators line the walls, sitting below the double-glazed glass windows. They creak and groan as though they were alive and fighting for life against the cold.

The soldier at the security desk eyes Aleksandr as he walks past, but he doesn't say anything. For his part, Aleksandr doesn't even bother with the pretense of showing his pass as his boots thunder on down the hallway. He's too damn cold to go searching through his pockets for his

ID.

As is his wont, Aleksandr doesn't take the elevator. He opens the door to the stairwell and unzips his coat, relishing the chance for some cardiovascular exercise to quell his baseline bitterness. He jogs up the stairs with his *ushanka* clutched in his hand. On reaching the seventh floor, he's out of breath but feels alive. He steps out into the reception area, turning his back on the accursed Roscosmos logo with its pandering to Western ideals and trekkie image. Had he taken the elevator, he would have stepped out facing the floor-to-ceiling logo. Turning his back to it is much more agreeable.

"Ah, there you are," Director Olenev says, standing by the conference room. An old chrome urn sits on a rickety table, keeping stale coffee warm. The director pours a steaming hot mug of burnt coffee and hands it to Aleksandr. "This will put some fire back in those bones."

"Thank you," Aleksandr says, nodding slightly in acknowledgment.

The director pours himself a cup, and together they walk into the conference room beside reception. Neither man bothers with sugar or powdered creamer.

Inside the room, a dozen support staff, engineers, and department heads sit quietly, waiting for their arrival. Alexi Romanov has a laptop out and is projecting his desktop onto a comically large screen at the front of the room. Everything is old except the projector, which casts an 8K image on the screen.

Genji Sokolov stands to greet Aleksandr. She shakes his hand, mutters some pleasantries, and takes her seat. Genji is in her late thirties and was selected for the deep space mission based solely on Aleksandr's whim. She's slim and petite, with jet-black hair pulled back in a ponytail. She hides her emotions behind a stony glare and despises makeup, which Aleksandr likes about her. She's professional above all else and that's what's needed for the *Vechnost* mission. She's loyal. She will do as she's told.

Director Olenev sits at the head of the table with Genji on his left.

Aleksandr takes the seat on his right. The symbolism isn't lost on anyone, as is obvious by the way even the department heads avert their eyes, looking at the two of them to be polite while avoiding direct eye contact.

Director Olenev says, "The Duma has approved our proposal for *Vechnost* as a three-phase deep space mission to the alien spacecraft. Secrecy is of the utmost importance. The Americans cannot get wind of our plans. We *must* launch before them. We must reach the alien spacecraft before them. Just as we did in the days of Sputnik and Gagarin, Russia will be triumphant in First Contact."

Around the room, people nod in agreement.

"Alexi, the floor is yours."

Alexi Romanov is a scrawny old man, balding on top, with grey hair cut close to his scalp, winding over his ears. His face is wrinkled. Aleksandr likes him because he's part of the old guard, having worked for Roscosmos before it degenerated into a puppet organization ferrying the Americans to the International Space Station. With the demise of the station, Roscosmos was reduced to satellite launches rather than exploration.

Alexi understands the true heart of Russian spaceflight. He remembers Buran, the Soviet alternative to the US Space Shuttle. He was part of the flight monitoring crew that celebrated the first ever fully-autonomous flight of the Buran into orbit and back to land. It's a feat of automation that defied even American ingenuity, but the Buran program was scrapped when the Soviet Union fell. The shuttle was left to rust in a hangar. For both Aleksandr and Alexi, the Buran represented the pinnacle of Russian space prowess. They feel it was superior to the American shuttle in every regard. That it was not only abandoned but ignored by politicians is a slight that neither man can forgive. Aleksandr always has time for Alexi.

"What we know, the Americans know," the old man says. "It is now a foot race."

"A space race," Director Olenev chuckles to himself.

"Yes, yes," Alexi replies. "And it is one we can win."

"Go on."

Alexi brings up an image that looks deceptively simple. On the screen, Earth orbits the sun in a circle. In practice, it isn't quite a perfect circle, but for the sake of the diagram, it's accurate enough. A single line extends from the sun, passing through Earth and reaching out further into space.

"Now that the alien spacecraft has rounded the sun, we can see where it is heading. And it is not heading toward Earth."

That gets everyone's attention. They look at the screen, perplexed as a dotted line appears to curl around the sun and head out well in front of Earth.

Alexi clicks his mouse button again. Two equilateral triangles appear on the diagram. One faces up, while the other leads down from the line passing through Earth and the sun. The tip of each triangle touches the circular path of Earth's orbit, but they connect a considerable distance away from Earth itself, almost a third of the way around the orbital path.

"These are Lagrange points for the Sun-Earth system," Alexi says. "They're stable points in front of and behind Earth.

"Gravity isn't the only factor in space. Momentum must be taken into account. Velocity is as important as gravity itself. Earth doesn't fall into the sun because it's moving so fast it falls around the sun instead. Earth is traveling at thirty kilometers a second. Our planet is caught by the Sun's gravity, but it's going sideways, so it never falls in. That's all an orbit is. Earth swings around the sun like a child swings around a maypole.

"Now, Lagrange points are the result of this tug-o-war between gravity and our momentum. The sun attracts Earth. Earth attracts the sun. But Earth is in motion. It's in equilibrium. This tug-o-war, though, spreads out all around the sun and Earth, forming flat spots. Lagrange points are where they cancel each other out. And this is where the aliens are heading. To one of these neutral spots."

Heads nod around the room, but Aleksandr doubts most of them understand. Lagrange points screw with his thinking.

Alexi says, "Think about a ship pushing its way through the ocean. Dolphins appear. They jump and splash, riding the bow wave. They surf ahead of the ship. It seems impossible, but for them, it's natural. In the same way, the aliens are heading to Lagrange point four. They're going to surf ahead of Earth as it orbits the sun."

Genji asks, "Why?"

It's a simple question, but it shows she's following the discussion. And it's a good question. Aleksandr is wondering the same thing.

"L4 is almost a hundred million miles from Earth," Alexi says. "Over a hundred and fifty million kilometers away. That's four hundred times the distance to the Moon!"

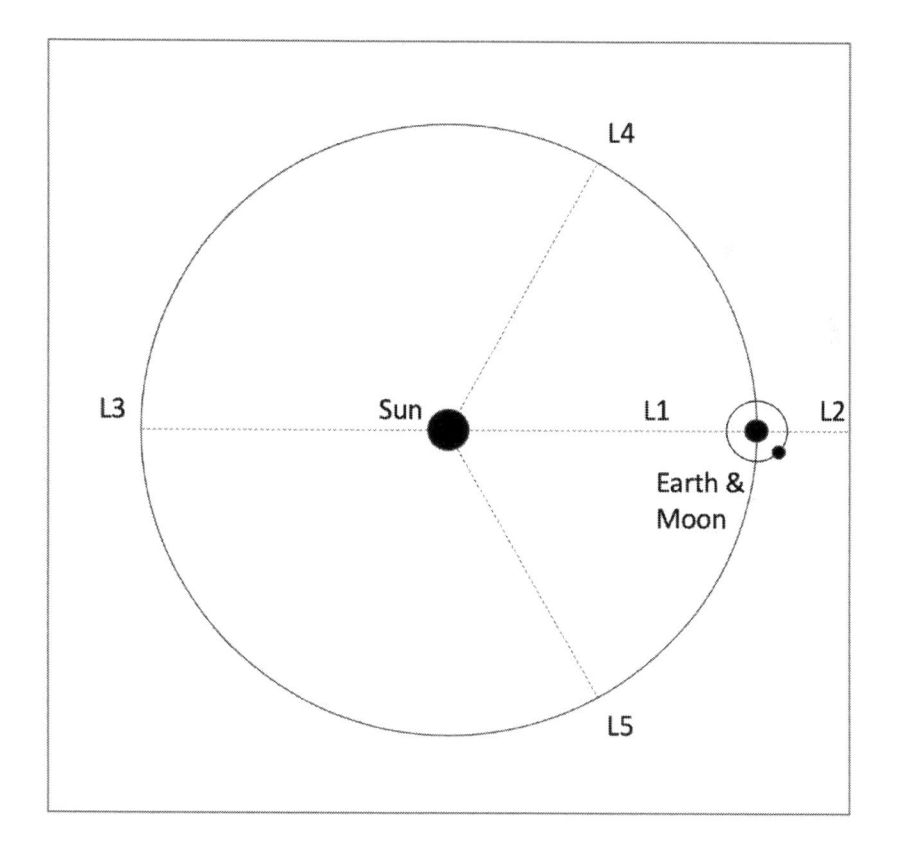

"That's absurd." Aleksandr is both impatient and unreasonable.

"Why? Why stop there?" he asks, repeating Genji's question, even though there's no way Alexi would know for sure. At best, he can guess. That's all any of them can do. And his guess is no better than that of anyone else.

"It's convenient," he replies. "For them, it's safe. They're keeping us at arm's reach. They can sit off in the distance while they prepare."

"Prepare for what?" the director asks.

"First Contact."

"Hmm," the director says. "Should we wait? Should we let them approach us when they're ready?"

"The Americans won't wait," Aleksandr says.

The director sips his coffee. "No, they won't."

"Can we do it?" Genji asks. "Can we rendezvous with them in deep space out at L4?"

"We can," Alexi says. "Distance isn't an obstacle. If *Vechnost* can reach the Moon, it can reach the escape velocity for Earth and glide forever if need be. And without using four hundred times the fuel. It requires a significant additional burn, but it's well within reserves if we use an assist to leave orbit. The challenge for this mission will be life support."

"How are we going to do that?" the director asks.

"To extend our reach, we need to be smart. We need to work within the limits of the Soyuz. And to do that, we will need three launches. The first from Baikonur. With the *Vechnost* launching from here in Vostochny. That will fool the Americans. They'll know that no one Russian launch could get us into deep space, but what they won't realize is that you'll rendezvous with the first launch. We'll put an oversized booster in orbit from Baikonur. You link up with it and ride it into deep space, conserving your onboard fuel for the return journey."

Aleksandr is confused. "You said there would be three launches."

"Ah, yes. The third launch isn't until later. Much later. It's to bring you back, but not from the alien spacecraft itself. If we strip the descent capsule on your Soyuz of its heat shield, parachutes and pyrotechnics, we buy ourselves mass that can be used for air, water and food. You have two modules, so living space will be fine. The command/descent module and the orbital module will be packed with supplies."

Genji asks, "If we have no heat shield, no parachutes, how do we land when we get back?"

"When you return, you'll enter a highly eccentric orbit around Earth. From there, we'll send up a Soyuz to rendezvous with you and bring you back."

"Ah," Aleksandr says, liking the simplicity of the idea.

Alexi says, "The Americans will go for a single shot. They won't suspect a multi-faceted approach from us. They'll think it too complex to pull off, but if we keep it simple, we can do this."

"I like it," the director says. "But the key to success is our launch schedule. We *must* beat the Americans to that alien spacecraft."

"Understood."

Launch

Crash is lying on his back in a simulator with the control panel of the *Odyssey* just inches from his face. Beside him, the Chinese taikonaut Wu Yúzé is studying a last-minute course correction forced on them due to a slow leak from the O2 tank. It's not a likely scenario given all the monitoring metrics gathered by the *Odyssey*, but NASA isn't taking any chances. Every possibility must be explored. Given they have a multinational crew that's largely unfamiliar with NASA hardware, the more exposure they have to fault detection and resolution, the better prepared they'll be once they're on their way to the BDO.

They've been training together for months now, although each day seems like a rewind of the last. There's so much repetition that their training is starting to feel monotonous, but that's good. It means their reactions are becoming instinctive.

Yúzé is slim. He's shorter than Liz. Crash isn't sure what the selection process was like for the Chinese, but his inclusion is welcome as both Crash and Pierre are six foot and lanky. The deal struck with NASA is that Yúzé will take the lead for communication, meaning the voice most heard during First Contact will be English spoken with a Chinese accent.

Liz has been slated for the first exploratory spacewalk examining the BDO, with Crash acting as the reserve, but Crash suspects this will be quietly reversed once they reach the BDO. America likes to be first, even if it's largely symbolic. For now, appearances are everything.

International tempers need to be placated.

Spacewalks are conducted in pairs, so Pierre and Yúzé will take the second shift planned for day three. Although it seems like they're getting the bum steer, the reality is that the initial spacewalk to investigate the BDO will probably be quite brief. Armstrong and Aldrin spent barely two hours walking on the lunar surface, while Conrad and Bean in Apollo 12 conducted two EVAs totaling almost eight hours. By the time Apollo 17 landed, the mission was extended to three EVAs, none of which lasted less than seven hours. Armstrong may have been the first person to walk on the Moon, but he never strayed more than fifty yards from the Eagle. Gene Cernan and Jack Schmitt covered an astonishing 22 miles in their dune-buggy-like lunar rover. If anything, Armstrong pulled the short straw.

If everything goes according to plan—and Crash can't think why it wouldn't—Adeep Gadhavi from India and Mikhail Ilyin from Russia will conduct the third and final EVA. The *Odyssey* is only carrying two EVA suits, so they'll be well-loved by the time Adeep and Mikhail climb into them.

One of the details that *never* makes the brochures is that astronauts smell. And those smells only grow over time, especially within the confines of an EVA suit. Spaceflight etiquette suggests rotten smells are quietly ignored. Given the toilet is a squat point at the rear of the capsule, that's easier said than done. Crash learned the best time for a fresh bag of coffee is when someone's taking a shit. It doesn't mask the smell, but the clash of conflicting smells and tastes is enough to distract his mind from pungent odors. By the time the third EVA takes place, Adeep and Mikhail will be so jacked up on adrenalin they probably won't notice the smell of sweat sautéing in the undergarments.

Yúzé farts.

As she's on the other side of Yúzé, Liz notices the smell first.

To simulate the cramped confines the crew will find themselves in during their 28-day outward journey to the BDO, the trainers have packed the simulator with sacks filled with foam as a substitute for supplies. As it is, they're going to be on strictly limited calories for the next two months, with the mission planners even going so far as to calculate their individual bone/muscle/fat loss. Crash is projected to drop from 210 pounds to 155 pounds at the point they touchdown in the Gulf of Mexico. He knows he's going to be dreaming of steaks for the next couple of months.

Several small fans in the hull circulate air, but it's stuffy within the *Odyssey*.

Liz raises her head and glances across Yúzé's back at Crash. He raises his eyebrows, unsure why she's trying to get his attention without saying anything. Then it hits and a smile comes to his face. For his part, Yúzé makes it obvious by trying not to be obvious. He shifts his weight as though he's uncomfortable, but it's a vain attempt to try to disperse the smell.

"Oh," Adeep says, turning away from them toward the open hatch. Mikhail holds his nose.

"Ah," mission control says in a slow drawl over the radio. "We're detecting a build-up of methane."

"Copy that," Crash replies, grinning. They know damn well there are no methane sources within the capsule beyond human bowels. If anything, it's impressive they can detect stray gas particles with such sensitivity. Although it smells bad to him, the actual concentration would still be in parts-per-million, barely affecting the capsule's atmospheric composition. Besides, with the hatch open to allow air to circulate, there's no danger of CO_2 build-up or any other noxious gas.

Poor Yúzé is embarrassed. His cheeks go red. He tries to focus on the controls in front of him, ignoring the comments.

"Ah, I've isolated the O_2 leak and shut the secondary valve. I calculate a 14-second course correction burn will return us to the optimal approach trajectory."

"We concur," Andrea says from their fake mission control, which is a desktop computer on a table set just outside the capsule. "Okay, let's take a break."

Adeep clambers out of the capsule, followed by Mikhail. Both men are laughing. Crash lets Liz climb over the pillows and sacks ahead of him to reach fresh air. Yúzé takes his time, following Crash out of the hatch, knowing he's about to be the butt of a few jokes. And jokes work on Earth. Up in space, no one will say anything. Down here, though, the prospect of eating a handful of peanuts while drinking a beer and reviewing the day's training allows for a bit of well-placed ribbing.

Adeep says, "After all that soda at lunch, I was burping like crazy in there."

"Me too," Yúzé says, playing along. "Only my burps came out of the wrong end."

Crash goes to add to the banter when he notices one of the senior managers marching across the floor toward them with a folder under his arm. He's got the kind of swagger that says nothing is funny anywhere in the universe.

"Director Summers wants to see you and Mikhail in her office."

"Okay," Crash says, unsure why he's so serious as the manager can see they're all quite lighthearted.

The manager escorts them across the broad concrete floor, which is unusual. They both know how to get from the hardware mock-up building to the central admin. It's a short walk across the road and down through the parking lot, but the manager follows them with his lanyard flicking around in the wind. Neither Crash nor Mikhail says much. It's cool out, but when they walk in the lee of a building, the warmth of the sun is pleasant enough.

Crash runs through a bunch of scenarios. He's had no question marks around Mikhail's performance. If anything, Adeep has been the wallflower. Adeep is capable but tends to cruise. As he doesn't speak much, Crash is never sure whether Adeep really understands a procedure or if he's bluffing. Mikhail, though, has been studious. And his English is impeccable. For Crash, that's important as it means there's no likelihood of misunderstandings.

The manager gets the door for them as they climb the steps of the admin building. Security guards eye them with suspicion. Every one of them is John-McClane-in-waiting, but this isn't the Nakatomi Plaza.

One of the security guards follows behind them as they walk up the broad internal staircase. Wonderful. Crash feels safer already. At first, Crash was confused by the summons to the director's office. Now, he's annoyed. What the hell is so goddamn important that a heavy hand is needed?

The security officer hangs back, but his presence casts a gloom over them.

Quietly, Crash speaks to Mikhail, saying, "Don't worry. You haven't done anything wrong."

"Wait here," the manager says, opening the door to the director's office and slipping inside. It's a command, not a suggestion. Will the security guard enforce it? What if Crash wants to go to the bathroom or get a drink from the water cooler down the hall? He's tempted to try just to be contrary, but the door opens again before the contrarian machinations of his mind resolve into action.

"The director will see you now," the manager says, holding the door open for them. Crash grits his teeth.

NASA Director Angela Summers is pacing at the back of the room, talking on her smartphone. She ignores them, looking down at the carpet as she strides back and forth.

The office is long, with the director's desk at the far end. By the door, there's a lounge suite and coffee table along with a picture book titled *Our Universe* showing a collection of images from Hubble and the James Webb Space Telescope, among others. The title, though, may need to be revised, given recent events.

Mikhail hangs back. Ordinarily, Crash would take a seat on the couch, but the temperature within the office is like that of a freezer. Warm air spills out of the vents above them, but it does nothing for what both men feel inside.

"Yes, yes," the director says, speaking into her phone and still not acknowledging that either of them has entered her office. "I have them here now... I understand... Thank you, Madame President... I will."

She ends the call and places her phone face down on the polished desk in front of her. Crash is expecting to be called forward and asked to sit in the chairs facing her desk, but all three of them remain standing.

"Did you know?" the director asks.

Crash isn't sure who she's speaking to as her eyes dart between them. He has no problem maintaining eye contact with her, but Mikhail is staring down at his shoes. His silence isn't convincing. He shakes his head softly. Crash is confused. Mikhail's motion is a lie. It has to be as he has to know something in order to deny any knowledge of whatever the hell this is. The director isn't fooled.

"You will be escorted from here to the airport and put on an international flight to Germany. From there, you'll fly on to Moscow. I'll arrange for your personal effects to be returned to Russia."

Mikhail nods, still avoiding eye contact with anyone. Crash turns to him, "What's going on, buddy?"

"Tell him," the director says.

Mikhail says, "*Vechnost.*"

The director says, "The Russians have launched a deep space mission to the BDO."

"What?" Crash replies. "How? When?"

"Yesterday. Two launches. Two hours apart. The two craft rendezvoused in space, and now they're on their way to L4. We're not sure of the specifics, but we can plot their trajectory. They're taking an S-curve, following the lines of least gravitational influence to reach the Lagrange point."

"And you knew?" Crash says, addressing Mikhail.

"It was a rumor. That's all. I heard there was a special project at the Vostochny Cosmodrome in Siberia, but *Vechnost* existed before the BDO. I swear. *Vechnost* was a moonshot. It was supposed to be a moonshot."

The director walks up to Mikhail, squaring off in front of him and forcing him to raise his eyes.

"What—did—you—know?"

Mikhail looks up at her with tears in his eyes. "I swear. On the life of my mother. I knew nothing beyond rumors. I was stationed at Baikonur—five thousand miles away. All I knew was that after the BDO appeared, senior technicians were called away to the east. Our best were sent to Siberia. It made no sense.

"You must understand. In Russia, no one trusts anyone. Questions lead to demotions. You stay quiet. You do your job. You keep your head down. Loyalty is rewarded, not initiative."

The director purses her lips. She pauses, thinking carefully about her next few words. Then her demeanor changes. Crash can see reason taking the place of anger. Whereas she was annoyed, now she's soft-spoken but resolved. There's no bitterness, only business to be conducted.

"Your flight leaves in forty minutes."

She steps past him, opening the door. The senior manager and security guard don't need to be told what's happening. They wait for Mikhail to join them. Crash remains where he is as the director closes the door on Mikhail.

"I'm sorry," he says. "I had no idea."

"None of us did," the director replies. "We all took the Russians at face value."

"Do you believe him?"

"I do. He's a patsy. He's their fall guy."

"And now?"

"Now, the Chinese are going ballistic. They're ready to walk."

"They'll go alone as well?"

"They'd like to, but I don't think they can. And that's the only reason they haven't pulled out already."

Crash says, "But we're still well over two weeks away from launching."

"Two days," the director says.

"But—"

"No buts. The President was clear. We cannot stand by while the Russians fuck this up for humanity. We need to get up there. Now."

"Sweet Jesus," Crash says, running his hand up through his hair.

"This isn't a space race," the director says. "It's about survival."

"And up there?" Crash asks, pointing at the ceiling.

"Your priority is to ensure First Contact is peaceful."

"What does that even mean?" Crash asks, shaking his head in disbelief. "What if we clash with the Russians up there?"

The director says, "I'll let you define peaceful anyway you need to—just get the job done."

"Understood."

Starship

Crash is distracted by the enormity of First Contact. It started as a vague notion while standing in front of a television in the astronaut's office. No one's explained his selection for the mission, but he's sure it wasn't random. He never sought the position and felt there were others that were more capable. He even discreetly said as much to the NASA director, who quietly assured him she had full confidence in his leadership. Months of training have rushed by. It was easy to lose himself in the minutia of mission planning, but now that he's lying on his back, strapped into a seat, staring up at a console, looking at pre-flight metrics and the image of the Starship ready to launch, the surreal has become real. He feels as though he's been swept downriver by a fast flowing current.

Crash doesn't even hear the countdown, but the rumble coming through his seat is unmistakable. Thirty-three Raptor engines roar in unison, with each one capable of producing over half a million pounds of thrust.

They're launching late, well behind the Russians. Even the US President cannot defy physics. The NASA director may have wanted to launch within two days of the Russians, but it was another ten agonizing days before the mission was ready. The team at SpaceX and NASA shaved off more than a week, but it may not be enough to get them to the BDO ahead of the Russians. Crash and his crew are going to be playing catch-up in space.

Adeep is the mission pilot. He's seated next to Crash. As

commander, Crash has decision priority, and with the Starship's flight profile being almost entirely automated, there's not much for Adeep to do beyond monitoring progress. For ISRO, the Indian Space Research Organization, though, it's a point of pride to have their most senior astronaut flying the American Starship on such an important mission. From NASA's perspective, it's an easy way to share some of the prestige of the moment with international partners.

"And we are clear of the tower," Adeep says, beating Mission Control to that milestone. Crash smiles, knowing Adeep has stolen their thunder by commenting on the position of the Starship's upper stage rather than the rocket as a whole. Mission Control wouldn't make that call for another second or so until the booster had cleared the top of the famed Mechazilla tower on Pad 39A at Cape Canaveral in Florida.

The reply is a calm and well-timed response.

"Copy that. We have you clear of the tower."

A shimmer runs through the Pegasus capsule. Originally, mission planners considered sending the bigger Starship directly to the BDO, but orbital mechanics and fuel constraints meant it would take fifty days to reach the alien spacecraft. The Pegasus was intended for a crewed fly-by of Jupiter and Saturn in 2040 using nuclear propulsion. The Pegasus design had already undergone shakeout tests in orbit before the BDO arrived, making it a good candidate for the mission. The idea of merging two different platforms was met with resistance by some within SpaceX and NASA, but the compromise gave the mission the best chance of success.

As it is, they're launching on the Starship Science-B configuration, where the upper stage of the Starship has been hollowed out and is little more than a fancy fairing. The Science-B configuration was designed for launching space telescopes and opens out into two pieces to release its cargo. The Pegasus is set on stiff rubber mounts, but the shaking within the cabin is still unsettling. It's coming from the sheer amount of raw power driving them and their overweight configuration into space.

The media raised alarm bells about the use of an experimental nuclear engine on the Pegasus near an alien spacecraft, but, as usual, the concerns were overblown. The term nuclear raises the specter of fireballs, meltdowns and radiation leaks. In reality, the NTRV rocket engine is a fancy kitchen kettle. Instead of a glowing electrical element boiling water, a coil of enriched uranium superheats liquid hydrogen. And just like a kettle, there's steam. Only the steam from the NTRV is a stream of super-heated hydrogen shooting out behind the spacecraft, pushing it in the opposite direction. Crash was asked if he had any concerns about being on a nuclear-powered spacecraft. His reply was, 'No. The only question I have is, why haven't we done this sooner?'

"Max-Q," Mission Control says as the booster pushes Starship through the atmosphere. As the rocket accelerates, the air pressure slowly decreases. NASA and SpaceX balance the upward force of the rocket against the air resistance, wanting to check the point at which these two opposing forces reach their maximum, exerting the greatest stress on the frame of the rocket. Once that maximum has been crossed, they can open up the throttle and roar into space.

Crash doesn't say anything, but Mission Control beat Adeep to that particular milestone, even though it was showing on his screen.

"Copy that," he says with a grin on his face. He doesn't care. He's off to become part of history.

The orientation of the rocket changes, shifting from vertical to sideways relative to Earth. By the time they're above the bulk of the atmosphere, the booster will be pushing them hard to the east, out over the Atlantic Ocean. Contrary to popular misconceptions, being in orbit isn't about reaching space, it's about *staying* in space. What goes up must come down. Orbits are the art of falling without hitting the ground. Gravity is always pulling spacecraft down, but if they're going sideways fast enough—considerably faster than the fabled speeding bullet—they'll fall without hitting the Earth. They'll fall around Earth. Crash remembers when he first learned this counterintuitive concept in high school physics. Far from floating in space, he knows he's falling in the equivalent of an elevator with its cable cut. But Earth isn't a flat expanse reaching into the distance. It's round. He and the crew of the

Pegasus are falling *around* the round Earth. Slow down, even slightly, and they'll fall back to Earth like a baseball hit into the outfield.

Most of the Starship boosters are recovered at sea, but for this mission, the booster is expendable, allowing it to push the upper stage with the Pegasus module well clear of the atmosphere.

"And staging," Adeep says as the hot-staging on the upper Starship kicks in, pushing them clear of the now empty booster.

"Farewell," Adeep says, watching as the elongated booster falls away behind them and begins tumbling back to Earth.

Once the Pegasus module separates from Starship, it will fire its nuclear engine to begin its journey to the alien spacecraft. At that point, the Pegasus capsule will become the *Odyssey* First Contact mission.

The *Odyssey* mission was named after the Greek myth written by Homer almost three thousand years ago, in which Odysseus, or Ulysses as he would later be known, sailed the Greek Isles for over a decade, exploring uncharted lands. On his journey, he encountered the Cyclops, a one-eyed monstrous cannibal, and the Sirens, who, through song alone, could lure men to their deaths. Crash hopes the BDO is far less entertaining.

As their capsule is still cocooned inside the upper stage of the Starship, they can't see anything out of the windows yet. High-definition cameras mounted on the hull of the Starship provide them with stunning views of Earth falling away beneath them. Already, concepts like the coastline become indistinct. Earth is a water world, and not just in terms of seas and oceans. Clouds carry water vapor high around the planet, obscuring pesky little things like islands and continents, which account for less than a third of the surface area. Sunlight reflects off both the clouds and the azure blue waters.

Over the next hour, they undergo two separate burns to circularize their orbit and prepare for their departure to L4. The chatter within the cabin and over the radio is professional, but the unspoken truth is they're racing into the unknown, following on the heels of the Russians.

Even though they're at least eleven days behind, their nuclear engine will help make up the difference. It's not a warp drive, though. And it needs to be able to get them back to Earth, so its use has to be judicious. The problem isn't that the NTRV doesn't have the thrust to make up for those lost days, but rather that they can't just punch their way straight to the BDO. They have to be able to stop when they get there. Every extra burn here needs to be countered with an additional burn there to slow down. The Russians have the advantage of coasting to a halt. NASA's projections have them closing the distance and making up most of the lost time, but whether they can beat them to the BDO is still being debated. It's about fuel. They've got to have enough to get back, and burning reserves just to win a foot race isn't smart as they need to ensure they have a contingency in case any emergencies arise. As it is, their motion is more akin to a skateboarder madly pushing with their feet and then coasting to the end of the road, hoping they've timed it just right to trundle to a halt in front of the stop sign.

Once the Pegasus is released and the *Odyssey* rockets away from the upper stage of the Starship, Crash will be able to relax. The thirty-eight-day journey to L4 is going to be cramped and boring. As commander, he needs to make sure the crew doesn't get on each other's nerves in the cramped confines of the capsule. And then... contact!

Questions

From within the claustrophobic living space of the Pegasus capsule on the *Odyssey*, Liz says, "This last question is from Jared Sanderson, a tenth-grader from George Washington High School in Columbus, Ohio. He's asking why can't you see the aliens yet?"

"Oh, they're out there," Crash says, tapping the window beside him while still facing Yúzé with the camera. "And we can see them on our long-range scanners, but we won't actually see them with our own eyes until the very last moment.

"Space is deceptively large. There's a whole lot of nothing and then something small, be that a star, a planet, an asteroid or a spaceship, and then there's nothing again—forever!

"How vast is space? Entire galaxies can collide without a single star hitting anything. When the Milky Way collides with Andromeda in four billion years' time, a trillion stars will soar past the roughly two hundred billion stars in our own galaxy, and not one will strike another! It's a bit like watching a sandstorm blow across the desert; only not one grain of sand will ever hit another. Out here in deep space, we need our instruments, or we'd never find the alien spacecraft. It's just too small and space is too big. Without electronic eyes, we'd be blind. We would soar past without ever knowing they were out there."

Yúzé turns the camera to Pierre, who's loosely strapped into the pilot's seat and working with the controls. He taps a nondescript dot on his screen, saying, "There they are. That's them—right there!"

Crash says, "And somewhere out in the darkness, they're looking at a dot on some other screen saying, here they come."

"Okay," Liz says as Yúzé turns the camera back to her. "That's the last question for now. We're about to enter a rest period before approaching to within a few kilometers of the alien spacecraft tomorrow. Then we'll all get to see them."

She smiles. Yúzé stops recording. The red LED above the camera lens fades to black.

"I don't understand why we're doing this?" Pierre says in his suave accent. "Why are we trivializing First Contact?"

"We're not," Crash says. "We're humanizing it. We're de-stressing it."

Liz says, "It might sound like that was for the kids. It wasn't. It was for several billion anxious adults."

Pierre nods, accepting that point.

Yúzé says, "Rest period? Huh? Really? Is anyone actually going to get any sleep on day thirty-eight?"

"No," Liz replies, dimming the cabin lights anyway.

"Besides," Crash says, looking at the metrics on one of the secondary monitors. "First Contact has already happened."

"They've beaten us, huh?" Liz says.

"Fucking Russians," Yúzé says.

Pierre says, "I'm showing only a single contact at four thousand kilometers. It's difficult to say for sure as they could be station-keeping on the far side of the vessel, being hidden in the radar shadow, but it looks to me like they've docked."

"What's our roundtrip comms time to Earth?" Crash asks.

"We're approaching seventeen minutes," Liz says. "Do you want to talk to Mission Control?"

Crash thinks about it for a moment. Between the flight of the *Odyssey* and the Russian *Vechnost* mission, no human has ever been this deep into space before. Even though their words are transmitted at the blistering speed of light, roughly three hundred thousand kilometers a second, the one-way transmission time is over eight minutes. If anything goes wrong out here with First Contact, they're on their own. Being beaten by the Russians doesn't bother Crash, as he thinks of them as an advanced team. They're human. He suspects they're motivated by the same hopes and desires as those onboard the *Odyssey*. How could anyone not think of First Contact as peaceful? All three spacecraft are almost a hundred million miles from Earth. It's a distance so insane as to defy reason. Crash wasn't kidding earlier when he said there's a whole lot of nothing out there.

Liz raises her eyebrows, looking for a response from him.

"No. If the Russians are broadcasting First Contact, I'm sure Mission Control will relay it to us. For now, let's get some rest. Tomorrow is going to be a long day."

Reluctantly, the astronauts prepare for a sleepless night as their space capsule continues drifting through the void, following a precise orbit intended to bring them to rest at Lagrange point four for the Sun-Earth system. Like curlers at the Winter Olympics, releasing a weighted bowl and watching it slide across the ice, the *Odyssey* is gliding into place without the use of her engines. In space, mass is everything, even with a nuclear engine. Their approach has been dictated by the demand to conserve what little mass they still have as fuel. Getting home is going to be as arduous as getting out to L4.

Crash turns away as Liz uses the portable bathroom at the back of the cabin. There's no privacy on their flight. Originally, the design of the craft allowed for a plastic shield to be drawn in front of the toilet, and not just for modesty but to contain the smell. Like so many things within the capsule, though, that flimsy shield was stripped out to conserve mass, which increases their fuel loading. If the *Odyssey* were a car, then they've increased their mileage by tearing the carpet from the floor and pulling the plastic trim off the doors.

After Crash has relieved himself, he unfurls his paper-thin sleeping bag, which is more for perceived comfort than actual warmth. He anchors either end with a clip placed on the hull. This will prevent him from drifting while sleeping. From a practical perspective, NASA provides sleeping bags to avoid *zombie syndrome*. When sleeping in weightlessness, a person's arms tend to float up like Frankenstein, and they sometimes kick and squirm while in deep rem sleep. To anyone that's awake, the effect is disconcerting. It's like watching a zombie horror film in real life. Confining astronauts to sleeping bags and, where possible, sleeping berths, allows them to rest and not freak anyone out with bouts of parasomnia, where they're acting out their dreams in their sleep.

Yúzé uses a sleeping mask to block out the ambient light within the cabin. The lights have been dimmed and tinted red, but they can still be distracting.

Crash lies in his sleeping bag without lying on anything at all. He drifts with the fabric pulled up over his shoulders. Occasionally, his slight motion causes the clips to go taut as he jostles around. Crash has his eyes closed, but his mind is wide awake. He's tired. It's been yet another sixteen-hour day, but the unknown plagues him.

Crash is tormented by the thought that they're not ready. Of course they're not ready. No one could ever be ready for First Contact with an unknown alien species that evolved a bazillion miles from Earth. At an intellectual level, Crash is prepared for peaceful coexistence. At an emotional level, he fears not only for his life but all of humanity. It's an irrational fear, but that doesn't make it any less real in his mind. And then there's the Russian wild card. What will the aliens make of *two* spacecraft showing up from entirely different, competing human cultures? Anxiety is a bitch, refusing to let him rest. Somehow, he drifts in and out of sleep.

In the red-tinted darkness, his eyes open. Liz has curled up in a fetal position within her sleeping bag, but she, too, is restless. They need their sleep. Knowing that doesn't help. She shuffles, unable to get comfortable—when being weightless is entirely comfortable. There's no discomfort whatsoever when you're soaring like a bird riding thermals. Ordinarily, Crash falls into a deep sleep while in space. It's the lack of sensory inputs. On this particular artificial night, however, his mind refuses to rest.

Perhaps Houston has sent them the Russian video footage? He should check again. It might be important to get that information sooner rather than later. Crash peers at the main console, willing it to spark to life with an urgent incoming message from Earth, but it remains dull and quiet.

Mission Control could have sent the results of the Russian approach but simply not flagged it as urgent. If so, then there's no rush. He should rest, but he can't. Without clambering out of his sleeping bag, he unclips the top fastener and leans forward. In weightlessness, he can pivot around the other clip beside his feet, swinging over effortlessly to the control panel. Crash taps the screen and it comes to life. The light isn't bright, but it's far brighter than what his eyes are accustomed to after almost two hours in the rest cycle, causing him to squint.

"Anything?" Liz asks, whispering. She peers at him with one eye. She's also suffering from disturbed sleep.

Crash scrolls through the log. He checks the file transfer folder and message bank.

"Nothing."

Liz whispers, "So either the Russians are staying tight-lipped, or Houston doesn't want to bother us."

"I guess," he says, powering down the interface and pushing lightly off the rim of the monitor. He reaches for the clip on the hull and reattaches his sleeping bag.

"Try to get some sleep."

"You too," he replies, settling.

Crash goes through a few yoga exercises, breathing in through his nose and out through his mouth. He focuses on relaxing each part of his body, starting from his head and working down. His lips are taut. His jaw feels stiff. It's not until he goes through the motion of focusing on each area that he realizes how tense his body is, being wound tight like a spring. His neck is sore. His shoulder muscles are clenched. Even his butt cheeks are rigid.

Slowly, his breathing allows him to rest. On a couple of occasions, he overthinks thinking about relaxing, and everything tightens again, but he's patient with his overactive mind and resets his routine. He loses count of how many times he starts again from the muscles on his face, neck and shoulders, but at some point, he reaches the calf muscles on his legs and finally drifts off to sleep.

"Hey," a gentle voice says, touching his shoulder. Crash wakes to the blinding lights of the cabin. He blinks, rapidly trying to take in what's happening. Everyone else is dressed. Their sleeping bags have been stowed. Adeep is upside down, sipping lukewarm tea through a straw from a plastic bag. Pierre and Yúzé are talking about something on the screen. Their voices aren't raised, but they aren't quiet either. Crash is surprised he was able to sleep through all the activity.

Liz says, "We let you sleep as long as we could."

"Oh," he says, squeezing his hand out of the collar of his sleeping bag and tossing his hair. "Thanks."

"Hey, commander," Yúzé says. "Good afternoon."

Crash smiles at that comment. He wriggles out of his sleeping bag and relieves himself at the back of the capsule before changing his clothes. The act of getting dressed is more symbolic than anything else. As they sweat less and their clothing floats around rather than hangs on them, the astronauts don't need to change their clothing for days on end. A few wet wipes replace the need for a shower. Crash listens to the others, glancing over at the screen as he brushes his teeth. Bacteria are the one organism that isn't bothered by zero gravity.

"We've got an approach vector from Houston." Yúzé's talking to Pierre as he draws with his finger on the touch screen. For a freehand sketch, his motion is surprisingly precise, following the computer-drawn arc sent up from Earth. "Two light burns, and we'll be station-keeping a hundred meters from the craft in about an hour."

"Damn," Adeep says. "This is it! It's all coming together! We're finally here!"

Crash rinses his mouth with a bit of water, swallowing rather than spitting it out.

"And the Russians?" he asks, pushing off the rear of the capsule and drifting over to join the others.

Liz is sipping coffee from a foil pouch. She's heated one for him. Coffee in space is a crime against humanity. It's tepid, being a mix of dried milk powder and instant coffee granules that has to be kneaded with lukewarm water before the straw on the pouch can be released. Fail to grind up the contents, and Crash knows he'll get lumps stuck in the straw or, worse, a mouth full of crunchy coffee followed by what could best be described as bathwater. Out of habit, he works his fingers over the foil packaging, but there's no crunch beneath his fingertips. Liz gives him a sideways glance as if to say, don't you trust me? He offers a quick smile before sipping on the contents. To be fair, as bland as it is, the caffeine hit is welcome, waking his mind from its lethargy.

"Houston sent up footage of the Russians approaching the BDO structure near the midships."

Yúzé plays a clip from the vantage point of the Russian *Vechnost* capsule as it drifts sideways along the outside of the alien spacecraft. Spotlights illuminate the hull of the vessel. Unlike spacecraft from Earth that are coated in layers of thermal insulation or smooth, painted panels, the alien craft is covered in corrugated metal, forming smooth waves and grooves. It's as though the vessel has been constructed from pipes rather than sheet metal. Crash is fascinated to look at the result of alien engineering.

"Does Houston have anything to say about that?"

Liz replies, "They think it's for structural integrity. Apparently, it's a design that better adapts to twists and any torque running through the craft."

"Huh."

"No windows," Pierre says.

"Nothing to see out here," Liz replies.

"Fair point."

Crash says, "No seams or welds or fabrication points. No panels or access hatches."

"Yeah," Yúzé says. "It's as though the whole thing came from some kind of extraction mold."

"Maybe it did."

The view of the alien spacecraft is marred by the crosshairs and guide marks added by the Russian camera. This footage was recorded by an old docking camera, which surprises Crash as he expected it to come from a high-resolution 32K camera dedicated to First Contact. The lower resolution makes it difficult to see the finer details. The Roscosmos logo is at the bottom right of the screen.

To be fair to the Russians, capturing high-definition images and video isn't difficult. Transmitting that back to Earth, though, is hideously complex and time-consuming. And in this case, it's then retransmitted back to them on the *Odyssey*.

As it is, the footage from their initial EVA will be transmitted to Earth in two phases. The initial "real-time" resolution will only be 640 x 512 pixels or about the same as a computer from the 1980s, like an Atari gaming system or a Commodore Amiga. NASA's use of artificial intelligence to enhance the image and upscale both colors and resolution will ensure the footage people see looks better than an old-fashioned video game, but it won't be until the slower high-resolution data dumps occur that scientists will be able to look at fine details. And that will be days later. Knowing the public's short attention span and impatience, the use of AI is the focus of the initial broadcast. One of the NASA analysts warned the government that subsequent highly detailed images could be called into question by conspiracy theorists because any deviation would be seen as deceitful. Crash laments how humans rush to conspiracies over facts, but he accepts that's someone else's battle to fight. He watches the footage from the *Vechnost* with intense interest.

On reaching the midship region, the Russian spacecraft examines a series of what appear to be radio masts or antenna arrays coming out of the side of the alien spaceship. Whatever they are, they surround the vessel, extending from it like a crown.

"And contact?" he asks, knowing the others have already reviewed all the footage sent up from Houston.

"The Russians are quiet on that point. Their footage ends with them approaching a ring of antennas extending from the hull. The shadows there suggest there's an opening in the vessel. We think it might be some kind of airlock for maintenance or a docking port. Best we understand it, that's where the *Vechnost* is at the moment."

"So they docked?" Crash says, confused. "They went onboard? And they're not crowing about beating the West to make First Contact?"

"Yep," Liz says.

Adeep says, "Something went wrong."

"Something went very wrong," Yúzé says.

Liz says, "Something they either don't understand or don't want to warn us about."

"Well, that's just great," Crash says. "And Houston?"

Yúzé says, "They've given you clearance to conduct the initial EVA."

"Me?" Crash says, pointing at himself. "The flight plan calls for Liz in the hot seat."

Liz just smiles at him and laughs, saying, "Bros before hoes."

"Not funny," he says. "Really, not funny."

Pierre says, "There was some discussion about your previous EVAs and the need for experience."

"Of course there was."

"And crashing," Liz says. "They figured if anyone was going to crash, it should be you."

There's an undertone of bitterness to her voice, but Crash doesn't hold it against her. Liz is frustrated. Their meticulously detailed plan has been junked because the Russians have gone silent, injecting uncertainty into an unknown encounter. For whatever reason, be that macho sexism or American exceptionalism, she's been bumped from her EVA mission. Experience alone isn't enough of a reason. They all know that. Any one of them could climb into a suit and clamber onboard that spaceship.

Crash says, "I'm a canary in a coal mine."

Liz nods. She knows it's nothing personal from him. They're professionals. They're all dedicated to following the mission directives, even if they don't agree with them. The days of the maverick astronaut are long gone. For them, there's trust in mission control. A change like this would have been debated at multiple levels and reasoned from a dozen different angles. It wouldn't have been made lightly.

Crash doesn't say as much, but he's not surprised by the change. He suspects this was the plan all along, and the Russians gave Mission Control just the pretext they needed to ensure America makes the next move.

Liz helps him clamber into his thermal undergarments in preparation for the EVA.

Pierre says, "I've located the *Vechnost*. It appears to be damaged. It's sitting right up against the hull of the BDO."

Pierre looks to the others, but no one replies. No one wants to give voice to their fears.

Panic

"Don't panic," Aleksandr mumbles into the microphone on his Snoopy cap as he clambers around in his EVA suit outside the alien spacecraft. "Don't *fucking* panic!"

But Aleksandr's not speaking to himself. He's talking to Genji Sokolov onboard the Russian *Vechnost*, only Genji's dead. Her body won't decay, though. He's not sure how long it'll take to freeze solid in the absurd cold of space, but it'll be measured in hours, not days. If anything, he expects she'll dehydrate first, losing a considerable amount of her mass to evaporation before she becomes an icicle. Like a grape in the sunlight, shriveling to become a raisin, her skin will recede from her eyes, nose and mouth. Her fingernail cuticles will be exposed as her skin shrinks and takes on a leathery texture. First to freeze will be her hair, which will become as brittle as straw in the sweltering heat of a hot summer's day in the seaside resort of Rostov-on-Don. After that, her ears, fingers and toes will freeze before her legs and, finally, her torso. What a waste.

"Stupid *fucking* bitch!"

How much will Roscosmos be able to recover from his EVA recordings? What will they think of his comments? No. They must not find out, as comments like these would sully his reputation. For now, he's not transmitting, so the only record is on his suit computer.

Aleksandr powered down the Russian capsule to conserve the batteries following the loss of the right solar panel. At some point, he's going to have to review his footage and decide what has been '*accidentally*' lost. Unsurprisingly, it'll be everything that shades his character. While he's thinking about it, he accesses the recordings on his wrist pad tablet computer and deletes the last ten minutes to be sure. He'll have to watch the rest to decide what's worth keeping.

In his mind, there's no conflict or ethical dilemma to his deceit. Even diamonds have flaws, but no one focuses on them. No one looks at the glistening rock on an engagement ring and asks about imperfections. In the same way, the focus of his life should be his successes, not the occasional point at which he has faltered.

Aleksandr rationalizes his decision based on what he considers '*mental bandwidth.*' Between the six US Apollo lunar landings, there were thousands of hours of video footage collected from training scenarios, the launch, flight, landing, lunar exploration and return. Most people have seen less than thirty seconds. Hard-core aficionados might have clocked a few hours. Since the turn of the century, no one's looked at all of it, of that, he's sure. Aleksandr decides it's not the amount of footage that's important; it's the significance of the events that are captured. He'll blame outages on faulty equipment, electromagnetic interference or corrupt files.

He bumps his helmet against one of the dozen or so equipment spikes rising out of the heart of the alien spacecraft and hits *record*. That bump will give him a plausible incident where extraterrestrial signals apparently interfered with his camera recording. He speaks as though he's been caught mid-sentence.

"—yet without knowing more, it's impossible to speculate on the nature of these radio dishes and antennae. The spikes themselves are reminiscent of cell towers... The dishes appear to be pointed in random directions, with several facing the sun itself, while others are turned sideways or out into deep space. These are the eyes and ears of the alien spacecraft.

"But it's the access tunnels on the hull that are most intriguing to me. The spikes and arrays extend from these, slowly tapering to a point roughly fifty meters away from the craft. The towers extend well clear of the hull. Like the sensitive instruments on our Venera explorer or the

US Voyager spacecraft, they're probably positioned out here to avoid interference from the vessel and its engines. They're a crown of thorns. That's how I'd describe these structures. Between them, they provide 360-degree coverage, extending from all angles around the hull."

Although Aleksandr could use his maneuvering unit to enter the nearest tunnel, he opts for handholds. It's old-school spacewalking. Some would object to touching the alien spacecraft, but there's nothing fragile out here. This vessel has traversed an inconceivable distance between star systems. His gloved hands pose no threat. For him, there's value in touch. Far from being someone wandering around within a museum, never able to touch the exhibits, he imagines himself as an explorer of an ancient temple. As it is, he needs only a light touch to propel himself within the nearest tunnel.

Aleksandr is looking forward to sending these images back to Earth. He can imagine the excitement they'll generate. Roscosmos wanted him to broadcast live, but Aleksandr is conservative. He'll broadcast only what he wants to be seen. And the delay will raise a sense of mystique around his exploration and heighten interest.

The spotlights on either side of his helmet come on as he drifts within the tunnel, pulling himself along the base of one of the spikes. His fingertips guide him on, pressing gently against the hull as he soars into the unknown.

Aleksandr isn't afraid of the dark. He's afraid of failure or, worse, being *seen* as a failure. It doesn't matter whether he's competent, but rather whether *other* people think he's competent. For him, pretense overrides fear. He's brave. That's the way he wants history to remember him.

"As yet, there has been no attempt at contact from the aliens... If they know I'm here, they're ignoring me... I can't imagine we would allow an alien astronaut to climb within one of our space stations... Where is everyone? After centuries in flight, are we left only with ghosts? Is that it? Have I entered a ghost ship?"

He brings himself to a halt. Darkness surrounds him. He should push on, but looking back, he can see sunlight reflecting off the towers extending into space.

"This is a dead end," he pronounces, not having actually reached the end of the tunnel at all. He turns, using his hands against the hull to guide him. Nerves betray him. His spotlights stretch along the curved sides of the tunnel, disappearing into the darkness.

"There's nothing down here," he says. "It's a maintenance tunnel. It's used to store the towers and antennae while the ship is traveling between stars."

Aleksandr tells himself he's not afraid, but he's almost a hundred million miles from the Russian Vostochny Cosmodrome in Siberia. No other human has ventured this far from Earth, not even the Americans in their *Odyssey*. Fear is elusive. It's the sweat on his brow, the tremor in his fingers and the tingle beneath his feet, warning of impending danger. He distracts himself, thinking about the international mission. As best he understands the flight path of NASA's *Odyssey*, the other craft is at least 12 hours behind him. Aleksandr is impatient. He wants to find something. He *needs* to find something. He *must* make contact. It must be him—for the glory of Mother Russia.

"I'm going to backtrack and head up to the bow of the alien spacecraft. There must be some kind of bridge or command center there. I'll upload what I have collected so far and transmit that back to Earth and then gather more data."

He turns his back on the darkness, glad to be rid of the unknown. Aleksandr focuses on himself rather than the alien spacecraft. It's his gloved hands he sees, not the slick skin of the alien metal, lacking any seams or joints. It's his spotlights that provide light. It's the rim of his helmet that frames the extraterrestrial vessel before him. It's his breathing he hears. It's his suit that provides warmth and fresh air. He's safe, cocooned in the thick material of his spacesuit. He feels invincible, like a superhero in some crazy movie with insane punches and kicks. Unrealistic is entertaining. And for him, the BDO is out there, beyond the confines of his suit. It's unrealistic. To him, it's a dream.

Aleksandr brings himself to a halt on one of the alien sensor arrays, perching on it like a bird settling on an aerial. Shadows stretch along the hull of the alien spacecraft, being cast by the distant sun. Like a rocket ready for launch, the BDO is a cylinder stretching for hundreds of meters on either side of him, only it's vast. The curvature of the cylinder is modest, peeling away gently. The slope reminds him of the immense Luzhniki Stadium. On those rare occasions when he gets back to Moscow, Aleksandr enjoys watching soccer being played at the Luzhniki Stadium. It's the atmosphere that defines the game. It doesn't matter how big the TV is in his father's home or how much the sound is turned up; there is nothing like the roar of a hundred thousand spectators rising in unison when a goal is scored. Walking around the stadium to find the correct gate is always daunting because of the tsunami of people all trying to get to their seats before kickoff. The curve of the alien spacecraft is strangely reminiscent of the space-age panels curling around the stadium.

Apart from the spikes and their associated tunnels, the hull of the spacecraft is nondescript. There are a series of nodules, each no larger than a basketball running in a line along the length of the craft, but they're the only blemish, and they only appear on one side.

The hull is corrugated like the old metal roofs from before the October Revolution. In the south of Russia, these metal roofs have rusted and been largely replaced with tiles, but they're still common around his ancestral home of Volgograd.

From a distance, the alien spacecraft appears as though it's a smooth cylinder, but up close, the corrugated metal looks as though it's designed to channel rain that will never fall in space. It baffles Aleksandr. He'll leave the finer points of the design to the scientists.

Aleksandr uses the maneuvering cold jets on his backpack to thrust along just a few meters above the alien spaceship, watching as the strange shape drifts beneath his boots. He passes the stricken *Vechnost* spacecraft. It's drifted up against the hull. Like the spikes, it, too, casts long shadows down the alien vessel.

Aleksandr brings himself to a halt next to the service module at the rear of the *Vechnost*. The Soyuz is comprised of three modules. The orbital module is a bulbous shape at the front of the craft, allowing for living space. The descent module is in the middle, being sandwiched between the orbital module and the service module, containing all the critical control systems. The service module at the rear holds the solar panels and engines and can only be accessed from outside the spacecraft. It contains fuel, water and electrical supplies for the rest of the craft but also has an auxiliary equipment bay. Aleksandr opens the bay and sets up an antenna. Once he's locked onto Earth, he downloads his footage so far and sets it to transmit back to Earth. Unlike the Americans, the Russians can't manage high data transfer rates, so it'll take several hours to complete. He leaves the data dump running and continues on along the alien spacecraft, heading toward the front of the vessel.

Aleksandr tries not to think about Genji, but he can't shake the image of her dead eyes staring blindly past him. He's only ever seen dead people in caskets before. They were all well-dressed and at peace—well, at rest if not at peace. Their eyes were shut. Their faces were relaxed. It was as though they were asleep. And it's no surprise to him that sleep is used as a euphemism for death. It's not sleep, but it's the easiest way to reconcile grief. Genji, though, looked distressed. Veins bulged on her forehead. Her mouth was open. It was as though she was trying to say one last thing, desperate to find life in words, if nowhere else. He wonders what raced through her mind in those final few seconds. The desperation, the anguish, the futility—they must have been overwhelming, and yet still she tried. As much as he may despise her for what happened, he knows this is a moment he, too, will face one day. It's not a question of if but when. Aleksandr is an atheist, refusing all gods, not just some. And when his last breath leaves his lungs, what words will he offer in sacrifice to a deity that neither hears nor cares? What anguish will seize him, imprinting on his face? Will he plead like Genji? Will he die out here a hundred million miles from Earth? Or will he succumb in a sterile hospital bed on the outskirts of Moscow? Or in the recliner seat of a rest home? Does it matter?

And what then? Aleksandr will be but a memory to his family and a byline in the history of Russian spaceflight. Oh, he'll be lauded as the first person to touch an artifact from another intelligent mind, a spacecraft created around some other star. Like Neil Armstrong, he'll be recognized as the first person to make contact with an extraterrestrial vessel, if not extraterrestrial life. But like Neil Armstrong, he too will be lost in every respect except that one act. All of his life will be simplified to one achievement. And like Armstrong, it was no real achievement of his personally. He was simply the one standing at the end of a very long line of people working toward a singular goal. Oh, he'll take the glory. Aleksandr has never shied away from glory, but for all his bluster, he knows it's hollow.

The *Vechnost* spacecraft passes out of sight along with any thoughts of Genji. Drifting on in the darkness, trapped in silence, listening only to his own breathing, Aleksandr resets his focus. It takes several minutes before he reaches the tip of the alien spacecraft, but there's a sense of exhilaration at seeing the hull drop away, revealing only the vast, lonely emptiness of space beyond the Bussard ramjet at the bow of the craft.

Aleksandr maneuvers to a halt. Before he turns to look at the front of the vessel, he allows his eyes to take in the stars beyond. This is reality. All those back on Earth—the billions watching for news of the *Vechnost* and the *Odyssey*—they think they're grounded, being surrounded by reality. They look up at the night sky, imagining the alien spacecraft revealing its secrets, but the real truth lies out among the stars. It's not the blue skies of Earth or the birds and the green trees or even the vast Russian steppes that define reality. No, it's the stars themselves. It's the stars that stretch into eternity, and even they won't make it that far. Even they are doomed to die. They may be billions of miles away and billions of years old, but they, too, have their limits. And him? He's but a speck of dust on this cosmic stage. He's Genji. He's dead already. On the scale of the universe itself, he's living his last moments, desperate to breathe, reaching out with his hands, struggling to speak, fighting against the darkness but doomed to fade into the cold night.

For Aleksandr, the stars offer a rare moment of clarity. His ego is meaningless before their grandeur. His arrogance is pitiful. His ambition is laughable, while his deceit is an admission of failure. All his efforts are for naught. Floating there, he feels small. And for Aleksandr, being small is humiliating, not humbling.

"No," he mumbles, knowing that one word has been captured on the mission recording but will never be understood. He refutes the cosmos. He's Aleksandr Krukov. He bows to no one. With that, he turns to examine the front of the spacecraft.

Canary in the Coal Mine

Adeep, Yúzé and Pierre put on their launch suits. These are lightweight, pressurized spacesuits capable of withstanding the vacuum of space but not the harsh radiation or the extremes of hot and cold. As long as they remain within the Pegasus capsule, they'll be fine. Crash and Liz suit up in their EVA gear, with Liz acting as his backup. She'll remain with the *Odyssey* on standby. Although she's wearing a life-support pack and an LCMU, she'll remain connected to the capsule via an umbilical cord like Yúzé and Pierre, but she's ready to deploy and assist him if needed.

Crash finds NASA's love of acronyms a curious oddity. Being an organization that is an acronym in itself, NASA loves obscure acronyms far more than actual names or terms. Rather than calling their spacesuits, well, spacesuits, they're wearing EVA suits or Extravehicular Activity suits. That Extravehicular is a mere one word and not two seems lost on the engineers. No one is going to simplify EVA to EA, though. That just doesn't sound right. It seems three letters are the minimum.

Their LCMUs could be called jet packs. Certainly, that's how the public sees them, but the Lost Crew Maneuvering Unit has retained its clumsy acronym even though Crash has *never* heard of an LCMU actually being used to rescue a lost astronaut. They're jet packs, but Crash learned the hard way not to use that phrase in front of the engineers. In their minds, such vulgar terms seem to lessen the technology.

Having both Crash and Liz in full EVA suits and LCMUs within the confines of the Pegasus capsule requires some jostling. Yúzé and Pierre help, being an extra set of eyes for them and steering them with gentle touches. Adeep stays out of the way at the back of the cabin, knowing he'll only make things more congested. Inevitably, Crash and Liz bump into each other. The thick padding and thermal insulation on their suits leaves them looking like the Michelin Man from the old car tire ads. The LCMU provides an additional layer of bulk, more than tripling the chest size of Crash. For Liz, the whole configuration approaches four times her chest size when outside a spacesuit.

The two of them have been trained to avoid proprioception, which is the sense of where the limits of the body lie. It's proprioception that stops someone from tripping in the dark or bumping into furniture—mostly. Both Crash and Liz were trained to *"touch their new noses,"* as the instructors put it. They had to relearn the boundaries of their extended bodies. Thick, bulky boots, padded arms, broad shoulders, a helmet that extends almost four inches above the crown of their heads, and the LCMU backpack have them inhabiting the bodies of giants. Everything that seems so simple in a tracksuit back in a training simulator in Houston becomes cumbersome when wearing an EVA suit with an LCMU. Pushing buttons, reaching for anchor points, adjusting visors, and even things as simple as flipping the procedure cards attached to their forearms requires a deft touch.

The LCMUs are the successor to the MMU or manned maneuvering units of the Space Shuttle era. To the uninitiated, they allow astronauts to fly around like Iron Man. In practice, using them is more akin to skating on ice. A slight burst here and a twist there will have them pirouetting in space without the need for constant thrust.

Over time, the mission parameters for the LCMU evolved to include tether-less spacewalks to repair solar panels and conduct extended EVAs, potentially spanning up to twenty-four hours. The current record is nineteen hours and is held by Crash during the refueling of the James Webb Space Telescope in orbit beyond the Moon. It's probably that particular spacewalk that had Houston bump Liz for Crash, as they know his experience will be invaluable. Spacewalks look easy, but they're comparable to a triathlon. Everyone starts strong, but it's endurance that matters. Over time, even little things can hurt. It's the sustained focus to maintain intense concentration over ten to twelve hours that makes them difficult. Mistakes are easy. And in space, mistakes are costly. On paper, Liz looks like a good option as she's clocked over two hundred days in space, including three spacewalks, but it's those final few hours when fatigue sets in that probably worry Houston. With Crash, they know what they're getting—for nineteen hours, at least.

Liz twists sideways and ends up floating beneath him like some doppelgänger/ living reflection. Even with a Snoopy cap on, her head looks tiny within the broad, white helmet. She speaks into the microphone wrapping around beside her lips.

"You good?"

"I'm good," Crash says, lying. His hands are shaking, but given his absurdly thick gloves with their rubberized palm and fat fingertips, no one can tell. If Pierre looks up at the metrics streaming to the console on the *Odyssey*, he'll realize Crash is in a state of panic, with his heart hitting a hundred and thirty beats per minute *before* the hatch is opened. Houston won't miss a detail like that, but they won't notice for another eight and a half minutes due to the communication delay.

Yúzé says, "And the hatch is open at station elapsed time four hours and fifteen minutes. Switching to First EVA time."

Ordinarily, mission elapsed time is calculated from the point of launch, but given they've spent a month in the depths of space, drifting toward L4, there's no point in saying it's day twenty-nine. Instead, the mission has been divided up into milestones, with the last being the point at which they rendezvoused with the alien spacecraft. From here on out, they'll track his EVA elapsed time as a separate activity. Someone back in Houston will stitch them all together into one seamless, continuous timeline.

The hatch at the pointed front of the cone-shaped Pegasus capsule opens outward. Darkness looms beyond. Crash reaches with his gloved hands, pulling himself forward. His breathing is heavy. He feels as though he's run a marathon and not as though one is just about to start.

Hands guide him on. Liz touches lightly at his suit, helping him forward, as does Yúzé from one side and Pierre from the other.

"I'm at the hatch."

There's no need to narrate his motion as the video camera on the side of his helmet is broadcasting to the *Odyssey* and on to Earth.

Drifting in space is akin to pushing off the bottom of the shallow end of a swimming pool and floating through the water. His body follows the motion of his hands. His LCMU bumps against the top of the hatch. A gloved hand behind him pushes him down.

With his waist extending out of the hatch, Crash pushes with his hands and glides through the opening into the void. His boots clear the lip of the Pegasus. He double-checks his LCMU controls. Power, water-cooling, electricity, oxygen exchange and CO_2 filters are all green. By touching any one of the symbols, Crash can examine the specific values, which will all start at 100% and include a runtime estimate, but he avoids the temptation to become preoccupied with something he already examined within the *Odyssey*. He's stalling. It's nerves. It's the fear of the unknown. What lies out there in the darkness? Mythical monsters? The Cyclops? Sirens?

"Anything from the Russians?" he asks, using the controls on his LCMU to right himself, turning from lying flat relative to the Pegasus to being upright. He turns on yet another axis, using his jets to face the three astronauts watching him from the open hatch. He should be looking at the alien spacecraft and the Russian *Vechnost* sitting up against the hull of the vessel. He's trying to settle his nerves. There's no reply. He tries to hide the frustration in his voice, but it seeps through the electronic transmission regardless.

"Sure would be nice if someone down there could reach out to the Russians and ask them what the *hell* is going on?"

"Sure would be nice," Yúzé replies. "We'll pass along your concerns."

Yúzé doesn't need to pass anything along. Houston will hear both of them in just over eight minutes. If NASA had anything to add, they would have done so long before Crash exited the Pegasus.

Crash takes in the enormity of the alien spacecraft. To him, it's a massive skyscraper in space. If anything, it's broader and wider. And like a skyscraper, it appears to be built in hundreds of repeating sections. There are no windows, but a curved line of nodules seems to indicate the equivalent of floors or at least layers within the craft. As the *Odyssey* circled the alien spacecraft on approach, Crash knows the nodes he can see are limited to barely a third of the circumference. Most of the cylindrical vessel appears seamless. Whether the exterior characteristics match the interior is impossible to tell.

"I'm approaching the *Vechnost*. At least one of their solar panels is damaged. It may be that they've lost comms."

"Copy that," Yúzé replies.

Crash picks a point between the spikes reaching out of the alien spacecraft, wanting to drift to the Russian vessel on the other side. He eyeballs his approach and drifts effortlessly between the pillars. Although he's able to look up and around within his helmet, he keeps his LCMU and suit facing forward. This limits what those on Earth will see, but from his perspective, it gives him a stable reference point during his flight. It's one thing to look along the alien trusses with their nodules, globes, radar dishes and antennae. It's another to lose his sense of orientation. A quick glance satisfies his curiosity, but for now, the focus is on the Russian craft and figuring out what happened to the Russian cosmonauts. He'll come back and satisfy the intense curiosity of billions of people and a whole bunch of scientists and astrophysicists once he's inspected the *Vechnost*. Understanding what happened to the Russians is important, as learning from them might keep him and his crew alive.

The *Vechnost* is resting up against the alien ship at the point the hull separates to reveal channels leading within the vessel. These openings line up with the trusses extending well beyond the craft. It's unnerving to see components that look like the result of human engineering on an alien spaceship. There are dishes and domes on the spikes, which extend easily fifty meters from the hull. As the girth of the vessel is circular, these reach out equally in all directions, forming a star shape. If anything, the tunnels leading inside the hull at this point on the craft appear to be bays into which these arrays can be retracted during interstellar flight. Perhaps they double as maintenance ports. Whatever their function, this is the place at which the Russians decided to enter the vessel.

The *Vechnost* looks dead. There are no navigation lights and no lights from within its windows. Solar panels extend from either side of the Russian spacecraft, but as it's in shadow, they won't be gathering electricity. On one side, several of the panels have been crushed, which is alarming to see.

The *Vechnost* is a modified Russian Soyuz, so it has three distinct compartments set in a row. The docking probe and hatch on the forward module appear damaged, but beyond that bulbous shape, there's the command/descent module, which will have an internal hatch. It's a clever design as damage to one section won't hinder another. Behind the command module is the equivalent of the service module on the *Odyssey*.

"Are you catching this?" Crash asks, pausing and allowing the image streaming from his camera to settle on the crumpled frame and broken panels. Bits of black solar cells float next to the vessel, having been torn free.

"What caused that?" Yúzé asks.

"Dunno. Don't want to know."

Yúzé doesn't reply. Rather than going straight in toward the Russian vessel, Crash conducts a wide pass, wanting to take in as much of the foreign craft as he can, knowing NASA will want detailed video footage. For that matter, this might be the first opportunity Roscosmos has had to assess whatever happened to their spacecraft and its crew. For now, the alien ship is a secondary consideration.

"The forward hatch is open," Crash says after circling the Russian vessel. He skims along twenty meters above the hull of the alien spacecraft, heading back toward the front of the Russian *Vechnost*. In space, a single, gentle burst of gas is enough to propel him like a hockey puck on ice.

"Slowing," he says, touching lightly on his LCMU controls. In addition to coming to a relative stop, he orients himself to face the open hatch. The Russian spacecraft is not more than ten meters up and to his left. Before approaching, he takes the time to survey where it is on the hull of the alien vessel.

"Yúzé, are you seeing this?" he asks, feeling his already madly beating heart race even faster. Scratch marks line the hull of the alien spacecraft, leading back to the *Vechnost*. It looks as though the craft has been dragged to its resting spot. There's a dent where the Russian spacecraft has collided with the corrugated hull of the alien vessel. The metal forming the scratches is shiny, having lost whatever tarnish or coating protected it from the harsh vacuum of space.

"Assessment?"

Crash wants to give Yúzé, Adeep, Pierre and Liz the chance to provide input. There's silence, but he knows that means they're conferring with each other. Yúzé is acting as the proxy for CapCom. Ordinarily, CapCom is an astronaut on the ground back at Houston, acting as the central point of communication with a team in orbit. As they're well out of real-time communication, Yúzé is taking on the local role. His job is to coordinate information from both the team in the *Odyssey* and anything coming in from Houston. Crash doesn't mind the delay. The thought of rushing into the unknown doesn't thrill him. He may have the nickname Crash, but that doesn't mean he wants to live up to it.

"The Russians are reporting they lost contact with the *Vechnost* shortly after their lead astronaut, Aleksandr Krukov, exited the craft. It's a little late, as they could have told us this about twelve hours ago, but their last communication is footage of Aleksandr entering one of the tunnels on the alien spacecraft. The spotlights on his helmet fade to black as he heads further in. Then there was a sudden loss of transmission. They don't know why. All their metrics were nominal up until that point. They've got more data inbound but say it will take time for them to process it."

"Wonderful," Crash says. He's being laconic. Given the jumble of information the Russians have reluctantly provided, it seems only appropriate to be sarcastic. He can't help but feel there's more they're not telling NASA. A little cooperation would go a long way to helping humanity. The idea that First Contact has descended into a competition between East and West is crazy to him.

"Two astronauts, huh?" he says, touching lightly at his controls and approaching the stricken Russian craft. "Only Aleksandr went into the alien vessel. There should be someone inside the *Vechnost*, right?"

"Correct."

Crash approaches the *Vechnost* at a quarter of a meter per second. It's barely a walking pace. His spotlights catch the partially open circular hatch, highlighting the thick metal and mechanical levers and seals. He's expecting to see spotlights within as the remaining astronaut sees the flicker of his lights and comes to investigate. Shadows stretch along the craft as he gets closer. There's a glass window facing out into space. That, too, would allow the light from his helmet to seep into the darkened interior.

"Four meters... three... two... coming to a halt."

Crash is so close he can reach out and touch the rim of the hatch. He'd rather not. A light touch on his controls and he aligns himself with the entrance, allowing his spotlights and the gaze from the camera on his helmet to peer within the Russian spacecraft. The hatch is open, but only just, with a gap of a few inches allowing him to see the tunnel leading to the forward cabin. There's no movement within the capsule.

"Assessment."

Yúzé replies without conferring with either Liz or Pierre. "Proceed with caution." Perhaps they'd already discussed the approach, but it would be nice to know all of them agree.

"Copy that," Crash says, feeling very aware of the darkness before him and the strange openings on the alien spacecraft immediately behind him. He breathes deeply, moving slowly, scanning with his helmet, realizing he needs their eyes and not just his own. Given the anxiety of the moment, it's too easy for him to miss something. He needs not only the crew of the *Odyssey* catching details but Houston as well, although it'll be a seventeen-minute round-trip delay before he hears any of their insights.

Crash arches his back, allowing the camera on his helmet to take in all aspects of the hatchway. There are scratches on one side of the hatch itself. His gloved hand reaches out, touching where paint has been scraped from the metal, giving those watching the video a sense of scale. Parts of the rubber seal around the inner edge of the hatch have been damaged.

Over the radio, there's a single word spoken in haste. "Hold."

Crash stays perfectly still.

"Liz is reviewing the footage of the Russian vessel at the point Aleksandr exited."

"And?" Crash asks.

"And it doesn't line up with the current orientation of the craft. It's off by almost a hundred and eighty degrees."

"It was facing the other way?" Crash asks, touching the dented metal on the outside of the *Vechnost*, facing out into space, away from the alien spaceship. "She flipped over?"

"That's what we're trying to assess," Yúzé replies, followed with, "Proceed with caution."

"Oh, you know it."

Before proceeding to open the hatch, Crash takes a good look at the hull of the alien spacecraft. The *Vechnost* is drifting not more than five feet from the corrugated surface. As his spotlight drifts over the battered metal, he spots a shadow move.

"There's a tether."

"Say again?"

Crash touches lightly at his controls, moving from the far side of the *Vechnost* over to the alien vessel. Although it goes against his better judgment, he turns his back on the stricken, darkened interior of the *Vechnost* to look at a thick cable leading back toward the spikes coming out of the alien spacecraft. As most of the cable lies up against the strange vessel, following the grooves in the corrugation, he didn't notice it until now.

Crash doesn't want to touch the cable, but he feels he needs to get a closer look for the scientists and engineers back on Earth. Without taking his eyes off the cable, he comes to within a foot of it. The gentlest touch on his controls brings him to a halt, allowing his camera to focus on the spiral strands of numerous metal wires forming steel ropes that curl around on each other. To him, it looks like the tension strands that hold up a suspension bridge.

"Human or alien?"

"Ah, we'll get back to you on that one," Yúzé replies.

Crash withdraws, turns and looks along the hull, visually following the cable to the point it disappears into one of the tunnels on the alien craft.

Yúzé asks, "Can you see how it attaches to the *Vechnost*?"

Crash turns back, using his jets to twist slowly in place, avoiding any sudden movements.

"Negative. The *Vechnost* itself is blocking my view. I've only got shadows. The craft is too close to the hull for me to investigate further."

Yúzé says, "Houston is online. They don't like what they're seeing. They're saying proceed with caution, but they want us to back off to five hundred meters."

"Ah," Crash says, feeling his hands tremble. "Leaving the canary to flutter around in the coal mine. Brilliant."

Whatever it was that spooked Houston, it's based on footage he collected seventeen minutes ago, footage they only saw eight minutes ago. Mentally, he tries to figure out where he was at that point. They're not talking about the cable. That's too recent. They have to be referring to the crushed solar panels. They are going to freak the fuck out when they realize it looks like the *Vechnost* has been harpooned.

Yúzé says, "You're the local commander. I'm happy for you to override that order if you feel it's necessary."

"No," Crash replies, realizing it's not just the safety of his crew that's at stake but the safety of his ride home. "Drop back to five hundred."

"Are you sure?"

"Yes. You don't need to be close to see the view from my helmet camera. Besides, sitting back a little, you may see things I miss, being too close."

"Copy that. Adeep is taking us back. We're in no rush. We'll be moving at one meter per second, so it'll take us a couple of minutes."

"Understood. Proceeding to the interior of the *Vechnost*."

"Copy that."

Crash appreciates the way Yúzé is complying with the direction from NASA back in Houston while still giving him options. One meter per second is a slow jog. It means Liz is still available to deploy at a moment's notice, and her LCMU can quickly negate the distance between them.

One of the advantages of being in space is that "*up*" lies wherever he wants it to be. On Earth, examining the wreckage of an aircraft is hampered by gravity. It's difficult to distinguish between cause and effect in an accident as the planet itself contributes to the damage. Over time, weather can hamper efforts further. In space, though, not only is the damage pristine—as though it only just occurred—Crash can examine it from every conceivable angle. The temptation he faces is to pull on the hatch and pry it open. Instead, he circles the hatch, slowly taking in the entire front of the *Vechnost,* looking at it from every vantage point. From his perspective, it's as though he's stationary and the craft is turning before him.

As he comes over what was the top when he approached the *Vechnost* but is now beneath him, his spotlights illuminate the shadows.

"What the hell could cause a dent like that?" he asks, pointing at the way the reinforced section around the hatch has crumpled. The thermal protection paint has scraped away from the metal, leaving it looking silvery in his spotlights.

Spacecraft are designed by compromising on priorities. They need to be sturdy and strong and yet lightweight. Reducing mass without reducing safety or mission goals requires exhaustive modeling and testing. In practice, what this means is that different parts of the spacecraft have differing degrees of structural integrity. Thermal insulation is more important than thick cladding. Around the hatch, though, where there are moving parts flexing and locking, not to mention the chance of an astronaut's boots or their backpack colliding with the hull, there's a need for more rigid structures. To see a dent in the reinforced area around the hatch is alarming.

"Something hit them."

"Or they hit something," Yúzé replies. "Let's be careful with our terminology. When presented with two options, we need to choose the most likely, not the most sensational."

"Agreed," Crash replies, appreciating Yúzé's level head. Being so damn close to the *Vechnost* it's too easy for Crash to think the worst. Yúzé's right. The most likely scenario isn't that the *Vechnost* was attacked but rather that it crashed.

Yúzé says, "The tether and scratches on the BDO have me wondering if this was an accidental burn. If someone panicked and punched the wrong button after they tethered, the two craft could have collided."

"Maybe," Crash replies, looking down along the hull of the alien spacecraft at the streaks on the metal. The spikes reaching out of the vessel are imposing and intimidating. Perhaps Yúzé's right. Perhaps the Russians panicked and crashed. Whatever happened, they were way too close. NASA's plans never allowed the *Odyssey* within a hundred meters. The Russians may have wanted to attach a tether to allow both astronauts to explore the alien spacecraft. Although his mind wants to jump to wild ideas about being attacked, this is a far more plausible scenario.

Using his gloves rather than his jets, Crash reaches out and tugs on a handhold. He swings himself around in front of the hatch. The sheered end of a bolt floats to one side. He grabs it, holding it up for the cameras and showing them the way it has been severed on an angle. It will give the scientists and engineers back on Earth an idea about the amount of force involved in the collision.

Crash braces himself, placing one hand on the Russian hull and the other on the hatch. Slowly, he opens the machined steel plate.

"The locking mechanism is intact," he says, peering sideways at the mechanical workings of the hatch. "It didn't sever or pop open."

"It was opened?" Yúzé asks.

"Looks like it," Crash replies. "And then left open."

"Why would Aleksandr do that?"

Crash runs his gloved hand around the edge of the hatch. His fingers come to rest on a slight defect. "There's a crimp in the rubberized seal. It's tiny, but it's abnormal."

"Enough for a leak?"

"Maybe. Proceeding inside."

Yúzé says, "First EVA elapsed time is thirty-seven minutes, and NASA astronaut Chris Williams is entering the Russian *Vechnost* spacecraft."

Against his better judgment, Crash flattens himself against the inside of the hatch. His helmet is facing down at the short tunnel leading to the cabin, limiting his view to just the curved metal below him. His spotlights, which cast an intense light, illuminating the finer details of the craft, now blind him, reflecting back off the chrome bands and joints within the Russian craft. As his helmet is down, he can't see anything ahead of him. He pulls gently, working his way through the narrow tunnel. It wasn't designed for a six-foot American wearing a NASA EVA suit and LCMU. Claustrophobia closes in on him, restricting him. He can't shake the sensation that he's going to become trapped in this metal tomb, unable to turn around and escape. His breathing is rushed. His heart races.

"Easy," Yúzé says, clearly watching his medical metrics as they spike. "You're looking good."

Crash has his arms above his head, feeling for handholds. He couldn't bring them back by his side if he tried. His padded shoulders and elbows wouldn't fit within the confines of the tunnel leading to the front module. His visor bumps against the tunnel. His ears feel blocked. To him, his breathing sounds wheezy, with the inhale being slightly higher pitched and shorter than the long exhale.

The forward cabin of the Russian spacecraft opens out around him. The hatch leading to the command/descent module is closed. Crash isn't sure what he expects. Too many dumb horror movies and space thrillers bounce around in his head. The shadows threaten to jump at him. He rights himself and looks around, allowing his spotlight to ripple over unfamiliar controls. Cargo nets hold white bags full of supplies against the side of the capsule, taking up most of the space, leaving him feeling claustrophobic.

Spacecraft might be designed for space flight, but they're built on Earth. They inherently have some gravity-centric aspects and a sense of up-down. Swinging around and aligning himself gives him some comfort. He might not recognize the characters written beneath the various switches and controls, but they're human.

"Pan to your left."

Crash doesn't ask why. He moves slowly, knowing Yúzé's spotted something important. When he sees it, his blood runs cold. Shadows stretch around the capsule, shifting with his motion. A woman's hand protrudes from beneath a sheet in what looks like the cargo bay within the forward capsule. Her body has been stowed.

As much as he doesn't want to, he pushes off the hull and glides over toward her.

Yúzé says, "That will be Genji Sokolov, the commander of the *Vechnost* mission."

"Aleksandr must have wrapped her body and secured her here."

Crash peels back the sheet, working it under several Bungee cords. Dead eyes stare straight ahead. Red veins darken the whites of her eyes. Her face is pale. Crash exposes enough to see the silver locking ring of her suit and padded shoulder. Like those onboard the *Odyssey,* she's not wearing a full EVA suit but rather a pressurized flight suit. As gruesome as it is, he continues to work the sheet back, exposing her body. Almost nine light-minutes away, the team at NASA and later her support team at Roscosmos will review this footage. Whether it'll be released to the public is questionable, but her family will want to know what happened to her. Crash is gentle, showing respect for the dead. He stops when he reaches her waist. Her left hand is gloved. Her right is exposed to the vacuum.

"I think this gives us a rough timeline," Liz says, surprising him, as so far, his communication has been exclusively with Yúzé. The two of them must have agreed to break with protocol. "The collision with the BDO damaged the forward hatch seal. The *Vechnost* lost pressure, probably without her realizing it until it was too late. She tried to suit up but lost consciousness."

"And Aleksandr?"

"He wasn't present. He must have already started his EVA."

"But he came back, right? He stowed her body."

Yúzé says, "Can you pan over the control panel again?"

"Sure."

Crash turns back to the series of panels grouped around the tunnel leading to the hatch.

"Top left. Is that an LED?"

"Yes," Crash replies. As helpful as his spotlights are, they're far too bright in the tight confines of the *Vechnost,* washing out the controls. Several LEDs glow dimly on the edge of his vision.

Liz says, "Okay, so Aleksandr saw what happened. He covered her body and powered down the craft to save the batteries. He probably swapped his EVA pack before reentering the alien vessel."

Yúzé asks, "What's he doing in there?"

"Making First Contact," Crash says. "Only he can't broadcast. He can only record while the *Vechnost* is powered down."

Yúzé says, "Well, that explains why he's gone radio-silent."

"Next steps?" Liz asks.

Crash covers Genji Sokolov's body again. He's in no rush to reply. He knows they can see his motion as it's captured by his camera. He wraps Genji, secures the straps, and, after almost three minutes, says, "It's time for this canary to enter the coal mine."

Inside the Tunnels

Crash pulls himself through the tunnel leading to the hatch on the Russian spacecraft. His LCMU bumps gently against the ring-shaped accessway. Sunlight catches the massive spikes protruding from the alien spacecraft, casting long shadows down the hull. To his mind, they're reminiscent of the old country telephone poles made from denuded pine trees as they're thicker at the base and narrow toward the top.

Liz says, "Roscosmos has given us the frequencies being used by the *Vechnost* mission. We're broadcasting, but Aleksandr isn't responding."

"Copy that... I want to get a better look at these structures protruding from the BDO."

Crash begins his exploration by soaring away from the alien spacecraft. He heads out along one of the spines reaching from the craft, drifting slowly so his camera gets high-resolution footage of the various cables snaking along the spikes, leading to nodes that look like those found on the radio masts of a navy warship. There's no value to him in what he's seeing, but he knows the scientists back on Earth will analyze every frame of footage.

Crash is aware of the way the light plays on the spike. Depending on his angle relative to the Sun, sections that appear as black as coal will suddenly reveal the ripple of an iridescent rainbow in the alien material. It's not metal, of that, he's sure. The texture is wrong. Instead of being smooth, it's hashed, almost like the weave of fabric or perhaps the backing behind fiberglass.

He heads up to the tip of the spike roughly fifty meters from the surface of the craft and pans slowly. By this point, the spikes reaching out of the hull have separated by roughly forty meters. From what he can tell, the equipment on them is largely the same. There are some differences in the placement of domes and radio dishes, and several of them point in different directions, but they look like the same basic rigging. The tip is rounded rather than sharp, as it appears from below.

"Ah, is the silence bothering anyone else?"

"From Aleksandr?" Liz asks.

"From them," Crash replies. "What is this? A ghost ship?"

There's no reply. No one wants to speculate on the unknown. For all their preparation, they're completely unprepared for First Contact.

Floating there, isolated from everything—the *Odyssey*, the alien spacecraft, the crumpled remains of the *Vechnost* and even Earth itself, Crash feels a sense of awe overwhelm him. Sunlight catches his gloved hand. As he raises his arm, shadows extend down to his elbow, rippling over the thick, crumpled fabric of his spacesuit. He's seen this dozens of times before during spacewalks, but this time it's different.

Crash has an unassailable sense of now. There's an immediacy to the moment he cannot express with mere words. It's the juxtaposition of everything around him, not just physically and emotionally, but even in terms of chronology. In his life, there is everything that lay before now and all that is to come following First Contact. At this exact moment, he's stuck in the middle of these two opposing narratives.

His childhood flashes by, dancing in his mind's eye. Somewhat ironically, his earliest memory is of crashing. He was five. He was riding his red tricycle down the driveway of his old home in Columbus, Ohio, but the slope carried him forward too fast. The pedals began turning as if they had a mind of their own, forcing his legs on. Crash lifted his feet from the black plastic, holding them clear, and the pedals became a blur. Ahead loomed the road. Cars rushed down the street. His mother screamed. His father ran across the lawn to grab him, but he was too far away. With split seconds to decide his fate, Crash swerved toward the grass. The front wheel turned too far, buckling beneath him. His tricycle flipped. And he crashed. He landed on the concrete driveway and skidded onto the grass, stopping by the curb as a delivery van roared past. Pebbles and bits of grit dug into his palms. Blood seeped from the cuts on his hands, but he didn't cry. He rolled onto his back and looked up at the clear blue sky.

It was the lack of tears that most upset his mother. She could see the grazes on his knees. She knew they stung, but Crash said he was fine. It was shock. As soon as she applied some ointment to his injuries, he howled and tears flowed, but in those first few moments, his mind was replaying the events that led him to the curb. Even at that young age, he was reassessing what he could have done differently. He should have stayed on the flat slab in front of the garage. He could have cut toward the grass sooner. He was wearing shoes. He could have put his feet down and pushed against the concrete drive to slow himself.

Crash is floating at the crossroads of history. Like Aleksandr, somewhere within the BDO itself, he's spanning two entirely different worlds separated by billions of years. Their lives are taking on importance that far outweighs that of any individual. Like Neil Armstrong holding on to the ladder with one hand as he stepped off the landing pad onto the dusty lunar surface, the smallest of their acts have ramifications for all of humanity. Crash is determined not to crash again. He's back on his tricycle. He's at the top of the concrete drive. He has decisions to make. Choices will unfold before him as he starts trundling down the slope. He needs to act rather than react. Lifting his feet from the pedals isn't good enough. He needs to make sure he doesn't get into that kind of frantic position again.

After an extended silence, the radio crackles in his ear. "Is everything okay?"

"Everything is fine," he replies to Yúzé.

The Sun illuminates the length of the alien spacecraft. Some sections are hidden in shadow, disappearing entirely from sight, blending in with the pitch-black darkness of space itself. Those he can see, though, scream of intelligence.

"Why no welcome mat?" he asks, rephrasing and repeating his earlier question.

"Say again," Yúzé replies.

"They're here. We're here. We know we both exist. Even though they're sitting off at L4, they know there's life on Earth, or they wouldn't have come all this way. And we've come out to greet them. Why is there no welcome mat? I mean, from what we can tell, the *Vechnost* suffered some kind of malfunction and collided with their craft. Even if they don't know the *Odyssey* is here—which I find hard to believe given all these radar dishes and domes—that collision should have triggered alarms. Someone should be investigating."

Liz says, "Houston raised this with us in one of their updates. The consensus down there is that L4 must be some kind of staging area for the aliens. They've been in transit for a long time, possibly centuries. They may need to reconfigure their ship or put together a shuttle or something, as there's no way that thing could enter Earth's atmosphere. JPL says, given its size, it couldn't even enter a Low Earth Orbit. If it did, it would be subject to differential gravitational stress that would twist the vehicle's superstructure and cause it to break up. They say the BDO wouldn't be able to get any closer than about a thousand kilometers—if that."

"Huh," Crash replies, drifting over to the next spike and beginning his descent toward the tunnels leading into the alien spacecraft. He takes his time. Gathering as much footage as he can of the various instruments on the spikes is a convenient stalling tactic. With a light touch on his controls, he descends toward the vessel, drifting parallel to one of the spikes. Rather than falling toward the craft, he feels as though he's coming up from beneath the vessel.

Yúzé says, "First EVA elapsed time is one hour and forty-two minutes, and NASA astronaut Chris Williams is entering one of the side tunnels on the alien spacecraft."

The spikes protrude from openings in the hull. The gaps are roughly twice the width of each spike, providing plenty of room for Crash to drift within the strange vessel. His spotlights catch the outline of sealed panels on the interior. He's reminded of the wheel well on his T-38. Hydraulics must be universal as he recognizes the shape of pistons. Given physics is the same everywhere, it's no surprise. He doesn't comment on it, knowing others will pick up on these distinctions. His focus is the unknown.

"We're expecting some kind of airlock," Yúzé says.

'We,' being the crew of the *Odyssey,* mission control back in Houston and eight billion people spread around a planet he can't even see at this distance. Crash doesn't reply. He's not sure what he expects. The SETI professor warned him against the danger of expectations clouding his thinking. Crash suspects human expectations will create an illusion within the strange interior of an alien spacecraft. He's not willing to assume anything. The pedals of his tricycle are whirring beneath his feet once again.

"Keep your eyes peeled for an access point like an airlock," Liz says, repeating Yúzé's comment. It seems Crash isn't the only one that's nervous. Will misplaced expectations be the death of him? Fight as he may, he knows they're right. There has to be some way of entering such a vast spacecraft. It makes sense there would be some kind of distinction between the wispy vacuum of space and whatever atmosphere these aliens breathe, and that would require an airlock of sorts. Although the act of respiration is an assumption on his part, it's reasonable, as on Earth, all complex organisms exchange gases using respiration. It's such an easy medium to exploit for convenient chemicals such as oxygen and, for plants, carbon dioxide. These aliens probably have some equivalent. Even animals without lungs need elements such as oxygen, like fish with gills or insects that breathe through holes in their thorax.

Crash is still unnerved by the lack of any greeting. No one else seems to be bothered by that, but for him, the BDO is a ghost ship.

Yúzé says, "Aleksandr got in there, so we're hoping it's easy enough to navigate."

Crash corrects them. "Aleksandr went somewhere, but we don't know that he got inside. He could have died trying. That would explain the silence."

There's no reply to that point.

Not more than twenty meters in, some fifty feet from the opening, the tunnel comes to an end. To his surprise, a curved cavern opens out before him. Crash turns slowly, allowing his cameras to take in the view around him. Ahead, a smooth, silver wall curls away from him in both directions, running the length of the craft, wrapping around the interior of the ship. Being shaped like a gigantic pipe, it's a broad cylinder disappearing into the shadows. All of the tunnels end at this point, joining in the cavern in front of the silver cylinder. There's a gap of about three meters or roughly ten feet between the cylinder and the outer hull of the spacecraft with its converging tunnels. Even if Aleksandr took some other tunnel as he explored the vessel, he would have ended up in roughly the same place.

From the *Odyssey*, Liz says, "It's in motion."

Crash was so busy examining the tube-like openings of the tunnels curling around the interior of the craft he didn't notice the subtle change in how the spotlights on his helmet reflect off the inner cylinder. To him, the vast silver metal panel looks nondescript. There are no welds or seams or hatches, making it difficult to sense its motion. As he watches, he catches a slight shimmer from tiny imperfections on the smooth, curved surface.

Yúzé says, "Seems we have another craft within the spacecraft itself."

"And it's rotating," Liz says. "Generating artificial gravity."

"Any estimates on size?"

"Adeep is running the numbers," Liz replies.

A dark patch whizzes past, racing out of the shadows through his spotlights and then curling back into the darkness.

"Was that an entry point?" Crash asks. "Can you freeze-frame that?"

"And we're timing it," Liz says. "If we can figure out the size and speed with which the cylinder is turning, we'll be able to give you an estimate for the pseudo-gravity it's producing."

Yúzé asks, "How the hell are you supposed to transit that gap? It's too narrow and moving too fast."

Crash looks down at a message on his wristpad computer. He taps the screen with his thick, gloved fingers. A blurred image comes up of a dark hole in the cylinder. It's circular, lacking any edges, and curls inward from all sides, looking more like a sink drain than an airlock. And it's shallow. It doesn't seem to lead anywhere. As Crash was turning, trying to capture an image with his helmet camera as it spun past, shadows hide the interior, but it doesn't look like a hatch.

"And there it is again."

Crash tries to pan with the motion of the cylinder, wanting to get better footage, but it doesn't seem to help. He's too close. He's only a few feet away from the internal cylinder, and the smooth surface is racing past like a semi on a freeway.

Liz says, "Okay. Adeep has done some rough calculations. He puts the diameter of the internal cylinder at approximately two hundred and fifty meters or roughly eight hundred feet."

"But?" Crash says, feeling there's more she's not saying.

"Ah, the error margin is fifty feet or so."

"So it's big. Damn big."

"Yep."

Crash pans from one side to the other, noting the smooth curve is reminiscent of the underside of a large ship, like the hull of a cruise liner or an oil tanker.

"Based on loose timings, he puts the rotation speed at fifty miles per hour or about eighty kilometers an hour."

"Makes sense," Crash replies. "Floating here, it's like standing too close to the train tracks as a freight train roars past."

"The simulated gravity within the cylinder is going to equate to just under half what you've experienced on Earth. It's similar to what you'd feel on Mars. Probably twice what you've felt on the Moon."

"How do I get in there?" Crash asks. "The cavity between the tunnels and the cylinder is too damn narrow. I couldn't get up to speed with my LCMU, not without crashing into the outer wall or one of the tunnels. It's the curvature. The LCMU is great in a straight line, but in these tight confines—nope, nope, nope."

Yúzé says, "How did Aleksandr get across?"

Liz says what Crash is thinking. "How do we know he didn't die in the process? I mean, the speeds involved here equate to a car crash."

"This is the end of the road," Crash says, watching the smooth surface racing past barely ten feet away within the darkened interior of the alien spacecraft.

Yúzé says, "Maybe we're thinking about this the wrong way."

"The axis," Liz says.

"Yes. This internal cylinder—this habitat—has to connect to the outer structure of the spacecraft at either end. It's turning around those two points."

"That's where the airlocks would be," Liz says. "At the points of egress and ingress."

"Okay," Crash says, turning in place and then applying a little thrust to send himself soaring back along the alien tunnel. In the distance, the spire extending into space catches the sunlight. It's strange, but that bizarre spike with all its bulk equipment is somehow reassuring. It's familiar. He moves slowly, conserving fuel and avoiding the need for course corrections should he get too close to the inside of the circular tunnel. As he drifts along, he reaches up, allowing his fingers to graze the smooth material. It's slick, reflecting the light around him like a mirror. As he approaches the end of the tunnel, the gap narrows at the point the spike protrudes into the vacuum. A light touch on the hull and he saves himself a burst of compressed gas, steering himself through the opening at roughly a meter per second. Given the LCMU can hit speeds equating to over fifty miles an hour, his motion is sedate.

Stars shine in the distance. As soon as he emerges from the

tunnel, though, the Sun washes out his night vision, leaving him surrounded by darkness. The stars are still out there, though. And he finds the thought that one of those stars is the *Odyssey* itself reassuring.

Crash drifts out to fifty feet. He makes sure he's well clear of the cylindrical hull of the alien spacecraft before changing direction and applying thrust to move toward the front of the vessel.

"I think those are fuel tanks," he says as the smooth hull of the craft drifts lazily beneath his boots.

"What are?"

"The whole thing. I think the spacecraft is that inner silver cylinder. Everything surrounding it is just one big fuel tank."

"What makes you think that?"

"The lack of access ports and hatches. The lack of windows and airlocks. It's sealed for a reason. There might be a combination of various fuels in those tanks, like liquid hydrogen, liquid oxygen, or even water, but I suspect they're using the tanks surrounding the cylinder to protect themselves from cosmic rays. The whole thing is like a hotdog wrapped in a bun."

"Huh," is the reply from Yúzé. He laughs. "I'm not sure your hotdog analogy is the most scientific way of describing an interstellar extraterrestrial spacecraft, but it sure will make the history books more interesting."

Paralysis

Molly is sitting on a wrought-iron seat in the shade, eating lunch on the edge of the South Lawn within the White House grounds. Lush green plants hide her from the secret service agents playing basketball on the court behind her. The court was originally added for President Obama but fell into disuse. Neither Trump nor Biden were ever going to shoot hoops. Newsom said he would, but he never wandered this far down the grounds. The secret service kept it alive. Occasionally, the Marines will play off against them, but normally there are only three or four agents doing layups.

Molly loves her secret garden. Technically, it's not hers, but she doubts many people know about this particular spot within the grounds. Who would have thought such a delight was hidden away in the middle of Washington, DC?

Goldfish swim in a pond not more than two feet from her shoes. Slate tiles line the path. The shrubs show signs of topiary, but it seems the gardeners rarely come into this area as the bushes are becoming unruly. To Molly, the unkempt look adds to the beauty and mystique of the closed-in garden. She's seen the First Lady and her entourage by the White House swimming pool and down by the fountain at the far end of the South Lawn, but never in this nook. Molly's tempted to mention it to her as she's sure if she knew about it, she'd find an excuse to sneak away with a good book and sit in the quiet solitude broken only by the bounce of a basketball and grunting nearby. For Washington, DC, that counts as almost complete silence.

Chief of Staff Susan Dosela walks down the narrow, winding path between the trees.

"There you are," she says with a warm smile. Molly's curious. How did the chief of staff find her? Molly's got her phone with her. She has to surrender it before entering the Oval Office or any of the SCIFs like the Situation Room, but otherwise, she keeps it in her purse. Has the chief of staff tracked her electronically, or are there cameras catching Molly's every move, even here in the garden?

"Hi," Molly replies, munching on a mouthful of tuna sandwich and trying to swallow. Should she stand? She shifts on her seat, and the chief of staff signals with her hand not to get up.

Molly asks, "Is everything okay?"

The chief of staff laughs. "There's an alien spacecraft far larger than any of our nuclear-powered aircraft carriers sitting off in the distance watching us, and you're wondering if everything's okay?"

Although she's trying to make light of the situation and be friendly, the comment comes across as awkward. To Molly, it's clear the chief of staff is trying not to be intrusive while intruding on her lunch break.

"Well, it's a beautiful day to visit Earth," Molly replies, smiling.

The chief of staff sits down opposite her in the garden. Sunlight dances through the leaves of the trees, rippling over her floral dress. This isn't a social call, even though Susan Dosela is trying to make it seem relaxed.

"The President wants to initiate a lockdown."

Ah, there it is.

"I wanted to give you the option," the chief of staff says. "You can stay, or you can go, but once the lockdown comes into effect, you'll be on one side or the other for the duration of First Contact."

"It's getting serious, huh?"

"The President is worried. The Russians are 12 hours ahead of us, but they're tight-lipped about their exploration of the alien spacecraft. We know their *Vechnost* mission crashed into the vessel. We're not sure how or why. The Russians aren't telling us anything, but we know at least one of their astronauts is dead and the craft is damaged. Whether it's still capable of spaceflight is unknown. As for the other astronaut, we presume they've made it inside the alien ship."

Molly puts her sandwich down on the plastic packaging it came in from the cafeteria. To continue eating seems wrong.

"I'd like you to stay," the chief of staff says, surprising Molly. "You've been a great asset during the lead-up to Contact. You're a fresh set of eyes and ears."

Although she probably doesn't mean anything by it, the term *asset* is manipulative. Molly would like to think she's rational and independent, that she's supportive and assertive. She doesn't want to be a wallflower or a tool, something that's useful for now but quickly discarded. The chief of staff seems to read the doubts lining her face.

"We're making history. You'll be there as my personal assistant."

Molly nods. "I'd like that. Thank you."

"Okay," the chief of staff says, getting to her feet. "You've got about twenty minutes before they sweep the area."

"Oh, right," Molly says, getting to her feet and following the chief of staff back along the path to the driveway circling the South Lawn.

"They're setting up cots in the East Room. You'll be assigned one in the Oval Office admin section. The staff there will be able to help with meals, washing, extra clothing, toiletries and stuff like that. If there's anything specific you need, like an asthma inhaler, just let them know."

"Ah, okay," Molly replies, only now realizing the lockdown is expected to last for several days, if not a week or more. She keeps pace with the chief of staff.

Marine One descends on the grassy lawn. The wind kicked up by the rotors sends a flicker of leaves and twigs cascading through the air. Tens of thousands of individual blades of grass are flattened by the downdraft from the helicopter. The chief of staff ignores the artificial hurricane as though there were only clear skies and a gentle breeze around them. Slick black tires and bulky hydraulics take the weight of the Sikorsky VH-3D Sea King. The helicopter powers down. The whine of the engines fades. Birds return to the trees. The rotors slow to a stop. Sunlight glistens off the polished paintwork. The door opens, and the aircrew descends the fold-down stairs. A Marine takes up the position of guard, standing to the right of the stairs, but no dignitaries emerge. The helicopter must be on standby in case the Secret Service feels the need to evacuate the President. As it is, the Vice President has been taken to Camp David as a precaution.

There's no immediate threat to the President, but they're taking no chances and don't want any delays. Molly suspects the crew of Air Force One is on standby at Joint Base Andrews, ready to take to the skies with the President if needed. It's details like these that leave Molly feeling unsettled. When faced with the unknown, the response of the government is to swing into action with whatever contingency is known. This is probably a rehearsed scenario for some other possibility, and they're bringing it into effect even though there's no precedence for what's happening.

There's no danger. There couldn't be. There's no way an alien spacecraft a hundred million miles from Earth would have any awareness of the United States of America, let alone its capital or the location of its leader. And even if they did, what could they do at such a distance? Light itself and all the radio waves and images being broadcast by the *Odyssey* take more than eight minutes to traverse the void between them.

The appearance of Marine One is overkill—of that, Molly is certain. And overkill worries her. For most people, taking precautions is smart. For Molly, precautions are a sign of intent. People do dumb things when they're afraid. As big and as mighty as the US Government may be with its armed services, the Senate, the House of Representatives, Judicial Branch and Executive Branch, it's still just a bunch of people. And in Molly's admittedly limited experience, grouping people together doesn't make them smarter. Grouping like-minded people together tends to amplify their blind spots. Where others might see contingency planning swinging into effect, Molly sees a typical knee-jerk reaction. Nothing about First Contact is predictable, but everyone's trying to predict what comes next. Bad assumptions are worse than no assumptions at all. And the basic assumption seems to be that First Contact is potentially dangerous.

Molly keeps her thoughts to herself, following half a pace behind the chief of staff as she walks around the circular drive toward the Oval Office. Molly would *never* cut in front of the Oval to get to one of the doors to the West Wing beneath the colonnade. Ordinarily, Molly keeps to Executive Avenue on the far side of the West Wing, where the main door is located. The chief of staff's office is in that corner, so it would be more practical for her to go that way, but the chief of staff is at home in the Oval. Molly, though, feels like an intruder walking up to the building.

As they step up from the grass onto the walkway flanked with columns, the chief of staff turns away from the West Wing. She walks out into the Rose Garden. The immaculately kept grass lawn is flanked by cherry blossom trees on the four corners and beds of roses running down either side. It's only once Molly steps past the bushes that she sees the President pacing the lawn. The chief of staff goes to her. Molly remains on the concrete path beneath the portico. The President is wearing a light blue pantsuit with broad heel shoes. They're not stilettos, so they don't sink into the grass, but they do leave peculiar divots where they've flattened the soft turf.

"There you are," the President says, turning to her chief of staff.

"Is everything all right?"

The President shrugs, letting out a laugh that comes across as a sigh.

Molly stands motionless, peering over the bushes. She's a statue. Chief of Staff Dosela is right, she really is invisible. Young, pretty female interns are a dime a dozen within the White House and the West Wing, and like her, they're from affluent or politically connected families. They're part of the furniture.

President Elizabeth Smith-Knowles looks exhausted. Her head hangs. Her shoulders are stooped. She's six feet tall without heels. With them, she towers over most men. Perhaps the heels are more of a power move than the pantsuit. They certainly got her noticed in the Democratic primaries and later in the presidential debates. The image of her lording over Senator Theodore Staggs from Texas was iconic. He wore a Stetson to the first presidential debate to look taller, only she made him look small, rising above the crown of his pale, felt cowboy hat. Between that and his arrogance, the Press labeled him Napoleon—and he hated it. Staggs still drew sixty-six million votes in the election, but the result was never in doubt. Now, though, Elizabeth Smith-Knowles looks defeated. She doesn't look presidential. She looks like a boxer in the twelfth round, stepping forward from the corner but tired of the fight.

"All angles," she says. "They're coming at me from everywhere. I can't do anything right. Every decision is wrong. And it's not just the Republicans. Even the Democrats are piling on."

"Who?"

"Senators Davidson, Johns and Summers to name the loudmouths. Ah, and in the House, the Homeland Security Committee is having a field day with this, as is the Science Committee. And they're chaired by allies. They're supposed to be on our side! On my side!"

"I know. I know," the chief of staff says. For Molly, it's telling what the chief of staff doesn't say. She doesn't offer any advice or make suggestions. She's a sounding board for the President.

"CNN is running with our recklessness in sending Crash Williams to represent all of humanity."

"It's just a nickname," the chief of staff replies. "He's actually quite reserved, but his name plays well with Republicans. They see him as one of theirs."

"It's not his reputation," the President says. "It's who he is—he's a privileged white male. Of course, he gets to make First Contact."

"But, but—"

"I've told them we have British, French, Chinese and Indian astronauts on the *Odyssey*, but it's an American that goes inside."

"You can't please everyone."

The President points at herself, saying, "Me? I can't please anyone."

"And you shouldn't have to. This isn't an election campaign. This is governance."

The President is disgusted with herself. "If I'd let the British woman go first, they would have hated me for it. I would have never heard the end of it. I had to push for him. I had to."

"They're assholes," the chief of staff says, and quietly, Molly agrees.

The President turns away from her. She's crying. She doesn't want her chief of staff to notice, but she does. Susan Dosela steps toward Elizabeth Smith-Knowles. For a moment, there's nothing between them. Neither holds any rank or office. They're two women struggling under the weight of expectation bearing down on them. Susan reaches out a kind hand, touching Elizabeth's shoulder. Given she's already turned away, Molly's expecting her to shrug off her friend, but she doesn't. She squeezes her eyes closed. Tears fall to the grass.

"*Icarus* worries me."

Molly squints. She's heard a lot of terms and acronyms thrown around over the past week, but not this one. Although her education didn't cover Greek mythology, she's vaguely aware of the story. Icarus wore wings that allowed him to fly like a bird, but he was warned not to be complacent. If he flew too low, the salt spray from the ocean would clog his wings and cause him to crash. Icarus was warned against hubris. His wings were held together with wax. Flying too close to the sun would cause the wax to melt, and he'd plummet to his death. But Icarus lost himself in the moment. He could fly. Icarus reveled in the ability to soar like an eagle on the wind. He couldn't help himself. He was invincible. He lost sight of himself before he lost flight. He became so caught up in the moment he forgot his father's warning, and it cost him his life.

"*Icarus* is your call," the chief of staff says. "Don't let anyone push you on it."

"They don't tell you about this, you know," the President says, drying her eyes. "It's not in any of the brochures or advertisements. Become President, they say. You can make a real difference, they say. And then 9/11 happens, or the stock market crashes, or a pandemic breaks out, or aliens arrive on your doorstep, and everything changes.

"We flatter ourselves. Everyone thinks they can be President. They all think they can do better. Johns, Summers and Davidson all think that way. Hell, I thought that way, right? That's why I ran for office.

"Then you sit behind the Resolute Desk. You see all the generals and admirals, the senators and representatives from the House. They come before you. Some haughty. Most humble. But they all come before *you* because *you're* the President. And you stare at that old, polished wooden desktop, listening as they speak. You notice the way the grain runs in the oak timber. And you think about how the Resolute Deck came to be in the Oval Office.

"The HMS Resolute sailed the arctic waters, searching for survivors from a failed British expedition to survey the North West Passage. Only the Resolute fell foul of winter. It became trapped in the ice as the passage closed. And as you sit there in the Oval Office, you think about the icicles clinging to the wood, the ice floes compressing the hull of that doomed ship, and the sound of wood straining as it's crushed by the pack ice. The sailors fought frostbite. They secured the rigging before abandoning the stricken ship and making their way across the ice, walking for hundreds of miles to the nearest island. And it's then you realize why this desk is in the Oval Office. It's a reminder. A warning. We think we're in control. We're not. We think we can command chaos. We can't. That desk is a reminder that I can make all the right decisions and *still* become trapped in the ice. That desk tells me that with every decision, lives hang in the balance."

She pauses. Far from needing a pep-talk, she's giving herself one.

"Being President doesn't make you the most powerful person in the world, it makes you the most humble. Sitting behind that old wooden desk, you realize how much you need everyone else to work together. You realize how tides and winds can run your ship into the ice floes. The weather can change—" She snaps her fingers. "—just like that! And this alien spaceship? It's the coming of winter. The question is, how will we navigate the Northwest Passage?"

Chief of Staff Dosela nods. Her eyes fall to the grass. Molly swallows the lump rising in her throat.

"*Icarus*," the President says. "I pray to God we don't need it."

"Me too," the chief of staff says.

With that, the President strides across the grass toward the side door leading into the Oval Office. She locks eyes with Molly, only just now realizing the intern has been standing there behind the bushes listening to this private moment between her and her longtime friend. She smiles. Molly's eyes drop away. She looks at her shoes. Freshly cut strands of grass stick to the black leather. She rubs her feet against the back of her leg, knocking them free.

"Come," the President says, walking past her and opening the door. "We've got work to do."

The Gods of India

The front of the alien spacecraft is roughly five hundred feet from the tower-like spikes containing the dishes and domes. On reaching the end of the smooth, largely featureless craft, Crash turns, taking in the whole vessel. He's drifted out to almost a hundred feet, allowing him to look down the length of the alien spacecraft. Its engines are facing the Sun, but it's slightly off-center, meaning one side of the vast cylindrical vessel catches most of the sunlight. Shadows stretch from the spikes along the hull. In space, colors tend to be washed out. It's the brightness of the sun dulling the sensitivity of the eyes and camera optics. Even with his golden glare visor down, it's as bright as the noonday at L4.

The tip of the vessel narrows like an hourglass pinched in the middle, with a scoop facing into the darkness of space. As the structure is largely hidden by the pitch-black shadows of the spacecraft itself, it's difficult to see details. Although the lack of aerodynamics is no surprise, it's still peculiar to see a bowl-shaped bow opening out like an upside-down umbrella facing the depths of space.

Yúzé must see him lingering on the strange device. "Adeep says they'll be collecting hydrogen while in flight. That looks like a Bussard Ramjet. It's basically a big collector. It probably has a magnetic field to help draw in wisps of hydrogen."

Crash says, "Collecting fuel along the way, huh? Nice."

He touches lightly on his LCMU controls and begins drifting in toward the neck of the hourglass, aiming for the point where the body of the spacecraft spreads out to form a cylinder reaching well over half a mile in length. As he enters the shadow of the massive craft, his spotlights come on automatically. Whereas the sides of the cylindrical spacecraft are smooth, the front is covered in box shapes and domes similar to those found on the spikes.

Crash uses his jets to halt his momentum toward the center of the craft, allowing himself to drift closer to the edge of the vessel. The ramjet doesn't extend across the entire front of the interstellar spacecraft, covering only roughly three-quarters of its circumference.

"Look at this," he says, allowing himself to float close enough to reach out and touch the surface. "There's pitting. The texture is rough. Sandblasted."

Liz replies, "That's got to be the result of plowing through the interstellar medium for what? Centuries?"

"I guess."

With a light touch on the hull, Crash pushes himself away from the vehicle and then uses his jets to continue toward the center of the vessel several hundred feet away. As he passes between the hull and the ramjet, he's surrounded by utter darkness. Sunlight catches one edge of the ramjet, causing the circular structure to shine like the crescent of a new moon. His spotlights are good for examining the craft up close, but they fail to illuminate the distant support struts and pillars of the ramjet, leaving them indistinct and murky.

As he passes between the pillars beneath the ramjet, his spotlights reveal smooth, continuous metal supports at the heart of the hourglass shape.

"There's a light," he says, steering toward a dim, flashing red beacon near the center of the craft. As he gets closer, he sees Russian letters on the side of several bags attached to the spacecraft by carabiners and tethers. They float inches above the bulkhead. The blinking light comes from a strobe attached to one of the tethers.

Yúzé says, "Well, we've found the point Aleksandr entered the spacecraft."

From within the confines of his helmet and feeling somewhat exposed floating in the darkness beneath the ramjet, Crash says, "It's the silence that bothers me. Both from him and the aliens. I feel like I'm entering a ghost ship."

"You're not," Liz says. "This isn't the Mary Celeste adrift in the Atlantic without any crew. It undertook a controlled braking maneuver and settled at L4. Someone or something is in control."

"All right, let's find them."

The Russian equipment has been set near a white structure directly below the center of the ramjet. Crash pushes off the surface. As if in slow motion, he floats above the circular opening. It's a mechanical pit, being spherical and set flush with the hull of the craft, almost like a ball joint with a hollow center. At a glance, he can see how the airlock works. Rather than a hatch that opens and closes to an internal room, the entire apparatus turns. And when it turns, the open face shifts by 180 degrees, closing to space while opening to the interior of the craft. With the entire airlock swiveling, it may not be the most energy-efficient mechanism, but there's no chance of a breach. The opening only ever faces in one direction. It must pressurize and depressurize as it turns. The eyeball-shaped interior of the airlock is considerably larger than the opening itself.

"Well, this gives us some idea of their size," Crash says. "I make the opening at ten feet in diameter, while the interior of the airlock is easily thirty feet across."

"Proceed with caution," is the only comment from the *Odyssey*. Like him, there's a mixture of excitement and trepidation with the unknown unfolding before them.

With a light touch on his controls, Crash enters the alien airlock.

Yúzé says, "First EVA elapsed time is three hours and fourteen minutes, and NASA astronaut Chris Williams is entering an airlock at the front of the alien spacecraft."

Crash examines the nodules and panels within the ball-shaped interior. "Looking for… Oh, it activates automatically."

He pushes off something that looks like a curved, padded seat running around the airlock and turns to face the opening he just passed through. Deep down, Crash wants one last, fleeting glimpse at the freedom of space, but there are no stars. The blinking Russian light catches the support struts of the ramjet blocking the view, casting them in an eerie red glow.

As the ball socket turns, the apparent aperture shrinks, disappearing from sight. A yellow glow illuminates the interior of the airlock, but it's not clear where it's coming from. His spotlights don't help as they wash out the light. He turns them off. It takes a few seconds for his eyes to adjust to the alien light. Once they have, he finds himself facing an identical ball-socket-like airlock leading to the interior of the craft. It's a clever design as it means the overall airlock mechanism is always open at either end, allowing easy passage in either direction.

Crash drifts across the gap, passing from one massive eyeball to the other. Before the second airlock begins rotating, the entire area is bathed in a brilliant violet light. Strobe lights flash around him, forcing him to squeeze his eyelids shut. From behind a thin veil of flesh, the veins in his eyelids are visible, being back-lit by the rapid flashes. He pulls down on his golden sun visor, wanting to shut out the sterile light.

"A—Assessment?" he asks, unable to hide the tremor in his voice.

Slowly, the light fades to a soft orange glow. He raises his golden visor.

Yúzé replies, "Ah, probably a standard procedure. Pierre thinks they're sterilizing anything that passes through the airlock."

The second sphere rotates away from the first sphere, allowing the entry lock to swing back toward the vacuum of space while the second sphere turns inward toward the interior of the craft.

"Breathe," comes over the radio from Liz.

"Yeah," he replies, feeling his heart beating out of his chest.

"You're looking good," Yúzé says. "Your video, audio and suit metrics are coming through loud and clear. We copy you entering the alien vessel."

As the spherical, ball-shaped airlock continues to rotate, Crash feels the pressure difference increase against the material of his spacesuit. EVA suits are designed for the extremes of a naked vacuum facing the harsh solar radiation on one side and the bitter cold of the shadows on the other. The outer cloth layer is thick, but it has a characteristic crumple when flexing in space. Now, though, it's slightly depressed. It doesn't crinkle quite as easily when he moves his arms.

"We have an atmosphere in here."

"Take samples," is the reply.

Crash reaches down to pull out one of a bunch of sample collection containers from his leg pouch, but he stops. The brilliance of the light flooding the airlock from within the interior of the massive vessel gets him to pause. Although his helmet is still facing down at his thick boots, his eyes rise to meet the light. He fumbles with a glass test tube, gripping it in his gloved hand as he stares out of the airlock. He raises his head, astonished by the sight before him.

"Oh—my—God," is mumbled by Liz over the radio.

"Yeah," is all Crash can say in reply. "We're gonna need a bigger sample collection kit."

Yúzé speaks with robotic precision, saying what needs to be said, but his voice betrays him. Like all of them, he's in awe of the sight before him and struggling to stay on task.

"First EVA elapsed time is three hours and eighteen minutes, and NASA astronaut Chris Williams has reached the interior of the alien spacecraft."

The circular opening of the airlock gives way to an atrium full of dark green grass and trees, streams and lakes, only the landscape is folded over on itself, wrapping around the inside of the cylinder. There's no top or bottom. No left or right. Instead, the entire vista is in motion, rotating with the cylinder itself. At a guess, the diameter of the open space above the trees and the rolling grass fields is easily eight hundred feet, if not more. Mentally, Crash does the conversion, realizing it's got to be almost two hundred and fifty meters across. To his mind, it's broader than several football fields set side by side. It's as though several NFL football stadiums, including the stands, have been stacked on top of each other and converted into a space habitat. The interior is long, stretching for easily half a mile into the distance.

"Wow! You could hold the Olympics in here," he mumbles. "Summer and winter."

By his estimate, seven or eight football stadiums could fit inside the cylinder, forming one vast habitat. In the center, an artificial star glows, bathing the habitat in a golden light reminiscent of sunset on a long, hot summer's day.

The airlock itself is stationary, but the outer lip beyond the airlock is in motion, being part of the cylinder.

Liz says, "*Rendezvous with Rama,* anyone?"

"The Indian gods are smiling on us," Crash replies. Like her, he's referring to the 1970s science fiction novel by Arthur C. Clarke in which a gigantic alien spaceship visits the solar system, with the interior of the spacecraft containing another world wrapping around on itself. In that novel, after working through Greek and Roman mythology to name interstellar interlopers, the fictional Spaceguard moved on to the Hindu pantheon, calling their BDO *Rama.*

Yúzé says, "It's an O'Neill cylinder—a space habitat."

Crash says, "Why leave your home world when you can take it with you?"

"Makes sense," Liz says. "If we were to undertake such a long-duration spaceflight, we'd want to account for the crew's psychological well-being. Nothing does that quite like nature."

"Only this is more than simply therapeutic," Crash says. "You could cater to medical concerns with a fraction of this volume. It's the entire ship! The whole damn thing."

"So it's a colony ship?" Liz asks.

"Maybe."

Crash holds onto a shelf within the airlock. He leans forward with only his helmet reaching out of the opening. Vertigo washes over him. It's as though he's peering over the edge of a skyscraper at a city park far below, only the park curls up at either end. And it's in motion, drifting by beneath him. The effect is disorienting. There's no up or down in space. His inner ear has become accustomed to swirling in crazy directions. Most days, he feels like a monkey at the zoo hanging from the wire mesh at the top of its cage. Now, though, with a sense of ground below him, his sense of balance is thrown into disarray. He feels as though he's toppling sideways, falling out of the airlock, even though he's stationary. It's all he can do not to be sick.

Down is an illusion. Down is a demon, deceiving him. If he looks to his left, he's looking down. Look to his right and he's also looking down. If he keeps his eyes in line with his body, down has shifted yet again in front of him. All ways are down—and that is disconcerting. A cold sweat breaks out on his forehead. His hands feel clammy.

From where he is within the airlock, the motion of the cylinder appears sedate. Far from a freight train rushing past as it seemed in the tunnels, from up here, the trees and lakes move with a steady cadence. Even though he knows there's no upside down in space, seeing trees turn over his head is unnerving. They pass out of sight, gliding beyond the confines of his helmet. At that point, they're horizontal rather than vertical, which messes with his sense of orientation.

Although it's difficult to see clearly from the angle he's on, looking down his end of the spacecraft, the outside of the airlock appears to be surrounded by struts reaching out in the shape of a star. They could be the spokes of a bicycle wheel with him at the hub. They're probably structural rather than aesthetic, but their motion heightens his vertigo.

Crash pulls himself back into the airlock, narrowing his view as he bumps into the rear of the chamber. It's a deliberate strategy to help him cope. The alien world beyond appears framed by the circular opening of the internal airlock.

"Are you okay?" Liz asks.

"It's overwhelming... It's like a portal to another world."

"It is," Yúzé says.

"Okay," Crash says, steeling himself in the moment. "How do I get down there? I mean, there's no elevator or ladder."

Liz replies, "You fly."

Crash laughs. "With the LCMU? It doesn't have enough thrust. I'll crash."

Liz explains her thinking. "Artificial gravity isn't gravity. It might look like it, but it's an illusion. Angular momentum is keeping everything grounded in there, not gravity. Float through that hatch, and you're as weightless as you were on the outside."

"Huh."

"Like a kid on a merry-go-round, it's the spin that throws everything outward, holding it in place. You could float a foot off the ground with no problem at all."

"But the ground?" Crash says, realizing there's more to her explanation.

"Oh, it'll be whizzing by like the M-Train Express racing through New York's subway, but you'd be fine. You'd still be weightless."

"So going inside is no problem. Landing, though. That'll be the challenge."

"Yes. The cylinder is rotating left-to-right as you look at it from the bow of the craft. To land, you need to match the rotational speed. Do that, and you can step down onto the grass."

Crash laughs. Talking with Liz has put him at ease. "You make it sound like a walk in the park."

She corrects him with, "A walk in an *extraterrestrial* park."

"Okay, so despite what I feel, I'm not going to fall. I'm just going to float."

"And your LCMU will work just fine. Close to the ground, you'll get some wind as the atmosphere is churned up by the motion of the trees, but it'll be in the direction of rotation and won't be any faster than the ground speed."

"Okay, let's do this."

Yúzé says, "Before you do exit the airlock, can you set up a mass spectrometer, atmospheric sampler and a relay point? I don't want to lose your signal in there."

"Copy that," Crash replies. He reaches into another of the bulky pockets on his legs and pulls out a device that looks like a security camera with an antenna. It's been designed as a signal booster as well as providing additional video footage. The battery is good for thirty-six hours. He powers it on and straightens the antenna, raising it above the slick, white body of the camera. There's a tab on one side he can grab with his thick, gloved fingers. Crash peels it back, revealing an adhesive surface. He sticks the camera to what he supposes is a bench seat within the airlock, lining it up so it faces the opening.

After drifting to one side, getting out of the way of the lens, he asks, "How's the view?"

"Can you twist it a little to your right and down?"

He does as requested.

"Perfect. We've got a good view of the airlock opening and the cylinder beyond."

"And?"

"We're streaming data now. Pierre is looking at the preliminary results... Hang on... Okay, we're looking at... I'll let Pierre explain it to you."

"Crash. The atmosphere around you is thirty kilopascals in pressure. The sea level on Earth is around a hundred. Thirty would equate to somewhere on the north face of Everest. Ambient temperature is barely above freezing. We're talking 2C or about 35F, so it's cold but not inhospitable. Atmospheric composition is 64% nitrogen, 32% oxygen, with trace amounts of ozone and a bunch of other gases making up the balance. In short, there's a lot of oxygen, far more than we see anywhere on Earth, so the low pressure is offset by an increase in oxygen."

"Is it breathable?"

Liz says, "Everything's breathable once. Even water."

"Okay, okay," Crash replies, loving her sense of humor.

Pierre says, "It's the particulate matter that's more interesting. That's anything other than basic gases circulating in the air."

"Microbes?"

"Microbes, dust, the alien equivalent of pollen, smoke or pollutants."

"And what can you see?"

"It's pretty clean but not perfectly clean. I wouldn't call it sterile. At a scale of 10 microns per cubic meter, we're looking at 15 particles that could cause lung issues. That's almost nothing, but they are unknown contaminants. We have no way of knowing how benign or harmful they could be. At 2.5 microns, or something like cigarette smoke, there are less than ten parts per million. While down at 1 micron, we drop to zero."

"And all that means?"

"All that means it's on par with Greenland for air quality, but I don't know what those stray particles actually are. They could be alien airborne viruses. Anything."

"All right, so no breathing the atmosphere."

"Oh, hell, no. Not unless you want First Contact to unfold like some B-grade science fiction movie."

"Hah. Okay. Point taken… I'm exiting the airlock."

Atrium

Even though Crash is soaring into the unknown within the alien O'Neill cylinder, it's reassuring to know that the team now has two video feeds, one from his helmet and the other from the signal booster. He's got one more portable camera in his other leg pouch, but he'll wait before deploying that.

He aligns himself so he's facing forward and releases a soft burst of compressed gas to propel himself through the opening of the airlock. Crash drifts forward at a walking pace. The floor of the airlock drops away beneath him, revealing the curve of the massive cylinder hundreds of feet below. Liz is right. There's no gravity. Technically, there's micro-gravity, but there's no overwhelming pull as he'd expect, given what he can see. Instead, he moves in a straight line at a constant speed, just as he did when navigating outside the BDO.

"Okay, this is pretty cool."

An alien world wraps around him, curling before him and folding over him. Roughly a hundred yards ahead, an alien sun casts light and heat over this miniature world. The plants vary from deep green to rust-colored and red. Some have black leaves, while others are a deep purple. It's as though he's emerged in a forest that has been scorched by fire. Blackened trunks rise from the dark soil, reaching toward the artificial starlight at the heart of the rotating cylinder.

Crash descends on an angle, taking in the surroundings. He can see the view from the relay point in the airlock behind him on his wrist pad computer and stays within the frame so the team on the *Odyssey* has him in view. As his altitude lowers, he's acutely aware of his descent. It's impossible to visually identify one direction over another as the ground is constantly in motion, but he can sense the lack of feeling within his inner ear. He's not plummeting toward the surface. Somewhat counterintuitively, it's reassuring to be floating weightless within an alien world.

A forest of what appears to be pine trees curls around one portion of the cylinder, but the growth is even and young. He levels out at a hundred feet and glides over the treetops. Unlike a forest on Earth, all the trees are the same height. They all appear to be the same age. The foliage is a deep green bordering on black. The trees catch the light in an extraordinary way. Leaves shimmer, reflecting the colors of the rainbow.

"This is new growth," he says. "It has to be. None of this could survive the 3G deceleration of the craft. And the lakes. The ponds. There's no way they could have withstood the spacecraft slowing down. None of this could be more than a couple of months old."

"I'm seeing crowning," Liz says. "That's where the branches of one tree give way to those of another, leaving a slight gap. It's common on Earth, allowing sunlight to reach the forest floor."

"So we've got convergent evolution occurring over billions of miles in space," Crash replies.

Liz says, "On Earth, we've got convergent evolution over hundreds of millions of years, resulting in things like eyes and brains evolving independently dozens of times. It's no surprise we're seeing similarities here."

"Same physics. Same chemistry," Crash says.

"Yep. And the same drivers behind natural selection."

Yúzé says, "If you look overhead, there's a meadow coming down toward you. If you want to land, that's the spot."

"Ah," Crash says, using his reaction controls to twist around and look up. "If I'm going to land there, I'm going to be flying blind. I'll have my back to the meadow right up until I touch down. This is going to be like landing a plane backward."

Liz says, "We're clocking the rotation of the cylinder at one minute and thirty-six seconds. If you line yourself up, we'll give you the *go* signal next time around."

"Copy that."

Crash uses his jets to position himself above a lake that curves with the cylinder. Seeing water bend beneath him is trippy, but as he moves into position, the meadow drifts by beneath his boots. "Descending to fifteen meters—fifty feet."

"Stay well above the trees," Liz says, although he's already taken that into account.

Yúzé says, "Adeep has been doing the math. At the point the lake first passes under your boots, fire your LCMU lateral thrusters on 75% for ten seconds. You're going to have to pull up at the last moment, but you should touch down at a walking pace."

"That meadow looks bumpy," Crash says, looking at the wristpad computer on his arm displaying the view from the camera in the airlock.

"It does," Yúzé replies. "Coming up on your burn in five, four, three, two..."

A thick tangle of trees and bushes rushes past a little too close for his liking, but Crash hits his thrusters. Deep water passes below his boots, curling as though by magic. As he accelerates, his altitude drops. Although he's moving in a straight line, the surface beneath him is concave, distorting his sense of height. His reflection ripples over the water. Although he's probably higher than he thinks, it feels as though his boots are about to dip into the lake. Suddenly, the grassy meadow appears. The ground beneath him slows, or it seems to slow as he reaches roughly the same speed. Long thin, slender blades of dry grass brush against his boots. As he's still weightless above the meadow, he uses the LCMU to adjust his orientation. Crash reaches out with his boots. The rubber tips touch the ground as his momentum brings him down. The wind passing through the grass causes him to misjudge his speed. His legs are pulled out from beneath him as they hit the ground slightly too slow. Crash finds himself running with the LCMU bouncing on his back and his legs struggling to match the pace. He feels as though he's careening out of control down a hill faster than his legs can carry him.

Crash trips. His hands rush up, trying to protect his helmet as he falls into the alien meadow. He skids to a halt. Dust swirls around him.

"Crash!" Liz yells over the headphones in his Snoopy cap.

"Yeah," he replies softly, lying face-first on the ground. He pushes off the grass with his hands, rising onto his knees before slowly getting to his feet.

"Well, that wasn't quite *one small step*," he jokes, referring to Neil Armstrong's immortal words.

Once it's clear he's okay, Yúzé says, "It's good to see you're living up to your name."

"No barrel rolls this time, huh?" Liz says.

"Nope."

Streaks of dirt line one side of his visor. He brushes them away with his gloved hand, but smudges remain. Standing there, Crash feels a sense of awe. Everything that was in motion is now still. He looks back at the distant airlock high above the curved plain. He figures he's roughly five hundred feet away and looking up at it at an angle of maybe thirty degrees. The radial lines leading to it appear artistic, as though they were painted on by an art-deco designer from the 1920s. The vast circular panel that makes up the front of the craft appears sky blue, while the spokes are a soft grey. The airlock itself glows like the moon.

Yúzé says, "First EVA elapsed time is three hours and thirty-seven minutes, and NASA astronaut Chris Williams has reached the inside surface of the cylindrical alien habitat."

The alien sun, which appeared as a single point when seen side-on from the airlock, spans three-quarters of the length of the habitat. It forms a glowing line in the middle of the cylinder, appearing more like a bar of molten metal rather than a star.

The grass swaying around him reaches up to waist height on impossibly thin stalks. The heads resemble wheat in that there are overlapping seeds forming the shape of pods. On Earth, such a plant would collapse under the weight of the seeds. Here within the BDO, they shift in unison, forming waves with the motion of the wind coming down from the forest. He walks on toward the trees rising out of the slope above him.

"It's really strange in here," he says. "I have steep slopes on either side of me, but I can't walk up them. I walk toward them, and they come down to greet me. It's quite surreal forever standing at the bottom of the habitat."

He's giddy with excitement, wandering aimlessly rather than walking with purpose. He turns, changing his mind, and walks away from the forest, wanting to explore the lake curling up the far side of the cylinder. With each step, the lake moves closer, slowly rolling back toward him, at least from his perspective.

"I've got to say, the prairies and plains of Earth seem like a waste of space compared to this place. Curling everything up like this is far more efficient. It's like rolling up a map on itself."

He pauses, craning his neck within his suit and turning slowly, taking in his surroundings, knowing that the sight before him is captivating not just the astronauts onboard the *Odyssey* but billions of people on Earth as well. He's aware there will be a mixture of reactions to his exploration of the cylinder. Most will find it fascinating, but some will react with fear, wondering what the intent is behind such a vast habitat. He knows his words can quell doubts.

"And it's strange having no sky. It's like standing at the base of a mountain, with broad slopes curling upwards. I've seen something like this before, in the Scottish highlands... If you go north past Inverness, you see massive rolling hills that have been carved out by ancient glaciers. Their approaches are smooth, devoid of all but tussock grass curling up toward the summit. For me, being here is like tramping through the highlands."

Although Crash could see the outline of mounds within the

meadow from the air, being at ground level, he gets a sense of the differing heights within the alien cylinder. The lakes are the lowest points. Narrow streams run down from the forest, passing through the meadow.

"There's some kind of hydro cycle," he says, walking over and looking at one of the streams. It's narrow enough that he can step across it with ease, but it runs deep, disappearing into darkness.

"So you think there's rain?" Liz asks.

"I don't know, but they've got water circulating for a reason. It could be pumped higher and released, but either way, it's an important part of their ecosystem."

Yúzé says, "I wonder if there are day/night cycles? If so, how long are they? That would allow for condensation to form within the habitat. It might not result in clouds or rain, but it could form dew."

Crash wades through the sea of alien wheat, stepping across the crevasses forming streams with water running down to the lake.

"Is this irrigation?" he asks, giving them a view of a stream that's not more than six inches wide but several feet deep. Although they appear jagged and haphazard rather than being a trench dug by a machine, the spacing of the streams every thirty to forty feet seems unusually consistent.

"Maybe."

"There are lines ahead," Yúzé says. "They might be paths. From the airlock, I can zoom in and see one not more than fifty feet ahead of you."

"In this direction?"

"A little more to your left."

Crash continues on. Behind him, crushed stalks rise, unfurling from his bootprints and once again reaching for the alien sun. They unfold without so much as a crease in their stalks, hiding his path through the meadow.

"You should be right on top of it."

Crash doesn't see anything beyond the unbroken meadow

stretching along the cylinder rather than around it.

"Oh, yeah," he says, stumbling out onto a gravel path. "Found it."

He crouches on one knee, reaches down and runs his gloved hand over the gravel. It shimmers, sparkling with the colors of the rainbow as it's moved.

"It's fine," he says, "but not like sand. It's more like crushed rock. The base color is sandy, but it glistens like glass."

"Some kind of silicate?" Liz asks through his headset.

"Maybe."

Crash stands and immediately sways. "Oh, that's not good. Not good at all."

Sick rises in his throat. He gags. It's all he can do not to vomit over the inside of the glass visor. He reaches up, touching the slick side of his helmet, wanting to hold his head but unable to touch anything other than his suit.

"Is everything okay?" a worried Yúzé asks.

"Ah, the spin. Damn. It's deceiving. I mean, I feel like I'm stationary, but I'm not. And when I rose, I was facing at an angle, staring down through the cylinder—and my inner ear went nuts. It's crazy in here. It's like stepping off a rollercoaster after a few hard loops. The world feels like it's in motion."

"And it is," Liz says.

"Yeah, but it doesn't look like it. There's dissonance, a clash. My eyes tell me one thing, my sense of balance tells me another."

Crash leans forward, resting his hands on his knees and slowing his breathing. Dirt clings to his left leg. He tries to dust it away, but it's embedded in the creases of his suit. Scratches line the thick fabric. His landing was heavier and harder than he thought. He composes himself, remaining bent over for a few seconds. The perceived weight of the LCMU on his back is reassuring.

"Just taking a moment."

Yúzé replies, "No rush."

When he straightens, his motion is slow. Crash makes sure he's facing in the direction of motion, looking around the cylinder instead of along it.

"There's no gravity," Liz says. "It feels like it, but there's none. Your comment about a rollercoaster is appropriate. The sense of gravity you feel is akin to rushing down the track into a series of loop-the-loops."

"Yeah," he replies. "It's not as easy to negotiate as it seems."

The gravel path is several feet wide with a concave curve. The edges are higher than the middle, but it's not a smooth curve.

"Any thoughts on the path?" he asks. "Does it give us some clue about their size?"

Liz replies. "Not really. Looking at how smooth it is, these paths could be designed for moving equipment around the habitat. Given the size of the cylinder and the way it makes you dizzy when you stand, I suspect they're probably shorter than us."

"Makes sense," Yúzé says. "They'd hardly design a habitat that was uncomfortable for them."

Crash walks along the gravel path. There are slight twists and turns. Banked corners mark changes in direction.

"It would be nice on a bike," he says.

"Ah, can you back up?" Yúzé says. "Those bushes to the right."

Crash turns and walks back to the dark bushes. Unlike most plants on Earth, there aren't any broad leaves. Instead, like a palm tree, stems open into dozens of thin leaves. They're thicker than the stems, catching more light, but lack the broad, flat expanse of leaves found on Earth. They're not as fine as pine needles, appearing closer to the leaves of succulents.

Yúzé says, "Adeep is reviewing your footage in slow-mo. He caught some movement back there."

"In the bushes?" Crash asks, feeling his heart thumping inside his chest. It's one thing to explore the flora of an alien world; it's another to run into the fauna. The rational side of his mind assures him the alien intelligence behind the habitat wouldn't stock it with harmful creatures, but that's quickly countered with—being docile to them could still be harmful to him. In particular, anything with teeth, claws or spikes could puncture his suit.

Rather than leaning in and taking a good look at the bush, he stands back. This isn't a movie. This isn't the time to do something stupid like pat an alien snake. In retrospect, his racing heart reminds him that coming down to ground level constitutes a kind of stupidity in itself. Due to the time lag between Houston and the *Odyssey*, no consideration was given to waiting for advice from NASA. He's sure they're passing along suggestions to the team in the *Odyssey*. If they're concerned about his exploration back on Earth, Liz and Yúzé have agreed to keep that warning to themselves. And he understands that rationale. There's no sense spooking him any further. They can see the spikes in his biometrics. They know he's dealing with the stress of the unknown.

"Can you get a closer look?" Yúzé asks.

Crash wants to say no. Instead of leaning over the bushes, he crouches, coming at them from the side, staying in the middle of the gravel path. He kneels. With his helmet drawing level to the top of the closest bush, he edges closer.

"Not seeing anything," Yúzé says.

On a hunch, Crash raises his hand above the bush. He waves his open palm slowly back and forth, casting shadows on the leaves. The bush reacts, closing its leaves over the stems and withdrawing its branches. No sooner has the shadow passed than the bush opens again.

"Fascinating," Yúzé says.

"It's a defense mechanism," Liz says. "On Earth, the Mimosa plant does something similar when touched."

"Why?" Crash asks, slowly drawing his hand back and forth through the air, watching as the alien plant reacts to the shade.

"Ah, for the Mimosa, it's a way of protecting its leaves against grazing animals."

"But I'm not touching it."

"Shadows precede touch," Liz replies. "The more sensitive it is, the earlier it reacts, and the more it protects itself. It's not difficult to see how this could evolve as a result of selective pressures."

Without getting too close, Crash twists his head, looking beneath the stems. He points.

"There are white dots on the underside of the branches. They look like insect eggs. The leaves close over them, protecting them."

"Could be seeds," Liz replies.

"So something feeds on this thing," Crash says, pushing off his right knee and getting to his feet. Once again, his inner ear swirls as he stands, but he keeps himself facing in the direction the cylinder is turning.

"Back on their home world, yes, but not necessarily here. You're safe."

And there it is. They're managing his fear. Her comment is probably a direct result of something said earlier to her by mission control. Liz doesn't know what is and isn't dangerous within the habitat—and neither does he. Anything that grazes on this bush should leave him alone, but trying to quantify risk in an unknown environment is impossible. Safe is an assumption, not a fact.

"Perhaps stay on the path," Yúzé says.

"Copy that."

Crash walks on toward the lake. Under the alien sun, his white spacesuit appears almost golden. Light plays on the aluminum locking rings by his wrist, causing them to shimmer like copper. Crash turns his gloved hand over, holding it up toward the light and looking at the way the grey rubber appears brown.

"The light in here isn't constant," he says. "It seems to surge. That's not something to worry about, right?"

"It's probably simulating the behavior of their local star," Liz replies. "Pierre has been looking at the spectroscopy results and said it approximates a red dwarf. They're known to have variable outputs, so perhaps they're simulating that to stimulate plant growth."

"Is radiation a concern?"

"Radiation is always a concern, but your suit will protect you."

And there it is again, misplaced optimism. *'Will protect you.'* There's no way in hell any of them know that for sure, but certainty is the best way to deal with the unknown. There's no point complicating uncertainty with even more uncertainty, even if it's a lie—a subtle lie and well-meaning, but still a lie. Crash accepts that, nodding slightly.

He walks on along the ambling path, following its curves as it passes through a region that looks like tussock grass with tall, spindly weeds popping up in the gaps. Crash works his way around the edge of the pond, which is the size of a public pool. He's not sure he'll ever get used to seeing water curl as though it were made from glass.

On Earth, unless a field has been graded for sport, there are always bumps and slopes, while pools and ponds appear perfectly flat. Within the BDO, the gentle curve of a lake gives it the appearance of glazed pottery. The glossy surface looks surreal, as though its shape is impossible for mere water alone to sustain.

He stops and crouches by the edge of the track. Keeping his balance is difficult within the cylinder so he kneels, giving himself three points of contact with the ground. Pebbles shift beneath his boots.

"What are you doing?" Liz asks somewhat nervously.

"Touching the water," he replies. "It doesn't look real. I need to know it's real."

"Ah, we wouldn't advise that," Yúzé says in his earpiece. "We don't know the composition. It could contain solvents or alien microbes that could dissolve rubber."

"I'm taking a sample," Crash says, ignoring him and pulling a test tube from his kit. He unscrews the plastic lid with meticulous precision. Then he dips it in the lake and watches as water swirls within. The tips of his gloves get wet.

"And I'm not melting," he says, trying to downplay their concerns. He's here to explore and collect samples. It's too late to be cautious now that he's on the ground. He holds the test tube up to the light. The water is murky. Sediment swirls within it, slowly settling.

Liz sounds more upbeat than Yúzé. "If this were Earth, you would have just collected around a billion microbial specimens from the average pond."

"And that's good, right?" he says, pocketing the sample and pulling out another test tube. He takes a sample of the soil above the waterline and stows that as well. Water drips from his gloves. As he goes to get to his feet, he notices something in the undergrowth on the far side of the path.

"Honeycomb," he says, pushing the grass to one side to reveal what looks like a beehive that's been split open and scattered over several feet. The edges are jagged, rising like termite nests from the ground and forming spires and miniature peaks. The sides, though, are unmistakable. Hexagonal cells form tubes in a broad mesh that looks as though it's made from wax. Horns reach up from the tips of the hive, forming spikes that appear as though they're intended to ward off predators.

"Do—*not*—touch—that," Liz says with slow precision.

"Are we thinking bees?" Crash asks, getting to his feet. The hive disappears beneath the bushes and swaying grass. Now that he knows what he's looking for, he can see the jagged tips stretching back toward the trees. Dozens of hives cover an area the size of a children's playground at the local park.

Yúzé says, "Ah, probably not bees as such, but something that lives in a colony. Honeycomb is an incredibly effective geometric shape. It's efficient. It maximizes the space available without compromising structural integrity. Hell, the insulation sandwiched within the hull of the *Odyssey* uses a honeycomb design. It's also used to hold the resin in the heat shield."

"So something built that as a nest."

Liz says, "Yes."

Yúzé says, "Recommend you continue on."

"Copy that," Crash replies, not wanting to run into the alien equivalent of a swarm of wasps.

Apart from the way the water curves, the only other unsettling feature of the pond is that it's perfectly still. There are no aquatic animals stirring in the depths or even wind forming ripples on the surface. The pond reflects the habitat curling over it like a dark mirror.

Crash walks on, following the trail as it winds around the pond. Gravel is crushed beneath his boots, leaving an imprint behind him. To his mind, the interior of the cylinder is a mix of wild, unkept regions and stretches that seem to contain agriculture, like the meadow where he landed.

"It's funny," he says, trying to lighten the mood. "But walking around within the habitat, it feels as though I'm going nowhere. I'm always at the bottom. From wherever I am, this alien world curls away on either side of me. I mean, I can see that forest up there clinging to the slope of the cylinder. And as I walk toward the trees, it feels as though the forest is coming down to greet me rather than that I'm approaching it. It's a peculiar sensation."

Liz lightens up. "You're like a rat on a treadmill."

"Hah, yes, exactly like that. I'm a hamster running around a wheel."

As he leaves the pond, mounds of red dirt come into view beyond the bushes. They're piled eight to ten feet high, forming uneven cones, making it difficult to see between them, but they haven't been dumped by a mechanical digger. It's clear they're nests of some kind as their sides are rough-finished and hard-packed, with only the occasional opening wide enough to reach within. And there's *no way* that is happening. Crash isn't sticking his hand anywhere out of sight. No one mentions the thirty or forty mounds, so he walks past them without comment, which is strange. It's as though no one wants to know what's buried within them. And on that point, Crash is in agreement. It's one thing to explore the habitat, it's another for it to awaken and come to life. Slowly, the mounds give way to a grassy field leading to the dark forest.

"Are you seeing that?"

"Seeing what?" is the rushed response of Yúzé.

"There's a haze in front of those trees."

"A haze?"

Crash points, extending his arm and looking down along his outstretched, gloved finger, wanting to help them identify the spot.

"It's a smudge," he says, confused by what he's seeing.

"Get out of there," Liz says, but her panicked response isn't helpful. Does she mean retreat along the path or flee for the airlock? And why? The only place with enough room to take off is the meadow, but that's well over a hundred yards behind him and beginning to curl overhead.

"Ah," Crash mumbles, turning side on and facing the scattering of mounds in the nearby field. As much as he wants to follow the advice Liz is offering, turning his back on the haze seems like a mistake. It's one thing to see a dark cloud. It's another to lose sight of it. Besides, quick lateral motions are not a good idea within the rotating cylinder. His inner ear is swirling again, threatening to make him sick.

Yúzé says, "Pull back to the pond until we can—"

To his horror, the black swarm rushes toward Crash. He can't run. His boots stab at the gravel, but the faster and harder he tries, the more he bounces roughly on the spot, barely making any progress. Crash is in an artificial form of low gravity. Rapid, frantic movements are akin to someone drowning and splashing in water. There's a lot of activity but no real motion. He feels as though he's running through waist-deep mud.

His heart is racing. His breathing is shallow. The curved visor wrapping around his helmet bounces on his shoulders as he swings his arms, trying to rush back to the pond.

The swarm reaches him. Tens of thousands of flying insectoid creatures the size of fruit flies buzz around him. He swats at them with his hand, trying to brush them away as they obscure his view of the path, darkening the air before him.

"What the—" he says as his right arm disappears from sight, being covered in a mass of pulsating, black insects clinging to the white material.

"The water," Liz yells over his headset, but he knows it's futile. Even if he makes it to the pond, his buoyancy in such low gravity means he won't sink beneath the surface. He'll splash around, but like tourists at the Dead Sea in Israel, he'll float all too well.

Crash trips. He's not sure what his boots stumble upon, but he finds himself falling to the gravel path. His motion is slower than on Earth, giving him fractions of a second to brace himself. He has his gloved hands out in front of him as he slides to a halt on the gravel.

Shadows close in around him. Tens of thousands of tiny insects cling to his visor, blotting out the alien sun. They clamber over the polycarbonate glass, forming intricate swirls like those in the clouds of a gas giant. Within seconds, the remaining light fades to complete and utter darkness.

Decisions

Aleksandr creeps through the shadows within the alien forest. Vomit has caked on his lower lip. The smell of sick permeates his helmet. Most of the spew has dried, but there are still wet patches near the locking ring. Tiny flecks of sick mark the inside of his visor, but Aleksandr ignores them. It's the goddamn rotation of the cylinder. It feels like regular gravity, just a little weaker, that is until he turns too quickly. Aleksandr has learned to slow his lateral movements. Turning with or against the rotation of the cylinder changes the motion of his inner ear. When turning with the cylinder, he feels as though he's caught in a stream. Turn against it, and it's as though the alien world comes rushing at him like a storm. He's been sick twice now and is determined not to vomit inside his helmet again.

Aleksandr watches from the grove of trees as the American astronaut flounders on the edge of the lake. A dark swarm circles around Chris '*Crash*' Williams, but it's biased, clinging to one side of his suit more than the other. The American panics, swatting the tiny creatures with his gloved hands. Of course, he panics. The unknown scares Americans. They thrive on processes and procedures. Everything has to be clearly defined. They have no room for uncertainty. For all his faults, Aleksandr thrives on ambiguity. A wicked smile reaches his lips. He could help, but he won't. Crash will be fine. They won't hurt him. He just needs to relax and let them do their thing.

Aleksandr takes hold of a pen on a short length of string and notes the time of the incident on the notepad on the inside of his left wrist. He'll erase this section when he gets back to the *Vechnost*.

Has the American discovered the decks beneath the habitat? From what Aleksandr can tell, Crash was heading toward one of the entrances when he ran into the swarm. Aleksandr has found four stairways leading to storage areas and laboratories. Now that he's seen the American, he realizes he needs to backtrack into the hold. There are corridors down there running the length of the cylinder. Crash entered through the bow airlock just as Aleksandr did, so the Russian decides to leave by the airlock at the stern. In his mind, it's about the priority of discovery. If Aleksandr retraced his steps to the front airlock, he could miss something significant at the base of the ship, something the American might uncover, but Russia must be first. The engines are down there. There could be much to learn for Mother Russia. In his thinking, everything he does is for his country and not his ego. In practice, there's no distinction between them.

He snickers quietly as the American brushes his arm, trying to clear the gnats from his spacesuit. Aleksandr could link up with Crash. He might need them later. Even though he was able to partially pressurize the *Vechnost* after the collision, the loss of the solar panel will limit the amount of electricity available to him on the return journey. Fuel isn't a problem. It's just a question of whether the hull integrity can be maintained. The damage from the collision was confined to the orbital module, leaving the command module unscathed, so Aleksandr isn't too worried. Besides, he wants to maintain a clear distinction between missions. Would the Americans even accept him? Would they allow him to travel with them back to Earth? Probably. For them, it would be a question of resources, but for him, it's a problem of pride. To ask is humiliating. Even if it costs him his life, he'll stick with the *Vechnost*. So long as it's functional, he'll bet on Russian ingenuity over NASA's engineering.

As he watches, the American gets to his feet. The swarm dissipates just as Aleksandr knew it would. Crash examines his arms and turns. He looks up at the airlock. He's done that a few times, particularly after he first landed. He must have set a camera up there, giving the crew of the *Odyssey* a view down through the habitat with its rotating cylinder.

"Hmm," Aleksandr mutters as though the volume of his voice was somehow significant. The American is roughly forty feet away from him, off on an angle of about thirty degrees, over on the slope near the curve of the pond. As with everywhere within the cylinder, Aleksandr feels as though he's at the bottom of the curve and the American is up on the wall. It's strange watching someone walking toward him without falling over. It's the angle at which the American appears to lean forward that's deceiving. In reality, Aleksandr knows Chris *'Crash'* Williams must feel as though he's walking perfectly upright, and everything else, including Aleksandr and the trees, is leaning on an unnatural angle. Such is life within the alien cylinder.

How much can the American transmit? Aleksandr doubts the clarity of any signal being sent from within the cylinder. The habitat is huge. Its rotation, its density and the surrounding fuel tanks will all weaken the signal. Is the American sending live audio and video? Aleksandr is curious about the American strategy for sending footage back to Earth. NASA must be vetting the video. Like the Russians, they'll want to control the dissemination of knowledge, particularly if there are any nasty surprises.

After powering down the *Vechnost*, Aleksandr has been forced to record but not send his exploration footage back to Roscosmos. Seeing Crash approaching the lower decks, he realizes he needs to get back to his craft and transmit the second cache of results. He *must* beat the Americans. The priority of discovery must be Russian, not American. Second place isn't good enough. Everyone remembers Neil Armstrong, Buzz Aldrin and Michael Collins as the crew of Apollo 11. No one knows who flew in Apollo 12, even though that mission explored far more of the lunar surface. No one cares. Aleksandr is determined that Russia will dominate the history books—Russia *and* Aleksandr Krukov. It's not fame he seeks but recognition, or at least that's what he tells himself.

Aleksandr keeps to the shadows. He heads to one of the other entrances winding its way beneath the habitat. He knows the pattern. The entrances are placed in a helical structure throughout the cylinder rather than in a line, meaning the entrance he's heading for is set roughly thirty degrees behind the one Crash was walking toward.

The entrances aren't obvious. There's no portico or shroud over them. Instead, stairs lead down from the surface, leading beneath the habitat. Once down, lights come on automatically, illuminating just those regions through which people and/or aliens move. From what Aleksandr can tell, the creatures that built this vessel are shorter than him. His helmet grazes the doorways and bumps against the ceiling. The American is taller. He'll need to crouch.

Stepping down into a stairwell in roughly one-third gravity is an unusual sensation. It's akin to falling in water. Aleksandr steps forward, and reluctantly, his boots drift down to the next step. Thankfully, all of the entrances Aleksandr has found face in the direction of the cylinder's motion, making the descent pleasant.

Aleksandr reaches the main corridor running beneath the length of the cylinder. He begins walking toward the rear of the vessel. Lights flicker on and off as he heads along the curved metal floor. Once he gets to the stern, he'll head to the airlock and return to his spacecraft. He'll batch up his records and transmit them before returning to explore further.

Modules and laboratories come to life around Aleksandr, reacting to his motion within the lower deck of the alien spacecraft. He feels conflicted. He doesn't want to miss anything important. He wants to explore and record as much as he can. Should he stay within the cylinder? Should he leave while he still can? Pride compels him to investigate the side tunnels. Patriotism tells him to send what he can back to Roscosmos.

Beneath the Surface

Crash stands there bewildered. He has his arms outstretched, looking at the folds of fabric in his suit. The swarm descends away from him, retracing his path and restoring the gravel that shifted when he fell. His visor is clean. The muddy smudge that ran down the left side of his helmet is gone. When he fell in the meadow, he dug up moist soil. The stains on his left arm and shoulder have been removed.

"They're cleaners," he says, turning and watching as the divot of gravel is repaired by the swarm, leaving the path pristine once again.

Liz asks, "Is that some kind of nano-tech? A swarm of robotic gardeners?"

"I guess," he says as the swarm hovers over the pond. It drifts toward the meadow, probably to repair the ground there.

Yúzé says, "Ah, we have a request from mission control to bring you back in."

Crash checks his metrics. "I've got a good sixteen hours left in the tank, plus reserves."

"I think they're worried about exposing you to harm. They want time to analyze the footage so far, store your samples, and then reassess the approach with a second EVA."

Crash hangs his head. He's disappointed. A recall feels personal, even though it probably isn't. NASA and the multinational team gathered in Houston wouldn't have seen the swarm yet. The time delay is too great. They had to make this call after seeing the honeycomb structures or perhaps the red mounds in the distance. They're worried. Damn, once they see him panicking, they'll feel justified with their recall decision.

Has he been reckless? Too reckless? The landing was rough. He could have damaged his suit. And that damage may take time to result in failure—and any failure would likely be fatal. Dozens of engineers and scientists would be analyzing his every step in here, wanting to understand how well his suit works in an alien environment.

Yúzé was right to be concerned about the water. Even now, there could be chemical or biological processes weakening the rubber seals, and he wouldn't know it until his suit failed. Then there's the swarm. On the surface, it seems all they did was clean his suit material, but there's no way to be sure they didn't damage it at a microscopic level, and he only has partial visibility of his own suit. Those things could have stripped away insulation in the folds and creases on the back of his leg, and he'd never know. His suit needs to be inspected. It's a pressure vessel, a miniature spaceship in its own right, and not a Halloween costume worn just for laughs. In all likelihood, given the uncertainty around the damage, it won't be used again to avoid the possibility of a critical failure. That will mean someone else conducts the follow-up EVA and not him. Even though the second EVA is scheduled for Yúzé, it'll probably be Liz they select. They're going to want to make sure the United Kingdom has its chance at exploration before China. Oh, there will be some technical reason or perhaps a practical excuse, but Crash suspects this is how things will play out. And as EVA suits are custom-fit, she, Yúzé and Adeep are the only options for the B-suit. Pierre and Crash are too tall. The A-suit will be retired. His heart sinks.

When the Apollo 13 disaster unfolded, Gene Kranz famously said, "*Failure is not an option.*" But he knew that was a lie, or at best, a hope. By that point, the Apollo 13 mission was already a failure. The side of the service module had been blown out into space. They were losing oxygen and power. It didn't take a genius to realize there wouldn't be a lunar landing, and there was a very real possibility the astronauts would die in space. Getting them safely back to Earth was wishful thinking. Failure was already a reality. But Kranz understood human nature. He realized he needed to instill belief in his team. He needed them to explore every possibility and fight for every chance to save the crew of Apollo 13, but he also knew failure was *always* an option, right up until the capsule splashed down in the Pacific and the parachutes drifted lazily to the ocean. *'Failure is not an option,'* is NASA speak for, *'We need to minimize the possibility of anything else going wrong.'*

"Copy that," Crash replies to Yúzé after an awkward silence. Reluctantly, he turns his back on the red mounds and the distant forest and walks along the path beside the lake. His shoulders stoop. His head hangs. He watches the fall of his boots on the shimmering gravel path. His suit casts a sullen shadow on the track.

"Ah," a subdued Liz says. "Can you give us a view of the fields around you?"

"Yes, of course," he replies, realizing they know he feels disappointed. His professionalism kicks in, and he pans his helmet slowly, taking in the broad, curving vista as he walks back toward the meadow.

"Take-off is going to be the reverse of your landing," she says. "You'll need to start by the lake and run toward the forest, firing your LCMU thrusters to propel you against the rotation of the cylinder. You should feel the artificial sense of gravity lessen as you accelerate. Running will become bounding. You'll be airborne before you've countered the rotational speed of the cylinder. Once you've negated that, you'll be weightless again, but you'll need to gain altitude. You need to clear the forest. You don't want any of the bushes or trees at ground level colliding with you or they'll bring you down."

"Understood."

Here's yet another reason to recall him. Given the very real possibility of microscopic damage to his suit during his landing, his fall on the path and from the swarm, any more mechanical stress could cause a catastrophic failure. If he clips those trees, he'll probably be fine, but it might cause an already-weakened material in the pressure suit to rupture. Downplaying genuine risks means relying on dumb luck. It's the same perverse logic that said the Space Shuttle Columbia's already been hit by falling insulation during a dozen other launches, so a tiny bit of foam might knock off a few tiles, but the spacecraft will be fine. The public might have been surprised by the loss of the spacecraft during reentry, but more than one NASA engineer bowed their head in shame, knowing the truth. They'd become complacent. They'd normalized something that should have always horrified them. Losing heat shield tiles with every launch was never going to end well. It was just a matter of time before the wrong tile was broken.

Yúzé says, "Rather than returning to the meadow, stay on the path. It'll be your runway."

"Quite literally."

Crash begins reviewing his flight controls. He releases a slight burst of gas from each of the thrusters, making sure they're not clogged. With each touch on the controls, the backpack threatens to topple him. He's going to have to accelerate gently and smoothly rather than in a quick burst or he'll lose his footing.

"Okay, preflight is good."

"Ah, just hold," Liz says, surprising him.

Yúzé says, "We were just checking the footage from when you came down and spotted something interesting on the edge of the forest."

"Copy that."

"Um, Pierre's been reviewing your initial pass over this region. There's something he wants you to check before liftoff."

"Sure," a surprised Crash replies. "What is it?"

"Stairs."

"Stairs?"

"Approximately thirty yards ahead of you. Up on the slope. Pierre got a glimpse of them from the air and also when you stepped out of the meadow. It's only now we realize what we're looking at."

Crash walks forward along the gravel path. He's curious. "What do they look like?"

"Ah, they seem to be flush with the ground... Yes, we can see them from the airlock as well. They're not obvious, but they are there, just beyond the bushes."

From where he is, Crash can't see anything that looks like stairs. He continues on, feeling a sense of excitement replace the disappointment he has in himself. As stunning as the atrium is with its alien flora, this is a starship. At some point, there has to be a bridge and practical compartments, like storage, engineering and crew quarters. And like the others, he assumed these would be in the bow or the stern of the craft, but it makes sense to have them as a subterranean layer within the habitat so they benefit from the artificial gravity generated by the cylinder. That's where he's going to find his welcoming committee. They won't be lounging around in the park. They'll be sitting in the command center.

The path opens into a small clearing, circling a set of stairs leading down beneath the habitat. Although the entrance is level with the ground, it's surrounded by a black metal rim several inches in height, probably to prevent any water from running in. Crash stops at the top of the stairs and peers into the darkness.

Yúzé says, "It's your call, commander. We're ready to bring you back, but you're so close. It might be worth taking a quick look while we still have you onsite."

"Agreed."

For Crash, this is the irony of being the mission commander. In theory, he has the final say on mission activities. In practice, space exploration is a team sport with the coaches back at mission control. The quarterback might get all the glory, but send them out onto the football field alone, and it quickly becomes apparent they need everyone around them working together to succeed.

The stairs are arranged so they face in the direction of motion as the cylinder rotates. Walking down them is akin to drifting between steps in a public swimming pool. Each footstep unfolds in slow motion.

As he descends the stairs and draws level with the rocky ground, Crash takes one last look at the curve of the cylinder wrapping around him and the distant airlock at the center of the bow, knowing there's an electronic eye up there watching him disappear into the depths of an alien spacecraft.

The stairs are broad, but the height between each step is only roughly half its depth. On Earth, stairs maintain a roughly 50/50 ratio, while he would guess these are closer to 70/30. What that says about the physiology of the aliens, he's unsure, but for them, this would be natural.

Crash steps down. His gloved hand touches the sidewall of the stairwell. He drags his fingers along what looks like a smooth plastic surface, but not for balance as much as grounding him in the moment. As the shadows grow around him, he reaches for his controls, wanting to turn on the spotlights on the sides of his helmet. Before his gloved fingers flick the virtual button on his wrist pad computer, lights come on around him.

Over the earpiece in his Snoopy cap, Yúzé says, "First EVA elapsed time is three hours and fifty-seven minutes, and NASA astronaut Chris Williams is descending into the basement layer of the alien habitat."

Crash stands at the bottom of the stairs. The ceiling glows, casting a warm, diffuse light over him not unlike that of the alien sun, but it's limited, only illuminating roughly twenty feet before him. He's reached a T-junction, allowing him to go in three different directions. To his left and right, a corridor runs the length of the habitat. Ahead, a narrow side corridor curves with the shape of the cylinder itself, disappearing from sight as the floor rises.

"We're getting inter—"

"Say again," he says, turning and looking up at the opening at the top of the stairs.

"Interference... Video dropping..."

"Okay," Crash replies. "I'm setting up the second repeater station."

He removes the remaining camera from his leg pocket and extends the aerial. Fiddling with tape while wearing gloves is frustrating. Even with a loose tab that's designed to be peeled away, he struggles to expose the adhesive strip on the underside of the unit. Crash fixes the repeater to the side of the stairway, nestling it up against the wall at waist height with the camera pointing down the curved corridor ahead of him. It's a limited view. He's tempted to reposition the camera longways, but he's more concerned about the signal getting through than the view being provided to the *Odyssey*.

"Better?"

"Yes. But your transmission still wavers in time with the rotation of the craft. When you're close, we get a clear signal. As you rotate away, the image drops out. Audio is fine. It's the video we lose."

"Understood," he replies, realizing they're probably going to be blind to him once he moves out of the line of sight. His suit will record any interactions, but they won't see them until he returns to the *Odyssey*. "I'm not going to venture too far from the stairs. I'll get a quick feel for the layout."

He bends down. His helmet scrapes along the low ceiling.

"Well, they're short."

He crouches as he walks along the curved corridor, feeling as though he's always at the bottom of the cylinder. He's walking, but he's going nowhere, or at least that's how it feels.

"There are compartments... I'm seeing hatches at regular intervals... no obvious way to open them, but they're consistent... Each one is roughly ten feet wide... then the pattern repeats... ah, there are symbols on the walls... they, too, repeat, slowly differing from each other... reminds me of walking through a hotel in Vegas or a corridor on a cruise liner... could these rooms be used for accommodation?"

"...zxyst again... not getting clean... audio good."

"Your audio is lousy," he replies.

As Crash continues along the corridor, hunched over and guiding himself with his hands out, touching the walls, the overhead lights continue to come on around him, surrounding him with warm light even though beyond their reach lies only darkness. He stops, looking back at the intersection. Already, the stairs have curled out of view. The warmth of the alien sunlight from above still marks their presence with a dull glow on the floor, giving him a point of reference.

With each step, the floor seems to rise to greet his boots. He reaches another intersection. Yet another corridor crosses his path, running the length of the cylinder from his left to right. If anything, these parallel corridors seem better for exploring as they don't disappear with the curl of the cylinder.

"I should probably head back," he says. "It would be easy to get lost down here. Given the size of the cylinder, it could take days to map out the interior."

He waits. There's no reply, not even the crackle of an attempt at a response. Curiosity compels him to wander on. Crash wants his time with the alien cylinder to be useful. He wants to gather meaningful data for those back on Earth. He decides to check out the far side of the corridor before turning back.

"Ah, there's glass up ahead. Just to one side. I thought it was a mirror, but as the lights come on, I can see inside one of the compartments... It's different... ceiling-to-floor glass... I can—"

He's interrupted mid-sentence. "Your audio is clean. Video is spotty... We can only talk when you're on our side of the cylzind grhaxed ornag..."

"Copy that," he replies, realizing they've got to time their messages to him. Knowing they can hear him and at least get some video, he moves up to the glass. The light from the corridor spills inside, but all he can see is the slick floor. Crash turns on his spotlights. Two brilliant white beams illuminate the darkness.

"Ah," he mumbles. "I think I've found the crew... Can you see this? Please tell me you can see this?"

Crash presses his gloved hand against the glass. His visor knocks against the window as he peers into the shadows. His heart races. Dark blobs hang from the ceiling within what looks like a laboratory. They're set at regular intervals, being spaced parallel to the corridor as well as stretching back into the darkness.

Looking further along the glass wall, he sees an opening. The thick window curves as it reaches both the floor and ceiling, opening out into an entrance easily fifteen feet wide. It's considerably broader than the hatchways and doors he passed earlier, making him think this is either to allow easy access for heavy equipment or because it's a thoroughfare and needs to allow room for aliens to pass next to each other as they enter and exit the lab.

"Stay with me," he says, even though such a notion is meaningless. He's on his own and isolated from his spacecraft.

Although the corridor is lit up around him, there are no lights within the laboratory. Crash steps into the broad room. As the floor curves with the cylinder, he can't see the far side, but what he can see extends for as far as his lights will reach.

Teardrop-shaped sacks extend from metal tubes crisscrossing the ceiling. They're organic rather than mechanical, being semi-transparent and roughly the size of one of the large yoga balls he's seen at the gym back in Houston. He doesn't say that aloud, as to his mind, it would sound like a silly comparison, but that's the only thing he can equate in terms of size. As the lights on his helmet pass over the skin of the closest sac, a creature squirms within, reacting to the glare. A tail runs over the inside surface, deforming the teardrop. Murky fluid swirls within.

Crash whispers. "I've seen this movie before... Pretty sure I know how it ends..."

He's joking. It's gallows humor, but it helps him suppress the rising sense of panic seizing his mind. His throat constricts. His breathing is shallow. Against his better judgment, he leans in close to one of the sacs, bringing his glass visor to within a few inches of the rubbery surface. Goo oozes over the skin, forming a mucus that pools at the bottom of the blob. Crash kneels, knowing his helmet camera is catching this in high-resolution detail. Beneath each sac, there's a floor drain. Secretions drip like blobs of honey. The cadence is irregular.

From where he is, his lights catch the underside of at least four pods directly in front of him and several on either side. They all drip at different rates.

Quietly, he says, "I'm really hating that sixteen-minute communication delay with Houston… I could really do with some advice right about now."

Liz replies, but her voice is garbled. Crash doesn't ask for clarification. The tone of her words was calm and measured. He interprets her mumbling to mean no sudden movements. The fixtures and anchor points on the floor of the alien lab glisten beneath his spotlights. Light reflects off the shiny chrome surfaces.

Crash pushes off his knee and steps to one side. His spotlights catch the edge of dozens of alien pods reaching back into the darkness. There's no end in sight. Several of the teardrops react to the light. Claws and boney tails appear, rubbing against the thick, leathery skin. The creatures within are agitated. As soon as their limbs are withdrawn, they disappear into the haze of fluids circulating inside the various eggs.

He backs up, steps sideways and examines another row of artificial wombs descending as swollen blobs from metallic apertures on the ceiling. A robotic worker moves on tracks, hanging upside down. It ignores him, focusing on the unborn aliens squirming in their sacks. Dim lights glow and shimmer on the robot. It's no bigger than a bat and, like the alien pods, seems content being upside down. Tiny probes extend from the mechanical body, pressing against the skin of one of the eggs. Immediately, the writhing within settles. A tail curls at the bottom of the teardrop sac, wrapping around the inside of the alien egg.

"There are hundreds of them," he whispers, struggling to swallow the lump in his throat. "Thousands."

Over his headset, he hears Yúzé. "—back! Pull back! Return to the *Odyssey*."

"Yeah," he replies. "That seems like a *really* good idea."

Uncertainty

Molly gets up from her seat and crouches, wanting to stay inconspicuous as she creeps forward and picks up a side plate. She uses silver tongs to pick up two neatly cut cucumber sandwiches and retreats to her seat on the curved inside of the Oval Office.

Chief of Staff Susan Dosela glares sideways at her for a moment and then takes one of the sandwiches from her plate, just as Molly thought she would.

Roughly fifty sandwiches sit on a polished chrome cart that's been pushed to one side within the Oval Office. The President likes cucumber on rye. She told everyone present to help themselves after she took three of the triangular sandwiches, but no one else got out of their seats. Molly is hungry. She's not starving, but she's hungry and she's not shy, even though she was a little distracting.

A large screen has been rolled into the Oval Office and positioned in front of the fireplace. Two broad couches face each other, forcing the military officers and scientists seated there to twist sideways to see the imagery coming in from the *Odyssey*.

Molly and the chief of staff are seated on the side of the curved room beside the door leading to the reception area and corridor. Their chairs are set at an angle to the screen. And they're uncomfortable—probably by design. Regardless of who's in the office, the US President is *always* busy and *always* running on a tight schedule. Seats need only serve for minutes, not hours. Several other dignitaries are seated in similar seats on the far side of the Oval Office, over by the French windows and the door leading to the Rose Garden. At least two of them are from NASA.

The President is seated behind the Resolute Desk with a plate of barely-touched cucumber sandwiches and a can of Diet Coke sitting on a coaster.

To her left, Senate Majority Leader Jill McMillan sits on a plush office chair rolled in from reception. To the President's right, Speaker of the House, Representative Tom Emmet, sits on a similar chair. Being Republicans, McMillan and Emmet have stonewalled most of the President's economic initiatives, labeling her a lame duck. When it comes to First Contact, the hostility has ceased, on the surface, at least, with both parties agreeing to a bipartisan approach to the arrival of extraterrestrials. That the President has given them equal billing with her in the Oval Office is telling. She's trying to stage manage them. Whether they'll allow that or not is uncertain. Molly has her doubts. For now, they seem to be brooding. Both of them have embossed folders with briefing notes that they've placed on the floor beside their chairs. As the two of them are within reach of the Resolute Desk, that shows some respect for the President, as they could have reached out and put the folders she gave them on the corner of the largely empty desk.

"*Well, they're short,*" astronaut Chris '*Crash*' Williams says from a distance of a hundred million miles. The view on the screen twists sideways as the astronaut turns his head, crouching as he moves within the narrow interior of the alien spacecraft. His helmet bumps into the low ceiling. Lights come on around him, but there's no light source as such. The walls are illuminated, but it is as if they're glowing from within.

Molly's still reeling from what she saw above the surface. The dark confines beneath the cylinder are a strange contrast to the exotic life flourishing within the habitat. Like all of those present, she's been held spellbound by both the similarities and differences compared to Earth. Seeing the distant curve of the landscape within the cylinder, including rivers and forests, has been exhilarating to behold. Even though the alien plants have stems and leaves, their colors are muted and darker than anything she's ever seen on Earth. Several of them looked purple, which was unsettling. The alien world is set under a warm, golden sun set like a rod in the sky. It's as though there's a gigantic fluorescent tube floating in the middle of the cylinder. Beneath the surface, though, sterile corridors and sealed compartments wrap around the interior of the massive cylinder. If nature rules above, below is the domain of machines.

"*I'm seeing hatches at regular intervals...*"

In contrast to the confusion of life within the vast, open cylinder, there's order and design to the interior of the spacecraft. The habitat appeared chaotic. The underworld has been planned with meticulous care, but where is everyone?

"*...the pattern repeats... ah, there are symbols on the walls... they too repeat, slowly differing from each other...*"

The President leans forward on the Resolute Desk. She sets her elbows on the polished oak surface. Her chin rests against her hands as she watches intently. The video drops in and out. Static appears. The images jump, giving the impression the astronaut is moving with a staccato-like rhythm, breaking up and then reconnecting further along the corridor.

"*...reminds me of walking through a hotel in Vegas...*"

The time delay between the *Odyssey* and mission control in Houston is over eight minutes. NASA has built in another thirty-second delay so they can cut the public feed in the event of a disaster. Watching an astronaut being eaten alive by a xenomorph isn't good for morale. They paused the video when the swarm descended on the astronaut and only reconnected once it was clear he was safe. The feed to the White House, though, is raw. Those in the Oval Office get to see the footage in real time and without any interruptions.

Chief of Staff Dosela puts her crust on Molly's plate, placing it next to Molly's half-chewed crust. They smile at what they know is long-past defiance of their moms to eat their crusts. Neither has curly hair, so perhaps there's some truth to the myth. Maybe not. Molly leans forward and slips the plate onto the floor beneath her chair.

The door next to them opens. The President's personal assistant enters with a manila folder. She walks over to the Resolute Desk and places a single sheet of paper in front of the President, then turns and leaves as quietly as she came. The President looks at the paper briefly before turning it over and sliding it to one side. Whatever's in that memo, it can wait. Nuclear war could be erupting between India and Pakistan, and it would still come in second place to the exploration of an alien spacecraft. The implications of the extraterrestrial presence within the solar system are vast, and not just for humanity but for all of life on the planet. Everyone wants to know what their intentions are.

"...*could take days to map out the interior...*"

For Molly, that's a key point.

The public expects First Contact to be a singular event, like shaking hands with a boyfriend's parents for the first time. The door to their home opens, and there they are, warm and smiling. First Contact, though, is torturously slow. It's really no surprise, though. Over the decades, the public has been spoon-fed astonishing scientific accomplishments as though they're picking up a candy bar from the tray at the bottom of a vending machine. Gravitational waves are detected from colliding supermassive black holes and it makes barely a splash in the news. That a team of hundreds of astrophysicists and engineers have spent decades collating precise measurements from thousands of pulsars at a distance of untold light years is lost on the public.

Modern life is a pop tart. If something takes more than thirty seconds in the toaster, it's a waste of time and people move on. The public sees stunning images from the James Webb Space Telescope, but what they don't see is a quarter of a century from concept to deployment. They'll never know how many times the project was redefined, redesigned and resting on the chopping block for cancellation. They'll never understand the extreme precision of the main camera, which is designed to operate at almost -400F, cold enough for oxygen and nitrogen to freeze solid. The resolution of the JWST is such that it could spot a single bee on the Moon from Earth. Its '*bees,*' though, aren't in hives; they're exoplanets and distant galaxies.

Molly knows she's guilty of indifference, too. Where she sees pretty pictures of Saturn's rings or a distant nebula, astrophysicists see tantalizing clues about the origin and evolution of the universe. When the astronaut says it will take "*days to map out the interior,*" even that would simply mark the beginning of his exploration. Although everyone is glued to their TV sets, smartphones or laptop screens, watching progress within the alien spacecraft with a sense of fascination, the science behind First Contact will take weeks, months, years, and perhaps even decades to unfold in the form of peer-reviewed research papers.

Molly watches the shapes and shadows on the edge of the astronaut's vision. As the light fades on the fringes of the video, it feels as though something is alive down there. Something's watching him. It's difficult to shake the idea of some monster lurking in the dark, about to leap out and grab him. Molly wonders how fast his heart is beating. She would have *never* gone down those stairs.

One of the other astronauts says, "*Your audio is clean. Video is spotty.*"

Up until this point, the basement of the cylinder has appeared entirely mechanical, which is a stark contrast to the habitat, but there's something in the distance that looks hazy and indistinct, blurring with the shadows.

Apart from the curve of the floor, the corridor could be that of a darkened warship. Although the astronaut described it as a hotel in Vegas or a cruise liner, it reminds her of the stark interior of a US Navy ship. As her father is a senator, Molly grew up touring ships that pulled into port for Fourth of July celebrations. For a teenage girl obsessed with K-pop bands from South Korea and beauty tips on TikTok, naval tours were torture. Walking down endless, seemingly identical corridors to inspect the engine room or visit the bridge was tedious. Sailors would walk past in uniform. And uniform was the right term. The differences between them were slight, if they existed at all. For someone like Molly, who spent hours with different eyeliners to get a colorful, blended cut crease before going out on a Friday night, such monotony dulled the senses. Molly feels the same way now, having seen the astronaut walking through the narrow corridors of the alien spacecraft. It's functional at the expense of any beauty or originality. And yet these aliens value the nature of their home world, having dedicated the bulk of their spacecraft to preserving their habitat.

Now, though, there's a distinct change. To one side, there's slick glass, to the other, the wall appears carved and ornate.

The video breaks up into chunks. The images stutter, struggling to move forward in time with Chris '*Crash*' Williams. His gloved hand reaches for a dark, glossy surface. It's glass, but the window reflects his thick, rubber fingertips back at him like a mirror. The shapes beyond are curved and organic.

"What is that?" the President asks, getting up from the Resolute Desk and walking toward the screen. Even the audio is garbled and choppy. She walks forward. It's as though her presence alone commands obedience, but the video stream from the alien spacecraft ignores the President's authority. Images stutter and shake.

One of the astronauts watching from the safety of the *Odyssey* is a woman. She speaks, but her words fail to reach Crash Williams.

Nobody dares breathe for fear of disrupting the broadcast.

"*We can only talk when you're on our side... of the cylzind grhaxed ornag...*"

Molly's heart races. Her palms go sweaty. She wipes them on her skirt. She fears for the astronaut.

"*Copy that.*"

There's no way he understood what that woman was saying. He's keeping both himself, the crew of the *Odyssey* and several billion people down here on Earth calm by remaining professional.

Although the corridor within the alien spacecraft is illuminated, the interior of the adjacent glass room remains dark. The circular outline of a white helmet reflects off the glossy surface. His eyes stare back at both him and them. As Crash moves closer, the lens on the camera struggles to identify what it should focus on. The astronaut's face blurs and then comes back into view. Beyond the glass, dark elongated teardrops hang from the ceiling, forming row upon row in the laboratory.

"Jesus," the President says, coming to a halt just a few feet from the screen.

"*Ah,*" the astronaut mumbles as his video cuts in and out. "*I think I've found the crew... Can you see this? Please tell me you can see this?*"

He walks sideways, edging his way along the glass, not allowing the camera angle to change, keeping the distended blobs in sight. He reaches an opening. A gloved hand grips the edge of the glass as he steps in front of a laboratory. The floor curves away on either side of him, as does the ceiling.

"*Stay with me.*"

He's going to die in there, and he knows it, or he fears that, and yet still he continues on. He has no regard for his own self-preservation. Molly needs to pee. She really needs to pee. Her bladder is trying to convince her that now is the time to leave the room, but she can't take her eyes off the screen.

Although the corridor is lit up around the astronaut, there are no lights within the laboratory itself. Molly barely breathes as the astronaut steps into the broad room.

Teardrop-shaped sacs hang from tubes running along the ceiling. They're semi-transparent and roughly the size of the sandwich cart off to Molly's right. The astronaut moves his head slowly, allowing his camera to take in all the detail, but their view on Earth is jagged and jumping, with images cutting in and out.

"What was that?" the President asks. "Can you back it up and zoom in?"

"Ah," the NASA Liaison Officer sitting beside the NASA Administrator on the far side of the room looks down at the laptop perched on his knees, saying, "I can replay sections for you on my computer, but that's a live stream. There's no way of pausing or rewinding it."

He points at his screen, beckoning the President over, but she remains transfixed by the images before her, wanting to see what comes next.

The astronaut leans in close to one of the blobs. Within the skin of the closest sac, an alien squirms, reacting to the piercing bright light. A tail runs over the inside surface, brushing against the leathery hide and deforming the teardrop. Murky fluid swirls within.

The astronaut whispers. *"I've seen this movie before... Pretty sure I know how it ends..."*

"Get him out of there," the President snaps.

"This is eight minutes old," the NASA officer says. "He should be out of there already."

Should is indistinct, but it captures the sense of helplessness they all feel. For all anyone knows, Crash *could* already be dead. His professionalism is infuriating. Frustrating. Like the President, Molly wants to shout at him, *"Run!"* Instead of retreating, he steps further into the laboratory. He kneels and bends forward, resting an outstretched gloved hand on the floor and allowing his camera to view the underside of the alien sacs. Goo drips into drains set into indentations in the floor. He shifts his head around low to the ground, changing the point at which both his spotlights and the camera are set and giving them a sense of depth. The view is skewed horribly to one side, leaning on an angle that makes it all the more terrifying.

The alien egg sacs droop close to the floor, but dozens of them are visible, stretching back into the shadows. They've been arranged in rows. Mechanical workers hang from the ceiling. They glide along tracks, tending to the brood.

From beside Molly, the chief of staff whispers, "It's a nursery."

Under her breath, Molly replies, "There's going to be a *lot* of them when they hatch."

"Not good."

The color fades to black and white as the astronaut pushes off his knee, getting back to his feet.

"Run," Molly whispers.

"No shit," the chief of staff replies under her breath. If anyone hears them, they don't react. All eyes are on the screen.

Crash Williams is methodical. Even though his footage is constantly breaking up, often sending only fragments of images in different corners of the screen or pixelated views of the amber sacs, he remains calm. He lines himself up between the alien eggs, and, for a moment, Molly worries he's going to push down the aisle between them, bumping against them to find the end of the room, but he sways, allowing his camera to catch the depth. Egg sacs react to the glare. Given these creatures are used to the soft, golden rays of their dwarf star, the cold, blue light is probably blinding even to the unborn. Aliens wriggle in their teardrop sacs. Claws and boney tails appear, rubbing against the thick, leathery skin. The creatures are agitated.

Molly wants to scream at him. The muscles in her arms go taut. She clenches her fists, holding them in her lap. Her fingernails dig into her palms, but she barely notices.

Spindly limbs brush against the amber skin of the sacs before disappearing into the hazy amniotic fluid within the teardrop eggs. A tail curls around the bottom of the nearest sac, wrapping around the inside of the egg, but the creature seems to settle. Is this normal for them? Is this akin to a lizard laying eggs and leaving them to gestate? Or is this some artificial replacement for an internal womb?

"*There are hundreds of them,*" the astronaut whispers. "*Thousands.*"

A male voice with a distinctly Chinese accent says, "*Crash. We want you to come back to the Odyssey. We've seen enough. Come back. Pull back. Return to the Odyssey. Do you copy? Over?*"

"*Yeah,*" Crash replies in barely a whisper. "*That seems like a really good idea.*"

He backs up, never taking his eyes off the sacs dripping within the laboratory. Once he's out in the corridor, he's surrounded by light again, glowing from the walls, but he never turns around. Instead, he feels his way back, watching as the doorway to the lab fades into the shadows. The view is skewed on an angle as he crouches in the low headspace. His helmet scrapes along the ceiling, causing an eerie noise to echo along with his heavy breathing. He mumbles to himself, but it's impossible to make out what he's saying.

On crossing the intersection of two corridors, he bumps into the corner and has to step sideways to continue, but he refuses to turn and look where he's going—and Molly is with him on that decision. If death is going to launch itself out of the darkness, better to see it coming in those last few fractions of a second.

Warm light spills down from above. He must have reached the stairs as the light around him is brighter than what's coming from the walls and ceiling alone. Finally, he turns. Molly never thought something as mundane as a staircase could bring such relief. The astronaut sits on one of the stairs, facing the darkness down the corridor. His knees are visible, as are his trembling gloved hands. He's talking to the crew on the *Odyssey*, but no one in the Oval Office is listening. The President has circled back to the Resolute Desk.

Senate Majority Leader Jill McMillan says, "Well, I've seen enough."

Speaker of the House, Representative Tim Emmet, says, "We need to start thinking about our next steps."

The President looks worried. Her hands are shaking. She hides the way her body is reacting by standing behind her chair and gripping the seat back. The generals and admirals stare at her, wanting to hear from her. She seems to react to the comments of the Senate Majority Leader and the Speaker of the House.

"*Icarus?*" she asks those present in the Oval Office.

General Mitchell Johnson sits upright on the edge of one of the couches, saying, "This is what it was built for, ma'am."

Icarus

"And the team? My team?" NASA director Angela Summers asks.

The President says, "Have them hold where they are."

"You can't leave them in there!"

The President looks at the NASA liaison officer sitting next to the director. He taps on his keyboard, passing instructions along to Houston, saying, "Yes, ma'am."

Summers looks horrified at being sidelined. She shifts in her seat, moving forward and perching herself on the edge of the cushion. The NASA director is on the verge of getting to her feet as she asks, "You're serious? You want to use *Icarus*?"

The NASA director is over by the windows overlooking the Rose Garden, leaving her physically off to one side and on the edge of the discussion unfolding between the President and her military advisors. The director's been deliberately sidelined. Molly is hit with a rush of anxiety. Not only does she want to understand *Icarus*, she feels the frustration of the director.

"We need to reason this through," the President says, avoiding a direct answer to the director's concern.

Molly wants to raise her hand and ask about *Icarus*, but that would be dumb. She's not in grade school. Chief of Staff Dosela seems to sense Molly's concern. She raises her hand slightly from her lap. Her fingers drift above Molly's skirt, spreading wide and signaling she should stay quiet. She returns her hands to her lap, but Molly notices she clutches her fingers. She, too, isn't happy about the NASA director being kept on the bench, but it seems she wants to hear the discussion unfold without any interruptions. Whether that's out of respect for the President or mere curiosity is impossible to tell. It takes all of Molly's might to remain seated and quiet. She has no idea what *Icarus* actually is, but the context isn't encouraging. It's something other than the *Odyssey* itself.

Senate Majority Leader McMillan says, "We have to be decisive. Now is not the time for doubts or uncertainty."

Molly is aghast. There's nothing but uncertainty in the images and audio they've received. Making a hasty decision might satisfy McMillan's ego, but it lacks clarity.

The Speaker of the House says, "We need to be strong. We need to make the tough calls."

What an utter bastard, Molly thinks. Whether the President realizes it or not, McMillan and Emmet are goading her, pushing her toward what they want, but it's not their decision to make. It's hers. She's the President.

General Mitchell Johnson agrees with them, saying, "We have a unique opportunity to deploy *Icarus*. Right here. Right now. We may *never* get such an opportunity again."

The President's eyes narrow. It's impossible to tell what she's thinking. She leans forward on the chair back, pushing it against the Resolute Desk. That she won't sit down is telling. Everyone else is seated. Molly doesn't think it's a power move so much as drawing a point of distinction. For the President, this is more than a mere discussion. Regardless of what she decides, she's about to change the future of humanity in a profound way, either by action or inaction. Molly can see the weight of this decision affects her deeply.

Admiral Dönmeyen says, "Ma'am, this is a political decision. We're the wrong ones to advise you. We only see military options. It's all we ever see."

The President nods in agreement. She purses her lips but doesn't speak.

NASA director Summers says, "First Contact is peaceful. We need to focus on that and not react out of fear."

Senator McMillan replies to her, saying, "The United States has always relied on peace through strength. There is no other way to be at peace."

The Speaker of the House agrees with her, saying, "Peace never comes from a weak hand."

"I can't believe we're having this discussion," Summers replies.

General Johnson says, "The military is politics by force, but this is different. We're not talking about policy decisions here. We face an existential threat."

"We've faced them before," US Air Force General Helen Solarim says. "The Cold War. The proliferation of bioweapons. The expansion of China. The breakup of Russia. But none of them have ever justified a first strike."

"First strike?" NASA director Summers says, getting to her feet and raising her voice in outrage. "This is First Contact! Not war!"

"Angela, please," the President says, holding out her hand and gesturing for her to return to her seat.

Democratic Senator McCluskey seems to be knowledgeable of *Icarus* as he says, "We need to weigh our decision carefully. We have a responsibility not just to our country or even humanity as a whole but to future generations. We have to make the right call."

"You want to kill them?" Summers asks.

"Neutralize," McMillan says.

Summers counters with, "Murder."

"Self-defense," the Speaker of the House says.

Chief of Staff Dosela rests her hand on Molly's knee. And it's needed. Molly's on the verge of jumping up and confronting what she sees as utter madness. She doesn't care who these people are. She clenches her jaw, gritting her teeth.

"Easy," the chief of staff whispers, leaning close to her ear and following up with, "Listen."

Listen?

Molly is furious. She's with Summers. This is outrageous. How can they even consider killing the aliens? They've done nothing wrong. And even if they had, how is such a heavy response warranted? What the hell is *Icarus*?

Molly sighs. As much as she doesn't want to admit it, Sue Dosela is right. She needs to listen and understand rather than react. And who's going to listen to Molly if she calls out in anger? No one. She'll be marched out of the room if she reacts. And then what? Nothing. She'll be excluded from the debate. She takes a deep breath, sitting bolt upright on her chair.

Sue Dosela taps her hand on Molly's thigh a few times before withdrawing her fingers. It's patronizing. And it's at that moment that Molly realizes why the chief of staff has kept her around.

Molly's useful.

Protocol and precedence restrict what the chief of staff can say and do, not to mention her friendship with the President from days gone by. Sue Dosela's joked about Molly being invisible, but it's more than that. Molly is a flexible tool. She's able to do things the chief of staff can't. She can speak when the chief needs to remain silent. Sue Dosela must see something of herself in Molly and realizes she can be useful at the right time. In a game of chess, pawns are more than mere sacrifices to far more powerful pieces. They can become queens in their own right. Molly doesn't feel used so much as on standby. Sue Dosela hasn't kept her around because she's the daughter of a US senator or helpful as a gopher. After seeing the way Molly handled the initial briefing with the President on her first day, the chief of staff has been preparing her for some other eventuality, probably one she can't even articulate for herself at the moment. Molly is the spare twenty dollar bill scrunched up at the back of her purse. For her part, Molly realizes she has to temper her indignation. Decisions made in anger are destined for regret. She pushes her heels against the wooden floor running around the edge of the room, biding her time.

"Let's not get ahead of ourselves," the President says. "We have a contingency—that's all. We need to discuss the ethics and morality of what happens next."

"They're helpless," the NASA director says.

"For now," General Johnson counters. "And then it's our turn. Then we're helpless. Is that what you want?"

"Let's play this out," the President says, holding her hands out and appealing for reason from all of those present in the Oval Office. "What are the various scenarios? What are the possibilities before us? War? Or peace?"

Aging Democratic Senator McCluskey says, "We have no idea about their intent."

"But we do," Summers counters. "The majority of their spacecraft is dedicated to life-support. It's not a warship. They intend to use *their* habitat, not ours. And the pressure difference, chemical composition and radiation profile suggest Earth is not a good match for them. They might be able to survive at Everest base camp, but they're not going to Hawaii without an environment suit. For them, it would be like dropping one of us in Death Valley at the height of summer."

The President says, "So they're not here to invade us or to conqueror us?"

"No."

"That's an awfully big assumption," the Speaker of the House says. "You say it's not a warship. We don't know what an alien warship looks like. Oh, but the habitat in that cylinder appears friendly. Hell, the Nimitz is a nuclear-powered aircraft carrier, and it has goddamn pinball machines! They play movies in the hangar, golf off the flight deck, and dive into the ocean from the aircraft elevator leading to the mid-deck. My wife, Julie, did yoga there during our last inspection. She said the women start their day stretching on the massive flight deck, watching the sun rise over the horizon. Sounds more like a cruise liner than a warship. It's not until bullets start flying that the real intent unfolds."

Summers says, "We've seen nothing that shows hostile intent."

"We've seen nothing at all," Senator McMillan counters, "because they're still growing in their pods. I think it's fair to say they settled at that Lagrange point a hundred million miles from Earth because they didn't think we'd be able to reach them out there."

"And that worries me," the Speaker of the House says.

"Why?" the President asks.

"It's a staging post. When we deploy our troops, we do the same thing. Sit off in the distance and prepare. Don't move in until we're ready."

Summers objects, saying, "They're not—" But she's cut off by Admiral Dönmeyen.

"The real problem is one of asymmetry."

"Explain," the President says.

"When the French and the English fought the Napoleonic wars, there was symmetry between them. They both had galleons on the high seas. They both had muskets and cannons and massive armies. Victory took decades to unfold and hinged on strategy."

The President nods. Although the admiral is longwinded, it seems his waffle is giving her some breathing space from the animosity of McMillan and Emmet.

"When the British shifted their focus to China, Asia and Australia, there was asymmetry."

"Because the Aborigines didn't have muskets," the President says, following his point.

"Exactly. Shields and spears were no match for muskets. Raiding parties were no match for disciplined troops. There was only ever going to be one outcome."

"And you think?" the President asks.

"We face a similar asymmetry. We don't know what weapons they have, but we know we can't match them."

Summers interjects with, "We don't know that they have *any* weapons at all."

"It would be naive to assume they didn't. No one would traverse the universe unarmed."

"We went to the Moon without muskets," she counters. "We came in peace. It was a stated goal of the Apollo program."

Senator McMillan says, "Intentions alone are meaningless. It's what follows that worries me. The pilgrims *came in peace*. Captain James Cook explored the Pacific *in peace*. Amerigo Vespucci gave us America as a name. He mapped the coastline of South America *in peace*. What followed, though, in all these regions, could hardly be described as peaceful."

The President says, "I agree with Summers. I think they're unarmed. For now, at least. They're certainly vulnerable. What right do we have to act against them?"

McMillan says, "This is our world, not theirs. We have the right to protect ourselves—to defend ourselves."

"But are we under attack?" Summers says.

"No," the President says. And for the first time since the astronaut ventured into the alien laboratory, Molly takes a deep breath. Her muscles relax. The President may be considering her options, but she's not been swayed by the arguments that are being put forward.

"Not yet," General Johnson says. He purses his lips for a moment, weighing his next comment carefully. "And since we're at peace, we should bring all our ships into port, let's say, Pearl Harbor."

The President isn't impressed with his snide comment, but she lets it slide. Her eyes, though, narrow.

"Ma'am," Admiral Dönmeyen says in a tone of voice that's trying to negate the tension in the room. "We can't lose sight of the real problem: asymmetry. At the moment, right now, we hold the upper hand with *Icarus*. That won't be the case tomorrow or next week. Then, we will be left clutching bows and arrows in the face of muskets and cannons."

"We have nothing to fear," Summers says, still seated on the far side of the Oval Office but sitting so far forward it's surprising she hasn't fallen off the edge of her cushion.

Senator McMillan says, "There's a lot of unknowns and uncertainty, but one thing we do know for sure is we need to be wary of them. To ignore that is a mistake. Saying we shouldn't is akin to saying a child shouldn't be wary of a busy road or a deep lake. There's danger there."

"What's the danger here?" Summers asks. "What is it you're afraid of?"

"Nothing. This isn't about fear. Danger need not be malicious. No one goes swimming with the intention of drowning, and yet people do drown. We have to recognize the inherent risk. We can't live in a fairy tale pretending there's no danger in First Contact."

General Johnson simplifies the discussion. "We have a contingency. We have *Icarus*. Now, we have a choice. We use it, or we lose it. That's it. That's the decision before us. Those are the only two options available to us. Because we will not have this opportunity again."

The President sighs.

Molly desperately wants to ask about *Icarus*. What the hell is it? Sue Dosela seems to sense that. She keeps her arm on her thigh but raises her hand slightly, signaling with her fingers for Molly to remain quiet and let the conversation continue to unfold.

The NASA director says, "We do not have the right to interfere with them and their development in those pods."

Senator McMillan says, "And yet we've entered their spaceship—uninvited."

"Think of what we could learn from their spacecraft," Admiral Dönmeyen says. "They've mastered fusion. They can fly between stars. Our scientists could reverse engineer their metallurgy. We could close the gap within decades, long before any follow-up craft arrives in our system. We could negate the asymmetry between us."

"Is this who we are?" the NASA director asks, although, from the look of disgust on the President's face, it seems she's also repulsed by the admiral's suggestion. "On Earth, we have cooperation between nations. Outside of that, there are rogue nations. Lawless. Is that who we are? Are we going to be the North Koreans of this region of space? If their intentions are peaceful, as I suspect they are, we're committing an act of war."

Senator McMillan says, "We cannot afford the luxury of debate when faced with the possibility of annihilation. The consequences of getting this wrong are too damn high."

The Speaker of the House has been quiet for the last few minutes, making notes in his folder, but he speaks up in support of Senator McMillan. "Why do you wear a seatbelt in a car? My wife finds them annoying as hell because of the way the belt runs across her chest, but still, she wears one. Why? Because the risk of a life-threatening injury in an accident is too great. And yet, if you're like us, you've probably *never* actually needed your seatbelt. And yet still you'll wear it. Why? Because the severity of the risk justifies the act."

"You cannot justify murdering them," the NASA director says.

The senator counters with, "If a Russian submarine surfaced in New York Harbor armed with nuclear weapons, there wouldn't be any debate about what to do. How is this any different? We cannot throw our hands up and surrender."

"No one is surrendering to anyone," the President says, gripping the chair back with white knuckles. That she hasn't made a decision worries Molly. The President is caught in indecision by the unknown—the unknowable future. What she needs is a crystal ball.

US Air Force General Helen Solarim seems to arrive at a similar conclusion. She says, "The question here is, who's right? For what it's worth, Madame President, the problem here is that both sides of this debate are correct, from their perspective, based on their assumptions. The problem is we don't know whose assumptions hold true."

The President nods in agreement with her point.

"And we won't know until it is too late," General Johnson says.

"What will it do?" the President asks, although Molly gets the impression the President knows precisely what *Icarus* will do. It seems she wants to remind those present of the consequences of this act.

"It's a neutron bomb," General Johnson says. "The actual blast radius is small. It won't damage their ship, but it will sterilize it. The radiation will kill all organic life within about fifty miles of the point of detonation."

"The morality of this worries me," the President says.

Senator McMillan says, "We have a duty of care to future generations. We're morally obliged to protect them, not the aliens."

"But we don't know their intentions," the NASA director says, pointing at the ceiling. "We need to be certain."

"In World War Two, we didn't build the bomb because we were certain. We built the bomb because we were uncertain—because we couldn't wait for the Nazis or the Japanese or even the Soviets to get the bomb first. We acted to protect ourselves and our way of life."

"But this is different," the director says. "We're not at war."

"Yet," the Speaker of the House says. "Do we have to wait for Pearl Harbor? Or can we attack the aircraft carriers while they're sailing across the Pacific?"

The NASA director shakes her head. "This is madness."

"Do we need a smoking gun?" the senator asks. "Or is pulling a gun on us enough."

"But they haven't—"

"Damn right, they haven't," the senator says, cutting her off in righteous indignation. "That's the goddamn problem! We've reached out with an olive branch, and they've ignored us. They could have responded to our hails for months now, but they chose not to. They could talk to our scientists, but they don't. They're silent. That's deliberate. That's *their* strategy for First Contact. Tell me, director—how is that not hostile intent?"

Molly swallows the lump rising in her throat.

"Do they know?" the President asks, pointing at the screen and changing the subject. She's leaning on the chair back, looking at the astronaut.

Chris '*Crash*' Williams is still sitting on the stairs, staring into the darkness. The folds in his spacesuit crinkle as he shifts his weight, moving his legs to get comfortable. Other than that, those in the Oval Office could be staring at a still image.

It's then that it strikes Molly. No one knows the true purpose of the *Odyssey*. Far from being a scientific voyage of exploration, it's been used as a Trojan horse for *Icarus*. Her palms go sweaty.

"No," the NASA director says. "The device is in the service module science bay."

"And it will kill them as well?"

"Yes."

"Do we—"

Molly shifts uncomfortably in her seat. Beside her, the door to the Oval Office opens. The President's secretary walks in with a thick red binder.

The President holds up her hand, signaling for her secretary to stop where she is. "Not now, Lisa."

"It's a P1, ma'am," the secretary says, "related to the mission. General Thurston..."

The President points at the polished oak on the corner of her desk. The secretary rushes forward, placing the folder there before retreating. It's clear, though, from the way the President ignores the folder that the current discussion is more important to her.

Chief of Staff Dosela slaps the side of Molly's thigh. Molly's confused by her sudden motion. The chief of staff is discreet but forceful, striking twice more in quick succession. Her determined taps have Molly on her feet before she's had time to think about quite what's happening. Somehow, she instinctively knows what the chief of staff wants from her. She ducks out of the Oval Office, squeezing in front of the secretary as the woman walks back through the door. Molly's motion is smooth and seamless and goes unnoticed by everyone else in the room.

Within fractions of a second, Molly finds herself in the reception area outside the Oval Office as the door is closed behind her.

"Is everything all right?" the secretary asks, confused by how Molly snuck out of the room.

"Everything is fine," Molly replies, lying. A smile lights up her face. Finally, she understands why the chief of staff has kept her around. She's not a gopher. She's a dispatch runner in the trenches at the Battle of the Somme during World War One. She can almost feel the shells falling around her, throwing up clods of mud and showering her with dirt. Molly needs to keep her head down and run like she's never run before.

Hold

"I need a moment," Crash says on reaching the stairs within the basement of the alien cylinder. Warm, golden light spills down from above. As much as he wants to flee and get back to his ship, he knows it'll take a marathon effort. Emotionally, he's spent.

"Understood," Liz replies.

Physically and mentally, Crash is drained. Fear is irrational. It drives him on, but Crash knows fear is an imposter. Panicking won't help. His primal sense of self-preservation may be screaming at him to run, but running is impossible within the alien cylinder. The artificial gravity is too low. At best, he'd bounce along like one of the Apollo astronauts on the lunar surface, but even that would be slow. Running is as much about gravity pulling down as it is about muscles pushing up. One counters the other. Crash knows that, even if he could run, it would only provide an illusion of reaching safety. Nowhere is safe. He's a hundred million miles from Earth. If those aliens hatch or are birthed or whatever and turn hostile, the *Odyssey* is no safer than his spacesuit. He's sailed here from Earth in a tin can. Comparing their ships is like having a dingy row up next to a nuclear-powered aircraft carrier.

He calms himself, breathing deeply. Although the thought of some monster lurching out of the darkness is overwhelming, Crash fights his fears. Professionalism is his only ally. Discipline is his friend. Fear is his enemy.

Crash turns and sits on one of the stairs with his legs out in front of him, resting in the junction of the corridor. The lights fall dark around him, leaving only the artificial alien sun above. Shadows are cast down along his arms. He looks at his trembling gloved hands, knowing everyone knows what he's feeling. There's no hiding his fear from the billions of people watching. He makes no excuses.

"Ah, I need to rehydrate and relieve."

"Understood," Liz replies. That she and Yúzé have fallen silent is telling. There's a lot to process.

Crash twists his head sideways within his helmet, reaching for a transparent tube located just beneath the locking ring. He raises his shoulder, edging the plastic tip closer and sips on tepid water mixed with electrolytes. It wasn't until he stopped that he realized how dehydrated he's become and how that was affecting his thinking. The throbbing in his head eases. His pulse slows.

Peeing in space never comes naturally. Crash is wearing an external male catheter beneath his liquid-cooled undergarments. It looks like an oversized, thick condom with a tube leading from the tip to a containment bag strapped to the inside of his thigh. As there's no pull from gravity in space, the bag contains cotton and chemically modified starches to wick away the moisture. In practice, it's good for four cycles. Crash, though, can feel the catheter resting against his leg. It must have come loose when he crash-landed. He's also wearing a diaper as a backup, but sitting in wet urine is never fun. As part of his pre-EVA activities, he abstained from eating for 18 hours and used a suppository to empty his bowels prior to suiting up. His diaper will hold feces if needed, but it is a distinctly unsettling squelching sensation he can do without. Besides, he really didn't want to be shaking hands with aliens while there was poop in his pants.

His shoulders sag as he relieves himself in his adult flight diaper. Warm fluid runs around the inside of his thigh before being drawn away by the material. No one watching will know. Oh, Liz and Yúzé will probably guess the moment based on the way he stares straight ahead and relaxes. They'll know. They've been there. Pierre is the only one that hasn't spacewalked, but he's done simulations in the tank back in Houston. No one makes it through those without passing urine. It's an unofficial milestone. The instructors don't talk about it much, but they know the importance of balancing effectiveness against human needs.

"Okay," he says, gathering his thoughts and feeling renewed. "Let's get back to the *Odyssey*."

To anyone listening, the use of the plural pronoun probably sounds strange on a solo mission, but Crash understands spacewalks are a group effort. No one is ever alone when walking in space. Someone somewhere is always there with them, whispering in their ear and watching their video feed, double-checking each action and providing a backup brain. The fatigue of a spacewalk is shared by all, particularly as Liz is suited up and ready to deploy in an emergency. She will have been closely monitoring every aspect of his EVA and considering her own response to the situations he's faced. She'll be thinking about what worked and what didn't when he touched down. She's lived this EVA with him.

"Ah, negative," Yúzé says. "We have a hold from Houston. Over."

"A hold?" Crash replies, confused. Holds during a spacewalk are normally undertaken during technical activities such as repairing a solar panel or deploying equipment when questions arise that require additional expertise. He could understand if the hold was to avoid some potential danger or to provide time for the *Odyssey* to relocate, or perhaps if some other mission parameter changed, but that's not the case. If anything, returning to the *Odyssey* was the next milestone, and that should have been straightforward. Perhaps they've spotted some subtle detail they need to clarify before he proceeds.

"A hold for what?" he asks.

"Ah, we've asked for clarification," Yúzé says, followed by a milestone comment. "First EVA elapsed time is four hours and twenty-seven minutes, and NASA astronaut Chris Williams is on hold at the base of the stairs within the alien habitat."

Somewhat surprisingly, the longer he remains on the stairs, the more his familiarity with the alien environment grows and the less he fears the darkness. Crash notices details he missed on entering the basement. The edges where the floor meets the walls and the walls meet the ceiling are rounded. It's subtle, curling barely an inch, but it's associated with smudges on the floor. Crash instinctively knows what he's looking at.

"Are you seeing this?" he asks, even though those four words are normally the harbingers of some shocking insight. This time, they're harmless. "Look at the curve running along the base of the wall and the marks on the floor. If I'm not mistaken, that's the wear of rubber wheels on some kind of heavy cart. And that curve running along the floor keeps the wheels away from the wall, centering the cart so it doesn't scratch the wall panels."

"Huh," is the surprised response from Liz.

"We look at this thing like it's a ghost ship, but it's not. It's not only functional, it's worn. It's functioning. We're seeing it in mothballs."

"Coming out of mothballs," Liz says, agreeing with him.

"She's seen service elsewhere."

"A lot of service," Liz replies as Crash leans forward and touches the floor, placing his gloved hand against a smooth curve marking where something has turned the corner perhaps hundreds if not thousands of times. "The wear is consistent. Could be automated. Some kind of self-propelled cart, maybe."

"Interesting," Liz says, and for a moment, they both lose themselves in the mundane. Little by little, the alien spaceship becomes less alien.

As he's sitting in a T-intersection with his back to the stairs, Crash can see in three directions. Darkness may fall within ten feet of the stairs, fading with the distance, but he doesn't feel claustrophobic. Having four points of egress, including the stairs behind him, he feels as though he has options on which way he could move if something did come at him out of the shadows, but that's not going to happen. This isn't some cheesy sci-fi movie. The darkness isn't a plot device to allow some acid-for-blood alien to creep up on him. If anything moves down any of the three passageways, the automatic lighting is going to engage, giving him not only some warning but visibility.

He relaxes, reminding himself that, apart from launch and reentry, nothing happens quickly in space. Patience is a technical requirement for astronauts.

"What's the first thing you're going to do when you get back?" Liz asks, and he knows what she's doing. The hold is being extended. With nothing left to discuss, she's distracting him.

"I've never been to Hawaii," he says.

"Oh, you should go. You should totally go there. It's beautiful."

"You've been?"

"Once. ESA held a conference in Waikiki."

"That's about as far from Europe as you can get."

"I think that was the idea," she says with a chuckle. "It was sponsored by JPL. Attendance at the breakout sessions was... sporadic, to say the least."

"Hah," Crash says. "I bet."

"Adeep says we should all go there when we get back."

"Sounds good to me."

Off to his left, there's a glow on the edge of his vision. The visor on his helmet allows him to see through roughly a hundred and eighty degrees, even though the camera focuses only on what's immediately in front of him.

Crash leans forward, looking down the corridor to his left.

"There's someone down there."

"Down where?" Liz asks. "What's your orientation?"

"I'm staring down the main corridor leading to the rear of the craft."

"What did you see?"

"Ah, you probably missed it as I turned, but I think it's the cosmonaut."

"Aleksandr?"

"The lights went on about fifty yards away as he crossed from one side of the main corridor to the other. He's moving on a parallel path."

"What did you see exactly?" Yúzé asks. "I've got Pierre reviewing footage. We didn't catch anything back here."

"A glimpse of a backpack. White. The lights faded pretty quickly around him. He must have been moving fast."

"Hold," Yúzé says, knowing Crash wants to get up and find the Russian cosmonaut.

"I think I can catch up to him," Crash says. "We're both going to be surrounded by a bubble of light down here."

"Hold," Yúzé says again. "I need Houston to weigh in on this." But Yúzé's not the commander. As the senior officer remaining on the *Odyssey*, he's assumed that role, but Crash is still technically in charge.

"By then, it'll be too late. He'll be gone," Crash says, getting to his feet. Lights come on around him.

Liz says, "We don't want you to get lost down there."

"I know. I know. But I can't let this moment pass us by. We need to compare notes with the Russians. As much as we may not like it, he's the only other human within a hundred million miles. We need to know what he's seen."

Disclosure

Molly feels frantic, but she knows she needs to appear calm. She takes a moment, straightens her skirt and tucks in her blouse so the white silk appears taut. Once she's composed, she walks away from the Oval Office. She's got to tell the news media about *Icarus*. The public has a right to know what's being considered in their name. The astronauts have a right to know they're carrying a nuke.

Molly takes the corridor to the West Wing lobby, wanting to exit through the main entrance leading to Pennsylvania Avenue.

Secret service agents walk past, eyeing her with suspicion, or is it just the guilt she feels for something she hasn't done—yet? With slick suits, fresh crewcuts and earpieces, they're anything but subtle.

"Is everything okay, ma'am?"

"Everything is fine."

Repeat a lie enough times, and it becomes believable.

She reaches the lobby and walks up to the security desk.

"Hi," she says, pointing at the picture of her face on the lanyard hanging around her neck. "I'm Molly Sorensen. An intern working under Chief of Staff Dosela. Ah, can I have my phone back? I—I'm not feeling well. I need to go home."

"I'm sorry, ma'am," the officer behind the desk says. "The White House is under lockdown. No one comes in. No one goes out."

Perspiration breaks out on Molly's forehead. She is as guilty as Lucifer himself. Her fingers shake. She feels a sense of dread. She may be faking illness to get out of the West Wing, but the claustrophobia descending on her at the thought of being detained feels all too real. Her fingers tremble.

"You don't understand," she says. "I—I can't stay here. I need to go."

The officer looks past her, glancing over her shoulder. An armed Marine walks over.

"Is there a problem?" he asks from behind her.

Molly's heart is racing. Before she can turn to face the Marine, she spots James Madden, the Director of the Secret Service. He marches over, looking as though he could kill her with mere thoughts alone.

"What is going on here?" he demands of her, and just like that, her bid for freedom is over before it began. What is it Chief of Staff Dosela thought Molly could do getting her out of the Oval Office only to remain trapped within the White House?

"I'm sick," Molly blurts out. She spins to face the Marine, feeling as though he's about to grab her and wanting him to keep his distance. "I'm feeling really bad."

Bad? Well, that's going to convince them. Molly chides herself. She's an amateur surrounded by hardened, seasoned professionals.

Director Madden places his hand on her shoulder. His grip is firm. His fingers feel as though they're made of iron.

It's now or never. Molly is out of options. She has to do something, anything. She's desperate. She cannot give up. The people—the public—they need to know about *Icarus*. The astronauts need to know they're carrying death onboard the *Odyssey*, but what can she do? She needs to get out of the West Wing. There are dozens of news crews camped out on Pennsylvania Avenue. They're close, so close, barely fifty yards away down the drive, but she can't get to them.

As she turns back to face Director Madden, Molly raises both hands to her face, making as though she's covering her nose and mouth out of distress, but she does something she hasn't done in almost four years. She sticks her index finger in her mouth, reaching into the back of her throat and touching her tonsils. The effect is instantaneous, as she knew it would be. Her stomach heaves. Her motion is involuntary. Her body spasms as she projectile vomits over the director's dark grey suit. Spew sprays from her lips. Droplets pepper the counter behind him. Four years of bulimia as a teen and endless counseling sessions mean she's not in any way incapacitated by what's happening. Far from feeling awful, her senses are heightened. She catches each and every reaction around her: the shock, the horror, the revulsion.

The woman behind the desk recoils, looking down at her uniform, horrified by how bits of spew have speckled her blouse. The Marine is only partially visible on the edge of Molly's vision, but he backs up several feet. He has his hands out wide as if in surrender, keeping his distance. She couldn't have gotten that reaction from him with a gun. Director Madden staggers backward, looking down at the sick that's sprayed across his suit. Bits of chewed cucumber and dark chunks of rye stick to his white shirt and tie. Vomit clings to his hands. Stringy bits of sick drip from his fingers.

"What the—"

"My brother," Molly blurts out, lying with utter ease. "He returned from the Congo last week. He's been—I've been ill. I—I—I."

The director points at the main door, yelling, "Get her the *fuck* out of here!"

The Marine takes her by the upper arm and marches her toward the door. For her part, Molly hangs back, resisting his motion, forcing him to force her on. She's reluctant. She knows she can't look too desperate or this could still backfire on her. Another Marine opens the door. He stands wide, staying well away from her as she stumbles out into the bright sunlight.

The Marine escorting her stops at the entrance, allowing her to walk out onto the empty driveway. Molly wipes her mouth with the back of her hand. A few stray flecks of sick have spotted her white silk blouse, but she did a good job of directing the stream at Director Madden. It'll take him a good five to ten minutes to clean himself up, and he, along with everyone else in the reception area, will be paranoid about catching ebola or some other exotic tropical disease. As she walks away down the drive, she can hear the commotion behind her as everyone swings into action to clean up the mess.

The external door shuts, and she's alone with her thoughts. Birds fly through the air, ignoring the security cordon surrounding the White House. Molly strides toward the front gate. She wants to run but doesn't.

A Marine walks out of the guardhouse onto the driveway. Molly's expecting him to stop her, but she can see another Marine in the flimsy hut talking to someone on the phone. The officer on the West Wing reception desk must have called through to explain what has happened.

Molly quickens her pace. Her shoes clatter on the drive. The clump of her heels jars her spine, but she doesn't care. She's got to get outside the security cordon. Already, several of the news crews have seen the activity on the driveway and are showing interest in her. If she can get to them, she can get the word out about *Icarus*. That's what Chief of Staff Dosela wants, of that, Molly is sure. As best she understands it, the chief of staff is trying to save the President from herself and her advisors by forcing her hand. If Molly can get this information into the public domain, it'll cause a backlash.

What right does Molly have to force the President to back down? None. The President has the right of a hundred million voters behind her, but even that doesn't give her the right to make decisions on behalf of eight billion people on Earth.

The Marine opens the gate, and without missing a step or slackening her pace, Molly marches through out onto the pavement.

Police cars block either end of the road. News crews working out of vans have set up satellite dishes and cameras, pointing them at the White House. Several reporters look at her, but they're only moderately curious. After some initial excitement at seeing someone leaving the West Wing, they've downgraded their interest. She's young. She's a pretty female intern in her early twenties. She's no one of note or significance. It seems their stares are driven more by the male gaze than professional interest. At best, she's eye candy. The chief of staff was right. She's invisible.

Molly spots a middle-aged woman standing over by a news van on the edge of the cordon. She's drinking coffee from a disposable cup. Their eyes meet. She knows. Molly's not sure how she knows, but she does, that much is apparent from the way the woman reacts, setting her cup down on a crate marked *Washington Desk* and walking over toward her. The woman calls out to her crew, sensing the importance of the moment. They look lethargic, barely interested in anything other than checking something mindless on their smartphones. The woman beckons to Molly. Perhaps it's the look of desperation on Molly's face. Perhaps it's the way her pace doesn't slacken, making it seem as though she's on the verge of bursting into a run. Maybe it's the conviction in her walk, zeroing in on this particular news crew.

By this point, Molly's passed behind several other vans and a bunch of police officers. She clutches her arms across her chest even though it's not cold.

"You okay, hon?" the woman asks, looking concerned.

"Are you broadcasting?" Molly asks, ignoring her question. "Can you broadcast on the move?"

The woman doesn't hesitate. She must be able to smell the Pulitzer Prize for Journalism hanging in the air.

"Mitch, Angela. We're rolling. Get the van started."

"But our equipment."

"Leave it. Jimmy from current affairs can pack it up."

The woman puts her arm around Molly's shoulder, comforting her as though she were dealing with the survivor of a terrorist attack and leading them to shelter. She brings her over to the open side of the van.

"What have you got, honey? What do you need to tell me?"

Molly doesn't answer. She climbs into the back of the van and takes a seat.

"I'm Jean Cranz, associate producer for XBC News Hour," the

woman says, stepping into the van behind her. "Mitch. Get in here with that handheld. Angela, get us back to the studio."

Mitch and Angela madly gather up tripods and cameras. They dump cables in boxes and lug them onto the scratched steel floor of the van.

"I'm Molly Sorensen. Intern with Chief of Staff Susan Dosela."

Jean leans out of the door and yells, "I want that goddamn camera running, Mitch!"

For his part, Mitch is busy dumping bags full of equipment in the back of the van. He slams the rear door shut and jogs around to the side door. Angela jumps in the front and starts the engine. Several deck chairs, a couple of studio equipment boxes and a tripod remain on the road with a bewildered-looking Jimmy from the van next to theirs protesting at being left to clean up the mess.

Jean closes the side door behind Mitch. He has a portable handheld camera with a large viewing screen and an oversized microphone covered in black fuzz.

Angela puts the van into drive and pulls forward slowly. Police officers wave them past their parked squad cars and outside the cordon.

"Are we transmitting?" Jean asks.

"I'm recording. And I have a clean internet connection with the newsroom. Cameron's online, monitoring the incoming feed. What's this about?"

As the two of them are sitting on seats that face each other, Jean reaches over and turns the camera lens toward her.

"My name is Jean Cranz with the XBC News Hour crew covering the reaction from the White House as the crew of the *Odyssey* explore the alien spacecraft. I'm joined here by Molly Sorensen, an intern working with the President's chief of staff. Molly?"

The van accelerates down the road. Mitch turns the camera back to Molly, who's seated next to Jean. She has no idea what she looks like. Given that she just vomited on the Director of the Secret Service, she guesses she appears pale and washed out. Molly's never been one for makeup, but she suspects her cheeks could do with some blush. She sweeps her hair behind one ear, composing herself. This is the first opportunity she's had to think since she ducked out of the Oval Office. She's been so focused on making it to this point that she hasn't had time to compose herself. She knows her argument needs to be coherent. If she rambles, she'll come off looking like a lunatic.

"I—I don't know if I'm breaking any laws by talking to you, but the people need to know."

Jean turns side on to her and reaches over, taking her hand. It's an insincere gesture that comes across as sincere in the moment. Touch is disarming. Molly talks to Jean rather than the camera, leaving her in side profile on the screen.

Molly says, "The President is watching the live broadcast from the *Odyssey* in the Oval Office along with members of the Joint Chiefs of Staff, a few senators and a team from NASA."

"And you know this how?" Jean asks, gently squeezing her fingers.

"I was there. I was sitting beside the door."

"Why were you in there?"

The van slows. Angela flips on the indicator. Jean breaks character. She snaps at Angela, saying, "No. Keep driving. Keep us on the move. And don't take the same street twice."

Angela looks at Jean in the rearview mirror and nods. She doesn't say anything. She seems to understand the importance of not breaking the moment, but for Molly, the illusion has been shattered. She's betraying the confidence of the President of the United States of America. There's no coming back from this. There's no way to know what impact the next few minutes will have on her future. Reality Winner leaked a single page of US intelligence to the Press, exposing the Russian interference in the 2016 US Presidential Election and was sentenced to five years in jail. Reality didn't do anything wrong, not ethically, only according to mindless regulations that ignore common sense. She was a whistleblower, and speaking out against the system has to be punished, or the system could falter, perhaps even fall. Molly knows her name is going to go down in history alongside the likes of Winner and Snowden.

Molly struggles to recall her White House induction and the numerous documents and disclaimers she had to sign. No one reads them. Oh, they're told to read them, but the legalese within the various pages is an incomprehensible wall of verbiage designed to dull any actual comprehension. NDAs are a contradiction in logic. How can anyone agree to something they cannot understand? That alone should render them null and void.

Jean prompts her. "And you were in the Oval Office because?"

What should she say? That she's the daughter of a US Senator and was offered a plum role because of her family ties? That's hardly going to give her credibility. And what will this do to her father's career? Is she sinking his ship as well?

"Ah, I was working on the communications team back when the BDO was nothing more than a curious observation by a bunch of college students and their lecturer."

Is that a lie? Molly likes to think of it as a summation, even though it's misleading. She was a gopher. She just happened to be the one the folder was handed to on that particular day. Were it not for the President's frantic schedule demanding that others help her decipher the often mind-bendingly complex issues thrust at her, Molly would have remained in obscurity.

"I was a gopher," Molly says, feeling she needs to clarify that point. "Someone that runs errands."

"And what did you see? What did you hear?" Jean asks.

Molly takes a deep breath. "The President and her advisors are watching a live stream from the *Odyssey* that's slightly ahead of what's released to the public. This allows them to truncate what's shown to everyone else."

"The blackout," Jean says, and Molly's eyes rise in alarm, surprised by the notion. "We saw Crash Williams walking down a darkened corridor, then the feed was cut. Four minutes and sixteen seconds later, we see him retreating down the same corridor to the stairs. What happened? What was he doing during that time? What did you see during those four minutes and sixteen seconds?"

"It's not what I saw that worries me," Molly replies. "It's what they want to do that's alarming."

"What did he see?" Jean asks, and Molly can see the intensity in her eyes. She, like everyone else on the planet, desperately wants to know what the NASA astronaut saw during that blackout period.

"Ah, he found a laboratory of some kind. There were eggs. Seeds. I don't know what to call them. Sacs of fluid drooped down from the ceiling. Imagine a basketball or bigger, something like a yoga ball or one of those balls people sit on at the office instead of a chair. Imagine dozens of those hanging from the ceiling, surrounded by goo. There are aliens growing inside that lab."

Jean's mouth falls open. Molly continues, feeling unsure of herself, but she's committed to full disclosure now.

"Um, there's a lot of them. Hundreds. Maybe thousands. It was dark, so it was difficult to tell, but there are row upon row of seed pods in there, all hanging from the ceiling. And you can see creatures squirming around within them."

Jean's eyes go wide, but she doesn't speak. Molly continues to ignore the impersonal, cold dark camera lens, preferring to talk to Jean.

"That's what's got everyone so spooked."

There's silence as the van turns a corner, weaving its way through Washington, DC. Jean senses the awkward pause, but it takes her a moment to say, "And?"

"They want to nuke it—the spaceship."

From the front seat, Angela lets an audible "*Fuck*" slip from her lips. From the look on Jean's face, she doesn't disagree.

"How?"

"The astronauts. They don't know," Molly replies. "They're carrying a nuke. A... What did they call it? A neutron bomb. It's not like a regular nuke. It's designed to kill life without destroying the spaceship. They want the spaceship. They want the alien tech."

Jean holds her hand out, splaying her fingers wide and gesturing that Molly needs to slow down.

"You understand what you're telling me, right? That the US Government is prepared to take unilateral action to kill the extraterrestrials onboard that spaceship?"

"And the astronauts," Molly replies. "Our astronauts."

"Jesus."

"They have no right," Molly says. "We know nothing about these creatures other than that they're intelligent and they're curious. They're intelligent enough to travel between stars, and they're curious about us. They want to learn. Right now, they're vulnerable. We have no right to kill them."

"And you're sure about this?"

"It's called *Icarus*. It's hidden in the science bay on the service module of the *Odyssey*."

"Why?" Jean asks. "Why would they do this?"

"They're afraid. The unknown scares them. Fear is the courage of cowards. They think they're being brave. They think they're making the hard calls. They're convinced they're protecting us, but they're not. They're blind."

"And the President?"

"She's in an impossible situation. What should she do? What's the right thing to do? Are they a threat to life on Earth? Is this the only chance we'll ever have to fight back? Or is this a gross mistake? Are we killing innocent intelligent beings for no reason beyond our own fear? Without a crystal ball, it's impossible to know what the future holds."

"And what do you think?" Jean asks.

"I don't know that any good can come from fear. Ask yourself, where does the real danger lie? I think it's in the status quo. We hate change. We avoid it. We want today to be the same as yesterday. Our lives, our economy, our stability relies on tomorrow being a repeat of today, but the alien spaceship threatens all that. It says tomorrow is unknown. And we don't want that. We don't like that. We want things to remain the same. We're comfortable where we are, but their existence says otherwise. Their presence says change is coming whether we want it or not. But there's a solution. Kill them, and nothing changes. Kill them, and we get to scavenge their tech. Kill them, and we have decades, perhaps centuries before we face them again. Kill them, and we can keep going as we always have. Kill them, and the turmoil is over. Then, the alien spaceship becomes a relic. It becomes something to explore instead of something that challenges our most basic notions about life and the universe."

Jean says, "Even though there's no threat?"

"Oh, the aliens threaten our lifestyle. We've never been answerable to anyone. We can do whatever the hell we want. No other species can question us and our decisions.

"Can an orangutan protest their forest being cut down? Just because we need toilet paper or palm oil or whatever. We need timber for *our* houses, not *theirs*. Can an elephant protest against climate change and their waterholes drying up? Can a dolphin protest against overfishing or fertilizer-runoff decimating fish stocks? But if there is another intelligent species capable of thinking and reasoning, challenging us? Well, that changes everything. And what will we do? Heed them? Ignore them? Lie about them? Fight them?"

"All of the above," Jean says with resignation.

"We need them," Molly says. "Because we won't listen to any reason of our own."

"Will she do it?" Jean asks. "Will the President activate *Icarus*?"

"I don't know. She might. She knows that whatever she decides, it will reach beyond today. Whichever way she goes, the implications will ripple outward for decades to come."

"We need to—"

Jean never gets to finish her response to Molly. Sirens sound, echoing off the buildings lining the avenue. The van swerves, taking a corner at speed. Tires screech, barely clinging to the concrete road. The passengers sway, rocking to one side. Angela is hard on the brake, but she's braking too late and taking the corner wide, straying onto the wrong side of the road.

Molly looks up. Red and blue lights flash across the buildings. A helicopter flies low over the city. Ahead, police cars block the road.

"What am I doing?" Angela yells at Jean from the front of the vehicle, clearly considering smashing the van into one of the cars in a vain attempt to break through.

"Stop," Jean says, turning and looking at the patrol cars racing up behind them. "Just stop. We can't outrun them. And we can't risk lives—ours or theirs."

Angela brings the van to a halt in the middle of the road, straddling the center line. Police cars rush in around them, cutting off any possible escape and blocking the rear.

"This is uncalled for," Jean says, staring down the camera. "The people have a right to know. Molly has acted in good faith, following her conscience. This is a violation of—"

The window on the side door of the van shatters. A baton breaks the glass. With a swift motion, the police officer wielding it clears away the broken window. Fragments of glass ricochet around inside the vehicle.

"Hands where I can see them," another officer yells with a gun drawn, pointing the barrel at Angela in the front seat. She has her hands up by the lining on the roof. The front door is opened, and she's grabbed by the upper arm. The police officer arresting her hasn't given her the chance to release her seatbelt. She rolls forward, unable to fall to the ground because of the taut belt. Angela's struck on the head as her hand fumbles for the release button on the seatbelt. Blood runs from a cut on her head. She screams but can't be heard over the chorus of police officers yelling. "Out! Get out of the vehicle! Hands in the air! On the ground! Get on the ground!"

All Molly can see is the darkened barrels of handguns being pointed at her from all sides. She no longer sees people behind the guns. These aren't humans. They're robots. Androids. They're following a script as much as any computer program. She's terrified. They're screaming at her, threatening to shoot at the slightest provocation, as if the twitch of her hand or the flex of her legs somehow threatens them.

The officer with the baton reaches in through the shattered window and unlocks the side door from within. He throws it open as more police officers surround the van with their guns drawn. Any one of them could fire by accident, and a split-second later, they'd all fire, cutting her down in a hail of lead. And for what? For lowering her hand to steady herself or for failing to respond to conflicting commands being barked at her? She's genuinely in fear of losing her life.

Jean gets out first as she's closest to the door. She has her hands in the air. As soon as her shoe touches the road, she's dragged away and thrown to the concrete. Her arms are wrestled behind her even though she's offering no resistance. A knee is planted in the center of her back, pinning her to the grit and grime on the side of the road.

Mitch is smart. He places the camera on the seat, leaving it facing sideways toward the street. The red LED is glowing, indicating that it's still recording and transmitting even if it isn't in his hand. The police officers are so focused on the two of them that they don't notice the camera.

Molly is next. She doesn't want to exit the van. She's afraid. She knows she's going to be hurt, possibly killed. Pain awaits her on the street. The officers are no longer yelling at her, they're growling like rabid dogs. Her mind is closing down, failing to interpret the sights and sounds before her, leaving only terror saturating her thoughts. The longer she waits, the more vicious they become. It's as though they're ready to tear her apart.

Molly steps forward. One shoe rests on the footwell, ready to step down onto the road when she's grabbed from the side. She didn't even see the officer pressed up against the van, standing beside the door.

Molly's arms are twisted up into the small of her back. Her shoulder feels as though it's about to pop out of its socket. She's slammed into the side of a patrol car. A gloved hand pushes her head forward, bending her over the trunk of the car and pressing her face hard against the sheet metal.

"Stop resisting," is yelled inches from her ears, but she can't help herself. She's in pain. She squirms, wanting to find relief, but that only provokes greater force, and she's pinned to the trunk with her face pressed up against the glass window at the back of the car. Another hand is pressed firmly in the center of her back, making it impossible to breathe.

"Don't fight me," the officer yells as cuffs are applied, but she has no choice. The pain surging through every fiber of her being demands release. She's not resisting him so much as trying to find relief.

Molly is jerked backward. The rear door of the car is opened and she's shoved inside, but not before her head collides with the door frame. Her ear catches the metal. The sharp crack stings. She's pushed down into the back seat and shoved sideways.

The car door is slammed. With her arms pinned behind her and her hands straining against the steel cuffs, she rights herself. Molly locks eyes with the dark lens of the camera still sitting sideways on the rear-facing seat of the van.

Tears roll down her cheeks as she stares at the cold, impersonal camera lens.

Aleksandr

Crash feels conflicted. He's standing at the bottom of the stairs within the massive extraterrestrial cylinder, staring into the darkness. He caught a glimpse of the Russian cosmonaut Aleksandr Krukov crossing the main corridor running the length of the alien spaceship. And just like Crash, lights came on around Aleksandr, illuminating his passage.

Crash only caught the flicker of light out of the corner of his eye. He turned in time to see the gentle gait of an astronaut in an EVA suit disappearing down a side tunnel roughly fifty yards away. He wants to go after him. His instincts say he should catch up to Aleksandr. Perhaps they can help each other, but he feels bound by his loyalty to Houston.

A general hold has been called by Mission Control. Crash knows what that means: someone somewhere is agonizing over a split decision. It's probably whether he should continue to explore the lower layers of the habitat or return to the *Odyssey*. They've put him on hold so he can pivot either way based on their assessment. As tempting as it is to think he has all the information he needs to make an independent decision, Crash knows that's a fallacy. Ego is intoxicating. Being an astronaut is humbling.

Crash remembers his time at Shackleton Base at the Moon's south pole. He was stationed there as part of ISLAND, the In-Situ Lunar Asset Nitrate Discovery project. At the time he was originally interviewed for the mission, he was dismissive. Who wants to go to the Moon? Everyone in the astronaut corps! But who wants to spend eighteen months training to mine for trace amounts of nitrates in the dark? No one. Working in the eternal night of the south pole, drilling into the regolith and dealing with dust so fine that even electrostatic repulsion struggles to remove it from a spacesuit held no appeal for anyone. Crash knew it would be dirty, filthy, dangerous work. Breathing in lunar dust is akin to inhaling finely ground-up glass. The long-term medical consequences are unknown, and no one wants to be the one that finds it leads to lung cancer or some other form of microscopic cellular disease.

The scientists told him that in-situ nitrogen recovery methods were the key to the exploration of Mars. They told him solar winds strip away volatiles, so these molecules could only be found in places that were in permanent shade or deep within the surface. They said that without nitrogen, there could be no continuous, self-sustaining presence on either the Moon or Mars, but the mission wasn't sexy. There were no mountains to climb, no flags to plant, no historic firsts to accomplish, just holes to be dug. Thousands of holes. When his submission to be part of the Venus flyby and the deployment of cloud monitors was rejected, Crash fell back on ISLAND as a way of getting off the planet.

Somewhat ironically, two tours with ISLAND at the Lunar South Pole paved the way for him to be selected for the *Odyssey*, as he was seen as dedicated to the mission rather than the glory of a plum posting. Going back a second time was seen as madness by the Astronaut Office but not by senior NASA management. Despite his nickname, Crash was seen as mature and seasoned. In reality, the scientists analyzing the results he dug up were kind, flattering him in their assessments to senior management. They knew that even in low gravity, it was boring, backbreaking work. Crash was the celestial equivalent of a laborer-for-hire. For him, though, it was a chance to learn what it really means to be an explorer. That's why he went back a second time.

Most astronauts only ever interact with mission control and other astronauts, limiting their exposure to the broader scientific community. Crash had a direct line to the astonishing brains behind the technologies that would make life possible on other planets, and he found that fascinating. He'd see them debating the different ratios within a mineral sample, thinking not just about the composition but the rate of loss, isotope decay and relative abundance compared to other molecules. To him, it was meaningless. To the scientists, it was a gigantic game of Clue being played out over billions of years. When they said it was *Miss Scarlett in the dining room with the lead pipe*, they were right. He had access to all the same information but was still thinking about *Colonel Mustard in the library*. For Crash, being humble became a default. Oh, he always knew he was intelligent, but for the first time in his life, he realized intelligence was no reason to be confident. Crash finally understood that confidence was more than a feeling. Confidence has to be based on facts. And right now, in the depths of the alien spacecraft, he knows he has none. As much as he doesn't want to, he needs to accept the hold because it's giving NASA time to make a considered, precise decision.

Without saying anything, he sits back on the stairs within the alien spaceship, resting his gloved hands on his thighs. His gut instinct says he should go after Aleksandr. His rational mind says to wait on Houston. His experience at the lunar base running ISLAND warns him there are probably dozens of details he doesn't fully understand. The only problem is the time delay. It'll take roughly sixteen minutes for Houston to see the footage and respond—and that's if they make a snap decision, something that's not likely.

Against his better judgment, Crash remains where he is, watching as the dim light from the side tunnel some fifty yards further down the corridor slowly fades. Aleksandr is moving away from him at a right angle, probably not on purpose. As Crash is stationary in the stairwell, with only the natural light spilling down around him, Aleksandr probably didn't even notice him.

"Ah, we concur," Yúzé says over the headset built into his Snoopy cap.

"We do," Liz says.

Crash is surprised by the comments he's getting from the

Odyssey. He'd talked himself out of the impulsive decision to chase after the Russian cosmonaut. He reasoned it was better to abide by the hold from Houston. From the way Yúzé and Liz are speaking to him, though, it seems they're confused by his reluctance and felt the need to validate his initial idea. They all know there's an inherent danger involved in going after Aleksandr. Crash could become disoriented and lose his way in the darkness. There should be other stairways, as the lack of a hatch or door on these stairs suggests they're designed for convenience. Besides, what are the chances he would randomly land in a meadow next to the only access point, or even one of only a handful? Given the size of the habitat, there should be dozens of them. He should come across them at regular intervals. And the stairway's position on a central corridor running the length of the cylinder seems deliberate.

Yúzé says, "We need the Russians to know we want to work together with them."

"And we need them to remain calm," Liz says. "We don't want them doing anything rash."

"Copy that," he replies, getting back to his feet. "If Houston calls an abort, let me know."

Crash doesn't need to say that, but it feels important to let both them and Houston know he's not going rogue. His initial reaction was to rush after Aleksandr, but now he feels settled. This is a deliberate decision by the crew as a whole.

He starts down the corridor. As it's set at ninety degrees to the rotation of the cylinder, it appears perfectly flat, which is quietly reassuring. Crash pushes off the walls, guiding himself on. It feels as though he's moving through water in the Neutral Buoyancy Tank back in Houston. Closed doorways line the corridor. Scratches mark not only the floor but the ceiling, with the wear marks matching each other. Whatever automated cargo moves through these passageways, it fills the entire space. Running into one of them won't be fun, but in low gravity, it shouldn't move fast, or so he hopes. And it should have some intelligence built into it. As the aliens are considerably more advanced than humans, there should be the equivalent of motion detectors for safety.

When he first descended into the heart of the spacecraft, the fear of the darkness dominated his mind. After seeing the alien pods, panic overwhelmed him. Now, though, he's become accustomed to the darkness. The spacecraft is in caretaker mode, awaiting the birth of its crew. Given the growth he's seen above in the habitat and how young and even it appears, it seems dozens of automated processes have kicked into gear in preparation for the crew. The lights that come on around him as he moves down the corridor make sense. Rather than powering up the entire ship, the craft is in some kind of standby mode, so the lights only come on as needed. For him, it's reassuring to realize he's working within a deliberate framework, just one designed by an alien mind rather than human.

Being more relaxed, Crash notices subtle details. Unlike a spacecraft from Earth, there are no joints or seams in the corridor. It's as though the entire length has been fabricated from a single piece of sheet metal. Perhaps there are seams and welds or rivets, but if there are, they've been machined perfectly smooth.

A light coating of something equating to grey paint covers the surface, making him wonder about the perception of these creatures. On Earth, no two animals see the same colors. Colors are a construct of the brain adapting to the sensitivity of the eyes. Where humans see red, dogs see brown. Where humans see black on the feathery coat of a raven, birds see iridescent greens and blues and scarlet. Where humans see blue, cats see grey. What do these aliens see, if sight is even a sense they have? Given that the flora in the habitat is tinted dark green to black, darker colors seem more natural and yet the corridor is a light grey. Somewhere some scientist watching the video feed is already working on this, of that, he's sure.

Crash reaches the intersection. He steals a glance back down the tunnel. The dim light of the artificial alien sun glows softly, marking the location of the stairs. He turns and looks further down the corridor and spots a similar glow coming down from above.

"I'm not sure how well you can see this, but it looks like there are stairs positioned every hundred yards or so, as I can see another one further along the main corridor."

"Good to know," Yúzé says.

"I passed several side tunnels crossing the corridor. I think this is the one Aleksandr proceeded down, but it's difficult to tell. I'll explore for no more than fifty yards and then retrace my steps."

Liz says, "It's nice to have a grid layout. Can you imagine if it was organic and the tunnels wound around without reason?"

"That would be bad," Crash replies.

"Yeah, and you'd be grzztl-hungang before shuxxxx-mann."

Although Crash feels stationary, crouching in the middle of the intersection, the way the radio drops out reminds him he's in motion, spinning around with the cylinder. The shifting distance between him and the *Odyssey*, combined with interference from the hull of the alien spacecraft itself, causes the signal to wax and wane.

He breathes deeply. Although he wants to catch up to Aleksandr, the lack of any ambient light ahead suggests the Russian has already moved well beyond him. Crash doubts himself. He should return to the stairs. He should wait for a response from Houston. Curiosity has him continue on, but he slows his pace. He's in no rush to run into another laboratory. He tries to still his madly beating heart by slowing his breathing.

Mentally, Crash maps his path inside the cylinder's basement level, keeping in mind the location of the laboratory with the alien pods he came across earlier.

Liz says, "Losing video... xxytz some still images... audio good... Pierre has mizzzzz-apped the interior of the habitat onto your path... uuuuu-underwater... interference."

"Copy that."

Being inside a metal cylinder with varying densities due to the layout of soil and water within the habitat is playing hell with his comms. Then there are the external fuel tanks wrapping around the cylinder, absorbing the signal and causing it to bounce around. The vessel's internal rotation complicates things even more. His recordings are going to be crucial as he suspects less than half of his transmission is actually making it through to the *Odyssey*. When he first arrived, he wondered why the Russians weren't actively transmitting their view from inside. Now, he understands why. If anything, the partial signal is probably frustrating and confusing those on Earth. There's a danger of misunderstandings or miscommunication arising from his fragmented messages. He's got to make sure he communicates with absolute clarity.

Crash edges along the side corridor. The walkway is narrow. It curves away from him, curling up toward the ceiling. As all the passageways are low, topping out at less than six feet, his helmet scrapes along the ceiling. When he was in the main corridor, he could lean on an angle to avoid bumping into the ceiling. Within the confines of the side passage, he has to crouch with his head down, restricting his view. He feels as though he's making his way through an abandoned coal mine. The radio crackles.

"Listen... here on *Odyssey*..."

Yúzé talks with a slow cadence, which is unsettling. Crash has been expecting an update from Earth, but the way Yúzé is speaking suggests he's trying to remain calm and get an important message through.

"...carrying *Icarus*... we need to depart immediately... no time... return in six hours... remain in the habitat... wait by the meadow."

Crash replies, "Ah, you're coming through in fragments. I'm not understanding you."

"Zztuurr... *Odyssey* to a minimum distance of five hundred kilometers... safe ddddd-deee-det-det-detonation..."

"You're not making any sense. Say again."

He continues on, feeling like Alice in Wonderland, crawling through a corridor that seems to narrow and constrict his movements, only he's in the dark while she was surrounded by light. He doubts his judgment. He should have remained by the stairs. He should return there.

"Warzzz *Icarus*... could detonate without warning... zshhhtzzz."

Ahead, beyond the reach of the automated lights around him, out on the edge of his vision, Crash spots a crumpled shape in the darkness: boots, legs, the folds of a cream-colored spacesuit, gloved hands, a backpack and helmet. An astronaut lies face-first on the floor.

"Neuuut... ombbb... science bay on the *Odyssey*... need depppart... xyzzys... no choice buttttt, buttttt, butttt..."

"I've found Aleksandr," Crash says, edging forward and ignoring the garbled call from the *Odyssey*. "He's down. He's injured."

As Crash pushes his way along the cramped corridor, he sees the familiar outline of a glass wall and a broad opening to his left. He's passing another alien laboratory, causing his heart to race. Row upon row of dark pods hang from the ceiling.

"He's not moving... Can you see this? I hope you can see this."

Although he wants to rush to the cosmonaut's side, Crash resists the temptation, wanting to understand what happened before moving into a potentially dangerous situation. The radio crackles in his ear.

Liz says, "Just returned... Arrtkkk on Aleksandr, with mmmzzzhhh."

"Yes, Aleksandr," Crash replies, looking down at the crumpled body of the cosmonaut.

Blood splatter lines the wall opposite the laboratory. Streaks of red mark where gloved hands have reached out, clutching at the wall as Aleksandr fell. The back of his helmet has been caved in. Splinters have formed in the white polycarbonate shell, revealing a layer of insulation within the helmet. Blood smears mar the cream fabric of the cosmonaut's spacesuit. A dark pool has formed beneath the Russian. A bloodied cylinder lies nearby.

"He's been bludgeoned," Crash says, kneeling next to the limp body and rolling it over. Eyes flicker. His visor has been smashed, but Aleksandr is alive. Scratches line his face, marking where glass has cut his cheeks. Blood seeps from a gash on his throat. He gasps, trying to breathe in the thin alien atmosphere. A feeble gloved hand reaches for

Crash. The cosmonaut tries to speak, but he cannot form words.

Within his helmet, Crash hears from the *Odyssey*. "Wwwhhheee and Aleksandr..."

"Yes. I have him," Crash says. "Aleksandr."

Liz says, "Repeat your last... Weehaaaaaave... on Aleksandr. We have eye-eye-eyes on... *Vechnost*."

"What do you mean eyes?" Crash asks, confused. "Aleksandr is dying. Can you see him on my feed? Is that what you mean?"

"N—No time," Yúzé says. "...with *Icarus*. Li—Li—Lah—Leaving... six hours... minimum."

"Negative," Crash says, confused not just by their response but the notion that the *Odyssey* is going to abandon him on the alien spacecraft. "You need to stay. I've got Aleksandr here with me. He's alive. Barely alive."

Blood runs from the cosmonaut's mouth. Aleksandr tries to speak. Bubbles form on his lips. Vapor drifts from his smashed helmet, condensing in the cool air.

"I need help," Crash says.

Yúzé's reply is frustrating. "...priority is *Icarus*..."

Liz says, "Nisssshhh choice... None. No choy-choy-cho-iiiice, Crassssshhh."

Crash grits his teeth. "The goddamn priority is an injured astronaut!"

Aleksandr looks at him with heartbreak in his eyes. Even with the light around them, his pupils are dilated. Tears pool in the corner of his eyes. Crash holds the cosmonaut's gloved hand and maintains eye contact, but deep down, he knows his efforts are futile. Aleksandr is dying. He's breathing, but his breathing is labored and shallow. His body is succumbing to both his injuries and the hostile, frigid environment. Even if Crash could get him up to the airlock, he couldn't return Aleksandr to either the *Vechnost* or the *Odyssey* without replacing his helmet and possibly his entire suit. It's heartbreaking to realize Aleksandr is going to die down here in the darkness.

"Easy," Crash says, watching as the light glistening off the cosmonaut's eyes slowly fades. "I'm here. I'm not going anywhere."

Normally, talking isn't possible in space without the use of a radio, but the atmosphere within the alien cylinder allows sound to travel beyond the confines of his helmet. His voice is muted, but he can see Aleksandr understands his words. There's recognition in his eyes. His lips tremble. Aleksandr tries to speak, but he can't.

One moment, Aleksandr is staring at Crash, locking eyes with him. The next, Aleksandr is staring through him, focusing on something beyond his helmet. His fingers go limp. His body sags. The muscles in his neck flop, causing his head to slip sideways within his helmet, leaving his eyes staring off into the darkness. And just like that, he's dead.

"I—I'm sorry," Crash says, still crouching beside the cosmonaut. Tears run down his cheeks. He releases his grip, allowing the gloved hand to sink back to the bloody pool on the floor.

There's no reply from the *Odyssey*. They should have picked up his audio, if not fragments of his video. They must have seen something—still images, at least—but they remain silent. What the hell are they doing leaving him down here?

Why did mission control call for a hold and then the departure of the *Odyssey*? It makes no sense. There has to be something else at play that worries them. As frustrating as it is, Crash understands the time delay between him and Houston means it is impossible for them to respond in the moment. Whatever course of action they've taken, they've based that on what, to him, would be old information. When they see what has happened to Aleksandr, they'll adjust their position, but by then another sixteen minutes will have transpired. And without the *Odyssey* acting as a relay, he'll be deaf to their advice. Whatever's spooked them, it must be something outside the ship. They've taken some kind of evasive action. For now, he needs to accept they've made the best call they can, even though it seems like madness to him.

Crash has his back to the alien laboratory. He's been so focused on Aleksandr that he hasn't thought about who or what attacked the

Russian astronaut. The cylinder lying ahead of the body is about the size of an oxygen cylinder from a hospital bed. Scratches and splatters of blood on the dull end reveal how it was used to smash open the cosmonaut's plexiglass visor. The force required would have been immense. What anger or fury could have provoked such an attack?

"*Odyssey*, do you read me? Are you hearing me? Come in. Over."

Silence screams back at him, leaving him feeling abandoned.

"What the hell, *Odyssey*? Come in. Over."

Crash gets back to his feet. His helmet bumps softly into the low ceiling. Staring down at the dead cosmonaut, tears continue to well up in his eyes and roll down his cheeks. He's confused. Nothing makes sense. Why would the *Odyssey* depart without him? If Houston was considering a general abort, why have him hold within the alien vessel? Why not retrieve him? What could be so urgent that they couldn't wait for him to egress? And six hours? What the hell are they going to accomplish in six hours? Where could they go in that time? They're a month away from Earth. Six hours is a meaningless distance by comparison. And there's nothing out here. Nothing beyond the alien spacecraft.

Crash senses movement behind him. He's been so fixated on Aleksandr and the departure of the *Odyssey* that he hasn't thought about himself. He's in danger. The hair on his arms rises in alarm.

Shadows flicker nearby.

Someone's watching him.

Something is stalking him in the darkness.

Tuna Sandwich

.

Molly sits on a thin mattress with her back against the wall and her legs up in front of her chest. Her arms wrap around her knees. The handcuffs have left bruises around her slender wrists. Being strip searched and dressed in Day-Glo orange fatigues has left Molly feeling ashamed. She'd like to think she did the right thing, but the way she's being treated brings nothing but doubt.

Her cell is six feet by eight, forming a rectangle. The bed is a concrete slab coming out of the wall. As the mattress is made from thin foam, without any inner springs, Molly can feel her bony ass pressing against the concrete. There's a toilet, a wash basin and a fixed desk extending from the wall, along with an immovable stool acting as a seat in front of the desk. Although it seems practical, the effect of all these items is to make the cell feel cramped. Her view of the outside world is a two-foot window that's only six inches wide. The world, though, as seen from the window, is a tar-sealed roof with a low concrete rim. Dark clouds loom overhead. Razor wire tops the exercise yard. She can't see the yard itself or any of the inmates, but she can hear them. Beyond that, there's a featureless three-story concrete building with hundreds of identical, narrow windows. Out there, somewhere opposite her, someone else is staring out of their cell at the razor wire and her distant, narrow window.

Molly lowers her head, resting her forehead on her knees. She's been told she's under suicide watch. No reason was given for this decision, but it means the lights around her are blinding. From the fading sunlight, the day is coming to a close. For her, though, the holding cell is brighter than the noonday sun.

She has no privacy beyond that which she imagines. The bars of her cell open out into the walkway. High on the ceiling of the corridor, well beyond the reach of anyone in the cell, is a camera. The red LED tells her she's being watched. Going to the bathroom is an embarrassment she's quickly moved beyond. Necessity demands that prudence is replaced with practicality. As far as she can tell, every fifteen minutes, one of the female guards does the rounds, walking down the corridor. Heavy boots clomp on the linoleum floor, announcing the guard long before she passes by. But why? Does the camera not work? After a bit of thought, Molly realizes it's all part of the institutionalization of inmates. The guards need them to feel helpless.

This isn't what she imagined when she walked into the White House on her first day as an intern. What would she tell herself if she had the chance to bump into herself on the way to Human Resources? Would future Molly tell past Molly to turn around and go home? As much as she hates the way she's being treated, Molly decides she wouldn't change a thing. She only hopes the astronauts have learned about *Icarus*.

The heavy steel door at the far end of the corridor opens. She can't see it, but she can hear it. And she suspects she'll be hearing it all night long. Although she could be mistaken, it seems a little early for the guard to be doing the rounds again.

This time, there are two sets of footsteps, and they're different. The clomp and squelch of boots are set in contrast to the click of office shoes—women's shoes. Molly was expecting to have her father visit, along with a lawyer. She was told they'd be given ten minutes to talk to her in a secure meeting room.

The guard walks up to the bars. Molly gets to her feet, more out of respect for authority than any sense of expectation. Compliance is the currency of jail life. As much as it grates on her, being difficult is dumb. She has to keep her ego in check or these sadistic assholes will make her life hell.

"Hands," the guard says, but the guard's alone. Whoever's accompanying her, they're shy, standing out of sight beyond the recessed alcove in which her cell is set.

Molly walks forward with her arms outstretched. She holds them just shy of the bars. The guard reaches through with a set of cuffs, attaching them to one wrist and then the other. Once they're locked in place, Molly lowers both her arms and her head. It's been less than a day and she's already suffering from learned helplessness.

The guard talks into the radio slung over her shoulder.

"Open cell 5H."

"Opening cell 5H," is the reply from whoever is watching from the control room. Deep within the concrete wall, there's a metallic clunk inside the locking mechanism, and the bars slide sideways.

"Come," the guard says.

Molly shuffles rather than walks. She doesn't need to, but the cuffs dull her sense of self, leaving her feeling like a shell. She watches the fall of her feet. The woman accompanying the guard is standing ten feet back in front of the empty cell beside Molly's. She's over by the far wall, staying out of sight from the cell camera, although there are corridor cameras that would catch her presence.

Molly doesn't raise her eyes. She turns away from the woman and walks beside the guard to the end of the corridor. A thick, heavy key is inserted into a steel plate on the door of the meeting room opposite the last cell. The guard winds the key, unlocking the hefty door. Molly walks in as fluorescent lights flicker on overhead.

"You have ten minutes," the guard says to the woman following Molly.

"Thank you," a familiar voice says.

Molly turns, seeing the President's chief of staff standing there. Her hair is ruffled. She's not wearing any makeup. Her features appear washed out under the bright lights.

"I'll be right outside," the guard says, closing the door behind them.

"Please, take a seat," Sue Dosela says, gesturing to the austere metal table in the middle of the room. Acoustic insulation lines the walls. It's old and scratched and dented. Molly can't look the chief of staff in the eyes. She sits.

The chief of staff places a brown paper bag on the table, saying, "Tuna, right? That's your favorite."

She opens the bag and pulls out a sandwich wrapped in plastic along with a plastic-coated cardboard box of juice with a straw stuck to the side.

"Sorry, there's no soda. They're a little paranoid in here. They won't let any metal in this wing."

With her hands still in cuffs, Molly reaches out and stabs the straw through the top of the drink container. She sips on the orange juice. It's sweet, and for a moment, she can close her eyes and imagine she's back home.

The chief of staff wraps her knuckles on the glass window in the door, getting the guard's attention. She points up at the camera in the corner of the interrogation room. The guard peers through the window and speaks into the microphone curling over her shoulder. The red LED on the camera goes dead.

"And now we can talk," Sue Dosela says, sitting opposite Molly.

For her part, Molly is starving. Her stomach is empty. Dried vomit still clings to one side of her chin, but she's beyond caring. She's been in the holding cell for at least six hours now without anything to eat and only tepid water from the tap on the basin built into the toilet to drink. She bites into the sandwich. Tuna and mayo dance on her tongue.

Molly's still in shock, and not just at seeing the chief of staff. The whole ordeal of being arrested and treated like a serial killer has left her mind reeling.

"Don't worry about a thing," the chief of staff says. "You did good."

That last comment gets Molly to stop mid-bite. She continues to chew, but at a slower rate, unsure what the chief of staff means.

"They got the message."

"The astronauts?" Molly asks, talking with her mouth full.

"Yes."

"And the aliens? Are they...?"

"They're alive. The *Odyssey* has departed from the BDO, at least for now. They're dumping *Icarus* where it can cause no harm, but it means we've lost contact with the astronaut within the alien spacecraft. For now, we're blind up there."

"I don't understand," Molly says. "This is what you wanted, right? That's why you tapped my leg and rushed me out of the Oval Office."

"Me?" the chief of staff asks. "Not me. The President."

"I—I don't..."

"You didn't think I'd do anything without her blessing, did you?"

"But..."

"You didn't see her make eye contact and flick her left wrist, huh?"

"Ah... I thought she was trying to get rid of her secretary."

"She was signaling me to release you."

Molly sits there with her mouth full of soggy bread and half-chewed tuna, with her lips gaping open, unable to comprehend what the chief of staff is saying.

"She needed an assist."

"The President?" Molly asks, talking as she chews.

"Senate Majority Leader McMillan and Representative Emmet, the Speaker of the House, were backing her into a corner. They're like rattlesnakes on a desert trail. They were squeezing her for a decision one way or the other when she knew what she needed was time. You gave her an out. She needed the public to push back on the military option."

"I—um."

"Officially, the President can't be seen to be slapping them down. It would be political suicide. She'd never get anything else through Congress or the Senate. She needed the public outrage to take *Icarus* off the table."

Molly takes a sip of orange juice. "And me?"

"You," the chief of staff says, allowing that one word to hang in the air before continuing. "We knew you had a hot head. We knew you'd go straight to the media, consequences be damned."

"What happens next?"

"I need you to be strong. You'll go to trial for violating the terms of your government service NDA. The judge will find you guilty but will drop the charges relating to the Espionage Act. The prosecution will ask for four years in jail, but the judge will sentence you to time served, which will be about three months. After that, you'll walk free."

Molly swallows the lump in her throat.

"If we get lucky and I can bury the media's interest in you, I may even be able to get the NDA charges dropped altogether."

Molly nods.

"And this," the chief of staff says, waving her hand back and forth. "This meeting never happened. I never visited you. The video of me in the corridor will be erased before I reach the main gate."

Molly lowers her head. She looks down at the handcuffs locking her arms together. She stretches her fingers out on the cool metal table.

"I've briefed your father. He understands. He'll be with you every step of the way. Don't worry about anything. We need to let due process run its course, but you're going to be fine."

Chief of Staff Dosela reaches out and takes Molly's hands. Her fingers are warm.

"You've done the President a great service, but it's one no one else will ever know. America thanks you. Humanity thanks you."

With that, the chief of staff gets up and walks to the door. The guard sees her approaching and opens it for her.

"And that's it? That's all?" Molly asks. The chief of staff turns her back on her, but Molly won't be dissuaded. She calls on their first meeting together back on day one, saying, "So, I get used and then discarded like a scrap of paper? Welcome to the White House, right? That's politics, right?"

The chief of staff pauses. She stands still in the doorway with the guard in front of her. She hesitates a fraction too long. Molly can see she's halting between two conflicting opinions. On one hand, she's got to follow political expediency. On the other, she's human. Molly's human. They both have feelings. Neither wants to use anyone or hurt anyone.

"Keep your head down," the chief of staff says in a soft voice, only turning slightly toward her. "Stay quiet. Do your time. Let me see what I can do."

Molly gets to her feet, taking one last bite of the sandwich before leaving the crust on the table.

The guard nods, signaling for her to leave the room.

Molly walks down the corridor toward her cell, only this time, her head is held proud. The chief of staff was right about her all along. Once, she might have been invisible, but now, she's important. She's played her part. The history books will capture her contribution to peaceful contact. They'll see her as a rebel. They'll never know the full story, but she will. Some will love her for her courage. Others will hate her for her betrayal. But she doesn't care what other people think of her. Molly only cares about what she thinks of herself. And she's proud to have done the right thing for both the aliens and humanity.

Looking in the Mirror

Crash stands perfectly still in the dimly lit corridor beneath the habitat. Within the confines of his helmet, he twists his neck, turning his head to one side, wanting to see the figure on the edge of his vision. The curve of his visor gives way to the padding on the inside of his helmet, obscuring his view. He edges sideways, wanting a better look, expecting to be struck on the back of the head like Aleksandr.

A NASA astronaut stands in the darkened doorway to the alien laboratory. White folds of fabric give way to the smooth, spherical curve of a lowered sunshade over the visor, something that doesn't make sense within the darkness. Like him, the astronaut's knees are bent, allowing them to crouch. Their helmet and shoulders skew sideways, rubbing against the low ceiling. Aluminum carabiners and belts hang from anchor points on the suit.

"Liz? Is that you?"

The NASA logo on the chest makes sense, but not the US flag on the shoulder. That flag should be British. And there should be an ESA logo as well.

Crash raises his hand, and the astronaut mirrors his motion. Is that it? Is he staring into a perfectly formed mirror? No, his sunshade is raised.

Crash activates the spotlights on either side of his helmet. Light reflects off the golden sunshade, reflecting his own image back at him as though caught by a distorted, fisheye lens.

"Who—are—you?"

Crash reaches out. His gloved fingers touch at the rim of the sunshade.

"Are you with *Icarus*? Was *Icarus* an alternative mission? A military flight?"

The other astronaut reaches up and rests his hand on Crash's forearm, wanting to prevent him from opening the visor.

"What are you afraid of?" Crash asks, ignoring the gesture and lifting the golden visor, exposing the clear plexiglass beneath.

His spotlights illuminate a blood-red skull within the helmet. Eyeballs stare back at him, not eyes with eyelids, just the balls themselves, bloodshot and motionless. Dark holes mark where the nose should be. Dozens of teeth grin at him, not hidden by a veil of flesh and skin. Blood drips from the jawbone. Muscles extend around the neck, connecting to tendons and flexing as the ghostly astronaut moves.

Crash recoils in horror, bumping into the body of Aleksandr in the hallway. He stumbles, falling back against the wall and sliding to the floor.

"No."

The astronaut steps forward, but its steps are stiff and slow. The motion of its arms is mechanical.

"No, no, no," Crash says, scrambling to get back to his feet and retreat down the hallway. Beyond the bloody astronaut, the spotlights on Crash's helmet illuminate dozens of alien pods, only there are no aliens within them. Adult humans curl inside the flesh sacs hanging from the ceiling. From their broad chests and shoulders, they're male. They're bald. They've curled upside down in a fetal position. Their heads are at the bottom of the sack, while their legs have curled up above them. They wriggle in response to the influx of light, squirming within the fluid-filled sacs.

"Oh, sweet Jesus, *Odyssey*. Where the hell are you?"

The bloodied astronaut reaches for Crash, holding out gloved hands, but behind the rubber and thermal insulation, Crash knows there's more of the fleshy pulp he can see within the helmet. Blood pulsates through veins creeping over the skeleton within the spacesuit. The eyes stare through him.

Crash backs up, stepping slowly toward the main corridor some forty or so yards behind him along the curved passageway.

"Easy," he says, with his hands out, wanting to avoid any sudden movements.

Lights come on automatically around him as he steps away with his helmet and backpack scraping on the low ceiling.

It's then he sees the name tag on the spacesuit. Navy blue letters have been sewn into a pale blue background and mounted on the chest plate. He's seen this dozens of times before, but only ever as a mirror image when suiting up while preparing for a simulated spacewalk in the Neutral Buoyancy Tank back in Houston. This is the first time he's been able to read this particular name tag properly.

C. Williams

It's him.

He's staring at himself.

"You're a... clone," he says, edging away. "A clone of me. But why?"

As he steps back, the automated lights along the corridor follow him, leaving the crumpled body of the cosmonaut to fade into the darkness.

He points.

"And him? Why did you kill him?"

Crash isn't expecting an answer. He doesn't want an answer. He's speaking to contain his own fears. If an answer came, he's not sure what he'd say in reply.

Crash has no idea what's behind him. His suit restricts his visibility. The narrow, cramped corridor is constricting, leaving him fighting a sense of claustrophobia. It feels as though the walls are closing in. The ceiling seems to get lower and lower. Crash wants to turn and run, but he knows he can't. Running isn't possible in the low gravity. And he doesn't want to turn his back on his doppelgänger.

What's behind him? An empty corridor, he hopes, but he has no idea. He's expecting to bump into something—someone.

He talks through his fears, wanting to slow down the encounter and avoid more violence.

"What are you doing here in orbit around our sun? Why did you come here? What do you want from Earth? Why clone me? And how? How did you copy me?"

Although these are questions to which he won't get answers, his mind casts back to the way the dual airlock saturated him with light. At the time, it seemed to Liz that he'd gone through some kind of sterilization process, but it could just as easily have been a process that harvests DNA from skin cells left over from when he donned his gloves or his helmet. It could even have been some kind of advanced magnetic imaging with a resolution far beyond human technology, able to read cellular components such as DNA. Regardless, they've done this for a reason, and that escapes him.

"What do you want from me?"

Crash reaches the main corridor. His clone staggers forward, but at a pace he can easily outdistance. Skin clings to the face, having grown over the flesh and bone at an astonishing rate. The body of the cosmonaut has disappeared into the darkness.

His mind casts back to Aleksandr and the look of pain on his face as he died.

"Are you replacing us? Is that it? Clone us and replace us?"

Now that he's in the wider main corridor, Crash turns his back on the clone and rushes toward the stairs almost fifty yards away in the darkness. He pushes off the walls and floor, bumping against the ceiling with his helmet and backpack.

A shadow blocks the light coming down from the stairs. Thick, white boots come into view, followed by gloved hands and the folds of suit material. A helmet appears along with a backpack, but this astronaut is facing along the curved corridor leading to the laboratory with the alien pods. They're yet to turn to face him.

"No, no, no," he says, seeing the astronaut step down onto the floor.

The flag on the shoulder. It's not the US Stars and Stripes. It's not Russian. A red cross sits in front of a red X on a white background with deep blue triangles in the gaps. This flag has flown on warships and castle battlements for over two hundred years. It's the Union Jack.

"Liz?"

"Crash!" Liz says, unsure where he is. She can hear him over the radio, but that provides no clue about his location. She turns slightly to her right and then back to her left, where he's bounding down the corridor with lights flickering on and off around him.

"Go. Go. Go!"

"Go where?" Liz asks, holding her hands out wide as he rushes up to her. She's got a point. Where can either of them flee to on the alien spacecraft? Nowhere is safe. And yet anywhere other than the darkened tunnels seems safe.

"Back to the surface," he yells on reaching her, although he needn't yell. She can hear him over her radio and even within the echoes rippling around them in the corridor.

Without hesitating, she turns and starts up the stairs, pushing off the wall, but she's not moving fast enough for Crash. He comes up behind her and bumps into her backpack, forcing her on in the low gravity. Stairs glide past beneath his boots.

Liz emerges into the habitat. She turns and rushes along the pebble path, heading toward the glassy pond and the open meadow. Her bulky LCMU and life-support pack sway on her back. Crash comes bounding out of the stairs and turns behind her.

"What—the—hell?" she says, coming to a halt forty feet further along the trail. She turns back to him. Long grass sways around her. The stalks are rust-colored, while the heads are a ruddy brown. The artificial sun blazes in the sky above them, casting a warm light upon them.

Crash is out of breath. He points back at the stairs.

"Clones."

"Clones?"

"They're not just breeding aliens down there, they're recreating us! I saw humans hanging from the ceiling in sacs filled with fluid."

"What? I don't understand."

"As adults," he says. Spittle flies from his lips, hitting the locking ring on the inside of his helmet. "Fully formed at birth."

"But why?" Liz asks, standing in the vast curved, alien wilderness. "Why would they do that?"

"I—I don't know... They... They killed Aleksandr."

"Aleksandr is alive," Liz says. She scrunches up her eyebrows, confused by his point. "I've seen him. He returned to his ship."

"No, no, no," Crash replies, feeling manic. "He's dead. I found his body. He was attacked from behind. His helmet was crushed. His visor smashed."

"You're sure it was him?"

"I held his hand as he died. I knelt there, staring into his eyes."

"Jesus," Liz says. "What are we dealing with?"

"I don't know... We've got to get out of here. Get back to the *Odyssey*."

"We can't. The *Odyssey* is gone. Yúzé won't be back for at least six to seven hours."

Crash staggers through the tall grass on the edge of the path, turning and looking up at the vast expanse of the habitat as it curls overhead, feeling overwhelmed from every angle. "W—Why?"

"He's burning through our reserves to get rid of *Icarus*."

"What is *Icarus*?"

"You don't know? As commander, he thought you knew."

"No," Crash replies, walking through the long grass on the edge of the path winding through the cylinder.

"It's a contingency. A nuke. They hid it in the science bay on the service module."

"A nuke?"

"Ah, it's a neutron bomb. Designed to kill anything organic. Us. Them. Everything in here. If things went wrong, the plan was to sterilize the BDO. Yúzé's pushing it into a lower orbit outside the Lagrange point."

"Things," Crash says, lingering on each of his words, "have—gone—wrong."

"No, you don't mean that. Surely, you wouldn't kill them, wipe them out before they've even hatched. We know nothing about them."

"They're cloning us," Crash replies. "Replacing us. Killing us."

"Tigers or leaves?" Liz asks, recalling their conversation with the SETI scientist back in Houston. "Are you sure about what you've seen?"

"I saw tigers," Crash says. As much as he tries to convey conviction in his answer, he's left with lingering doubts. Uncertainty clouds his mind. He needs certainty, but there's none to be found.

"What are we going to do?"

"We've got to get out of here while we still can," Crash says, pointing at the sloping curve of the field leading to the smooth arc of water forming the pond. "We lift off. We return to the airlock. We wait up there for the *Odyssey*."

"And then?"

"I—I don't know. We leave. We're not capable of handling this. First Contact is over."

Within his thick gloves, his fingers are shaking uncontrollably.

Life as a Bat

Crash slows his breathing. He draws in through his nose and out through his mouth, desperately trying to calm himself.

After squeezing through the dark, claustrophobic interior of the alien spacecraft, the habitat feels immense. It really is another world. Hundreds of feet above him, a forest hangs upside down, threatening to fall, but it's an illusion. Those trees are as secure as the shrubs and bushes around him. Water sticks to the inside of the cylinder, curling around it like a dark mirror, reflecting the warm light from the artificial alien sun. Fields and meadows stretch into the distance, winding along the length of the habitat, being loosely linked by paths that curve around various ponds and streams. Bushes rise in clusters. Red mounds break through the undergrowth. Their rough-hewn shapes are visible between the trees of the forest. Stalks of what looks like wheat sway with the wind coming off the slope, forming waves similar to those found on the swell of the ocean.

The stark contrast with the dark, narrow corridors and laboratories beneath the cylinder leaves Crash feeling lost. Nothing feels right. Everything is deceiving, even their voices over the radio. When Liz speaks, the speakers in his Snoopy cap make it seem as though she's standing next to him when she's easily thirty feet away, over by the edge of the nearest lake.

The vast, open atrium spans hundreds upon hundreds of feet. Crash looks up, wanting to find reason rather than fear, wanting to think clearly rather than panic. He needs to think with clarity. Trees form stalactites above him, leaning down toward him, defying gravity, only there is no gravity. Their branches reach toward the artificial sun. Behind Liz, a thicket of shrubs extends horizontally from the curve of the cylinder without drooping as he'd expect on Earth. In space, no way is up. Within the alien's O'Neill cylinder, all ways are up. Regardless of where they are, up is always above them.

The habitat is coming to life. Monkey-like creatures move through the trees hundreds of feet up on the curved slope of the cylinder, swinging between branches. The same creatures probably inhabit the forest directly behind them, but from below, their movements are obscured by the canopy. With each passing second, the cylinder is becoming more of a world than a spaceship. It's the Garden of Eden. But it's misleading. The horrors beneath the surface seem like a nightmare compared to the lush extraterrestrial atrium spanning easily half a mile, curling around them.

"What are we going to do?" Liz asks.

Crash can't find any alternative. "We need to get the hell out of here."

It's not a solution. He understands that. His impulse is a reaction, but what else can he do? He can't turn his back on the stairs. He positions himself so he can see Liz, but he's wary of the horrors beneath the ground. He's expecting another astronaut to appear, one that hasn't originated from Earth.

Liz walks through the grass, approaching the lake as they prepare to take flight within the alien habitat. Dark water curls up the far side of the atrium, bending and reflecting the light around them like glass.

Crash backs up on the gravel path, preparing to use it as a running track/runway.

The vast curving structure surrounding them is imposing. Seeing an entire world stretching overhead is breathtaking. Crash knows what Liz is feeling—the awe, the beauty, the surreal distortion of nature unfolding like a Salvador Dali painting. The sheer size of the alien structure is humbling, and yet, beneath the surface lies the crumpled body of a cosmonaut.

"I just can't believe this—all this is destructive," Liz says, turning and taking in the length of the habitat. "It makes no sense."

Golden rays of light dance through the leaves of trees on the far side of the path. Long, slender trunks reach for the warm light, with a crown of leaves branching out to form a canopy. Insects stream up and down the trees, forming highways running in both directions. Although at a distance, they resemble ants, they're bigger and far more dominant. On Earth, ants climbing a tree would be barely noticeable. Here, they form swarms rushing about the trunks, hiding the smooth surface of the alien plants. They're busy and industrious, no doubt driving some critical process within the alien ecosystem.

"What was it the professor said?" Liz asks as Crash checks his controls, lining himself up to rush against the rotation of the cylinder and take to the air.

"Expectations are dangerous."

"And what did you expect down there in the darkness?"

"Not clones."

"But when you saw them, what was your reaction?"

"Aleksandr was murdered," Crash says, feeling defensive. "He's dead!"

"Is he?" Liz asks. "Or is he onboard the *Vechnost,* powering up the capsule?"

"That's the clone. It has to be."

"Do you really think a clone could operate a Russian spacecraft?"

"What are you saying? That he killed himself? He killed his own clone?"

"It's a possibility," Liz replies.

Crash points at the airlock set high in the center of the bow. "It's also possible his doppelgänger is impersonating him out there."

Liz says, "But how would it know about his spacecraft? How would it know where it was, let alone how to power it up? I'm telling you, that was Aleksandr out there."

"But why would he leave the habitat so soon?" Crash asks. "I mean, his EVA suit should have been good for at least twelve hours."

"I dunno. Maybe to transmit results. Maybe to get more equipment."

"What was he doing when you saw him?" Crash asks.

"The last time I saw Aleksandr, he'd restored power and looked as though he was gathering tools from the external bay on the Soyuz service module. I think he intends to come back."

Crash doubts himself. He wants to leave, but running from something he doesn't understand isn't a solution. It's convenient and easily excusable, but not honest. Deep down, he knows he's giving in to his fears. That's the answer Liz was looking for. What did he expect down there in the darkness? Fear itself. The worst of his nightmares. Was any of it even real? Perhaps he was hallucinating, bringing his own paranoia to life. He couldn't help it. Everything he saw reinforced that notion, but there's dried blood on his suit.

The professor was right. Expectations are dangerous. They blur reason. Damn it, Crash thinks, he knows what he saw down there. He watched as Aleksandr died in his arms. And he saw a zombie reaching for him within the confines of an EVA suit, but where the hell did that suit come from? If it's a ruse, it's elaborate. If the goal was to kill him, there are easier ways to do that than cloning and chasing him. And it hasn't followed him to the surface. Not yet, anyway. And as for that spacesuit—once those creatures killed either him or Aleksandr, they could salvage an original. Why go to the trouble of fabricating a seemingly perfect copy?

Liz must sense his discomfort. "If we leave, we learn nothing."

"But we survive," he says from behind the curved glass of his visor.

"You're assuming this is an either/or situation, that we either live or die. What if there are other possibilities?"

Crash doesn't want to debate this with her. Not here. Not now. Deep down, though, he knows she's right. Life is lived in color, not black and white. When are there ever only two options?

"Liz," a familiar voice says over the radio, but it takes Crash a moment to recognize the speaker.

As strange as it may seem, he only ever hears himself through the resonance of his own skull. Whenever Crash speaks, he hears not only the sound coming from his lips but the vocalization reverberating through his own body to his ear canal. The result is such that he's never liked hearing recordings of himself. They never sound quite right. It's the lack of that internal resonance that's missing. His Mom and Pop are always so proud when he makes the news or speaks on a panel, but Crash has never been able to shake the feeling it's someone else speaking other than him.

"Liz, please," the voice repeats. It's at that moment Liz realizes it's not Crash that's talking to her over the radio. She must see his lips are still. She turns and looks across the field with its grass swaying in the soft breeze. There, on the edge of the clearing, stands an astronaut in a pristine white NASA EVA suit with an LCMU on his back. He steps out of the stairway and turns toward them, walking slowly along the crushed rock path with his golden sun shield raised, revealing familiar features behind his visor.

"Wait," she says, backing away from Crash. Liz steps through the waist-height grass, moving at an angle away from both of them. Her eyes, though, say what her words can't express. She's looking at Crash, but she's focused on his arms and gloves. She's alarmed. She's seen something she missed up until this point. Crash looks down at his own arms. Dried blood stains the folds in his white suit material. Blood has coagulated on his gloves.

"I can explain," he says, holding his hands out and trying not to appear threatening.

"No, no, no," she says, increasing the distance between them.

"It's not what you think."

"Clones, right? That's what you said," she replies, pointing at him and then at his doppelgänger some fifty feet away up the curved slope. "How do I know who you are? How do I know what really happened down there?"

"Aleksandr died in my arms," he says, trying to show her what happened from the stains on his suit.

"Oh, I don't doubt that," she replies. "But I doubt who died and how he died."

"He was dying when I got to him."

"Was he?"

The other astronaut holds out a gloved hand, beckoning to her and saying, "Liz. Don't be afraid."

She keeps her distance from the two of them, saying, "You could both be clones."

"It's me," Crash says, holding his hands in front of the thick chest plate on his spacesuit, but seeing the blood on his arms, he can understand why she doubts him.

"Tell me something," Liz says. "Tell me something only the real Crash would know."

Before Crash can reply, his doppelgänger says, "We met at Ellington Airfield. Andrea was taking you up in a T-38."

"What? No," Crash calls out in alarm. "Don't believe him! You can't believe him."

"He's right," Liz says, edging her way through the grass toward the stairs.

"I was going to say that," Crash says, pleading with her. "Please. No!"

"You're not seeing reality," the doppelgänger says, addressing Liz and echoing the words of the SETI scientist they met in the park back in Houston. "You've got to put aside your preconceptions. They're dangerous."

"They are," Liz says, and Crash can see she believes him. He's got to think of some way to sway her back to him, to convince her he's real—he's the original.

"You're British, but you were raised in France," Crash says, no longer pleading with her but rather laying out facts without any emotion, drawing on their meeting with the SETI scientist as well. "You don't like Dr. Pepper. You prefer Sprite."

Liz softens. "Actually, I prefer Diet Coke, but Sprite is okay."

"But you prefer savory to sweet for a snack. You ate the Extra-Cheesy Doritos instead of the Skittles."

"I did."

For Crash, this is madness. They're standing within an alien cylinder, surrounded by exotic flora, bathed in golden light from an artificial sun, watching as water curls up and overhead in vast lakes without falling, and yet they're talking about junk food back on Earth, but somehow it's working. Liz can see they both know the same details. She placed her trust in personal knowledge, but now she must realize she has no reason to trust either of them as they both remember the past.

"It's me," Crash says. "I'm the one that launched with you from the Cape."

"Do you believe him?" the doppelgänger asks with an equally convincing voice, causing her to doubt herself. She halts between them, resting her gloved hands on the stalks swaying around her. Crash can see she's trying to ground herself.

The doppelgänger draws on the conversation with the SETI scientist once more, asking her, "What does it mean to live life as a bat? Can we ever really know?"

"You," she says, turning to face him. "You're the bat!"

"No. You are," the clone says, smiling. "At least, from my perspective."

"We're bats to each other," Liz mumbles. "Aliens..."

"Yes."

It's at that point Crash understands. He can see the realization washing over Liz as well. From within her helmet, from behind a thin plexiglass visor, she speaks with clarity, talking to an entity from another world.

"You—You could never understand us. Our reasoning. Our emotions. Our thoughts and feelings. Our experience of consciousness. What it means for us to be alive."

"Your senses," the doppelgänger says, dropping all pretense. "They're unique. Colors. Smells. Sounds. These are sensations we have not experienced. Vocal chords are an interesting mechanism for communication."

Crash stumbles forward on the path. Fascination has replaced fear. "You could never understand what it means to be human without being human."

"Correct."

"And the lie? Your deception?" Liz asks, backing up toward Crash in his bloodstained spacesuit.

"*Your* deception. The last of your kind killed one of us."

"Aleksandr," Crash says, realizing he held the hand of a dying clone within the depths of the alien spacecraft.

There's something about this clone's terminology Crash finds unsettling—*your kind killed one of us*. His comment is personal. Whatever he is, this clone is not expendable, no more so than any human.

"We have rushed communication, wanting to understand your intrusion."

"Us?" Liz says, tapping her own chest.

"We're the bad guys," Crash says to her. "We've invaded their spacecraft."

"The nature of your intrusion is disturbing," the clone says. "As a species, you are..."

"Complex?" Liz asks.

"Contradictory," the clone replies. "You're driven by emotion."

"Fear," Crash says.

"It's your first reaction," the clone replies, walking slowly toward them. "Fear overrides reason."

From their perspective, the clone is walking down a curved path, slowly approaching from the slope.

"We meant no harm," Crash says. "We were curious."

The clone comes to a halt no more than ten feet away. For Crash, seeing himself is unsettling, but not because he feels like he's looking into a mirror. On the contrary, that would be more comforting.

In high school, Crash broke his nose while playing baseball. It was a humid Saturday in the middle of a blistering Ohio summer. He was on second base, joking around with the fielder, and the ball caught him on the cheek, breaking the bridge of his nose. He doesn't remember too much about what happened immediately after that, as the pain drowned out both sights and sounds, but there was blood. A lot of blood. He was carried from the field and taken to the local hospital. Coming from a middle-class family, the sudden influx of emergency medical bills threatened to bankrupt his dad, so his nose was never set properly. Even now, there's a kink in the bridge, and the nostrils lean slightly to one side, while his right cheekbone is higher and more pronounced than the left. It's subtle. Most people don't notice, or if they do, they simply accept that *that's Crash*. For him, though, it means pictures and mirrors depict entirely different people. He sees himself in a mirror but a stranger in a photo, as his features appear reversed. Whatever full-body scan he passed through within the airlock, the aliens have decided to replicate him not only biologically but in terms of his physiology as well. His clone has the same crooked nose, but to his mirror-trained mind, it leans the wrong way—only it doesn't. Crash wants to reach out and touch his clone. His fingers flex within his gloves. This is the first time he's ever seen himself the way everyone else sees him.

Crash says, "We just want to understand you."

"You're perplexing. Love and hate. Fear and curiosity. Anger and kindness. How is it these contradictions reside within you at the same time?"

Liz ignores his question, asking, "Why did you come here? Why have you come to Earth?"

"To hide."

Liz looks confused, but Crash intrinsically understands what the clone means. This is him speaking. An utterly alien intelligence is using his thoughts, his feelings, his emotions, his memories and experiences to communicate through a perfect clone of him.

His mind casts back to the sunny afternoon when Liz rushed into his office to announce the arrival of the alien spacecraft. His first reaction was to hide what he was doing on his laptop, but not out of guilt or embarrassment or anything like that. He hadn't done anything wrong, and yet he instinctively hid his game of *Wordle* from her. She wouldn't have cared what he was doing. She wouldn't have thought anything of him missing the clues for that day's word puzzle. She would have barely noticed, but he *had* to hide. For him, it was a gut reaction, not a reasoned, logical response. He hid because flopping at *Wordle* doesn't match the outward persona of a seasoned astronaut. He hid because he felt he needed to be seen to be successful and not flawed—not human. He hid because humans live behind a mask of pretense, pretending to be perfect when no one is faultless. He hid because of the way she saw him as someone larger than life. And it's that last point that resonates in his mind.

"They're not gods," he says to Liz.

"What?"

For her, his comment is a confusing leap of logic, but from the few words spoken by the clone, Crash understands its intent. He's astonished by the accuracy of the alien's communication. Far from mere words, it's communicating with unparalleled precision by drawing upon body language and vocal inflections, along with his attitudes, experiences and memories. Instead of being longwinded and potentially confusing, it can use just a handful of well-chosen words to communicate with astonishing depth.

Crash looks his clone in the eye, saying, "They knew there was life on Earth. They wanted to observe us without being seen, but they didn't realize how far we've come in terms of technology."

"But why hide?" Liz counters. "Why not talk to us? We're smart.

We're intelligent."

"All complex life is intelligent," Crash replies. "You think dolphins don't know who we are and what we're capable of? Or chimps? Hell, cats and dogs manipulate us into caring for them. From their perspective, we're useful fools. We're their slaves. A wagging tail and a soft nudge, and we go all gooey inside."

"But that's different," Liz says.

"Is it?"

"We're different. We're clever—ingenious. We can communicate with clarity."

Crash recalls their conversation with the SETI professor in the park, knowing full well his clone remembers it too. "And yet, gorillas use sign language. Prairie dogs can identify people by the clothing they wear, warning others of a specific danger with a few yelps that say, red shirt or black hat. Cuttlefish talk with a rainbow of colors rippling over their skin."

"But those aren't words."

"Aren't they? Why not? Only because we say they're not."

"But why would they hide?" Liz asks, stretching her hand out toward the clone and appealing for a response from him. The clone, though, is curiously silent. He seems to know Crash understands him. He looks him in the eye, encouraging him to take his logic further with a slight smile.

Crash smiles. Looking at his seemingly identical twin, he can see the creature understands precisely how it has set off this chain of reasoning in his mind. And it's observing them, relishing how they work through the logic of First Contact together. Crash suspects his clone knows what he's going to say before the words leave his lips. It knows him so well it can anticipate his line of reasoning. Communicating via clone is masterful, allowing the alien behind the clone to steer him to the conclusion it wants him to reach with just a few well-placed words. Crash shakes his head. Deep down, he wants to be the contrarian and not allow himself to be manipulated, but he understands there's no malice. He returns to his earlier point.

"They're hiding because we need gods."

"I don't understand," Liz says.

Oh, boy, he thinks, just wait until she runs into her own clone. Then she'll understand. For him, there's a recursive sense of awareness when talking to himself as a clone. Once she realizes that, she'll marvel at the effectiveness of their strategy just as he is, standing there in the cylindrical alien habitat.

"Your friend is correct," the clone says, just as Crash knew it would because it's precisely what he'd say if he were in its place and wanted to help him convince Liz.

"We want things," Crash says. "We're like a cat meowing for food or purring, wanting to be pampered. We wouldn't be content with them just being. We'd want their attention, their technology."

"Why is that a bad thing?" Liz asks.

"Because they're not gods. They came here to observe us, not change us. They understand it's not their place to play god with us. They respect that we need to stand on our own feet."

"So they'd hide from us?"

"Like we hide watching animals in the wild, leaving them undisturbed, wanting to understand them on their own, without our influence."

"Like a researcher watching a cougar from behind camouflage netting?"

In perfect unison, using the same tone of voice, both Crash and his clone say, "Yes."

"Ooooh-kay," Liz says, switching her gloved hand back and forth, alternating between pointing at each of them. "That's creepy."

Again, in perfect unison, both of them say, "I know." Only Crash follows up with a laugh, adding, "Pretty wild, huh?"

"Life as a bat," Liz says, raising her eyebrows.

"For them," Crash replies. "Yes! For us, this is normal, I guess."

Behind the clone, another astronaut emerges from the stairs, stepping out onto the gravel path. He's shorter. His spacesuit is made from a different type of fabric and appears cream-colored when compared to the sterile white of the NASA EVA suits. Three stripes on the shoulder form a flag. Red, blue and white stripes leave no doubt about the country of origin, but who is this? Is this the Russian cosmonaut Crash saw in the tunnels? Or is this another clone?

"Aleksandr?"

Over his headset, Crash hears English spoken with a Russian accent.

"Ambition drives you. Greatness. Adoration."

"Yes," Liz replies, not making any excuses for humanity. "We struggle with our impulses. All of us, to one degree or another."

The Russian clone asks, "Is reason always subordinate to ego? How is it that you've reached the stars?"

Crash is unable to reply. He's stunned. The Russian clone is emulating Aleksandr, understanding his motives and intents. To comprehend humanity, the aliens have adopted human form, inheriting not only human bodies but human memories and idiosyncrasies as well. It's as though researchers were able to inhabit the clones of specific dolphins rather than study them while in captivity or while swimming alongside them with scuba gear. The aliens are able to communicate on the level of humanity as humans, understanding the foibles and cognitive biases that blind most people. For them, the clones are research vessels. They're interfaces with a bunch of primates from the third planet in this particular star system. The aliens are able to bridge misunderstandings and avoid the disconnect between *Homo sapiens* and their species by immersing themselves in humanity.

Liz says, "Our science. It allows us to avoid our own biases and prejudices. Well, at least in theory. We—"

Crash cuts her off. He doesn't mean to, but his intense curiosity gets the better of him. He asks the two of them, "Where are you?"

"Me?" both of the clones reply in unison, pointing at themselves with an identical gesture, one that's perfectly synchronized. "I am here and there. I am within and without. I am with you and alone."

Crash and Liz look at each other. The implication is clear. Like an Air Force pilot flying a drone via remote control, the alien is manipulating each of the clones, and yet it's more than that. He's inhabiting them. His brain is capable of controlling both of them simultaneously and independently.

The choice of terms used by the alien is revealing. On Earth, a soldier flying a drone over enemy territory remains safe in the control room back at the airfield. Here, though, the alien being seems omnipresent, being both with them and yet still inhabiting his own alien body somewhere beneath the surface of the habitat.

"And the other one?" Crash asks, articulating a question for which he feels he already knows the answer. "I held his hand."

"He died, so I was awakened."

Crash swallows the lump welling up in his throat.

Whatever link connects these creatures with their human clones, it conveys more than mere audio and video as a drone pilot would experience back on Earth. If a missile brings down a Reaper or a Global Hawk, the operator sees static on the screen, removes their headset, grabs a coffee, and waits for the ground crew to launch a replacement. Here, though, it's more than a mere link. The clones are biological extensions of the aliens themselves. It wasn't a clone that died in his arms. The intelligence he saw behind those eyes, the disbelief, the terror and heartbreak was that of an alien dying of shock. A tear rolls down his cheek.

"You were awakened early," Liz says.

"The pods I saw," Crash says, pointing at the gravel on the ground in roughly the position where he found the laboratory.

"We will not be ready for some time," his clone replies as the Russian clone walks up beside him, standing next to him on the edge of the path. "I was rushed. I am—premature."

Liz turns to Crash, shaking her head in disbelief. "We're talking to a child."

"In your terms, yes. I'm vulnerable. I'm in need of returning."

"To develop further in your pod," Crash says, realizing how humanity has fucked up First Contact by rushing to the meeting.

"It is..."

"Difficult?" Liz asks.

"Painful," the American clone says. "Our flight computer—or that's the closest equivalent in your language—it roused me. Forced me."

"I am so sorry," Liz says, clutching her gloved hands in front of her.

"And her?" Crash asks, pointing sideways at Liz. "Are you cloning her?"

"It takes time, but yes, a communications vessel is being prepared."

"And will you command her?"

"Breathe with her," the clone says. "Understand her."

Liz shakes her head, astonished. "I—I—I."

Another figure appears on the edge of the forest, high on the curved slope, just beyond the stairs. A Russian clone steps into view, walking down the gravel path. Like the others, his motion is casual and relaxed, so Crash doesn't think anything of his presence within the vast, cylindrical habitat.

"We will withdraw from your spacecraft," Crash says. "We will wait for your people to—"

Without warning, blood explodes within the helmet of the closest Russian clone. One moment, his face is clearly visible behind the polycarbonate glass. The next, brilliant red blood sprays out within the confines of the helmet, coating the inside of the visor. Blood, brains and goo stick to the smooth inner surface, slowly dripping down in the low gravity.

The sound of a gunshot echoes within the habitat. Immediately, the hive of activity in the surrounding trees stops, with the various insectoid creatures coming to a halt.

The clone falls forward, moving in slow motion as it collapses to its knees before plummeting face-first on the gravel. Blood drips from a hole on the edge of the helmet, marking the path of the bullet.

Liz yells, "Nooooo!"

Crash is already on the move. He leans forward at an angle that, on Earth, would see him fall flat on his face. Within the alien habitat, it allows his boots to gain traction. Gravel shifts beneath him, kicking up behind his boots. He runs like a linebacker with his shoulder down and his arms out, ready to sack the quarterback. He's so low his gloved fingers touch at the path, directing him on.

The cosmonaut that emerged from the forest has his arm outstretched. A handgun points at the clone of Crash Williams. For his part, the American clone has his arms up, grabbing at his helmet and screaming in pain. The death of a linked lifeform causes him untold distress. The clone rocks his head back. His eyes are pinched shut. Veins strain on his neck as he yells within the confines of his helmet.

A second shot rings out.

A bullet punches through the back of the remaining clone's helmet. Blood squirts from the side of his neck, spraying over the lining on the inside of the helmet. The bullet exits through the polycarbonate glass, punching a tiny hole in the visor. Vapor rushes into the frigid air. Cracks splinter through the glass.

Crash drops his shoulder. He has no intention of stopping to help the wounded American clone or drag him to cover. Crash charges, knocking the clone off his feet and sending him tumbling into the grass. As heartless as it may seem, Crash has only one objective: the shooter. Nothing else matters. As long as Aleksandr has that gun, they're all in danger.

Aleksandr must see the old, dried blood on Crash's suit and realizes he's from Earth. He lowers his aim. He has no intention of killing the American astronaut. He speaks over the radio, having switched to their frequency.

"They're an abomination—all of them."

Liz rushes to the wounded clone's aid. She crouches, with just the top of her backpack and helmet visible above the swaying grass.

Crash collides with Aleksandr, knocking him off his feet. The gun clatters to the gravel path. They fall on the edge of the track. Crash grabs the Russian, taking hold of the loose folds on his arms. Fighting within a spacesuit is more like wrestling than boxing, with both men struggling to pin the other.

"We must kill them," Aleksandr yells, pushing Crash away and causing him to roll and stumble backward in the grass. "All of them!"

"We need to listen to them," Crash counters, regaining his balance and charging back at Aleksandr. The Russian cosmonaut scrambles across the gravel, reaching for the gun. Crash grabs his backpack and hauls him to one side, tossing him into the grass. Aleksandr rolls. He turns over, lying on his backpack with the gun in his hand, pointing it squarely at Crash.

In that instant, Crash knows what is about to unfold. He feels a profound shift within his soul. His life is not his own. Not anymore. He dares not blink. Decisions made in hundredths of a second will determine both life and death, but not just for the two of them—for every intelligent being on the alien spacecraft and potentially billions of people on Earth if this should escalate into an interstellar war. Crash should halt where he is. He should stop and raise his hands and plead for reason, but the trickle of blood dripping from the cosmonaut's mouth suggests he's beyond mere logic. Hatred glistens in his eyes. Anger lines his face. Bitterness curls on his lips.

Crash lunges for the gun. Aleksandr squeezes the trigger. The barrel recoils. A bullet explodes out of the pistol, moving faster than the speed of sound within the thin atmosphere. Crash feels it tear through his body before he realizes quite what has happened. The bullet punches through the front plate on his suit and breaks his ribs. The steel tip tumbles within him. The projectile mushrooms on contact with his body, ripping through his lungs within a fraction of a second and exiting beneath his shoulder blade. The shard of hot metal embeds itself in his LCMU. Thick, warm blood oozes from his wounds. He staggers forward, shuffling with his feet, barely able to stand.

Aleksandr is still lying on his back in the grass. He shows no regret. His eyes narrow. It's not that he's enjoying watching the American die so much as that he seems perplexed that Crash would rush him. Aleksandr has no remorse. He has a mission to fulfill—a mindset, a belief. With his spare hand, he pushes off the ground, getting to his knees, keeping the gun trained on Crash, who's no more than a few feet away from him. For his part, Crash braces, locking his knees together with his legs pushed out wide. It's the only way he can continue to stand.

Liz yells, "Crassssshhh!"

She pushes through the long grass, rushing toward the two men. Aleksandr turns the gun on her. He's up on one knee, having swiveled to face her. He stares down the barrel of his pistol at her.

Crash feels unduly weak. Raising his arms takes a herculean effort. It's as though he's lifting absurd weights at the gym. Life is draining from his body. Blood bubbles from his lips. He grabs Aleksandr by the shoulder. The cosmonaut turns to face him. Crash grabs the gun, wrestling it from his grasp.

"No," Aleksandr snarls, snatching at Crash's hand, but his thick gloves make fine movements cumbersome. His fingers glance off the sleek metal.

Crash brings the gun up under the rim of the cosmonaut's helmet, pushing it hard into the thick fabric and the suit's locking ring for no other reason than that's the only way he can hold the gun steady as his strength fades. His legs tremble, threatening to give way beneath him. With his other hand, he holds on to Aleksandr's shoulder, using the cosmonaut for balance. Once Liz reaches them, he'll give her the gun. Aleksandr, though, grabs his glove.

The gun goes off.

A single bullet tears through the locking ring, deflecting within the helmet. It grazes the cosmonaut's forehead and tumbles, digging into the bone. The Russian's skullcap is ripped off his head as the bullet exits through the top of the helmet. Brains splatter against the white lining. The slightest touch of the supersonic projectile has liquified both grey and white matter alike. Ripples reverberate through the Russian's brain like jelly, destroying hundreds of millions of neurons and killing him in an instant.

Aleksandr looks up with dead eyes. He collapses, falling backward, folding over on himself and crumpling in the grass.

Crash tumbles to the ground, barely able to prop himself up on the gravel as he leans sideways on his backpack. The gun lies on the path. Steam rises from the barrel in the cool air.

Liz bounds over. She crouches by Crash, taking his gloved hand as he chokes on his own blood. Beside her, the alien clone mimicking Crash stands inert. He's removed his helmet along with his gloves. He has his right hand up, pressing against the side of his neck, controlling the bleeding from the torn tissue where the bullet grazed him. As he breathes out, vapor drifts from his lips.

"Easy," Liz says, lowering Crash to the dirt and trying to make him comfortable. "Hang in there. Hold on. We'll... We'll do something."

She turns, looking up at the clone, but he's unmoved. Like Crash, he must know nothing can be done. He stands there silently with his head bowed. Blood seeps between his fingers. Beside him, a ghost appears. Is this a lucid dream? An illusion? Crash blinks, unsure what he's seeing as his life fades. The ghost, though, takes form. Translucent skin shimmers in the golden light of the artificial sun. Crash pinches his eyes shut for a second before opening them again. He can barely focus on the surreal creature standing before him.

His heart struggles to beat, starving his brain of oxygen. As he lies there dying, is he imagining what he wants to see? Is the creature before him merely the construct of his failing mind clinging to life?

The alien is short, barely four feet in height, with almost entirely transparent skin. Nerves and arteries extend around a brain set in clear jelly. There's a skeleton, but the muscles attached to it are invisible, distorting but not blocking the light. A tail flicks behind the alien. Cords reach from eight dark eyes, winding their way back toward the bulbous folds of the brain. The creature has arms and legs, being bipedal. Claws extend from the alien's thin arms. The translucent skin of the creature catches the light like a halo, glistening softly in the warm rays of the elongated star at the heart of the cylinder. In folklore and ancient scriptures, it would be neither an angel nor a demon but rather one of the neutral orders, such as the cherubim or the seraphim. To him, it's supernatural, almost divine, even though he knows the alien is real. And he understands its intent. It knows his life is slipping away, and it's giving him a glimpse of what he's dying for, allowing him to see who he saved.

As the alien moves, the curved habitat behind it appears distorted and blurred. Whether that's from the tears welling up in his eyes or the creature's clear organs is difficult to tell.

Crash struggles against a lump rising in his throat. It's only now he realizes that when the alien is in motion, the clone is perfectly still. When the clone moves, the alien becomes a statue. Whatever consciousness inhabits this strange creature seems to dance between bodies.

Liz turns to see the alien but quickly returns her gaze to Crash. He chokes on his own blood, trying to swallow the dark fluid rising in his mouth. The ghost stands there inert as the clone kneels on the other side of Crash. A bare hand rests on the bloody hole in his EVA suit, returning the kindness he showed in the darkened corridor beneath the surface of the habitat. Their eyes meet. He's staring at himself, and yet he's not. Compassion wells up between two sentient beings separated by hundreds, if not thousands of light years and billions of evolutionary steps undertaken on entirely different worlds.

"Me," Crash says to Liz, spitting blood from his lips. He looks deep into her eyes as he speaks, clutching her hand in his. "M—Me. I—I'm the clone."

"What?" Liz says, looking at the clone opposite her and then back at Crash. "I don't understand what you mean?"

"Him. Take him with you. He's me."

Liz lowers her head, breaking eye contact with Crash. Tears roll down her cheeks.

Crash coughs. Blood splatters on the inside of his visor.

"D—Destroy the video. No one must know. He—He's right. Fear... Fear destroys reason... They—They'd... Humanity will be afraid. Afraid it's going to be replaced... Just like Aleksandr... They cannot know. They won't understand."

Within her helmet, Liz nods. She understands what he's asking of her. Her lips tremble. She tries to speak, but words fail her. Her fingers shake, but his don't. His hand goes limp. His eyes stare past her, gazing at the ghost and the way the warm light radiating from the artificial sun at the heart of the habitat shimmers on the alien's skin. Crash releases his last breath. His head slips to one side, going limp. Blood trickles from his lips as his gloved hand relaxes, releasing her fingers. And with that, he's dead.

Liz leans forward, rocking on her knees and resting her helmet on his chest. Tears fall to the inside of her visor as she sobs, whispering, "I will. I will take him with me. I promise I will."

The End

Epilogue

"Trust," Liz says, standing on a podium in the East Room of the White House. "We cannot lose sight of the need for trust on both sides of First Contact."

Liz, Crash, Yúzé, Adeep and Pierre are seated at a long table on a raised platform at the front of the room. It's been four months since First Contact and almost a month since they arrived back on Earth. Liz has been itching to address the public, but the President has shielded them from attention until now, saying the focus needs to be on the science of First Contact, not personalities.

Microphones have been strategically placed on the desk between the astronauts. They're dressed informally in their blue flight suits. Given the crystal chandeliers hanging from the ceiling, the golden drapes surrounding the windows and the ornate cornices running around the edge of the room, the astronauts are out of place. They look like mechanics about to work on a classic car.

The President stands at the side of the stage with the NASA Executive Director. Although they're not speaking at the press conference, their presence is telling. Nothing is haphazard. Even though this was an international effort, the US is sending a clear message about its continued leadership. In Liz's thinking, this debrief should have been held at the UN.

Painted portraits of Presidents and First Ladies adorn the walls, being mounted in gilded frames. For Liz, walking into the White House was overwhelming, but that was always the intention.

The audience has been divided with the press seated behind the dignitaries. There are ambassadors, members of the US House of Representatives and US senators present. This is a press conference held at arm's length. The astronauts have been briefed on what they should and shouldn't talk about, while the press can be cut off by simply withdrawing the microphone boom stretching over the audience. When it's overhead, they can ask questions. As it moves away, their voices fade.

Two rows from the back, a reporter from the *Washington Post* raises his hand. The boom swings over the audience, lowering near him. Camera angles are deceiving, making the conference look much more open and inclusive than it is.

"Yes," Liz says, pointing at him and playing along with the general script.

"Can we hear from Chris Williams? He was the first person inside the habitat."

"The second," Liz says, following her brief to remain in charge of the discussion. "The Russian cosmonaut Aleksandr Kurkov was the first human to enter the alien spacecraft. Crash was second. I was third."

"Can we hear from the commander?" the reporter asks. Crash was always going to be the focus of media interest on Earth.

The clone of Crash Williams leans forward, approaching one of the microphones mounted on the table in front of them. He touches the scarring on the side of his neck. The flesh is angry, still somewhat raw. Stitches are visible.

Crash speaks in a soft voice, but his tone is like that of gravel turning over within a cement truck. It's an act but a convincing one.

"I'm still recovering... can't speak much."

He sits back, surrendering the microphone on the table to Liz.

"I can speak for Crash," she says.

"The Russians are contesting your version of events," the reporter calls out as the boom mic recedes above him.

"We didn't bring a gun onboard," Liz replies. She turns sideways, gesturing to Crash and adding. "We were lucky to get out of there alive."

"So the Russian cosmonaut attacked you? But why?"

"He claimed the alien vessel for Russia. He felt we were the aggressors. We weren't. He shot Crash. Thankfully, between the two of us, we were able to overpower him, but the gun went off in the struggle, killing him."

"So it wasn't on purpose," the reporter asks, standing so his voice can reach the microphone. An uncertain boom operator looks to the floor manager, wondering if he should recall it entirely and move on to the next person.

"No," Liz replies, knowing both the reporters and the dignitaries in the grand ballroom have already been presented with a detailed, written account of the incident. She tries to move the conversation forward, saying, "Of course, it wasn't intentional. We're astronauts. Not soldiers. We came in peace, not in conquest."

A murmur runs through the audience. Liz ignores it.

"With the extraterrestrial spacecraft now in a geostationary orbit over twenty-two thousand miles above Earth, we can move to the next phase of First Contact: sharing cultural and historical information."

Unbeknown to everyone but Liz and Crash, this was the most contentious point of First Contact on the BDO. Even after the original Crash saved the life of his clone, the aliens wanted to withdraw. Their mission was scientific. Their brief was to observe but not interfere.

Liz pleaded with them to reconsider their objectives, pointing out that they could be a force for positive change within humanity. The aliens accepted that Crash and Aleksandr represented the contradiction that is *Homo sapiens*. Like Yin and Yang, between them, they represented the best and the worst of humanity—hope and fear, love and hate, kindness and anger, ego and humility. The aliens accepted that this contradiction defines humans in general. They realized that once seen by humanity, they could never observe humans unseen, but they could shape First Contact, using it to encourage good within humanity. Liz told them the clone of Chris '*Crash*' Williams was ideally placed to view First Contact from both perspectives without anyone knowing otherwise. They liked that as it fit their brief. Their spacecraft might be under observation by human technology, but humanity would have no idea a clone was walking among them, collecting untarnished information about them.

"What about the missing ninety-seven minutes?" someone calls out from the back of the room. The moderator, standing behind Liz, steps around toward the front of the stage, apparently ready to have that particular reporter removed. Liz breathes deeply. This was supposed to be a triumphant interview, not an interrogation.

"No, it's okay," she says, holding her hand out and wanting to address that point. "Before we left Earth, one of NASA's SETI scientists warned us—warned all of us—that expectations were dangerous. They told us our fears, our assumptions, our expectations, and even our eyes themselves could be misleading. And they were right. Nothing up there made sense. We saw a stationary spacecraft, only to enter it and find a spinning core generating artificial gravity. We found a habitat teeming with life, heated by an artificial sun. These were things we simply could not have imagined before we left Earth. We weren't prepared for what we faced. Not physically, not technically, not emotionally. And as you all saw, in real-time, our communication would drop in and out with the internal rotation of the habitat.

"When the *Odyssey* departed with *Icarus*, we lost the ability to transmit back to Earth. We could record, but even that ran into interference from the alien spacecraft itself. We did what we could, but there were black spots, points where our equipment failed."

Another murmur ripples through the audience.

"I know, I know," Liz says, holding out her hands and trying to appear open and honest. "There are conspiracy theories. There are *always* conspiracy theories. What happened during those ninety-seven minutes? Well, I can answer that. I was there. Pretty much what happened during the other twelve hundred and fifteen minutes that did survive our exploration. We lost an hour and a half, but we have over nineteen hours of footage from within the habitat."

The boom swings across to another reporter.

"But those ninety-seven minutes include the death of the Russian cosmonaut Aleksandr Kurkov."

"They do," Liz says, turning to Crash. Without speaking, he gestures with his hand, leading his index finger from behind his ear and forward beside his face. Liz picks up on this point, saying, "But I'll remind you, we were ambushed by Aleksandr. Chris Williams was shot from behind. We have his original helmet. The damage is clear. After the return of the *Odyssey*, I retrieved a spare from storage and evac'd him back to our capsule, but he was shot while his back was turned."

The reporter asks, "So he was breathing the alien atmosphere for? Hours?"

"He was," Liz replies. "And it was cold. I could see the vapor forming on his breath."

"And he was fine being exposed to the alien biosphere?"

"He was," Liz says. "Our exobiologists have examined the soil specimens and plant material we collected and concluded that the two ecosystems are so vastly different as to coexist without interacting."

The reporter nods, satisfied by that answer, which Liz notes was also in the debriefing provided to them weeks ago.

"Please," Liz says. "I know there are doubts and rumors and conspiracies out there, but I'll remind you, the single most extensively documented event in human history is the Apollo program. There were literally cameras everywhere for over a decade. From launch to landing, all of the Apollo missions were broadcast on open channels. Hundreds of millions of people from all around the world tuned in to watch Neil Armstrong step out onto the lunar surface, and *still*, there are detractors. People say, *oh, we never made it to the Moon* when we made it there six times over four years! Hell, we took a beach buggy to the Moon, and *still*, there are doubters.

"First Contact is too important to be surrounded by lies. The latest so-called theory I heard is that the US military is receiving laser weapons from the aliens. Not only is that absurd, it's the exact opposite of what's happening. The aliens are committed to peace. They refuse to share any technology with us that could be used for war. They'll share medical imaging tech, food amplification tech, water purification tech and energy harvesting techniques, but nothing that can be weaponized. They're not interested in helping any of us until they've helped all of us. Their focus is on the gross inequality and poverty that afflicts *billions* of people on this planet, not on making billions of dollars.

"And they're not dumb. They've flown halfway across the galaxy to get here. They've got a pretty good view from where they are up there. They see us for what we are. They're not going to play into anyone's hands down here."

Several of the senators squirm in their seats. Consciously or unconsciously, this is not what they want to hear.

Liz says, "First Contact is a new beginning for us. We need to embrace that. We can't fear change. Thousands of years ago, the Apostle Paul said, *When I was a child, I spoke as a child, I understood as a child, I thought as a child; but when I became a man, I put away childish things.* And he was right. It's time for us to let go of the past and grow up as a species."

The moderator steps forward, taking charge of the meeting and saying, "Okay, thank you for those questions. As you know, we have a full day of activities here at the White House, including a follow-up panel with the scientists on the UN First Contact Committee. Lunch will be held in the State Dining Room in fifteen minutes."

Several ushers and Secret Service personnel position themselves in front of the stage, making it clear that neither the astronauts nor the President are to be approached.

Liz and Crash walk down the side steps leading from the stage. The President greets them with a warm, friendly smile and a handshake.

Liz says, "Ma'am. Is there somewhere quiet we could talk?"

"Oh, uh, sure," the President says, turning to her chief of staff, Susan Dosela.

"You're free for the next hour," the chief of staff says. She turns to the aid standing beside her, saying, "Molly can take you and the astronauts up to the residence."

"Yes," the President says. "Let's go up to the Treaty Room. It's quiet in there and quite comfortable."

"Good," the clone of Crash Williams says with surprising clarity in his voice. "There is much we need to discuss."

Afterword

Thank you for taking a chance on independent science fiction. If you've enjoyed this story, please take the time to rate it online and leave a review on Amazon or Goodreads. Your opinion counts. Your review will help others decide whether they should pick up this novel.

I love the classics of science fiction. *Ghosts* was inspired by Arthur C. Clarke's 1973 novel *Rendezvous with Rama*, which went on to win the Nebula Award for Best Novel, the Hugo Award for Best Novel, and the John W. Campbell Memorial Award. Like *2001: A Space Odyssey* (which inspired the name of the NASA spacecraft in this novel), *Rendezvous with Rama* redefined the hard science fiction First Contact genre. It examined a plausible, realistic alien encounter, considering not only the physics involved but also the inevitable politics and religious implications.

Genetic Differences

One of the points made in this novel is that, regardless of race, gender or any other metric you choose to measure, the differences between us are insignificant. There are eight billion of us on Earth, and we're 99.9% identical at the genetic level! We are but one species divided by everything we have in common.

Lagrange Points

Lagrange points are gravitationally-neutral points in space. It's not that there's no gravity acting on these points but that the various gravitational influences balance each other out, resulting in a roughly net-zero force.

Whenever you see an image of Lagrange points, you have to remember the image is static, but *nothing* is static in space. Everything is in motion, and that's the key to understanding how Lagrange points work.

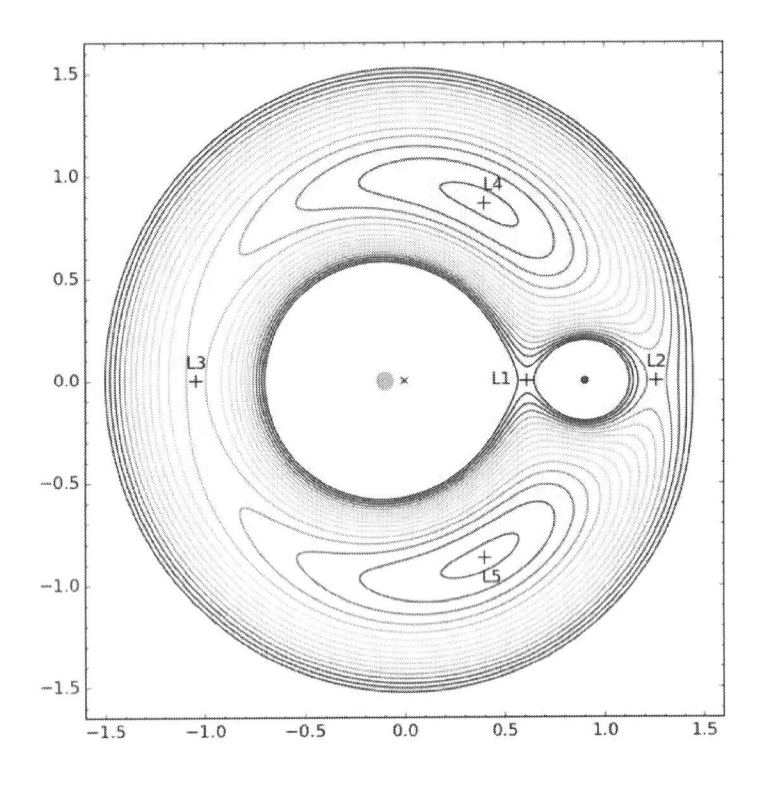

Lagrange points with Earth orbiting the Sun

Take L4, which is used in this story. In this image, we're looking down from the north (or perhaps up from the south) at Earth as it orbits around the Sun.

It seems counterintuitive that L4 could be ahead of Earth (and L5 behind it), but remember, *everything* is in motion. Nothing can get to L4 or L5 without *also* orbiting the Sun at the same speed as Earth. But it's not just the Sun tugging on objects in this position. Earth is also influencing the motion of objects in space. Once there at L4, the pull of both the Sun and Earth forms a stable point in the gravitational tug-o-war.

Lagrange points are a bit like two kids on a seesaw. If the bigger kid (the Sun) scoots toward the center of the seesaw and the smaller kid (Earth) sits further back on the other side, they can reach a point of equilibrium where they're evenly balanced, and neither's feet can reach the ground. You could place a marble in the middle of the seesaw and it would just sit there. It wouldn't roll in either direction. That's a Lagrange point. The position of the marble is stable because the crossbar is balanced between the opposing downward force of the two kids on the seesaw.

BDOs

In this story, the alien spaceship is given the fictional designation BDO or Bright Data Object. This is a made-up, tongue-in-cheek reference to a science fiction trope known as the BDO or Big Dumb Object.

Normally, BDOs describe plot devices/MacGuffins within a science fiction story that serve no purpose other than to drive a sense of mystery. They're left unexplained by the author and often leave fans with unanswered questions.

Examples of BDOs include the monolith in Arthur C. Clarke's *2001: A Space Odyssey*, Michael Crichton's *Sphere*, the origin of the dome in Stephen King's story *Under the Dome*, Larry Niven's *Ringworld*, the Sophons from Cixin Liu's *The Three-Body Problem*, the alien presence in my novel *Anomaly,* and even the proto-molecule in James S. A. Corey's *Leviathan Wakes,* which later became the TV series *The Expanse* (although in subsequent books there are explanations that tie up some of the loose ends, the creators of the proto-molecule and star gate remain mysterious). In *Ghosts*, I have a *big object*, but hopefully, it doesn't fall into the *dumb* category of being an inexplicable plot device without any real function. It's a habitat for a bunch of alien scientists sent to explore our world.

Spin Rates

In this novel, the BDO has an internal cylinder rotating to provide artificial gravity. This is based on a radius of roughly 400 feet or 125 meters, giving the cylinder a diameter of 800 feet/250 meters, rotating at 50 mph or 80 km/hr to produce 0.4 gees, which is just under half the gravity experienced on Earth but slightly more than what is felt on Mars (which is 0.38 gees). The Moon, by comparison, has 0.17 gees.

The entire cylinder would rotate once every minute and a half to maintain the sensation of gravity. Revolving at rates of over 1.4x per minute will leave most people feeling a little sick, although, over time, the body will adjust to rates as high as 10x per minute. Rates under three times per minute are considered practical and would be comfortable. The closer someone gets to the center of a rotating cylinder, though, the faster they turn and the more they'll feel the disorienting Coriolis Effect, which would upset the inner ear, leaving them dizzy and probably vomiting every time they turn their head one way or the other. For this reason, I had the axis revolving around the airlock, leaving the airlock itself stationary relative to the outer hull of the spacecraft.

Red and Black Plants

In this novel, the alien habitat replicates its home world, which, based on the artificial sunlight within the cylinder, is presumably in orbit around a red dwarf—a star that's much fainter than the Sun.

What would plants look like on such a planet? Instead of being green, they'd probably be dark red or black, as these are better frequencies for absorbing energy from such a star. We've even found extremophile cyanobacteria with chlorophyll here on Earth that extend the limits of terrestrial photosynthesis, harvesting light at wavelengths up to 750 nanometers (reaching into infrared). Based on this, I've speculated that the alien plants would be orange, red and black (with black being how we would perceive infrared pigmentation).

The Nature of Fear

I enjoyed exploring the nature of fear in this novel. Here's some of the background research behind the story.

Rhesus macaque monkeys are renowned for being afraid of snakes. In 1964, scientists compared wild monkeys with those raised in captivity in a controlled experiment and found those who had never seen a snake before weren't bothered by its presence. Once they were exposed to wild monkeys with snakes nearby, they learned the appropriate response. This suggests that at least some fears are social constructs.

Fear, though, isn't always learned. We're more afraid of ancient threats, like heights or the dark, than we are of modern dangers, like guns, even though guns are far more dangerous than a darkened room. This suggests there is an evolutionary instinctive element to fear.

As far back as the 1840s, Charles Darwin noted how fears emerged as survival instincts in his children.

"When [my son was] nine weeks & three days old... I happened to sneeze—which made [him] start, frown, look frightened & cry rather badly— For an hour afterward, every noise made him start,— he was nervous.— I think he certainly has undefined instinctive fears."

On a trip to the zoo, Darwin later noted, "[his two-year-old son] had no fear of any bird, though large, like the ostriches & noisy like the gulls... [His] fear [of large four-legged animals like buffalo, though], has certainly come without any experience of danger or hurt."

In this regard, we see that fears and phobias are both inherited and learned.

Depending on the complexity of their brain, it seems all animals experience at least an instinctive response of self-preservation that can be likened to fear in humans. The key point, though, is—regardless of origin—fears are never rational. Even predators as imposing as the Great White Shark experience a kind of fear. Marine biologists have documented how the presence of Orcas in the seal-feeding grounds of

Great Whites will cause sharks to flee for the rest of the season! The smell alone is enough to drive them from the region.

Fear induces a disproportionate response to danger. It advocates caution above other necessities for survival, like hunting for food, causing even Great Whites to turn and swim away with an empty belly. In a similar manner, impalas roaming the African savannah are far more afraid of lions than is warranted. Only one in five lion hunts are successful, whereas cheetahs catch one in every two animals they chase, while wild dogs bring down four out of every five animals they attack. As lions are opportunists, they'll let cheetahs, leopards, wild dogs and hyenas bring down impalas and then steal the kill. Logically, impalas should be far more afraid of cheetahs and wild dogs, but they're not. They fear lions. The lesson is clear: fear is not logical.

In this novel, I wanted to explore how our fear of the dark and fear of the unknown could cloud First Contact and cause misunderstandings to arise.

Collective Intelligence

We tend to think of intelligence as an attribute of an individual. We say this person's smart or that person's dumb, but *all* intelligence is collective. No one's intelligence stands on its own, making IQ tests redundant. Understanding our collective intelligence is far more important than any individual's numeric test results.

While researching this book, I watched a YouTube video by a prominent and uber-intelligent science communicator with a Ph.D. who was investigating IQ tests. They did a number of practice exams before taking their formal IQ test, which to me, highlights the fallacy behind these tests. If you can practice and get a better outcome, then the test doesn't measure your latent, innate intelligence at all. I'd go so far as to say IQ tests represent a failure in understanding what actually defines intelligence.

When you look at intelligence from the perspective of biology, it becomes apparent that intelligence has evolved at multiple levels over billions of years. Even something as simple as bacteria can be thought of as intelligent. They use quorum sensing to communicate and function as a colony. Place food on key locations on a topographical map of your state or country, and mere slime mold can design a more effective rail system than humans, even though slime doesn't have a nervous system. There are no neurons, no thinking or reasoning at all, but the results are astonishing.

Evolution has incorporated intelligence at *every* level of life, from the individual cell to body tissue, organs, the individual's mind and then society itself (something that isn't constrained to humans or animals, even plants can be thought of as having social groups).

The premise that each level of life has an underlying form of biological intelligence is known as abstraction. Although it might sound obscure, basically, what this means is the complexity at one layer is hidden and simplified for the next layer up.

Computers are a great example of abstraction. At their heart, they're nothing more than zeros and ones rushing through logic gates. That's abstracted into CPUs, GPUs, RAM, etc., but you—the user—don't need to worry about CPUs, GPUs and RAM because that's abstracted yet again by the operating system itself. The complexity is hidden and simplified, allowing you to concentrate on more important functions. When you move the mouse across your desktop and click on a folder, nothing even remotely similar to that is happening within the computer. You're working at a simplified, abstract level. In the same way, our lives are an abstraction built on biology.

At each level of life, intelligence is baked into the system to solve problems. And by solving these problems, the next level up doesn't have to think about what the lower level actually accomplished. This is why you don't have to worry about your heart beating or your blood cells being replenished. The biological intelligence latent within those systems frees you up to concentrate on higher, more abstract forms of intelligence.

Remarkably, though, the most "*intelligent*" species on the planet (*Homo sapiens*) breaks down at the level of the individual, leading to dysfunctional societies when other species cross this particular boundary with ease.

Our collective intelligence is contradictory. On one hand, we have developed astonishing achievements by working together, such as landing people on the Moon, developing drugs to combat cancer (a failure at one of the lower levels), music, poetry, art, etc. On the other, we're blindly consuming our way to oblivion. Our obsession with (perceived) individual brilliance has led to arrogant ideologies, selfishness and greed, keeping us from having a functional collective intelligence on par with even the humble honeybee. If aliens were to visit Earth, I would expect this would be one of their key takeaways from observing us in the wild—because we are very much still in the wild. They'd see our individual intelligence as somewhat contradictory and dysfunctional, hindering our overall collective intelligence.

If you're interested in learning more about this concept, I highly recommend the YouTube video The Beauty of Collective Intelligence by Michael Levin.

Extraterrestrial Lifeforms

Although we've never encountered extraterrestrial life, we do know roughly what alien life will be like. Physics applies limits to chemistry. Chemistry applies limits to biology. Biology adapts within these constraints via natural selection. And this leads us to the conclusion that not everything we can think of forming alien life is necessarily possible. Yes, we need to be prepared for lifeforms that are exotic and wildly different from us, but that's already true here on Earth! Think about how vastly different an octopus is from an eagle or a bacterium from a blue whale. And yet, even here on Earth, there are limits to the astonishing diversity of life.

As an example, we're not likely to find aliens with biological wheels. We don't see cars evolving in the wild because a creature with separate moving parts isn't pragmatic. From the perspective of biology, legs are much more practical than wheels. For an animal such as a giraffe to evolve wheels, it would need millions of gradual, beneficial steps leading to a wheel. Half a wheel isn't useful, whereas half a leg or half an eye still provides an organism with the benefit of some mobility and the ability to see vague shapes to avoid predators.

An animal with wheels would need a biological way of growing a freely revolving part, not to mention the means of providing nerve impulses for control and nutrient/blood supply to the wheel without veins and arteries being tied in knots. Although this is practically impossible, it has occurred on a microscopic scale with bacterial flagella tails. These wiggle around like a propeller blade, but they're strictly limited by physics, chemistry and biology—and they don't scale to larger animals.

When considering extraterrestrial life, there is a lot we can infer based on the constraints of physics, chemistry and biology, along with the astonishing range of diversity we observe on Earth. What we don't observe here on our own planet is telling as it hints at the limits of natural selection.

When it comes to extraterrestrial life, we can expect to see convergent evolution, where life converges independently on the same practical solution from entirely different evolutionary pedigrees. And the reason is simple: the same physics, the same chemistry, and the same biological influences will often lead to the same solution.

Perhaps the best example of convergent evolution is the body shape of sharks and dolphins. At first glance, sharks and dolphins look related. They have astonishingly similar streamlined bodies with seemingly identical dorsal fins and pectoral fins, and yet their evolutionary pedigree couldn't be more dissimilar, with dolphins being mammals like us.

Sharks are hundreds of millions of years older than even the dinosaurs, while dolphins evolved from land animals with semi-aquatic habits similar to those of the hippopotamus only about forty million years ago. With four hundred million years between them, sharks and dolphins evolved the same basic body shape because of the constraints of physics when moving through water.

In the same way, useful adaptations like sight have evolved forty times independently of each other here on Earth because seeing is a wonderful survival trait. Porcupines (which are mammals) and echidnas (which are marsupials) look almost identical despite being entirely separate animal species, having evolved in completely unrelated geographical regions (being the Americas and the continent of Australia).

Humans and koalas have almost identical fingerprints because both species benefited from the extra grip provided by these grooves and indentations in the skin of their hands.

If such unlikely convergence can occur on Earth, it's reasonable to expect similar convergence with life that evolved elsewhere as the same laws of physics and chemistry will constrain alien biology.

In this novel, I've described bipedal aliens not to be anthropomorphic (or human-centric) but because it makes sense in terms of convergent evolution. Freeing up one set of limbs for fine motor skills while the other provides locomotion undoubtedly set *Homo sapiens* on the path to accumulating greater and greater dexterity and developing tool use, so it's reasonable to assume this could happen elsewhere, like sharks and dolphins converging on the same body type.

Plant life is the bedrock of our ecosystem, turning sunlight into chemical energy. Again, it's entirely plausible that this is an area where we would see convergent evolution in an alien biosphere because photosynthesis is so astonishingly effective at supporting ecosystems.

Kroger's?

If you live in the US, do you shop at Kroger or Krogers or Kroger's? Technically, the name of the store is Kroger in the same way as Walmart or Dairy Queen are singular terms, but because Kroger is a surname, our lax approach to speech leads to us saying Krogers or, more correctly, Kroger's, meaning a store (originally) owned by the Kroger family.

You might be wondering why I bring this up, but it's because, as an author, I need to find the balance between being grammatically correct and accepting of cultural oddities like Kroger's. In the same way, do you buy a box of Cracker Jack or Cracker Jacks? The singular form is technically correct, but to our ear, the plural sounds better, so we tend to gravitate to that. In light of this, I've used the plural/possessive forms of terms like these within this story. Even though they may be incorrect, they sound more natural and so flow better for readers.

Children's Garden

In this novel, Chief of Staff Susan Dosela finds Molly in a small, secluded garden near the White House South Lawn (where the Marine One helicopter lands). The Children's Garden is near the basketball court, not far from the fountain in President's Park. The garden was a gift to the White House from President Lyndon Johnson and his wife in 1968. It's a rare, secluded spot offering privacy within the White House grounds. The garden features a goldfish pond and a shaded area with ornate, white cast iron chairs. Footprints and handprints of various President's children and grandchildren have been embedded in the stones making up the walkway. I loved finding this on Google Maps and thought it would be a nice inclusion in the story.

If you're curious, use Google Street View to explore the South Lawn and see if you can find this beautiful garden. If I was in the White House, I would sneak away here to have lunch in quiet solitude.

Life as a Bat

What does it mean to be you?

What does it mean to be conscious and alive?

In the words of philosopher David Chalmers, "How does the water of the brain turn into the wine of consciousness?"

One of the concepts explored in this novel is that it is impossible for us to understand the conscious experience of others, let alone the experience of other species. The absurdity of this notion is captured in the realization that we can never experience life as a bat—and that places fundamental limits on our understanding of consciousness as a whole. Although this might sound like an obscure reference, I've taken it from a famous thought experiment from the 1970s.

While exploring the subjective notion of consciousness, American philosopher Thomas Nigel proposed that there's no objective measure that can define what it is like to experience life. I am me—

that's all any of us have to go on. Or as René Descartes famously said, "*Cogito, ergo sum*. I think, therefore I am."

Thomas Nigel used the concept of life as a bat as an extreme metaphor to make the point more obvious, suggesting that although we can imagine the viewpoint of a bat and understand all its senses, we can never actually experience life in the same way as a bat. We will always lack its internal perception of reality.

Science seeks to examine natural phenomena from an external perspective by means of observation. To use a literary example, science works in the third person, while consciousness is only ever experienced in the first person. And this raises an interesting question—can consciousness ever be understood from a purely objective perspective? Imagining life as a bat suggests the answer is no.

Humans and chimpanzees share an astonishing 98% of their DNA, and yet look at how difficult it is for us to communicate with them or understand them. Then consider how remarkably intelligent dolphins are and yet how absurd it is to try to talk with them. In this novel, I've adopted the idea that to avoid misunderstandings, an alien race might clone humans so as to effectively communicate with us.

Contrary to what you see in Hollywood, the vast differences between us and any extraterrestrial species would be so extreme that we may not be able to communicate directly with them. Sharks sense their surroundings using electrical impulses; oilbirds, shrews and rats use echolocation like bats. If we were to encounter aliens using something similar instead of sight, it would complicate communication as they simply could not read anything that was written down. Using clones as a surrogate is one possible alternative to bridge such a celestial evolutionary gap.

Nuclear Rocket Engines

Few terms invoke as visceral a reaction as the word *nuclear*. Even peaceful applications have been plagued with challenges, from how to deal with radioactive waste products and disastrous accidents like those at Chernobyl and Fukushima. When they're properly designed and managed, though, nuclear reactors release less pollution and radiation than coal-fired electric stations.

As rocket launches carry an inherent risk of catastrophic failure, space agencies like NASA have avoided nuclear power where possible. The prospect of a rocket exploding during a launch, showering the region with radioactive material, isn't a good look. There have, however, been some exceptions. Several of the Mars missions, including Viking, Curiosity and Perseverance, have used upwards of a hundred pounds of plutonium each to produce electricity. Needless to say, during each of these launches, there would have been some very nervous mission controllers.

Nuclear-powered rocket engines were proposed as early as the 1950s, but the concept was seen as an unnecessary risk when compared to the performance of conventional rockets. Recently, though, NASA has revived plans for an in-space-only version of the nuclear rocket that I then used in this novel. Not only will this drastically reduce the round-trip time to Mars, but it will also open up the exploration of the wider solar system. With a nuclear rocket, we could put Mars-like rovers on the surface of the moons of Jupiter and Saturn to search for signs of life, something we couldn't accomplish today using chemical rockets.

Thank You

Thank you for taking a chance on an obscure Australian science fiction author who hails from New Zealand. Your support of my writing is deeply appreciated. By purchasing this book, you're giving me the opportunity to write the next one, so I'm grateful for your kind support.

I'd like to thank a bunch of beta-readers who helped me with quality control, including John Stephens, David Jaffe, Terry Grindstaff, Steve Bell, Chris Fox, Scotty Davis, LuAnn Miller, Melinda Robino and Gerald Greenwood.

If you've enjoyed this novel, please leave a review online.

If you'd like to chat about this or any of my novels, feel free to stop by my virtual coffee shop.

If you'd like to learn more about upcoming new releases, be sure to subscribe to my email newsletter. You can find all of my books on Amazon. I'm also active on Facebook, Instagram and Twitter.

Keep looking up at the stars in awe. If there's life here, there's life elsewhere. It's just a matter of time before we find evidence for life beyond the bounds of Earth.

Peter Cawdron
Brisbane, Australia

Printed in Great Britain
by Amazon